The Final Pairing

Fabulous Five Series
Book 2

Virginia C. Hart

ISBN: 1503290522
ISBN 13: 9781503290525

For my sister Jessica...
I don't tell you often enough how truly special and important you
are to me.
It's always been easier to express my true feelings with my writing.
These words are for you.
I love you!

Prologue

Patrick

Letting out a frustrated sigh, I walk back toward my family beach home with an abundance of emotions. God, it's so hard walking away from Suzanna! Actually, walking in general is a bit difficult, seeing as I'm now sporting a raging hard on. Even after four years, that girl can get me all out of sorts with just one look. Of course I took it a lot further than just lustful eye hockey. I couldn't help myself. There she was looking more beautiful than ever and I couldn't control myself. I just had to reach out and touch her. When that wasn't enough, I pressed my body right up against her tiny frame. But even that couldn't curb my desire. So what did my greedy asshole self do? I kissed her. Her soft lips were pulling me in like a magnet. It began as something soft and sweet at first. However, when she didn't push me away, I deepened the kiss and shit, if she didn't kiss me right back. I would have died a happy man in that moment. All too soon, the moment ended and reality crashed backed down. If things were different, I wouldn't be walking away from her now. I'd stay and fight for the only woman I want in my life. But I can't be selfish and put her in the middle of my fucked up life, especially since my life has been so perfectly planned out for me.

Screwed-up Perfection! Now there's an oxymoron for you. Too bad it's the first thing that comes to mind when describing my life. Actually, it fits me to a fucking tee. For example, I'm a twenty-three year old college graduate getting ready to start law school in the fall.

I'm engaged to Katelyn, a beautiful girl who comes from a powerful family with political ties. Actually her father has guaranteed me a successful life upon completion of law school. Not to mention my dad, who owns our family law practice and is priming me to take over. Tonight, surrounded by family and friends, a fabulous party was thrown as a celebration of my recent engagement. So why am I so frustrated and angry with my life? Because all of that is the screwed up part. The perfection part...that's what I just walked away from and left standing on her front porch.

Suzanna is my perfection. She is the girl who still holds a place in my heart after all these years. Even though she left me our senior year of high school, I don't think I ever gave up hope that one day we would find our way back to each other. Tonight, I couldn't control myself and gave in to my desire to kiss her. The best part is she kissed me back. Her soft sweet lips were like an electrical current zapping every nerve ending in my body. Had I been less than a southern gentleman, I would have pushed her up against the nearest wall and explored every inch of her insanely sexy little body. The all consuming need to hold her, kiss her, touch her and be inside of her is frustrating the hell out of me.

Chapter One

Patrick

Six months ago...

"Hey, we don't have to call it a night yet. You wanna go grab something to eat? Or we could just go to my house and watch some TV," Landon says breaking the uncomfortable silence between us. We've been sitting in the cab of his truck for about five minutes, neither one of us wanting the night to end. I haven't made a move to exit his truck and make my way into my house. Even with the lack of conversation, I don't feel as lonely sitting here with Landon as I will inside my own home.

It's not that I will be alone inside of the house. My father's car is parked in the open garage so I know he is home. Physically. However, my dad has been emotionally checked out since my mother passed away in a car accident that happened years ago. Dad never has dealt with his grief in a healthy way. Instead, he decided he would live his life inside the bottom of a liquor bottle. I don't know the last time I saw my dad without a drink in his hand and a buzz. Lately, the few times I have been home, which have not been frequent, Dad basically drinks himself into oblivion until he passes out. The few conversations we have usually occur in the mornings while he is nursing his hangover. Obviously, in his conditions, whether drunk out of his mind or hungover, our little talks never get beyond a quick question and answer session. I keep my answers short, usually just yes or no, and he doesn't have the mental capability to delve any deeper into the happenings of his only son's life. That, or either he just doesn't care. He hasn't cared about much ever since the accident that killed my mom.

"Yeah? I could eat I guess," I answer really wanting to take Landon up on his offer and extend some much needed time with one of my best friends. "Think James will want to join us? I bet he hasn't made it home yet." We have all been back in our hometown celebrating the Christmas holidays with our families. Since we all went to different colleges after graduating from high school, the holidays are the only times we get to spend time with each other. During our early college years, we would visit each other at the different campuses occasionally. However, as we each entered the core course work for our respective majors, the visits became less frequent until they stopped all together. We call and text each other every now and then, but it's just not the same as spending time with my best friends. These guys mean so much to me. I think of each of them as a brother. They were both there for me when I lost my mother and helped put me back together after Suzanna left during our senior year of high school. I owe these guys so much for everything they have done for me.

"Sure, I'll send him a quick text. What're you in the mood for? Breakfast at the Venus?" Landon asks just as he reaches for his phone which is sitting in the cup holder of the console between us. Right before Landon is able to grab his phone, the display lights up indicating an incoming call. I read the illuminated screen before Landon can pick up the phone and answer. Runt, otherwise known as Chloe, is calling. She is the youngest member of our close knit group of friends from our high school days, referred to as the Fabulous Five. Now why in the world would Chloe be calling Landon this late at night? As far as I know, Landon isn't dating anyone seriously, but he has been going out occasionally with Leslie, who also went to our high school. He assured me it was nothing serious. But from the looks Leslie was giving Landon tonight at the bar, I question just how serious it is. If Leslie had any say in this so called relationship, she'd be sitting co-pilot in Landon's truck rather than me. Granted the old Leslie would have vacated her position in the passenger seat and positioned herself right over Landon's cock, straddling his body, the steering wheel be damned. Supposedly, Leslie has been enlightened and no longer spreads her legs for any guy who looks her way, or so I hear. Well, I'll believe it when I see it. I'd also wager some money on the fact that Leslie's idea of the exclusivity of their relationship is entirely different from Landon's.

I just can't figure out how Chloe plays into to all of this and why she is calling Landon. I wonder if they have something other than friendship going on. I seriously doubt it though, because Landon was totally against dating within our group of friends. He only tolerated my relationship with Suzanna. I guess he was right on the money with his assessment of how that would end. Suzanna left me midway through our senior year, moving to the beach to follow her dream of becoming a professional golfer. She left me high and dry, breaking off our almost two year long relationship with barely a goodbye. Needless to say, I was devastated. It took me a long time to accept that we were over. Landon and James watched as I completed my senior year behind a mask of depression. Landon and James both kept me busy during the summer after graduation until I could finally escape my hometown where I had to deal with my drunken father and the ghost of the only girl I loved.

I haven't spoken with Chloe in a while. When Suzanna and I split, so did the Fabulous Five. The battle of the sexes ensued, and the boys rallied with me, while Chloe chose Suzanna's side. I know Chloe, James and Landon have tried to maintain their friendships. However, I couldn't stomach seeing and talking to Chloe, knowing she was still so close to Suzanna. The few occasions we have all been in each other's company, everyone with the exception of Suzanna, that is...because Suzanna didn't just leave temporarily. She bolted out of Florence and I don't think the girl has stepped foot back in this town. Anyway, it took all the will power I had not to question Chloe like a detective, trying to find out any information about Suzanna. I just wanted to know how she was doing. How was her golf going? Is she happy? Is she dating anyone? Okay, so I really didn't want to know about the dating part. What I really wanted to know was why the hell did she leave, basically like a thief in the night, never to return? What the hell did I ever do to her that she completely cut off all contact not only with me, but with Landon and James as well? There I was, a foolish high school boy who thought I had found my one true love. God, how I loved that girl! Even after all these years, I still love her. I thought she loved me too. I guess I was wrong.

Trying not to make it too obvious that I am eavesdropping on Landon and Chloe's conversation –hell, he has to know I'm listening, I'm sitting right here beside him-I do my best to stare out of the passenger side window and try not to stress over the fact that Suzanna could be with Chloe right now while she's talking to Landon. Of course I'll never ask, not only because I know Suzanna wants nothing to do with me. She's made that abundantly clear the last four years. But I don't want Landon to think I'm still that pussy-whipped eighteen year old boy pining for a girl who broke his heart. With the little discretion available in the close quarters of the truck cab, I listen to Landon's side of the phone conversation. It's not like I can help it or have much of a choice.

"Hey Runt. What's up?" Landon asks. Chloe must give him an answer he doesn't like because Landon tenses up in his seat. His free hand grips the steering wheel so tightly, I think it may break under his strength. And Landon definitely has some strength. It looks like Landon has spent the majority of his college years inside of a gym rather than a classroom. I hope it's not Chloe specifically that has Landon so mad. I know I'd hate to be on the other side of his wrath. "Are you hurt? Did she –" Landon never finishes realizing I'm still in the truck. As soon as the words about Chloe being hurt come from his mouth, I whip my head in his direction no longer caring that I'm invading his private conversation. "Okay, just calm down. I'm coming over right now. You gonna be okay until I get there?" Landon asks as he cranks his truck shifting the gears into reverse ready to leave. I guess our plans for a late night breakfast have been detoured. "Be there in a few minutes. Hang in there Runt. See you soon." With that, Landon ends the call.

"Need me to tag along?" I ask in hopes that whatever personal hell Chloe is going through, I'll be happy to help just to escape the loneliness that awaits me inside my house.

"Nah, she's just having a rough night and asked for some company. You don't mind if we take a rain check for the breakfast do you?" Landon asks impatiently. He is still stressed out about Chloe's phone call and I can tell he wants to throw me out the truck so he can hurry and get to her. Taking the hint, I open the truck door.

"No problem man. I had a great time tonight. I don't get to see you or James nearly as often as I'd like. Let's make plans to get a guys weekend together before the semester gets away from us and finals begin." Once we graduate, who knows where we will all scatter across the state or the country? Personally, I've got my heart set on moving from my beloved south to the cold and cloudy skies of Bristol, Connecticut. I've worked my ass off during my college career studying all the ins and outs of sports journalism. Not only did I attend and complete the required work of all my classes, I interned at the local newspaper in the sports department. I've covered everything from the small, feel good story of opening day at little league baseball to the big, in-state college rivalry game between the two state universities in South Carolina. Any story I could get my hands on, I took the job and wrote until it was the best damn sports story ever written. With all this being said, I built a pretty impressive portfolio of work. Submitting my best stories and resume complete with raving reviews from the editor of the local paper and the dean of the school of journalism, I applied for my dream job to become a reporter and writer for ESPN. It is actually looking very promising. Not only did I receive correspondence through the mail requesting more samples of my work, but they have also requested to set up a date for an unofficial interview over the phone. I'm crossing my fingers that I'll finally get the job that I've worked so hard for, and get to make a living doing something I love.

"Sounds good. We'll talk more soon, but I really need to bolt, like now," Landon says, the anxiety evident in his voice.

"Yeah. See you Landon. Goodnight," I say as my feet hit the ground getting out of the monstrosity of a truck Landon uses for transportation and to wipe out the ozone layer. Doubt he heard me. It's a miracle he didn't run me over with how fast he put the pedal to the metal leaving my driveway. I'm starting to wonder if Landon doesn't have feelings for Chloe other than those of a friendship variety. He sure was in a hurry to get to her. I just hope she's all right. As I watch Landon's tail lights disappear down the street, the darkness settles in and the quiet takes over. I'm confused, feeling polar opposite emotions. I'm happy to have spent some time with my friends. It was good to get out tonight and just be a normal college senior. I didn't have to worry with the stress of studying to maintain my near perfect GPA. Nor was I thinking about the future and what type of job awaits me after college. I was just shooting the shit with my buddies and enjoying the hell out of it. But I'm also sad. Not for the most obvious reason that the night ended too soon for me. But sad because things are going to change and once again I'll have to adapt to being an adult. Not that it's a new character trait I have to hone and develop. My adulthood started long before I ever wanted it to or it should have. I've had to act like the adult ever since my mom died and my dad became a shell of a man that he used to be. I'm sad and grieving not for the physical loss of my mother. Nor is it because when I lost my mom, essentially I lost my dad as well. Right now, I'm sad because I'm grieving the loss of my childhood which was unfairly taken away from me. And if I'm being honest, I'm still missing the girl who I continue to love and grieve the loss of our relationship.

Tossing my keys onto the foyer table, the clinking sound of metal to wood echoes throughout the silence of the house. Not that I'm worried about making noise. Usually by this time of night, my father has drained his bottle and is passed out cold. I don't think the roaring sound of a tornado ripping through our neighborhood would wake him in his comatose state. I walk into the kitchen to get a glass of water before I head to bed myself. I plan to rise bright and early and drive back to my apartment on campus in the upstate. My two bedroom apartment, although barely furnished, with little décor or personal knick knacks, still feels more like my home than this huge house. I want to get back and get set for my final semester in college. I still have more applications to send out, should my number one choice, ESPN, not pan out. I also want to avoid the crowds of students coming back from break all at once in a couple of weeks. I plan to go to the bookstore as soon as they reopen and get everything I need for this semester before things get too crazy. Hopefully, the local paper will have a story they want me to cover. This time of year, the focus is mainly on college hoops and which teams will make it to March Madness. High school basketball is close to being over and the playoffs are getting ready to start. Maybe I'll catch a few games before school begins and write a story, whether the paper asks me to or not. Writing is cathartic for me. It lets me escape the reality that is my life for just a while. I have more written pieces sitting in my apartment that have never been printed or published. Whenever I feel the depths of depression weighing down on me – thoughts about my dead mother, my drunken father, or Suzanna – I take a pencil in hand and just start writing anything that comes to mind, other than the aforementioned. The sports world always has interesting stories to tell. Not just the statistics of players or the outcome of a particular game. I am intrigued with the individual players and what makes them tick. What obstacles, if any, did they have to overcome to play? What motivates them to do their best on the playing surface in front of numerous fans? How is their home life? There is always a back story to be found. Usually these stories by far overshadow the details of the play by play and final score of just a game and are, in my opinion, the best stories. However, very rarely will the paper publish one of my soft articles, stating that the readers are only interested in the end result of a game. Eventually, I would love to make a living writing my "game of life" articles.

My writing thoughts are interrupted and I almost choke on the drink of water I just inhaled when I hear my dad's voice coming from the darkened corner of the kitchen.

"Hey son," he says, causing me to almost drop the glass in the kitchen sink. I whip around and see my father sitting at the kitchen table. He is slumped in the chair, shoulders sagging, while his elbows rest on the table. He looks tired. Physically drained, actually. He reminds me of a kid who just lost his favorite toy and has exhausted himself looking for it only to come up empty handed. I examine my father and see that the drinking has not only deteriorated our relationship, but has aged him tremendously. I used to think of my father as this bigger than life man. Standing a few inches over six feet, he was always someone I looked up to literally and figuratively. Before my mom died, he kept his body in great physical shape, working out several times a week either before or after work. Now, he looks frail, all muscle mass he once had gone, turned into flab. Dad used to enter a room, commanding authority with his reputation and his physique. Now, if he ever entered a room outside of this house, I'm sure he would be a laughing stock to his peers. I'm not sure he even has anyone he could call a friend anymore. Since my mother died, the only friends Dad associates with is Jack and Jim. That's pretty pathetic when your only friends are in the form of an amber liquid inside of a bottle.

Feeling sorry for the old guy I entertain this idea that my dad might actually want to converse with me. "Um, hey Dad. It's kinda late for you to be up." As soon as the words leave my mouth, I regret them. Dad, if it's possible, looks more defeated after hearing that his son just confirmed that his normal routine of passing out before ten each night is an event to bring up. Trying to smooth over my former statement, I cautiously walk over and sit with my dad at the kitchen table. The dim lighting from the bulb over the kitchen sink is the only one on. Even so, I see from up close what the last few years have done to my dad. And it's not good. I wish I hadn't wandered over into his close proximity to witness the utter defeat written across his face. We sit in silence, each of us waiting to see who will break the standoff that is occurring in our kitchen. From the looks of it, Dad is a nervous wreck. I watch as a row of sweat beads dot his brow. His hands tremor and shake even though he clasps them together on the table. The man looks sick. And just then the revelation hits me. The lack of alcohol, in a glass or lingering from his breath, is absent. For some reason this startles me because I haven't seen him without his best friend in a long, long time. Apparently, whatever he plans to say to me tonight is important enough for him not to slur his words. My impatience for this so-called father son bonding attempt overflows and I ask, "Dad, are you okay?"

Dad lifts his head and his blood shot eyes meet mine. "No, Patrick. I am so far from 'okay' that I don't think I'll ever get back."

I take a minute to let his words sink in. My first thought is that he is giving up. What? I don't know. Maybe he is giving up the hope that we will ever have a relationship. It's not like he seems to care that we don't have the normal father and son interactions that we used to. It's hard to remember that my dad and I actually used to have a good time together. Memories of parent/child golf tournaments at the club and tossing baseballs in our front yard have almost been forgotten because they hurt too much to think about. They make me realize that I not only lost one parent to a horrific accident, I may as well have lost both. Panic grips me when I think of actually losing him for good. Is my dad thinking of giving up on life? He has pretty much done that already, living his days secluded to this house, drinking away his sorrows. But at least he is still here, a breathing, physical being on this earth. The thought that he may be giving up to join my mom in death unnerves me. Granted, I haven't been too willing to repair our strained relations due to my responsibilities at school and just bitter anger that I have been holding onto. However, the little hope I have that we can get back to being a family will disappear if Dad is really thinking of ending it all.

"Dad, hey, let's talk about it, okay?" I ask, praying that he isn't thinking what I'm thinking, which is the worst scenario.

"I don't..., I can't...." Dad struggles to form a coherent sentence even in his rare state of sobriety. He breaks eye contact and stares at a scratch on the table.

"Are you sick? If so, we can get you some help. I can make you an appointment to see Dr. Morris this week. I'll even stick around to take you if you want," I say trying to get to the bottom of the problem.

"I am sick, Patrick, but there's not a cure in the world that will help me. I'm a sick bastard. The things I've done...I can't... Look, you wanna help. Good, I need your help. Although, I don't deserve it. God, what a horrible, despicable father I have been to you! And here I am pleading for you to help me out of the shit I have made of my life." Dad finally lifts his head and I wish he hadn't. I see the sheen of wetness coating his eyes and I'm sure he is about to break down crying. I can't watch my father cry. A grown man, I have looked up to for the most part, breaking down in a crumbling mess is too much to watch.

"Dad, don't get upset. Whatever is wrong we can fix it...together. I'll help you any way I can. Just please don't do this," I say waving my hand in his direction indicating that I can't deal with the tears. I hear Dad sniff and watch as he wipes his hands across his face, trying to pull it together. "But I can't help you if you don't tell me what's wrong. And frankly Dad, you're scaring the shit outta me right now."

I watch Dad compose himself as best he can and wait patiently with bated breath to hear what I may have just agreed to. Dad remains silent, every so often glancing toward the cabinets in the kitchen that houses his liquor. Obviously, baring his soul is harder to do sober and I can see the effort it takes him not to go straight to the bottle. I'm tired and I'm in no mood for the theatrics of a big build up, so, although I know I'm feeding his addiction to get the answers I need, I don't care. I stand and go straight to the cabinet to grab my dad's drug of choice. Pouring him a big glass of the amber liquid, I place it in front of him on the table. I watch a battle wage in my dad's eyes. I can see he wants to resist, but needs the liquid courage to carry on this conversation. Slowly, his trembling hand reaches out and takes the glass, lifting it to his mouth. It's like a relief consumes him immediately as the burning liquid goes down his throat into his body, bringing only a calm only another alcoholic can relate to. He doesn't stop until he finishes the entire glass. When he reaches for the bottle for a refill, I snatch it away, feeling braver and demanding the answers he is gonna give me. It's like bribing a kid at a candy store. And I'm sick to my stomach having to use this torture on him, but hell, what else can I do?

"Not another drop until you tell me what it is you have to say. You get me, Dad?" I ask, although I don't need an answer. I know the enticement of another drink will have him spilling his guts in a matter of seconds.

"Patrick, I'm sorry."

He might as well make a list because there are several things that he needs to apologize for. I remain silent to hear how he plans to elaborate on his apology.

"I've been a shitty father. I wasn't always like this, but ever since your mother..." he can't even finish his sentence. I see the effort it takes for him to talk about what happened to Mom. I know he never really dealt with his grief, burying it deep down and numbing the pain with alcohol. I watch the grief contort his facial features. Trying to read his every expression, I watch as other emotions –embarrassment, shame, and guilt – appear as his jaw tics and his brow furrows. As though he senses the emotions he is showcasing, he turns his head to look across the kitchen and away from me. After a few moments he decides to continue. "Your mother, God bless her soul, was one of the best people to ever walk this earth. I was so lucky to have known her and loved her. She gave me everything. She loved me, confided in me, and took care of me. She gave me you. She made us a family. But when she was gone, God, I didn't know how to keep on going. I needed her like I needed my next breath. But she wasn't here and well, you know how I coped in her absence. I failed. I failed as a husband, a businessman, a friend. But my biggest failure was as your father. I should have been there for you emotionally when you were dealing with her loss. But I was so caught up in my own pain, I couldn't see beyond it. I didn't want to feel anything so I starting numbing myself with alcohol. And now, I can't live without it. It just hurts too much to see everything and everyone I have lost through sober eyes."

Dad has never talked about his substance abuse before. And he has never shared his feelings about my mom and how it affected him. He has kept all that bottled up inside for so long. I wish I had urged him early on to express his feelings and talk about them rather than hide behind them in the bottom of a bottle. Maybe then, we would not be sitting here having this conversation now.

"Do you want to get help? Like rehab, or something? Maybe you should talk to someone, a professional counselor or something."

"I know, and I will. Just, right now there is some other stuff I have to deal with. And the only way to deal with it is to involve you. Patrick, you are going to hate me, if you don't already. But I don't have any other choice."

"I don't hate you, Dad."

"If not yet, then you will. Just let me get this out, okay. Then you can yell and scream and hit me if you want. But son, it's the only way to save this old, wretched man you once called a father." Dad sighs heavily, like the weight of the world is sitting on his shoulders. I wait, knowing I'm not gonna like what he has to say next. But he is my dad, the only immediate family I have left. And whatever he has to say, and however I may be involved, I know deep down I have to help him.

"The law firm is in trouble. When I say trouble, I mean it's about to collapse. In my not so business oriented state over the last few years, I inadvertently let some things slide. I lost more clients than I brought in. My reputation of being 'the kick ass lawyer in town' went down the drain. Where I should have poured all my liquor. But I kept on drinking, forgetting client meetings and court dates. Finally, the lawyers I had working for me left as well, getting other jobs in town. I can't say I blame them. Not only was I bringing down myself, but everyone associated with the firm. Patrick, I was so close to losing everything I had worked for. I thought I was going to have to file bankruptcy and close the firm."

"Dad, why didn't you tell me sooner? I would have given you the money to help with bills or whatever. You know I have it." Turns out, I was the sole beneficiary of my mom's hefty life insurance policy. I guess when she bought it, she believed she would outlive Dad and I'd be the one left to inherit her money. Luckily, Dad never contested the policy. He made sure it was invested wisely and that I used it only for school and living expenses, plus a small allowance each month for incidentals. It has grown to more money than I'll ever need, especially if I get a good paying job after graduation. Plus, I never planned on living off of her death money. It just seemed wrong. I keep it as an emergency fund. Hopefully it will continue to grow and I can pass it down to my children one day. That way I know my mom will have a connection to my future family even though she won't ever get the chance to meet them or be a part of their lives.

"I don't want your money, Patrick. I said the firm almost collapsed and went into bankruptcy. But, fortunately, or unfortunately, depending on how you look at it, I got an offer to sell the firm."

"Who in their right mind would want to buy a firm that is on its last leg?" I ask, not really understanding where this conversation is headed.

"Well, you remember Judge Bostick, from Greenville, right?" The way Dad spits his name out I can tell there is some animosity between the two, which is surprising. Judge Bostick and my dad were college buddies and later roommates during law school. When I was younger and Mom was still alive, we used to vacation with his family. We would spend at least a week a year together, either during the summer at the beach or during the winter months in the mountains skiing. As I got older, and so did the Bostick children, the vacations stopped because we could never coordinate a perfect week when our entire social and sports schedules coincided.

Judge Bostick founded his law firm immediately after graduating. He worked hard and gradually made a name for himself in the upstate. Now, his firm is one of the biggest in South Carolina, with offices in Greenville, Columbia and Charleston. He left his firm in the hands of managing partners and became a judge some years back. He also served his city and state in several political capacities. Rumor has it that one day he may make a run for governor, but no official announcements have been made.

"Yeah, Dad, I remember the Bostick family. But what in the hell do they have to do with the problems you are having with your firm?"

"Well, looks like Jonathan, Judge Bostick to you, has made an offer to buy my firm," Dad answers but then discreetly looks away. I'm not sure what he doesn't want me to see. Maybe he is embarrassed that an old friend, who started his own law practice, just like my dad, is now capable of buying my dad's firm. The firm that means so much to him since he started it from the ground up. I remember going there as a small child when Dad would work crazy long hours trying to make a name for himself and win cases. Mom and I would have to take him dinner frequently just so he would take a break to eat and we could actually get to see him before we went to bed. As I got older, the firm grew substantially and Dad was able to spend more time at home with his family. I can't imagine the beating his pride is taking now. Especially knowing that all his hard work and the name he built for himself has been destroyed by his own doings. And then to top it off, he has to watch a man he considers a friend come in to clean up his mess, essentially robbing my dad of any dignity he has left. But something is not sitting right with this whole bail out. Why would Judge Bostick, a big wig in the world of South Carolina law, with mega offices in the metropolises of the state, want to buy a small firm in Florence?

"So, are you going to sell? Is this the only way out? Cause, I gotta say Dad, I don't understand what Judge Bostick would want with your firm. Not that it's not a great firm and has had serious success in the past. But why a firm in Florence? Aren't the other parts of the state, the bigger cities where he is already established, enough? You know, my offer still stands to loan you the money you will need to get things back to the way they once were. You don't have to sell, Dad."

"Dammit Patrick, yes I do!" Dad yells. I watch as the little control Dad has maintained up until this point shatters. Dad reaches for the bottle of Jack and refills his glass. I sit back stunned at his outburst and don't dare try to stop him from getting his fix. He takes several large gulps until the glass is once again empty. He stands from the table and starts to pace the length of the kitchen. I can tell he is angry. But really? All I did was offer him another way out rather than selling his hard work and career. "Look, I'm sorry but I've been dealing with the financial fallout of my actions for a while. It is at the point that no amount of money will fix what I single handedly destroyed," Dad says looking more defeated than I've ever seen him.

"Okay, so you sell. Then what? Will you continue to work for the firm while it's under new ownership?" I ask hoping that my dad still has a job. His drinking is bad enough now. If he has to sit around all day with nothing to do, who knows what level his addiction could skyrocket to.

"We have agreed on a very generous price. And yes, an offer has been extended to me to do some legal work if I want. However, this is not quite a done deal yet. Judge Bostick has some stipulations and conditions before the deal can be finalized. Patrick, just remember that I have searched every possible solution to the problem I'm in and this is the only one that works. Please, please, I beg, if you ever loved me, forgive me now. I don't have any other choice." Dad finally sits back down and takes my hand in his. I don't think the man has touched me or shown me any type of physical love since I was a boy. Even when Mom died, Dad never even hugged me. He would check on me occasionally, even ask how I was doing. But his channel of expressing love in any shape or form died right along with my mother.

"Dad, I don't understand why you need my forgiveness. Sounds to me like you got this all worked out. As long as you are happy with the purchase price and can continue to work, I don't see why you just don't accept the offer. What else does Judge Bostick want from you?"

"You, son. Judge Bostick wants you."

Chapter Two

I sink to my knees and feel the cold dampness from the ground seep through my jeans. The discomfort barely registers seeing as how I am almost numb to the physical elements affecting my life. I wish someone would come and punch me, a hard right hook connecting with my face. Maybe then the physical pain would outweigh what I'm feeling emotionally. How do you continue to cope when you find out your life is nothing more than a pawn being played by two men? What's more disconcerting is that one of those men is my own father.

The sun is just beginning its accent into the sky. It's still fairly early and the crisp morning air makes it difficult to breathe. I should have grabbed a jacket before storming out of the door in my hurried attempt to leave my father. December in the south can still be bitterly cold even though we don't have to deal with the snow and ice that accompanies the northern winter weather. But I was in such a rush and state of anger and shock, I wasn't thinking to protect myself from the winter elements.

After the first time listening to my dad tell me all the gory details of the deal to save his firm, I laughed. I mean gut wrenching, doubled over laughter that left tears in my eyes and cramps in my midsection. It took me a good ten minutes to calm down and look at the stoic look on my dad's face. He was definitely not laughing and found no humor whatsoever in the situation. So I asked him to tell me again about this absurd plan that he cooked up with Judge Bostick. The second go around didn't differ from the first except this time I contained my laughter and looked on in stunned silence as he began to elaborate once again that it was the only option to save his ass. When I couldn't quite grasp each detail of the plan, I asked him a final time to tell me in excruciating detail every facet of the deal and what it would mean to me and my future plans. This time it was finally sinking in that basically I was fucked. I was so angry that I had been pulled into the mess Dad had made of his life, I stormed out the house and took off avoiding a potential knockdown, drag out between father and son.

I had one of only two choices. Turn my back on my father and let his reputation and all his hard work die, which would probably kill him. He may be dead on the inside, but he still was the only living parent I had left. We may not have been as close as we used to be, but he was still my father. Second choice, not that it was really much of a choice at all, I would have to give up on every dream I ever had concerning the future I envisioned for myself. I would become the property of Judge Bostick, both as a future employee and as a family member. If I accepted the terms of the deal, Judge Bostick guaranteed that my father would remain employed and well compensated. Meanwhile, I would be living in my own personal hell.

I desperately needed someone to talk to. Someone who would hear this incredulous story and give me much needed advice on how to proceed. However, I was embarrassed to present this fucked up scenario to any of my friends. I know they would find what my father was trying to persuade me to do preposterous. I felt the same way. But what they couldn't understand is the length a child will go to save the only living person who had been there since taking his first breath. Our tumultuous relationship since Mom died should have been a factor in my decision making. And it was, because should I agree to help and be a part of this deal, I would have some conditions of my own that would have to be met. First priority, getting my dad the help he so desperately needs. I needed him to get sober and start to deal with his bottled up feelings about losing Mom. Maybe this deal would bring the dad I once looked up to back. Maybe this was a sign that not all was lost when my mom passed. If I could do this for my dad, maybe a lifelong relationship between father and son would develop and everything I had given up to fix his shit would be worth it just for that.

I place the rather small, pathetic flower arrangement I bought at the twenty-four hour Piggly Wiggly at the headstone of my mother's final resting place on earth. I know she isn't still under the ground. Her bones may be there encased in the beautiful casket I watched be lowered in the ground, but her soul is in Heaven hopefully watching over me and ready to give me much needed guidance. "Hey Momma. Sorry about the flowers. It was all I could get during the middle of the night." I brush off the dried leaves and dirt from her grave stone. Her grave is taken care of on a weekly basis. Aunt Betty arranges weekly flower deliveries and ground maintenance so that her sister's grave is a reflection of how my mother lived her life. With the little sunshine of daybreak I can see that my mom is being well taken care of. "I miss you Momma...so much! I wish you were here now so you could tell me what to do." Of course, I know if my mom was still with us, this problem I find myself in wouldn't exist.

After driving around for hours, visiting places of my childhood, I ended up at the cemetery. I knew the only person I could talk to about this was my mother. Some people might think it is silly talking to a piece of concrete, but I find that I feel the closest to my mother when visiting her grave. I feel her presence and I believe that she can hear me when I talk to her. If only she could talk back. But I don't have to hear her voice to know exactly what she would say. Among all the things my mom taught me, her lesson of unconditional love rings in my ears. No matter what I would do as a rambunctious boy or a hormonal teenager, she always ended every confrontation we had with the assurance of how much she loved me.

When I first stormed out of the house, I drove my Jeep aimlessly around town. Somehow my subconscious felt I needed a walk down memory lane and before I knew it, I had parked in front of the little league baseball field where I played ball every spring as a child. I remember watching my mom sitting in the stands cheering me on as I went up to bat. Whether I hit a homerun or struck out, she would clap and yell my name all the while giving me an encouraging smile. Sometimes my dad would show up if the game lasted long enough for him to finish his work. On those rare occasions, he would cheer right along with her, but it was my mom's voice I always heard out on the field. Mom never showed up to a game empty handed. Win or lose, our team always had a post game celebration with the sweet treats my mom baked and provided. Mom officially became the team parent of every sport I played.

When I had outgrown little league and the local park, I spent most of my extracurricular time involved in school sports. So in my walk down memory lane, it was only fitting I make a stop by the local high school. When I wasn't studying, I was playing any sport available. I started the year on the football team. Granted, football wasn't my best sport. That was more Landon's territory. Landon's big, bulky physique was perfect for the football field where I, being more the tall, lanky type, really had to rely on the padding we wore under our uniforms. Of course, Mom was always a nervous wreck while she watched us play. But she never shied away from supporting me in my endeavors, always at each game cheering me on. I asked her to chill out with the "Go Patrick" yells because however supportive she was being, it was a tad bit embarrassing to a teenager. And I needed to retain my level of coolness that all high school boys think they possess. Once football season ended, it was straight into basketball. In the spring, I would participate in our school's baseball program. Mom was always there at both home and away games. She not only became my biggest cheerleader, she became the cheerleader of all my teammates. She was especially supportive of my teammates who didn't have parents or brothers or sisters in the stands to cheer them on. I think this is when I became more attentive to the lives of my fellow teammates rather than their performance on the court or field. My mom always encouraged me to get to know my teammates on a personal level and build friendships. This is how my interest in writing began. I would focus on the person, not just the player. What I found was that while I loved sports, some of my teammates needed the sport just to survive what was waiting for them at home. Sports became like a savior to some of my friends and without it, those friends may have never finished high school, much less gone on to college.

I find that my mom really shaped the way I see the entire world. She was the one always there cheering me on in my sports life. She was the one who helped me with homework and studied with me for tests. She was the one I called on when I was having a crap day and she was definitely the one I told my happiest news to. When I walked through the doors of my home, it was always her I was calling out for.

Somehow, in my middle of the night journey, I found myself parked beside the golf course of the country club. I rarely come to the club anymore. Not just because I don't live in town now. Even when I come home on those very infrequent visits, I just don't have the desire to indulge in all the club has to offer. Being at the club fills me with memories both good and bad. It's here that Suz and I began our relationship and shared our first kiss. I remember going home to get ready for our first date. Mom, ever so insightful, knew immediately something was up. I was so excited and a little nervous. I casually mentioned to Mom that Suzanna and I were going out to dinner. Of course Mom could tell this wasn't just two old friends sharing a meal, which was obvious when there was no mention of Chloe, Landon or James joining us. She fawned over my appearance and ran through her whole spiel about manners and being the perfect southern gentleman. All the while, she tried, unsuccessfully, to hide the smile that lit up her face at the news of a possible romantic relationship between me and Suzanna. How would I know that what began on the golf course that day would become a beautiful relationship of love only to end in heartbreak? This is also the place that Suzanna and I had our last intimate encounter, just days before she broke things off and left town, leaving me sad, angry and confused. I was a mess and needed my mom more than ever when Suzanna left me. Of course, this was after the accident that took my mother's life. My dad was no help, spending most of his time at work. When he wasn't working, he was drinking. Had he been available, I don't think he would have understood what I was going through. He never asked about my relationship with Suzanna. Even when Mom was alive, he didn't seem to take the interest that she did in my personal life. There was no way I was going to confide in him and spill my guts about a broken heart. Fortunately, I had my best friends, James and Landon. They let me talk when I needed to and didn't push for information when I would shut down. They were just there to help me finish the last semester of senior year and kept me focused on college. I knew deep down that they too were mourning the loss of a friend when Suzanna left. All five of us, Chloe included, had been inseparable since childhood. I tried not to blame myself for the destruction of our group of friends, but I did. When Suz and I entered our relationship we knew that our friendships would be at risk should things not work out. However, I never fathomed us ending. For me, Suzanna was it. She was my forever. Even years later, I still consider her as my future. I figured we would both complete college and mature into adults. Only then would I track her down and find out why she left me. Really, it didn't matter to me. If she was willing to give it a go again, I would be all in, no questions asked.

Focusing back on my surroundings, I look at my mother's grave and wonder what she sees in my future. If I help my dad and agree to this deal with Judge Bostick, everything I planned for my future vanishes. Would Mom want me to give up on my dreams? I don't. Of course I learned in my short twenty three years that you don't always get what you want. I want my mom here on Earth with me, but that's not the case. I want my dad to be sober. I want him to be the man he was when my mom was alive, not the washed up, bankrupt lawyer and depressed drunk he has transformed into. I want my girl back. I want to feel her soft skin pressed against mine and wrap her in my arms. I want Suzanna to be mine. But of course, she is off somewhere concentrating on golf and she is definitely not mine. There is so much I want but don't have. Should I continue to deny myself by letting go of my dreams to help my dad? He needs me. I remember how he used to be so independent, never relying on anyone else. But now, he has nowhere else to turn. I know what it feels like to need someone, but they don't come through for you. I need my mom, yet she isn't here. I need Suzanna, but she isn't here either. Have I ever needed my dad? It was always Mom I turned to in crisis. Had I turned to Dad more in my youth, would he be in the situation he's in now? I'm not that ungrateful of a son that I don't realize the sacrifices my dad made for Mom and me. It was his hard work that kept a roof over our heads, afforded us membership to the club and gave Mom the freedom to stay home and focus solely on the family. The reason she was always present at every sporting event I played was because Dad was slaving away to ensure our financial stability. Now all his hard work is at risk of being destroyed. I have the chance to save him. Maybe becoming his savior, I'll show him the gratitude I selfishly have been holding in.

The deal looms at the forefront of my mind. Going over each detail, I'm still reluctant to accept. Sure, I won't be seeking my dream writing job right after graduation, but law school isn't such a bad idea. I could still continue to write while earning a law degree. Who knows? Maybe after law school and working for Judge Bostick, I could use the law degree to become a sports agent. Or I could use my legal knowledge and become an analyst for ESPN. There are plenty of opportunities a law degree would provide and I could still concentrate my career in the world of sports. I'll just have to be patient. I realize that if I'm going to help Dad, I don't necessarily have to give up my career dreams. I just have to put them on hold for a while. However, the other part of the deal is harder to digest. I fish in my jeans pocket and pull out my mother's engagement diamond. I didn't realize that Dad had saved her ring for me to give to my future wife until he gave it to me earlier tonight. Her diamond is beautiful. Set in platinum, a total weight of two carats cut in a round solitaire shines brilliantly in the early morning sun. I never thought of what it would be like to slip a ring onto a woman's finger, asking for her hand in marriage. Okay, so that's not quite true. Years ago, I did entertain thoughts of a future with someone in particular. Now, looking at my mother's ring, there is only one person who deserves to wear her diamond. Unfortunately, Suzanna isn't part of this deal. No, if I want to save my dad, I'm required to get married. Supposedly, I'm going be a part of the Bostick family by the end of this summer, marrying Judge Bostick's only daughter, Katelyn. I barely know the girl. Sure I remember her from our family vacations, but I haven't seen her in years. Dad assured me she is on board with this arranged marriage.

For whatever reasons, she agreed to marry an almost complete stranger. This leads me to believe that her life may be just as fucked up as mine. That or she too is being bribed. Since I'm considering this arrangement, however, wondering exactly what century I'm currently living in, I realize that whatever her reasons or mine, the final goal is the same. We are trying to save and protect someone close to us, someone we love.

Putting the ring back inside my pocket, I stand getting ready to leave. I guess I'll head back to my father's and give him my decision. "Thanks, Mom. I always seem to see things with a little more clarity when you are close. I know in my heart that I have to do this, although just for the record, I don't want to. If it was you, I wouldn't think twice and agree immediately. I know I shouldn't play favorites, but Mom, Dad just hasn't been himself since you left. Maybe this is a way, granted a preposterous, screwed up way, but nevertheless a way to bring Dad back. I know you would help anyway you could, never considering what you would be giving up. But that was you, Mom. Always putting others first. I'm gonna put Dad first this time, not because he asked and feels like it's his only way out. I'm doing this because it's what you would do. And, I'm doing it to make you proud. So, I hope you will watch and guide me while all this plays out." I lean down and kiss the top of her headstone. "Bye, Mom. I'll see you again soon. I love you."

I walk back to my truck with a new purpose. I'm not at all excited about what I'm about to do, but I feel needed by the one man who never needed anyone. If I can help my dad pull out of his grief and depression, then get him some help to beat his alcohol addiction, I'll accomplish something for both me and my dead mother. Pulling away from the cemetery, I drive back home with a determination to fight for my family, my one living parent. I'm getting ready to help my dad and accept the conditions of the deal Judge Bostick has offered. I just hope I'm not making a deal with the devil.

Chapter Three

Suzanna

Present day...

One foot in front of the other. That mantra is the only thing that is going through my brain as I make my way down the stairs and away from Wyatt and the opened door of his apartment. My legs are trembling, but I continue to walk at an even and steady pace toward my car. I don't stop and wave to the neighbor walking her dog. I don't slow down for the oncoming car making its way across the parking lot. And I definitely don't look back. The only thing I see ahead of me is my car and my means of escape. Finally, *finally*, I make it to the driver's side door and thank myself for forgetting to lock the vehicle in my haste to see Wyatt upon my arrival. Sliding onto the seat, I can barely stick the keys into the ignition because my hands continue to shake. I force myself to take some deep breaths and eventually start the motor. Astonishingly, I manage to back my car out of the parking space without getting t-boned. I never once look in the rearview mirror for oncoming traffic because I refuse to take one look back toward Wyatt's apartment. I have no idea whether or not he is still standing there watching me leave. For all I know, he is making his way down the hallway toward his bedroom for more between the sheets action with Bridgett. That thought alone makes my stomach twist into knots causing me to want to vomit. I'd vomit all over my lap before I stop my car from peeling out of his apartment complex parking lot.

Miraculously I manage to drive away from Wyatt's home and make my way through downtown Columbia without causing a traffic accident. I hold the tears at bay until I accelerate onto Interstate 20 heading east toward the beach. The despair that I have controlled up to this point bubbles over and violent sobs rack my body. How could I have let this happen? Up until a month ago, I guarded my heart very carefully, never allowing myself to love another man. But Wyatt cracked my armor and I stupidly let him in. Granted, I had gone into the relationship still broken from memories of my first love, Patrick. The news of Patrick's engagement had sent me into a deep downward spiral that I wasn't sure I would recover from. However, Wyatt had been there to pick up the pieces and help me mend. In the process I had grown to love Wyatt, and I thought the feeling was mutual. What a dumb blonde I was! I guess if anyone was to blame it was myself. I let my emotions go uncontrolled and barreled head first into a fast and frenzied paced relationship thinking that I could feel what I once felt with Patrick. But just as Patrick had been taken away, now the same was happening with Wyatt. What a fucking mess!

If I didn't believe in guardian angels before today, I do now. My blurry vision from the onset of tears didn't deter me from driving down the interstate. Once I reached my hometown of Florence, I still had over an hour's drive time before I was safely back at the beach house. Funny, how each time my heart was broken I would escape to my little slice of heaven by the sea. When things ended with Patrick during our senior year of high school, I moved to the beach under the assumption that I was concentrating on my golf game. Sure, I had been fortunate to be accepted to the prestigious junior golf academy to finish out my senior year and focus on the sport I loved. But truthfully, my reasons for leaving then had absolutely nothing to do with golf. I would have never chosen golf or anything else over Patrick. It really wasn't even a choice I had been allowed to make; I had been forced to make it. The terrible things that happened that one night at the country club had been the deciding factor in my leaving the love of my life, and that night has continued to haunt me to this day, even over four years later.

For the briefest moment I think about stopping at my childhood home. But after one look in the mirror, I quickly dismiss this idea. My puffy, tear stained face and red rimmed eyes would be a dead give away to my parents that something is terribly wrong. Plus, I really didn't want to hear the 'I told you so' I was sure my parents would give me. Mom and Dad were more than surprised to hear about my relationship with Wyatt during my college graduation just over a week ago. They both thought the relationship had progressed too fast and that there was no possible way that I had fallen in love in a month's time. Even I had questioned the time frame of my declaration of love. But the feelings I had locked away since Patrick had been unleashed with Wyatt and I was head over heels in love with the man. Not that it matters now. Once again love had kicked my ass! Dismissing the parental visit, I continued eastbound toward the beach. Once Florence was behind me, my despair had transformed into anger. I was so angry with Wyatt and how he so easily dismissed me from his life. Not to mention the lame excuse of not being able to deal with a long distance relationship this summer. We had discussed that the distance would be hard to deal with, with him in New York completing a summer internship in international business, and me in South Carolina concentrating on my golf game in preparation to go pro. But we had agreed that what we had was worth fighting for and we were both willing to suffer through the distance this summer to build for our future together. Obviously, the distance excuse was a farce, since what Wyatt had really been hiding was stretched out in his bed. Bridgett, my former college teammate and obsessed Wyatt freak. She had basically been stalking Wyatt before and even after we started dating. I have to give her credit for her persistence, even if she is a slut! Well it looks like she finally got what she wanted. Ugh! I can't think about her anymore or that sick, nauseating feeling would be creeping back soon and I couldn't afford to stop my travels.

Hoping the radio would take my mind off the train wreck my life has become, I scan the stations for a distraction. The first few notes of Journey's "Don't Stop Believing" fill the car before I quickly change the station. Hate to break it to you Journey, but this girl stopped believing a long time ago, only to be taught a lesson once again that you shouldn't believe in love or any fairytale endings. More sappy love songs played on various stations and they were quickly replaced with a new song. The last station I found had the audacity to play Pink's anthem "Try". Memories flooded my brain of how Wyatt had begged me to try a relationship with him. We had started out as friends many years ago, and had maintained that friendship. Wyatt and my best friend, Chloe, were the only two people who knew my deepest, darkest secret from the moment it happened. I owed Wyatt my life, because he had saved mine on that terrible night four and a half years ago. After a night of heavy, celebratory drinking in honor of my invitation to LPGA qualifying, Wyatt and I had taken things from friendship to the bedroom. I was willing to let that be a one-time sexual encounter, not that that was my normal behavior. Up until that night, I had only slept with Patrick. Wyatt convinced me that we could have something more and urged me to try. Well, Pink, see what happens when you open your heart yet once again and try? Having enough of the try lecture from Pink, I slammed my fist into the radio so hard it not only silenced the sounds, but shook the entire dashboard. "Ouch!" Apparently, I had resolved to physically harming myself now.

The rest of the trip I alternated between states of depression, sadness, anger and numbness. I relished the feeling of numbness because then I couldn't feel anything at all for Wyatt. Soon the salt air of the ocean was upon me and for a brief moment I felt a sliver of peace come over me. This was my safe haven, the beach. Whatever my moods, being surrounded by the ocean and inlet had a calming effect on me. As my car made the last leg of the journey from hell down Atlantic Avenue, I tried to erase the images of this morning with anything more pleasant. Involuntarily, my fingers brushed over my lips and a tingling sensation raced through my body. Thoughts of Patrick's lips brushing over mine as we embraced each other on the front porch last night came rushing back. Whoa, where did that come from? Had it just been last night that I had attended his engagement party, been threatened by his jackass father, and then spilled my deepest secret to my brother? And hadn't it been just this morning that the small amount of joy I allowed in my life with Wyatt came crashing down all around me? Talk about life taking a turn for the worst! Finally, emotionally and physically exhausted, I turn my car into the driveway of my family beach home. Luckily, our house guests from the weekend have already left and only Flynn's and Chloe's cars remain parked under the raised beach house. Granted, I love my dear friends, James and Landon, and I was glad that we all reconnected over the weekend after years apart. But I didn't want anyone to see me in this state of mind. With one deep breath, I grab my purse and exit the car hoping the ocean breeze still holds a magical cure for another of Suzanna's broken hearts.

Chapter Four

With the exception of the ten minutes it took for Wyatt to break my heart, I had spent five hours trapped in a car on my round trip from the beach to Columbia and back. My body ached as I stepped out of my car and stretched. With a heavy heart, I trudged up the stairs to enter the house, secretly praying that Chloe and Flynn would be anywhere, but inside. I needed their support and comfort, however, the wound was still too raw and I didn't know if I had it in me to rehash the events of this morning. When I graduated just over a week ago, I had been so optimistic about my future knowing that I had a significant other to share it with. Living at the beach alone this summer seemed tolerable knowing that I would be sharing my daily experiences with Wyatt. I looked forward to our daily chats and texts, and I couldn't wait to hear about his experiences in New York. We were both following our dreams and sharing those experiences with each other. Even though we would be states away, the time apart would bring us that much closer. But now, my summer at the beach, regardless of how much I adore this place, suddenly seems lonely. I should be used to being alone since I basically lived that way during my college years, focusing only on my studies and golf. But Wyatt had opened up something I forgot existed, and I actually was beginning to find some hope that I could share my life with someone other than just family and friends. Now that hope was fading fast. Damn him!

The tears I thought had long dried up during the drive returned as my optimism slipped away. Emotionally wrecked, I entered the quiet house. Maybe my silent pray of an empty house had been answered. At least something today might go in my favor. Hanging my head low, I walked through the living area toward the solidarity of my bedroom. I was halfway there before the slightest movement caused me to stop in my tracks. Glancing toward the couch, I couldn't believe what my eyes were seeing. Legs and arms so entangled, I didn't know where one body began and the other ended. Chloe was sporting her red, skimpy bikini that was barely covering her private parts. She was lying atop my brother, Flynn, who was bare chested, wearing only a pair of swim trunks. Both of them seemed to be caught in the moment because as I stood there and watched the peep show, that was slowing turning into a porn movie, they continued. I guess they had not heard me enter the house over their moans and groans. As if a switch had been turned, my sadness turned to anger in the blink of an eye. How dare they be all lovey, dovey, groping and sucking while I was in the depths of my misery! The voice that I thought would be soft and scratchy due to my unlimited amount of crying surprised not only Chloe and Flynn, but, also me.

"Un-fucking-believable!!!" I shout.

Chloe jumps up adjusting her bikini top to quickly cover her ample chest. Damn, I hate to admit it, but I'm jealous of her girls. It doesn't mean that I want to see them in their state of bare glory. "Suzanna? What are you doing here?"

Did she just have the nerve to ask me what I was doing in my own house? What the hell? "Last I checked this was *my* beach house!" I smart back. Flynn has finally made it to a sitting position trying to adjust his swim trunks that are, thankfully, hiding his excitement from a few minutes earlier.

"I think what Chloe means is, why are you at the beach now instead of in Columbia with Wyatt? I thought he wasn't leaving until tomorrow."

Just the mention of his name is like a knife slicing into my skin. Even though I am simmering with anger, the waterworks start again. Both Chloe and Flynn watch with concern as I try to wipe the tears that are clearly evident. I can't seem to manage my emotions as they fluctuate between sadness and anger. Chloe cautiously starts making her way toward me, arms outstretched, ready to comfort me in a hug. I don't want her comfort or her pity. Here she is getting everything she has ever wanted. Chloe has been crushing on my brother for years, despite the fact that he only ever saw her as his sister's best friend. Unlike me, Chloe didn't let her obsession with Flynn stop her from pursuing other romantic interests with other men, even though no one would fill the spot in her heart she reserved just for him. From the look of things, Flynn's wandering eye concerning the female population has finally landed on Chloe this weekend, even though Chloe brought a date to attend Patrick's engagement party. I know I should feel happy for Chloe, finally getting my brother's attention, even though I know he will eventually leave her with a broken heart just like the string of other girls in the southeast. Both Chloe and I know Flynn is somewhat of a man whore, not the least bit interested in forming a committed relationship. He is a soccer star, getting ready to show his stuff in the European leagues this summer. So what the hell is he doing, leading on Chloe the way he is? I am a complete mess and don't have the time or energy to put Chloe back together after Flynn will no doubt leave her in pieces. She has wanted this thing between her and Flynn for so long, only to start something and have him take it away from her when he goes overseas. That would leave both me and Chloe mending broken hearts! Ugh, could this day get any worse?

Before Chloe can reach me, I turn and storm out of the living area into my bedroom. Not bothering to undress, I throw my purse across the room and crawl under the covers of my bed. Chloe rushes in the doorway, followed closely by Flynn. "Suzanna, what's wrong?" she asks.

"What's wrong? Well, let's see. First, Wyatt tells me upon my arrival that he no longer wants the whole long distance relationship thing. Second, I find Bridgett butt naked, draped across his bed. And third, I come home a complete wreck to find you dry humping my brother. So to answer your question of what's wrong with me, well, I'm sick and tired of running into not one, but two whores today!"

I hear Chloe gasp as she stands frozen in her spot just inside the doorway of my bedroom. Okay, I know that was a little over the top rude. I basically just called my best friend a whore and lumped her in the same category as Bridgett the slut. But I am beyond angry at any and everybody. Flynn rushes around Chloe, stomping toward my bed. "Don't talk to her that way! She's your best friend," he yells.

"Oh my, if I wasn't present for this I might not believe it. Flynn, my man whore brother, taking up for a girl. Not your normal style, huh? I thought this was the time you were pushing the girl out the door with a 'thanks for tonight, but don't call tomorrow' spiel. Guess you didn't get far enough inside Chloe's red bikini to send her packing just yet!" Wow, I can't believe I just said that. Pretty sure the angry side of my multiple personalities is back full force.

I take a moment to quickly glance at Chloe. My harsh words have brought her to tears and she is slowly backing out of the bedroom. Flynn, on the other hand, is livid, his anger radiating off his tense body. "I don't know what the fuck happened to you today, but your anger is directed toward the wrong people. Don't ever, EVER, talk to me or Chloe again that way! I don't care what you think about me, but you will regret saying these things about Chloe. Now apologize to her, now!"

"GET OUT!" I scream. Not much of an apology, but I can't take anymore drama today. I know I am way out of line with both Chloe and Flynn, but I am hurting so much and I guess I just want others to hurt with me. Childish behavior at its best, but I don't want to be an adult. I just want to be left alone and suffer silently with my misery.

"Suzanna," Flynn speaks with concern rather than anger lacing his voice. "We'll leave you to be for now. We love you and we care about you. Please let us help you get through whatever happened to you today."

His words slice through the anger and the layer of sadness is covering me, again. I nod, and then turn my back to him burying my face in the pillow before he can see the tears that finally escape my eyes. Between my silent sobs, I feel Flynn cover my body with the bed comforter and walk out of the room, closing the door behind him. I hear hushed voices outside the door, Flynn trying to comfort Chloe while she cries. I know I am the source of her tears and I feel guilty for causing her pain. I am glad that Flynn is with her, holding her while she aches from my harsh words and the worry I know she harbors for my failed relationship with Wyatt. I will apologize and beg her forgiveness. Chloe has been my best friend forever and helped me through the pain of leaving Patrick. Now, single again since Wyatt has so easily dismissed me from his life, I know I will need Chloe more than ever. I hope I haven't pushed her away with my angry rant. Alone in my bedroom, I cry until there is nothing left and sleep finally consumes me.

Chapter Five

What day is it? I peel my greasy hair off of the pillow my head has been permanently glued to for the last...how long has it been? I remember coming back to the beach house and cursing out my best friend and brother and then I closed myself up in my room and have been camped out on my bed ever since. The only time I have left the safety of the covers is to go to the bathroom or sneak into the kitchen for a drink. Chloe and Flynn have checked on me frequently, bringing in food that never gets eaten. Who knew a broken heart affects your appetite? I haven't eaten anything since Wyatt decided to end our month long relationship. That statement almost makes me laugh. Who is this depressed after only a month of dating? But it wasn't just a relationship. It was love and I'm still in love with him, despite the way he crushed my heart into too many pieces to count. I am a twenty-two year old depressed and pathetic woman. And I'm sick of feeling this way!

With the energy of a slug, I slowly get out of my bed, stretching muscles that have been in a lethargic state since becoming a hermit. Whoa, is that reeking smell coming from me? Taking another sniff, I decide that my first priority is a shower with lots of soap and shampoo. On my way to the shower, I peek out the window to see the sun starting to set across the inlet. Another day of my miserable life is almost over. Trying not to concentrate on my broken heart, I shower for longer than ever before, wishing the water could clean my darkened mood as well as my body. I refuse to cry any more. Surely, the well of tears is dry by now. Plus, I'm sick of who I have become. I wish I could go back and be Suzanna, the girl who just played some spectacular golf. The girl who let no one bring her down because she refused to let her heart care deeply about another man again. My chaotic emotions have been all over the place going from sad and depressed to angry and mad. I just want to live again and be happy. Happiness seems to be eluding me. It teases me for moments in my life, but then makes an abrupt exit. While the much needed shower invigorates me, I make the decision to take back my life. I will search for my happiness again. And I will find it.

Hours later, I still haven't found my happiness in the bottom of a tequila bottle. However, the warm burn of the alcohol streaming through my blood brings the euphoric feeling of numbness. Now numbness, I can deal with. No pain, no crying, no misery, just numbness. I lie on my back on the wooden planks that make up our dock. Staring up at the stars, I'm trying to identify the constellations that I learned about in my astronomy class, but all I keep seeing are Walt Disney characters. Just as I'm piecing together a picture of Mickey Mouse, I hear footsteps crunching over the grass. As the sound gets closer, I also hear the very identifiable heavy breathing of Darth Vader. Now at this point you may think I've ventured off into an alcohol induced la-la land, placing myself right in the middle of a Star Wars episode. I wish! Unfortunately for me, I'm still very present in the reality of my life. As the smell of cigarette smoke comes into play, I hear the loud clip clap of Darth Vader's nails on the dock as she approaches. Darth Vader, real name Raquel, is the ugliest English bulldog you have ever seen. So ugly, she is actually cute. Raquel is the beloved pet of my beach next door neighbor Mrs. Sylvia Stokes. Mrs. Stokes has been the grandmother I never had, since both my parents' mother and father passed either before I was born or shortly thereafter. As long as we have been coming to the beach house, which is all my life, Mrs. Stokes has stepped into the grandparent role. I'd love to say that she is the sweet, doting kind, baking cookies and knitting sweaters for me and Flynn. However, Mrs. Stokes showed her authority by giving us unsolicited advice while corrupting us with cigarettes and booze. When I moved to the beach during my senior year of high school, Mrs. Stokes made sure I was taken care of and never let me wallow in my misery. I never told Mrs. Stokes the real reason I left my hometown and she never asked. Although, with her many years of wisdom, she was perceptive enough to know that I didn't just drop everything to further my golf ambitions.

Turning my head to my uninvited guests, I watch as Mrs. Stokes takes a seat on the bench puffing on her 120 Virginia Slim menthol while Darth Vader gets up close and personal with my face, sniffing and drooling. "Ugh, Darth Vader, leave me alone you ugly mute!"

"Now Suz, you know she doesn't respond to that silly name you and Flynn call her. Don't hurt her feelings. You'll give her a complex not to mention sexual orientation confusion. She's a girl, not some guy dressed in a black cape with a mask. Come here Raquel, Suzanna doesn't know what she's talking about, baby!"

Oh my God! Her attentiveness to that dog gets worse and worse every damn year. At least the bitch listens to her owner because Darth Vader quits giving my face a bath with her spit and curls up at Mrs. Stokes' feet.

"Speaking of hurt feelings, I'm a little disappointed you didn't invite me to your one person tequila party on the dock. Can't an old woman get a drink around here? What happened to you young people's manners?"

"Here," I say handing her the almost empty bottle, "I'll trade you." Mrs. Stokes takes the bottle and sits it beside her on the bench. She reaches in the pocket of her 1980's hot pink wind suit and produces a leather, blinged out cigarette case. Producing the long skinny cigarette she hands it over to me with the lighter. I light the cigarette inhaling deeply while the minty tasting smoke travels down my throat into my lungs. Now, I'm not one to partake in the cancer sticks every day. But I do love me a social smoke, especially when I'm drinking. And I've done quite a lot of that tonight. Mrs. Stokes is the extreme opposite. I don't think I've ever seen her without a cigarette imbedded between her lips. "You know these things will kill you, right?" I ask as I watch Mrs. Stokes take a hefty gulp of my liquor.

"Well, if I'm gonna die, might as well die happy. You got anymore of this because your bottle is running a little low?" she asks in between her second and third swigs.

"Nope, that's the last of it I think. Unless Flynn is hiding his own stash somewhere in the house. I wasn't expecting company."

"What's got your panties in a wad? Must be bad if you're out here all alone having your very own private pity party."

"I don't want to talk about it," I say hoping that will be enough to derail this conversation. But knowing Mrs. Stokes like I do, she will be persistent until she can come to her own conclusions.

"Ah, must be a man. Just like all those years ago when you escaped down here. Who you running from this time, Suz? Can't be the perfect Patrick. I hear he is engaged to another woman," she says bluntly with her raspy smoker's voice.

"I'm not running from anyone. I'm actually taking up permanent residence here this summer to practice for qualifying. You did hear I got invited to compete to be on the professional tour, didn't you?"

"Well yes, I do believe your mom and dad mentioned that when they called me to make sure I'd check up on you. Also, Chloe called and invited me to your surprise party, but I was out of town and couldn't make it. God only knows how, but I got roped into taking care of my wicked sister-in-law who is suffering with gout."

I suddenly can't control the giggle that escapes. Somehow, in my hazy, alcohol induced brain, the word 'gout' seems extraordinarily funny. Mrs. Stokes watches on as my giggles develop into full blown laughter, as I roll side to side holding my belly. Mrs. Stokes' lips twitch upward and before long we are both in hysterics.

"I'm sorry," I say trying to catch my breath. "I don't mean to laugh at your sister-in-law's medical condition. But gout? Who gets gout anymore?" This only starts the laughing all over again. Finally, after minutes in fits of giddiness, we both calm down. "Thanks, I really needed that. I haven't laughed that much since I got back." Suddenly, the reason for my sadness comes back to the forefront of my thoughts and it's definitely not a laughing matter.

"Oh dear, Suzanna. Really, what's got you so down? I thought with the news of potentially joining the tour you would be ecstatic."

"I am. It's just, I don't know. A lot has changed and I'm trying to deal with it all and concentrate on golf," I say even though it is a very vague answer.

"Like you need to concentrate. You are so gifted when you have a golf club in your hands. You have natural talent that will get you on that tour. So don't try and tell me your golf concentration is the reason this liquor bottle is empty."

"No, the reason it's empty is because you drank it all!"

Mrs. Stokes gives me one of her 'I'm not in the mood for this shit' looks.

"Alright, nosey neighbor. If you must know, yes it has something to do with a certain man. And no, before you get all blunt again announcing Patrick's engagement to me, which I already know about and attended the damn party, it doesn't have to do with him."

"Well, that's another topic of discussion we will address later. I want to hear all about the engagement shindig. Just another party I had to miss on account of the gout!" Mrs. Stokes smiles and I return it. "So if this doesn't have to do with Patrick, who are you running from this time?"

"I am not running!" I shout. "Ugh, just the opposite. He ran away from me. All the way up the eastern seaboard to New York. And even though I was fully committed to endure the long distance relationship deal, he apparently wasn't. So much so, he had a naked girl in his bed when he told me to further convince me that I'm obviously not what he wants. Do you now get why I'm in desperate need of a thousand pity parties? And next time you want to join, how about you bring your own booze."

"Whoa, snippy much these days Suz?"

"Sorry, but yeah, I've had better days. It's just I really thought this was the one. Wyatt, well, he was everything to me. I've known him for years, but we just got romantically involved a little over a month ago. And you don't have to tell me. Mom and Dad and Flynn and practically everybody who knows me say it happened too fast. They can't believe that two people could fall in love in such a short amount of time. But, I did. I guess, maybe he didn't," I say the sorrow in my voice lacing the night air.

"Suzanna, I believe two people can fall in love in a month or less. Didn't I ever tell you about how Ernie and I met? Oh, it was love at first sight. It didn't take me two seconds to fall completely head over heels for that man. I was visiting one of my dad's hotels and he was working as a janitor. Ernie, God bless him, he worked his whole life and made me the proudest woman on this planet. Anyway, Ernie didn't come from much and I, well, I was the heir to the real estate fortune that my family had acquired over the years. After an encounter on the hotel elevator, I knew Ernie was my one and only. We started seeing each other secretly because Lord only knows what would happen had my parents found out their only daughter was dating a hotel janitor. But to me, Ernie was so much more than the label attached to his part-time job. He was a hard working college student trying to make a life for himself. Unfortunately, our secret dating didn't last long and, just like I knew they would be, my parents were livid. They even forbid me to see Ernie again. Now, you know what happens when someone forbids Sylvia Inman Stokes to do anything. Well, I left with Ernie after he was fired from the hotel and we went and made a life together in North Carolina. He finished school with a business degree and worked in the oil business until he formed his own oil company. And the rest is history. Ernie sold said oil company to Shell twenty years after he had incorporated it. We never had to worry about money for the rest of our lives. Finally, after Ernie made his millions, my parents tried to make peace with us. But by then, it was too late. Sure, I talked to my parents but the relationship was strained right up until they passed away. But I don't regret one single second I spent with Ernie and my decision to be with him. I knew the moment we locked eyes the very first time at my dad's hotel that I was in love with him. So no, Suz, I don't think you're crazy for falling in love with Wyatt in such a short amount of time. Usually those are the best, long lasting love stories."

Wow, I never knew Mrs. Stokes had a soft spot. I have never heard her speak of Mr. Stokes more lovingly before. Sure, I knew Mr. Stokes in my early childhood before he died of a heart attack about ten years ago. I remember going to his funeral and thinking how strong Mrs. Stokes seemed, never shedding a tear. Looking over at her now, I can see the misty sheen in her eyes as she remembers her late husband.

"Now, enough about my love life. I want to hear about yours. Tell me about this Wyatt dude. What's his last name? I might know his people," Mrs. Stokes says turning the attention back to me.

"You won't. He doesn't come from money."

"Suzanna, just because I have more money than God, doesn't mean I don't know people who don't. Didn't you listen to anything I just said about me and Ernie?"

I sigh heavily, because I really don't want to talk about Wyatt. It hurts too much. But Mrs. Stokes just showed me she actually does have a heart and I guess I can entertain her curiosity.

"His name is Wyatt McCain. I have known him since I was a junior in high school. He worked at the country club as a bartender while attending Francis Marion University. We were friends right up until I moved to the beach during senior year. After that we lost touch. Chloe still saw him until he quit the club and moved to Columbia to work on his master's degree at USC. When Chloe and I lived together in college, we all started hanging out again. Just recently, things went from platonic to romantic. Until it was time for him to leave and he decided the long distance thing wasn't going to work for him. And that's about it, end of story."

Mrs. Stokes stares off into the sky trying to figure out whether or not she knows Wyatt or his family. It wouldn't surprise me if she did, the woman knows almost everybody. "I don't think I know any McCains. But he sounds like a good man. What made him leave and move to New York?" she asks more curious than I think I've ever seen her.

"He is working at Galloway and Meads brokerage firm. Fulfilling an internship that will complete his masters program in international business. He was one of only five chosen to participate in the internship from students all across the country," I say pride clearly evident.

"Now, Galloway and Meads I do know. Quite the reputable firm. Ernie and I had some dealings with them with our 401k's and retirement packages. It's an accomplishment to be associated with them. You know, Wyatt reminds me a lot of my Ernie with how dedicated he is working toward his career. Sounds like Wyatt is a smart man. Well, smart when it comes to business. Maybe not so smart when it comes to women?" Mrs. Stokes jokes trying to lighten the mood.

"I agree. He's a dumbass!" I say, but don't really mean it.

"Ah Suz, I can tell you still harbor some serious feelings for this boy. You sure about what he wants when it comes to you? Maybe he was giving you an out so that you can focus on golf."

"Well, I might believe that if only I had his words to evaluate. But the naked bitch in his bed left no room for any other conclusion than he doesn't want me, nor did he love me. Because, how can you love someone and do something like that?" I hear the question I just spoke and suddenly feel extremely guilty. Wasn't it just the night before I left to see Wyatt that Patrick's tongue was down my throat? And here I am calling Bridgett a whore for being in Wyatt's bed when I never saw him touch her. Yet, I had Patrick's hands all over me only hours before seeing Wyatt. Who's the whore now, Suz? Maybe you shouldn't be name calling.

"Well, as damning as that scene might have been, there's always more to the story than what's right in plain sight. Have you talked to Wyatt since the breakup?" Mrs. Stokes asks almost like she has some mindreading skills.

"No, I haven't turned my cell phone on once since I got back. I really haven't talked to anyone about this. Not even Chloe or Flynn."

"Why not? Aren't they here at the beach with you?"

Ashamed to tell her about how I mistreated my best friend and brother when I arrived home, I look away just in time to see none other than Chloe and Flynn walking across the lawn toward us. Mrs. Stokes must have heard them coming because she also turns her head in that direction. Useless Darth Vader looks up, but must deem them uninteresting because she settles back down, laying her head in a puddle of her own drool.

"Well, speak of the devil. Chloe and Flynn, we were just talking about you two," Mrs. Stokes greets them as they make their way to the dock.

"Hi, Mrs. Stokes. Glad to see you made it back from your visit with your family," Chloe ever so politely addresses Sylvia.

The reference to Mrs. Stokes' visit with her sister-in-law sends me into another fit of giggles. Mrs. Stokes joins my hysteria while Chloe and Flynn look at us both with amusement. "Looks like you gals have been having a party without us," Flynn says with a smirk on his face.

"I'm just here making sure Suzanna doesn't fall into the inlet and become a shark's snack. I'm glad you both are here. I don't think it's safe for Suzanna to walk the plank and get to dry land all by herself. I know my old bones aren't worth shit and couldn't possibly help her. So I'll leave it up to you two to get her back to the house and all tucked in. Good luck, you're gonna need it." With that, Mrs. Stokes throws her burned down cigarette in the inlet and pats Darth Vader on the head. "Let's go, Raquel. I've got a gourmet dog biscuit with your name on it." Darth Vader stands and stretches her short, stubby legs before coming over and giving me a goodnight lick to the face.

"Gross! Go home Darth Vader!" I yell wiping the slobber from my cheek. Mrs. Stokes cackles all the way up the dock and across the lawn, Dark Vader following at her heels.

"Night Suz, we'll talk more tomorrow. You guys take good care of the girl...she's a bit fragile."

"Ugh," I groan as I push up to a sitting position. Whoa, the stars seem to start moving and I find myself getting dizzy.

"Hold up sis. Let me help you." Flynn leans down and picks me up planting me firmly on my feet. I immediately start to sway to the left before Chloe comes to that side and stabilizes my body. Leaning against both her and Flynn, I slowly make the trek from the dock, across the lawn and inside the house. Chloe and Flynn never let me falter. When I make it to the bedroom, Chloe helps me with my clothing while Flynn goes in search of aspirin and a bottle of water. "Here Suz, you better go ahead and take these before you pass out."

Flynn hands me the goods and I quickly swallow the meds with a big gulp of water.

"Thank you," I say through a throat that is heavily clogged with emotion. "And I'm sorry, so very, very sorry." I manage to get out my apology before the waterworks take over. Peeking through wet lashes, I make eye contact with both Flynn and Chloe. "You guys didn't deserve my wrath the other day and I'm sorry for all the things I said. I was in such a bad place, and I still am, but you have to believe that I didn't mean anything I said. I love you both so much and nothing would make me happier than for you two to be together. If that's what you both want. Please, please forgive me. I'm an idiot." I sob the entire time and pray that they are able to understand my words through my tears.

Chloe comes over and hugs me while Flynn kisses the top of my head. "Suz, you've been through a lot and although neither I nor Flynn understand what all went down with Wyatt, we will never hold irrational words spoken during emotional distress against you. Now, you are trashed and I think you need a good night of sleep before we begin to hash everything out. Just know we both love you very much and, no matter what happens, everything will be okay."

With that, Chloe releases me and tucks me in. Right before my head hits the pillow I hear both her and Flynn leaving my bedroom. Flynn pauses at the door, "Night sis, sweet dreams." He turns out the light and closes the door just as I pass out for the night.

Chapter Six

W hen will I ever learn? Tequila does nothing for a broken heart. Not only did I wake up with the same ache in my heart, but I now have to contend with an ache in my head. Damn alcohol! Each morning when I wake up I reach over and touch both sides of the bed only to find them empty and cold. I know that Wyatt isn't with me anymore, but old habits die hard. Before leaving Columbia, the best part of each day was waking up snuggled close to Wyatt's warm body and cuddled in the safety of his arms. Of course I knew that would change when we decided to both follow our dreams. Wyatt would be spending the summer in New York working as an intern in a highly prestigious investment firm while I would be concentrating on my golf game trying to make the pro tour. However, even though we would be states away from each other and the physical contact was impossible, the fact that we would have each other in our hearts twenty-four-seven was something that I could deal with until we were back in each other's arms. But he isn't mine anymore and my heart is empty. Just like my bed.

I thought I had been doing better with the whole Wyatt doesn't want me anymore fiasco. Well, better is very relative. I had spent countless days locked up in my bedroom at the beach house alone. It was easy to try and take my mind off the heartache with music and mindless television. I guess last night when I had had enough of staring at the ceiling and walls of my bedroom, I sought the solace of the inlet and stars, having my own pity party on the dock. Of course I didn't get my alone time like I thought I would. My nosey neighbor, Mrs. Stokes, crashed my party and drank all my tequila. But worst of all, she had me rehash the memories of love and betrayal, making me tell her all about Wyatt. Not that I haven't thought about him constantly since I returned from Columbia where he surprised me with our out of nowhere break up. But this morning the pain is fiercer just having talked about him last night. I realize I can't stay holed up in my room the rest of my life. I have got to get back to the land of the living. But living without Wyatt in my life seems unbearable. Last night was the first time I actually explained to another human being what went down with my love life. I haven't even told Chloe or Flynn what happened since I returned. I vaguely remember them putting me to bed last night in my drunken state. I don't know exactly what I said to them. But they deserve some answers as to why I have been acting like a lunatic. Not only that, they deserve an apology, as well, for my bad behavior when I interrupted their love fest on the couch.

I know that Flynn and Chloe are right outside my bedroom door in the kitchen having breakfast. The unmistakable sound of Flynn's NutriBullet, his pride and joy smoothie blender, reverberates throughout the house. Flynn never travels without his favorite kitchen appliance. He blends a variety of food items (that you would never eat together normally) in his blender each morning. Such things like spinach, berries and raw eggs. He swears that his concoctions taste delicious and are packed with nutrients that keep him in tip top athletic shape. I'll just take his word for it because I refuse to try any of his morning blends. Raw eggs and spinach... that's just disgusting! Speaking of disgusting, my mouth tastes and feels like I just drank one of Flynn's special smoothies. Running my tongue over my teeth, I feel and taste the coating of grime from last night's tequila and the grossness of morning breath. I slide out of bed and decide to begin my post Wyatt life today. Just as soon as I brush my teeth. After brushing twice and then using mouthwash, I tame my long blond hair as best I can and throw it all into a ponytail. With my personal hygiene priorities taken care, I walk out into the kitchen to face Chloe and Flynn.

Both Chloe and Flynn are sitting at the kitchen table having breakfast. Flynn of course is slurping on some green liquid he blended up earlier, while Chloe is drinking coffee and getting her sugar quota for the day by eating her daily Pop-Tart. Both Chloe and Flynn are sitting in comfortable silence, Flynn reading from some sports magazine while Chloe taps away on her iPad. I walk silently to the kitchen counter to retrieve a mug and pour myself a cup of coffee.

"Well, good morning Sybil!" Chloe says still not taking her eyes off the electronic device in front of her. I watch Flynn smirk behind his magazine while I look on in a state of confusion.

"Huh?"

"Yeah, Sybil. You know the girl with like sixteen different personalities. I think you're on your way to having that many since your return from seeing Wyatt. Wanna recap? Okay, let's start with before you left. You were happy and excited and actually smiling. Remember what that felt like Suz, to smile? That was actually my favorite personality. Then you return the raging bitch, tearing both me a Flynn a new one, calling us every name in the book. Didn't like that so much! Then you become a recluse, hiding away from the world in your bedroom for the past three days. When you finally break out of the bedroom, you become the drunken Suz who is actually entertaining, although sad. So what's it gonna be today Suz? Because Flynn and I have a bet going on and I'd like to win."

"Sybil? Really, Chloe? That's the best you've got?" I smart back not enjoying the recap of my emotional rollercoaster ride these last few days.

"Oh, feisty Suzanna. I like this one," Chloe says with a chuckle.

"I think my fav is drunken Suz. All huggy and lovey. Especially like the part when you gave us your blessing to go 'fuck like rabbits' and make a niece or nephew for you to love on," Flynn says adding in his two cents to this bizarre conversation. Chloe's eyes about bug out of her head at Flynn's statement and I can see a hint of fear and embarrassment in them. She quickly hides her emotions and leans over to slap Flynn in the chest for his antics.

"Did I really say that to you two?" I ask not quite remembering all I was blubbering on about last night before I passed out.

"No, you didn't. Flynn is just trying to rile us both up. Now come over here and reveal the real Suzanna for the first time in days," Chloe says patting the kitchen chair beside her.

I walk over and sit down at the table with my brother and best friend. Guess now is the time to finally get real with them and not hide behind my multiple personalities Chloe so bluntly pointed out to me. "Okay, I get it. I haven't been myself since returning from my visit with Wyatt. But Chloe, you really need to stick with drama and leave the comedy routine to someone else. Your Sybil joke lacked any humor."

"Was it that bad? I thought I nailed my delivery," Chloe asks seriously concerned with her acting skills.

"Yeah, it was that bad. But, hey, at least it got Suz to sit here and finally talk to us sober and not cuss us out," Flynn says patting Chloe on the back to comfort her injured pride due to her terrible comedic skills. I haven't seen Flynn be so attentive to the opposite sex without trying to get in their pants. I don't doubt Flynn would love to get in Chloe's pants. But the expression on his face has more to do with fondness toward Chloe than sex. I wonder how far their relationship has progressed while I was living as a shut in. I don't have too much time to ponder my questions concerning their love life because Chloe immediately pushes for more answers concerning mine.

"So Suz, what exactly happened Sunday at Wyatt's apartment to send you back here a complete mess?"

I tell them everything that happened from the time I walked into Wyatt's apartment until the time I left. I explain, in detail, how my excitement to see Wyatt wasn't reciprocated. I tell them word for word how he tried to convince me that he no longer wanted to pursue a long distance relationship with me this summer. Holding onto the strength I didn't know I possessed, I proceed with the morbid story and tell them how I found a naked Bridgett in Wyatt's bed. That's when it was crystal clear that what Wyatt and I had was all a lie and I left him behind and came home to the beach. Flynn and Chloe listen

The Final Pairing

until I finish and we all sit quietly while they comprehend everything I said and I try hard not to break down in a heaping mess.

"Wow, I don't know what to say," Chloe finally speaks breaking minutes of silence. "I would have never thought Wyatt could do something like that to you. Are you sure you got the whole story?"

"I didn't need the whole story in words, Chloe. I saw it with my own two eyes. Can't explain a naked woman hiding in your bed while you try to break up with your girlfriend. Believe me, if I wasn't buying his 180 degree turn from 'yeah, let's be apart this summer so we can follow our dreams and plan a future together' to 'nah, I've rethought things and decided I'm not really into the whole dating from states away thing', then the fact that Bridgett was stretched out all nice and cozy between his sheets did it for me. Wyatt sure knows how to hammer his point home!" I say, emphasizing that I know *exactly* what I saw.

"Okay, so you saw the worst thing possible after hearing Wyatt's lame excuse to not further your relationship due to long distance. So how did you leave things?" Chloe continues with a calmness I didn't expect. It is actually pissing me off. Had this happened to her I would be fuming mad at the dirt bag that caused her pain. I guess with Wyatt being a friend of hers she is having a hard time believing he could be so cruel. But I'm supposed to be her BFF, where the hell is her loyalty?

"I just left. Told him goodbye and left, never looking back," I said trying to keep the tears at bay. I am so sick of crying, but having to say goodbye to Wyatt was one of the hardest things I had ever done.

"Have you spoken to him since Sunday?" Flynn asks. He seems way too calm also. I want him to show some of that brotherly protection he is so eager to pull out anytime, even if someone just hurts my feelings. After hearing my story of betrayal, I thought for sure I would have to contain him from flying out the door in search of Wyatt to beat his ass. But no, he continues to sit down and listen like I just didn't get my heart smashed into a million, gazillion pieces.

"No, and I don't plan to talk to him ever again. He said all he had to say Sunday morning. I don't want to hear another word that comes

51

out of his mouth." Okay, so that is a lie. I miss hearing his voice so badly. But I don't think anything he could say would explain how he intentionally hurt me to prove the point that a long distance relationship was something he couldn't deal with. "Not that he would try to contact me after he basically dismissed me from his life so cruelly, but I haven't even turned on my cell phone since returning."

"Well, no need to state the obvious," Flynn mumbles under his breath.

"What the hell is that supposed to mean?" I ask them both.

"While you were living like a hermit, all locked up in solitary, Chloe and I have been fielding calls from just about everyone you know," Flynn answers sounding annoyed.

"I don't understand. I haven't told anyone except you, and well, Mrs. Stokes last night. Why would anyone be trying to get in touch with me?" I ask totally confused.

"Suzanna," Chloe says, talking to me like I'm a child, "just because you got your heart broken and tried to stop existing, doesn't mean the entire world stopped on your behalf. There are people who love you and care about you and you've been ignoring everyone. Your parents have called several times to check on you. Coach Moore and Drew called because you missed your last golf lesson. And yes, Wyatt even called to make sure you made it back to the beach safely."

Wyatt had called Chloe and Flynn? What did he say? And my parents? Oh God, what they must be thinking. I can hear them now with the 'I told you so' comments. And I had blown off golf? Golf was the only thing constant in my life. Something I had to look forward to. Something to build a career on. And here I was throwing it away because I was broken hearted. I sound pathetic even to my own ears. I had to know if everyone saw me as the pathetic girl who couldn't keep a man.

"What did you tell Mom and Dad?" I ask Flynn. I'm surprised they both hadn't driven down to the beach to jerk my ass out of bed if they knew I missed golf lessons.

"I told them, as well, as your coaches that you came home with a summer cold and weren't feeling very well. I had to assure Mom that

Chloe and I were taking good care of you or else she would have driven down herself to check on you and nurse you back to health. But you have got to make a quick recovery and call them soon or they are likely to suspect that there is more to this than just a little cold," Flynn says. I hated that he and Chloe had been put in the middle of my drama and then they had to go and fabricate a lie just to keep my parents and coaches off my back. I hated it, but I was so grateful. The last thing I needed was my parents breathing down my neck.

"Thank you. You didn't have to lie for me, but I'm glad you did. I'm not ready to tell anyone about my break up with Wyatt. I promise I'll call Mom today and assure her I'm feeling better."

Flynn nods, "Sounds good. And while you're at it, give Coach Moore and Drew a call too. They want to reschedule as soon as possible to get all the playing time in you can before qualifying rolls around."

"Yeah, I'll call them too and set up something for tomorrow."

"Tomorrow? What about today, Suz? It's beautiful out today. If they can't fit you in, I'll go play with you. Chloe, you up for some golf with me and Suz?" Flynn asks.

"I've got some things to take care of today but if all goes well, I can meet you later this afternoon and maybe squeeze in nine holes," Chloe says.

"I can't. I just can't go golfing today," I say hanging my head down so they can't see my shame.

"And why not Suz? What's wrong with you that you can't start living your life again right this minute?" Flynn replies sounding frustrated.

"I just need one more day. I know you won't understand but just give me one more day to let this settle in and then I'll get back to normal," I beg hoping that Flynn will just drop it. I feel like if I get back into to my old routine that it will finally sink in that Wyatt and I are completely finished. Like I'm leaving that part of my life behind and in the past. I know we are done and the relationship we shared is over, but knowing it and living it are two completely different things.

"Whatever, Suz!" Flynn mumbles then throws his hands in the air like he's had enough of this conversation. "I'm going for a run. I'll be back soon." I watch as Flynn stalks across the living room toward the front door.

"Flynn, wait!" I scream.

"Look Suz, you're right. I don't understand. How can you give up on your dreams because your love life isn't quite working out like you so perfectly planned it? You are too talented to throw away a lifetime of hard work and dedication on the golf course just because some guy decided he didn't want to continue a relationship with you. I know it's hard to see past the pain right now, but you'll be in a world of pain if you let him take away not only your heart, but also a promising career. So wallow all you want, but just know a man is never worth giving up on yourself." Flynn doesn't wait around for me to respond. He said his peace and left out the front door to go pound the pavement and hopefully work out some the frustration of dealing with his emotional sister.

"Well shit, now Flynn's mad at me. Could my life get anymore miserable?" I say on a sigh.

"Flynn's just concerned. You had us both very worried while you refused to talk to either of us and shut us both out. I think he doesn't realize the extent of what's going on with you. He never has had a real relationship based on love like you have had. He doesn't understand what happens when your heart is broken and you can't fathom getting up the next day because the pain is so intense. But he's trying to be there for you. He just wants you to be happy. He equates your happiness with golf success. Remember, he never saw you and Wyatt together so he just doesn't get how in love the two of you were. I, however, saw it and lived with it. That's why I find it hard to believe that there isn't something deeper, something we are missing that caused Wyatt to act so out of character." Chloe appears to be deep in thought trying to come up with something that will explain Wyatt's actions.

"I know what I saw Chloe and there doesn't need to be an explanation. He can't explain this away," I say seeing the picture of Bridgett lying in Wyatt's bed that is now burned in my brain forever.

"You know I believe you Suz, so don't ever question that. But you know some things aren't always what they appear to be," Chloe says with caution. I think of Chloe words and remember hearing the exact same words from Mrs. Stokes last night. I would love to believe that the naked girl I found in Wyatt's bed was just a figment of my imagination or an apparition that vanishes as quickly as it appears. But I can't deny what I saw. If there is any doubt that I may have misread things then that would just lead to hope. And I'm not ready to let even a sliver of hope seep into my brain concerning me and Wyatt. He is currently off in New York working on securing his future. Now, I need to start doing the same. But before I can finally move on, I have to know what exactly Wyatt said to Chloe when he called.

"I don't want to talk about what I definitely saw at Wyatt's apartment any more today. However, I am curious as to why Wyatt called you. You did say in addition to my parents and coaches that Wyatt made the list of Suzanna's concerned citizens, right? So what did he have to say?" I ask Chloe looking her directly in the eyes so that she could see I was being dead serious in knowing every last word she had with Wyatt over the phone. It is the least she can do since I just poured out my heart to her and Flynn over breakfast.

"At first he just asked if you made it home safely. After reassuring him that you arrived all in one piece, he asked how you were doing. Before I was willing to give him any information about your emotional state, I started asking him questions. He was very vague, never giving me any details about what transpired between you two. He said that I needed to hear the story from you. He didn't try to explain himself or excuse his behavior. He just said that things had ended and that he wished you the best. However, Suz, the man was devastated. I could hear it in his voice. The only relief I heard from him was when I told him that you were safe and sound in your room. Now that I've heard your side of the story, it just doesn't make sense. Why would he intentionally set out to hurt you, but then call me constantly checking on you? That's the only reason why I'm questioning any of this."

Chloe has a point. I'm sure if I turned my phone on it would be full of texts and voice mails from Wyatt trying to check on me. But what would he have said once he found out I actually made in back to the beach and didn't end up in a ditch along I-20? Would he try to apologize? I can almost hear him now. *Glad you made it home safely, and yeah, sorry about you finding the naked slut in my bed.* Or how about *I'm a cheating a-hole and I hated for you to find out this way, but better to find out now rather than later.* Oh and here's my favorite, *See Suz, all this time you thought I loved only you, well, I've been seeing Bridgett the entire time. Why else would she be at the bar constantly and answering my phone when you called?* If those were the kinds of messages I would receive when I turned my phone back on, I'd rather just chunk the mobile device in the ocean. I can't imagine Wyatt actually saying any of those things to me. Because deep down I know he could never do that to me. But I can't go back and erase what I saw. Sure there is probably an explanation. The only one that makes sense is that in a moment of weakness, Wyatt caved to Bridgett's persistence and slept with her. Even if it was just a one-time thing, it doesn't change the fact that he cheated on me. That nagging voice in the back of my head keeps saying, *Didn't you do the same thing...cheat, when you were locking lips with Patrick on your front porch?* I don't want to think of myself as the bad guy. I am only giving Wyatt that label.

Shaking my head to clear it of the disturbing thoughts, I glance back at Chloe who is watching me closely. I don't know what she thinks I'm gonna do. Considering I have shown her all of my multiple personalities in the course of a just few days, she has every right to question my next move. But I don't think she ever expects me to turn the tables.

"So, what's going on with you and Flynn?" I ask abruptly changing the subject. Chloe's eyes get as wide as saucers. She opens her mouth to say something then shuts it quickly, obviously thinking things through before she says anything out loud. It is no secret that Chloe has always had an attraction to Flynn. Even as his sister, I can see why women flock to be around him. He is a gorgeous man. His athletic body is ripped with muscles from head to toe. We share the same silver blue eyes that we got from my Dad. However, I got my Mom's fair coloring with blonde hair and fair skin while Flynn inherited the darker tones from my dad's side of the family.

His brown hair has a natural wave and hangs perfectly around his face and over his ears in a longer style that my mom always thinks needs trimming. His skin radiates a golden hue all year long from his hours of training in outdoor sports. He towers over my petite frame, standing a little over six feet tall. So, of course, I can understand Chloe's attraction to the man. But seeing Flynn being so affectionate toward Chloe this morning kinda threw me off. Even I know of my brother's sexcapades, giving him the title of man whore. The boy has never had a serious girlfriend. And he doesn't hide the fact that he is not the least bit interested in acquiring one. He uses women to scratch an itch. Once they are done fulfilling his needs, he no longer has any use for them. Sad, however true.

"There is nothing going on with me and Flynn," Chloe says trying to use her voice to convince me. It wasn't her voice that gives her away, though. The fact that she is finding her coffee cup so interesting that her eyes are glued to it while she speaks, rather than looking at me, tells me she is lying.

"Come on, Chloe. I'm not stupid. I did walk in on a soft porn episode that was starring both you and Flynn the other day. I know I interrupted you two then, but I haven't a clue what's been going on since. Plus, I found the interaction between you two this morning during breakfast rather confusing. So do us both a favor and cut the crap. What's going on with you and my brother?"

"Really Suz, there is nothing between me and Flynn. Yes, you saw us in a passionate moment that could have easily escalated had you not walked in. It was a mistake, to let our lust for each other take over. I'm glad you came home when you did. The man is hard to resist sometimes." Chloe takes a deep breath and I watch as the corners of her mouth lifts slightly as if she wants to smile at the memory of her and Flynn being intimate. But just as quickly the smile fades and Chloe spaces off into deep thought, scrunching up her brow. Whatever she is remembering puts a scowl on her pretty face. Coming back to the present she addresses me again. "But since then we've both been concentrating on getting you back to your old self. We really didn't have time to worry about anything else."

"I'm sorry about the way I reacted to the situation I walked in on. I was in a bad place and took out my anger at the two of you. You know I'd approve should you and Flynn try to give this thing between you a shot," I say apologizing again for my emotional outburst the other day.

Chloe lets out a hooting laugh that I find holds not a bit of humor. "Suz, there is not, and never will be a thing between me and Flynn. I've already got your broken heart to look after. I don't need one of my own to try to mend. Besides, Flynn will be leaving in a few short weeks for Europe to play soccer. Now you and I both know he isn't the least bit interested in a long distance relationship. I'm not even sure what you would call a relationship separated by an ocean. Maybe impossible? Yeah, that's it. Impossible. Of course that could describe any romantic relationship involving Flynn. We both know he isn't into that sort of thing," Chloe says trying to make light of the matter. But I hear the disappointment in her voice and I know, even if Chloe can't admit it, she'd like for things to be different.

"Well, I'm glad you two can maintain a friendship." I want to say more. However, I think she may be wrong about the feelings Flynn has for her. I have never seen him act the way he did this morning toward a girl. But if I say anything, that would only give her hope. She and I don't need false hope at this point in our lives. So I leave it at that and close the subject. "Hey, I think I may have attempted an apology last night during my inebriated state, but I'm not sure. And I owe you a big one. So I'm gonna try this again. Chloe, I'm so, so sorry for calling you all of those ugly names. You know I didn't mean any of it. You are far from being a whore. Not even close to that category. I was just really angry and I took it out on the last person who ever deserved it. So please accept my apology and forgive me."

"Suz, you were forgiven the minute the words flew out of your mouth. I know you better than to think you would say such a thing and actually mean it. Plus, I've been called a whore previously and believe me your version didn't hurt as badly as the one before. My skin has gotten tougher in my old age. Don't worry another second about it. It's all water under the bridge now. However, never, ever associate me in the same category, good or bad, as Bridgett. You got it?" Chloe asks with a smile on her face.

"Got it. But who in their right mind would ever call you a whore and actually mean it?" I ask confused as to where all this is coming from. I know Chloe better than anyone and she is far from being promiscuous.

Chloe turns to walk away having ignored my last question. I can see she is trying to avoid answering but I'm not letting her get away this time. She has been the best friend in the world to me through all my drama over the last four years. She knows all the dirty details of the secret I've kept hidden from everyone for so long. If someone intentionally hurt her, I'll take a golf club to their face. Nobody better be hurting my sweet Chloe! Grabbing her arm before she can leave the table I ask again, "Chloe, who called you such a hurtful name?"

I watch as pain flashes in her eyes and I can tell she is afraid. Of who, I have no idea. But being the great actress she is, Chloe masks her emotions quickly and soon her face breaks out in a big grin. "Suz, I was just joking. Trying to get you to let go of the guilt you were feeling from saying those things to me the other day. Man, I really need to work on my jokes. I'm 0 for 2 today!" she says with a laugh. I know I'm not getting any other information from her on the subject so I let it go, for now. Vulnerable Chloe is rare, but it happens. And when it does, I'm going to be there and get those answers she refuses to give now.

"So, we good?" I ask.

"Yeah, we're more than good. Now come over here and give me a hug," Chloe says opening her arms. I immediately go to her and hug her back. I am so blessed to have a friend like Chloe. I will choose to focus on the good things in my life rather than the bad. Still embraced in each other's arms, we hear the front door open and watch Flynn walk inside.

"Room for one more? I think this calls for a group hug," Flynn says as he runs our way giving us no time to prepare for the onslaught of his sweaty arms wrapping up us both and pulling us against his equally sweaty chest.

"Ew, gross. Let us go you sweaty, filthy man!" Chloe squeals. This only encourages Flynn to antagonize us more, tightening his hold and rubbing his wet hair across our faces.

"You stink, Flynn. Come on, please release us now," I beg through my laughter.

"You girls know you love it!" Flynn teases, but lets us go and laughs with us.

"Now, I've got to take a shower. Thanks a lot Flynn," Chloe snaps trying to act perturbed at the situation. Flynn cocks an eyebrow like he knows she not only enjoyed the hug, but would most definitely enjoy much more.

"Let me know if I can be of any assistance to you in that shower you're getting ready to take. I'm always at your service, Chloe," Flynn says in a teasing manner. However, if Chloe accepted his assistance I'm sure there wouldn't be any teasing involved. The sexual tension between those two is so thick I decide I need to escape to my room just to get some air.

"Hey guys, I'm gonna go and finally turn my phone on. I guess I need to call Mom and Dad and get in touch with my coaches. Flynn, are you sure you are available this afternoon? If so, I'm thinking why not take advantage of this beautiful day and play a round." The smile on Flynn's face would have me dropping my panties if I wasn't his sister. Good thing Chloe's back is turned as she walks into her bedroom for that shower. Had she seen that handsome face light up with his smile, she would definitely accept his offer of shower assistance.

"Yeah, I'm good. Any time is fine with me. Go make your phone calls and then we'll get lunch and play this afternoon. And Suz...I'm glad you're back."

"Thanks, me too."

Chapter Seven

I drove my ball from the tee box where it landed in the middle fairway, setting me up for the perfect second shot on the par four ninth hole. Flynn's tee shot had drifted off to the left landing in the rough right beside a cluster of pine trees. I'd been killing it today. My drives were longer than normal and my putting was still in excellent shape, always being the best part of my game. We were halfway through our round and I was already beating Flynn by six strokes.

"Damn Suz, are you trying to rub it in?" he asked as he watched my tee shot roll into perfect position half the distance to the green.

I shrug and give him an apologetic smile before putting my driver back in my golf bag. This is where I need to be today. The golf course is my constant in life. It brings me peace and structure when I feel like the rest of my life is out of control. We are an hour into our play and I have barely thought of Wyatt the entire time. Okay, so sometimes he would pop up in my thoughts, but I tried to push him away and solely concentrate on getting that little white ball in the hole in as few strokes as possible. The way I was playing today, you'd never know I was plagued with any distractions. Maybe the need to over-compensate on my concentration of golf was working, not just as an advantage to my game, but also as a way to overcome my sadness concerning my love life. This is probably the only time I would ever think of my break up with Wyatt as a positive.

Flynn fired up the golf cart and we headed down the path to prepare for our next shot. "Maybe you should stick to soccer and leave the golfing to me," I teased. Flynn tried to give me the stink eye, but couldn't contain his smile. He knew I was right. Thank goodness he was a great sport. And a wonderful brother who knew I needed to clear my head and pushed me until I caved to come out and play a round. I didn't know how much I needed to get out on the course today. Not only was I getting the much needed practice that I had to have before qualifying, but I was feeling somewhat back to the old Suzanna. Of course, while I loved golf, the game would never love me back. And it sure wouldn't keep me warm in my bed at night.

We finished the front nine and I still had a commanding six stroke lead. Although, Flynn's competitive side was beginning to surface. How he managed to par the last hole after his misfired tee shot was nothing short of brilliance, earning him a high five from me. I'd better keep my mouth shut about Flynn's golfing abilities until I had this round wrapped up. Only then would I brag about my win. Before setting off to start the last half of our round, we stopped by the clubhouse for a short break.

"You want anything, Sis? I'm gonna grab a beer and some snacks," Flynn informed me as he parked the golf cart.

"How can you possibly be hungry? We just ate a huge lunch!" I said still very full from the shrimp po boy and fried pickles we woofed down at Creek Ratz earlier.

"Hey, I'm still a growing boy! I assume you aren't interested in a snack. How about that beer?" Flynn asks.

I'm never one to drink alcohol while golfing. While most people enjoy the occasional cocktail while playing golf, especially during the heat of the day, I take the game way too seriously to cloud my mind with alcoholic beverages.

"I'll just take a water thanks."

"Okay, coming right up. I'll be back soon," Flynn says as he walks into the clubhouse.

I follow Flynn into the clubhouse to use the restroom. When I finish, Flynn is waiting for me on the cart already enjoying his refreshments. Before taking off for the tenth tee, I check my phone for any missed calls or texts. I just turned the thing back on this morning after Chloe and Flynn told me they were tired of playing my secretary. I'd only had time this morning to check the messages from my parents and coaches. Secretly, I didn't want to listen to the many messages that had been left by Wyatt. Nor did I read any of his text messages. The voicemails and texts had begun as soon as I had left his apartment. Scanning through, I saw that the last message from him had come in late last night. I assumed he wouldn't try to contact me since he was busy leaving for New York early Tuesday. But I guess he arrived safely. Apparently, since exiting the plane, and the return to full mobile phone access, he resumed trying to contact me with more calls and texts. I can't believe he has yet to give up trying to explain his infidelity. I guess I'll find out later how Wyatt left things when I finally listen to and read his messages. Since there has been no contact today, I am reluctant to hear his final words because I know how much they are going to hurt.

"Finally turned that thing back on, huh," Flynn states as I stare at the screen thinking about Wyatt.

"Yeah, I thought it was time I contacted Mom and Dad and Coach Moore," I say pushing Wyatt to the back of my mind. "Mom bought the story of my summer cold and so did Coach. Thanks for covering for me. I don't want anyone to know how pathetic I've been acting over my broken heart."

"Sure, not a problem, Suz. Did you listen to all the messages?" Flynn asks as we make our way to the tenth tee box.

"No, not yet. I was excited to get out and play some golf with my brother and didn't want to alter my mood with messages from my ex. Besides, looks like my phone is full of them and it might take awhile to listen to them all. I'll get to them later tonight when I have more time and some privacy."

"Okay," Flynn responds. I know he wants to say more but we need to tee off before we hold up the foursome behind us. Flynn makes an excellent drive and waits for me to have my turn. My mind is more focused on Flynn's reluctance to say more on the subject of my unchecked voice mail that I end up hooking my shot to the left.

"Shit!" I say jamming my driver back in my bag. I climb onto my seat beside Flynn and he takes off never saying a word. I thought my misfire at the tee would at least get him to make a snide comment.

Finally, I can't take it anymore. "What? I know you want to say more about Wyatt so just go ahead and say it. I'm not gonna fall apart out here on the course."

"Suz, we are having fun today. You are doing great and we haven't talked about Wyatt or Patrick or your attack or anything that you've had to deal with recently. I just want to keep it that way and finish our round," Flynn explains.

"But you obviously have more to say or else you wouldn't have brought up the voicemails from Wyatt. Please, just tell me. I can't concentrate knowing you are holding back. I mean, look at my last shot!" I plead.

"Honestly Suz, I think you shouldn't even listen to or read any correspondence from Wyatt. I'm so angry at what he has put you through. But I know how hard headed you can be and that eventually you'll give in and see what he said or wrote. I'm just asking that you give it a little more time. You just decided to venture out of that bedroom you've been holed up in for the past three days. You're back to playing golf and I thought we were having a really good time. I don't like to see you all depressed like you've been. I'm just scared that if you hear his voice it will cause you to revert back to your recent state of depression and isolation. I don't think I can take seeing you like that again. Neither can Chloe. So, just consider holding off for a few days if you can. Or if you have to listen to the voicemails or read the texts, let me or Chloe be there to help you through them. I don't want you facing whatever he has to say alone."

"So you don't think I should listen to the voicemails at all?" I ask.

"I didn't say that, although I don't know what good if any could come out of torturing yourself. You said it was over between you two. Is there anything that he could say that would make you change your mind?" Flynn asks looking at me curiously.

"I don't know," I answer honestly. I told myself that infidelity would be one thing I could never accept in a relationship. But the words from Chloe and Mrs. Stokes keep playing back in my mind like a broken record. Sometimes things aren't always as they seem. If Wyatt could explain why I found a naked Bridgett in his bed then maybe we would have a chance to build our relationship again. Then again, he pushed me away. He never wanted me to see Bridgett in his apartment. He told me as soon as I entered that he no longer wanted to pursue a long distance relationship and was trying to get me to leave before discovering who was in his bed. Maybe he just didn't love me enough to continue dating.

"Just think about it. You don't have to make a decision now. We still have the back nine to play and I plan to kick your ass this afternoon," Flynn teases trying to distract me from my wandering Wyatt thoughts, getting me to focus back on our golf game.

"Okay, I'll consider not listening to the many messages from Wyatt, although it will be hard. I promise if I do cave, I'll let you or Chloe be there to help me through whatever he has to say," I reassure Flynn. "Now about kicking my ass...I don't think so buddy. Come on, let's play on."

"Gladly," Flynn says relieved to get back to playing golf and leaving the drama behind. "Hey, this whole phone conversation got me sidetracked. When you were checking your phone, did you happen to hear from Chloe?"

"Actually, I was going to call her. I thought she said she'd meet us on the course after running her errands. But I haven't heard from her. Know anything about what she was busy doing today?" I ask glancing back at my phone to make sure I haven't missed an incoming text or voicemail from Chloe. I switched my phone to silent mode during our round of golf.

"Not a clue," Flynn says just before hitting his next shot sending it soaring then landing it on the green.

"Nice," I say giving him some well deserved praise. That was an excellent shot. I grab my iron and line up to make my attempt for the green. My ball soars through air not only landing on the green, but rolling only a few feet from the cup.

"Show off!" Flynn says nudging my shoulder as I take my seat next to him and we drive toward the flag. I have time to send a quick text to Chloe before we finish up the tenth hole.

Hey, thought you were meeting us at the course. Finished with your errands yet?

We finish the next three golf holes before I hear back from Chloe.

Sorry, got busy. I'll just meet y'all back at the house. Happy hour on deck?

Yeah, sounds good. See you soon.

"Chloe's not going to make it. She says she'll just meet us back at the house. I wonder what in the world she is doing today?" I ask no one in particular.

Flynn just shrugs, but I notice the interest in his eyes at the mention of Chloe. I spoke with Chloe earlier about what I walked in on happening between the two of them, but I haven't gotten Flynn's side of the story. He's had to deal with my love life so much recently it's only fair I try to get to the bottom of his.

"So, I wanted to talk to you about Chloe," I start, but get interrupted immediately.

"Nothing to talk about, Suz," Flynn says trying to close the subject. Not so fast buddy.

"Didn't look like nothing. I was sure what I walked in on was heading in the direction of something very far from nothing," I say hoping he'll give me some details. I definitely don't want sexual details, but I would like to know how they ended up tangled together on the couch.

"Maybe, but my crazy sister decided to cock block me, so like I said it was nothing," Flynn deadpans with disinterest.

"Flynn, Chloe is far from nothing. And if you ever insinuate that just because you didn't get a chance to get completely in her bikini, I'll knock you so far into next week you won't know what hit you! Now you better start explaining how you two ended up in each other's arms. Start talking!" I angrily demand.

"Whoa, Sis. Okay, fine. Not that it's any of your business."

"I disagree. It is my business. You're my brother and she's my best friend. When I find you two in the middle of a very intimate moment then it becomes my business."

Flynn glances in my direction and takes note of the serious expression on my face. He knows I'm not letting this go. It may not be my business, but I love them both fiercely and I want to know if I need to intervene before either or both of them gets hurt. Finally, Flynn decides it's best to just tell me before I bug him to death.

"Chloe and I were the only ones left in the house. We were making breakfast and couldn't help but brush up against one another. You know how small that kitchen is at the beach house. Anyway, one thing lead to another and we found ourselves giving into a moment of lust. I mean, we were both barely dressed. I had on my swim trucks and she was sporting that hot red string bikini," Flynn pauses and I watch as his eyes glaze over. I have no doubt he is currently picturing Chloe in said bikini. After snapping my fingers in front of Flynn's face to bring him back to the present, he continues. "Well, you know what happened next. We caved and took advantage of an empty house. Empty, that is, until you walked in. End of story."

"And if I hadn't walked in? How far would it have gone, Flynn?" I ask knowing good and well there would have been no stopping that freight train. I was privy to Chloe's secret attraction toward my brother. Surprisingly, I never thought Flynn ever noticed Chloe as anything other than my best friend. I had seen the looks he gave her over the weekend and the playful teasing between them. But that was just Flynn's nature. Always the flirt. I never imagined he'd take it to a physical level with Chloe. Especially, knowing how he doesn't do romance or relationships. There is also the fact that he is moving across the Atlantic Ocean in a few weeks. Chloe doesn't need to start something with Flynn just for him to leave her so soon. Believe me, been there and done that. It's not very fun!

"I think you know the answer to that Suz!" Flynn says like duh.

"Really, you'd treat her like something you picked up at a bar? Just some random girl to hook up with? You can't do that to Chloe, Flynn. She's different." I warn him.

"Dammit, Suz, I know she's different. That's why I'm glad you stopped things from going any further. It was a mistake," he says and turns so that I can't see his face. Just saying it was a mistake seems to cause him pain. I can hear the hurt in his voice. I'm starting to believe that Chloe and Flynn are fighting a losing battle. Both calling their physical interaction a mistake, but neither one of them believing it. I think Chloe and Flynn are trying to convince themselves to stay far away from each other. Because the reality of the situation seems to be that if given the opportunity to be together, their relationship would be so much more than physical. Sure, the physical part would be hot. Hell, I saw that with my own two eyes. However, I think they have realized that there might be more than just physical attraction between them. And that's what's scaring the shit out of them both.

"Oh my gosh, you like her! You actually have feelings for Chloe, don't you?" I ask shocking us both.

"Don't get all drama queen on me, Sis. I wouldn't necessarily classify them as feelings just yet. However, I have come to see Chloe in a new light this weekend. And no, it's not just because she is stunningly gorgeous as witnessed in that sweet dress she wore to the engagement party Saturday night. Or how she fills out every inch of that damn red bikini, leaving little to the imagination," Flynn says with a smirk. I slap his shoulder which only instigates him more. "And it's definitely not because of how responsive she was under my touch. Her skin, so soft and smooth, pebbling into goose bumps when I laid my hands on her. And the sounds she made when I pressed up against‿"

"Stop it! I don't want to hear the details Flynn. Sexual and physical graphics aside, just tell me what else contributes to this new enlightened attitude you have for Chloe," I beg.

"Well, beyond the beautiful package she presents on the outside, I have come to find just how beautiful Chloe is on the inside also. It still amazes me that she kept your secret all these years. Not that I ever thought she would tell anyone. It's just that she had to go through it with you all this time. Helping you cope immediately after the attack had to have been hard on her. Then you decide to move away and leave her to deal with the aftermath in Florence. I'm sure she was bombarded with questions about you leaving even more than I was. Then she had to deal with not only her best girlfriend moving away, but the suspicions that her best guy friends, Patrick, James and Landon, had. I know playing the middle man, or woman in this case, couldn't have been easy.

Even after all of that, she continued to stand by you for years during college, waking in the middle of the night to your screams of terror from the persistent nightmares that still plague you. Her loyalty to you is something to be in awe of. And she never once asked for help. I mean, she couldn't really, because you refused to tell anybody, not even your family. I just find what she did to help you during the last four years remarkable. I guess that's why I was so forceful and angry with you after all the ugly things you said to her when you returned from Wyatt's. You should never take the kind of friendship Chloe has given to you so freely for granted. You don't know how lucky you are to have her in your life."

"Yes, I do. And I thank God everyday for her. Believe me, if it hadn't been for Chloe, I don't think I would have survived after my attack," I state with tears in my eyes.

"Suz, don't cry. I wasn't trying to make you feel guilty again. You know we have both forgiven you for your uncharacteristic outbursts. I'm just trying to convey these strange feelings I'm having concerning your best friend. I don't really know what to make of them," Flynn says with a pinched brow. I really think this may be the first time ever he has had feelings about a girl that were unrelated to sex.

"I'm not crying because I feel guilty. I'm crying happy tears. I'm just so happy to have Chloe and you in my life. That's why I hope you don't take what I'm about to say next the wrong way. Please, don't do anything that would jeopardize my friendship with Chloe. You are my family, so I'm kind of stuck with you. Plus, I'll always put family first. But Chloe, she's like a sister to me, even though we don't share the same blood. If anything happens between the two of you and it doesn't work out, I don't want to be in the position where I am forced to choose. I don't know how I would even be able to make a choice. Just be careful, with your heart and hers. Lord knows, I have enough heart break that we can all share. No need to go and create your own."

Flynn chuckles, "Yeah, Suz, I think you drew the short straw when it comes to relationships. I promise you I'll be careful with Chloe. You don't have to worry. Remember who you're talking to?

I think I didn't get dealt the boyfriend gene. I'm not even sure I'm equipped with any of the romantic qualities required for someone to even to want to put me in that role. I assure you, Chloe is safe with me."

Flynn may think he isn't ready to settle down with just one woman, but he is mistaken. I know from experience that once that love bug bites, it bites hard. Breaking down barriers that you once tried to hide behind for fear of getting hurt. Even though I hurt everyday with just the thoughts of Wyatt, I'd never go back and change a thing. Sure, it was a whirlwind romance, from start to finish only lasting a little over a month. But the time was so full of love and passion and lust, it could fill probably years of Flynn's random conquests. So yeah, Flynn doesn't even know what is in store for him. Or maybe he does know, now that he has admitted there might be some interest in Chloe. I can't wait to see my brother in love. Who would have thunk it?

We finish our round and as expected, I won. Although, Flynn did make an amazing comeback, birdying five holes on the back nine. I still was victorious by four stokes. Flynn took his loss in stride being the amazing brother he is. After an exhausting conversation about Wyatt and Chloe, we veered the talk around lighter topics. He talked about school and how although he is only eighteen credit hours from finishing his accounting degree, he is on top of the world about going overseas to play soccer. However, I don't think my parents are quite so eager for him to leave behind his studies to concentrate on a professional soccer career. Flynn is not only gifted athletically, he is brilliant as well. His almost 4.0 GPA remains intact even after hours of extracurricular activities involving playing for the University of Alabama soccer team and suiting up to be the long kicker for the infamous Crimson Tide football team. He had the chance to go to several schools where soccer was king but choose to attend U of A at the wishes of my dad, where every sport takes a backseat to American football.

Although he still got to play soccer, he wasn't recognized nationally had he played for teams who were ranked in the top ten every year. The only reason he was given the chance to play overseas is because his soccer coach sent tapes of his play to a variety of leagues both here in the states and in Europe. I hope all works out for Flynn and he gets the chance to show off his amazing abilities this summer. I'm sure Flynn would make a brilliant business man in the future, but I know he won't be happy sitting behind a desk nine to five every day.

Gathering our gear, we walk through the pro shop to exit the club. Drew is the behind the desk tapping away on the computer. I pull Flynn over with me to say hello. Flynn met Drew during my first paddle board lesson. "Hi Drew," I call out as we make our way over to the counter.

"Oh, hi Suzanna. Glad to see you're feeling better. Dad said you had a cold and missed your golf lesson earlier this week," Drew says with sincere concern.

"Much better, thank you. You remember my brother, Flynn," I say in way as a reintroduction.

"Yes, good to see you again Flynn," Drew says and extends his hand.

Flynn accepts his handshake. "Same to you. We have got to get Suz back on that paddle board soon. That was great entertainment."

I give the obligatory eye roll to my brother for his constant teasing. "Be careful little bro, next time I'm signing you up to join in on the lesson!" I threaten.

"Speaking of lesson, we need to get you scheduled before the summer season is in full swing. I usually get swamped right around the first week of June when all the public schools let out for the summer. Want to schedule something now? I've got my calendar with me," Drew says searching under the counter for his day timer.

"Yes! I meant to call you this morning after I got off the phone with your dad. Since I missed my golf lessons earlier this week, boy is he making me pay. I'm scheduled to play thirty six holes tomorrow and eighteen holes on Friday."

"Wow, my dad's a slave driver!" Drew chuckles. "Well I have some time Friday afternoon if you think you'll be up to it after all that golf. Or I could set up something for over the weekend. What do you think?"

"Let's shoot for the weekend. Saturday works for me and I think my parents will be in town so we'll have a full audience again. And definitely bring an extra board for Flynn. We'll see if his paddle boarding skills are any better than his golfing skills," I tease.

"Ouch, Sis. You're beginning to hurt my ego," Flynn fake pouts. I watch as the women in the pro shop openly admire my brother's masculine physique and handsome face. I know a silly comment about his golf game will not touch his ego with all the female attention he freely gets. And I know he enjoys being the object of women's desires, basking in the attention. I guarantee his ego has barely been bruised, ever.

"So your golf game was good today, huh? Or was your victory due to the lack of competition?" Drew comments getting in on the brother-sister banter.

"Actually, Flynn is an excellent golfer. I was just on fire today. Must be beginners luck since I haven't played in a while."

"Drew, she's not exaggerating. Her drives were incredible. And her putting was precise as ever," Flynn adds bragging on his sister. I love it when he compliments me, pride written all over his face.

"That's great Suzanna. Just what Dad wanted to see improve in your game. He'll be happy to hear about the distance and accuracy of your drives today off the tee box," Drew says.

"Thanks Drew. I'll be sure to tell and show him at our lesson in the morning. Do you plan to up the competition in the morning or should I drag Flynn along again?" I ask.

"Would y'all stop dogging my golf game? Geez!" Flynn starts to complain. His good sportsmanship can only take so much. Plus, we are both exhausted from the heat and are in need of a shower and some dinner.

"I'll be ready to play in the morning. I might only get to play the first eighteen holes since I have paddleboard lessons scheduled for the afternoon."

"You might want to cancel those lessons and pick up and dust off that guitar of yours," comes a voice I don't recognize. Both Flynn and I look around the room, but have yet to determine where this unidentified speaking person is. And a guitar? What else does Drew excel in? He already is an excellent golfer, studious graduate student, and basically rules the water on a paddle or surf board. Now, someone's telling me that he plays a musical instrument. Unbelievable. The swinging doors from behind the counter where Drew sits begin to open. The doors divide the sales counter from the equipment room where golf technicians work on tweaking club heads and grips. As a professional golfer, it's a must to know someone who can make your clubs mold to your body like they are a natural extension. The doors open and at first I still haven't seen anyone yet, that is until I take my sight which was focused at the normal eye level for an adult and look down. Rolling through the doors, in a blinged out motorized wheelchair is a beautiful, yet quirky looking woman. Her hair is dyed with hot pink strips that contrast to what I'm assuming is her natural blonde color. Her eyes are a beautiful emerald green, so striking, even hidden behind a pair of black cat eyed glasses, you can't help but take notice of them. I notice her casual dress, a grey t-shirt that says 'Honk If You Like My Wheels' paired with cut off jean shorts. The colorful appearance continues to her toes which are painted an electric blue and hard not to notice in a pair of rhinestone flip flops. "Beau called and said he and the guys scored a gig at Dead Dog this weekend and they want you to open," she says breaking my rude jaw dropping staring aimed at her. I glance over at Flynn and nudge him with my arm because he is doing the exact same thing.

"Really? Awesome! I haven't seen those guys in months. I guess since they are playing again they've found a new lead singer. The band plan to stay at the house?" Drew asks. I think we may likely have been forgotten and I feel uneasy standing in the middle of this conversation.

"Didn't say, just asked for you to give him a call. Now, quit being so rude and introduce me to your friends," the pink haired girl says turning her attention toward us. She pushes some controls on the arm of her chair and before I realize what's happened she has maneuvered herself around the counter faster than a race car driver at Darlington Speedway. I glance down and find her parked in front of us staring curiously.

"Suzanna and Flynn, as if you had any other choice, meet my sister Callie. Callie this is Suzanna Caulder and her brother Flynn," Drew says sarcastically making the introductions. I stand motionless taking in this unique creature. It's not like I've never seen someone in a wheelchair. It's just usually the person is old and wrinkly, not uniquely beautiful and so full of spunk. Slowly, I extend my hand remembering all my ingrained from birth southern manners and break the awkwardness.

"It's nice to meet you Callie. Forgive me for being a little caught off guard, but Drew never mentioned having a sister, much less one so, so..."

"Crippled!" She answers my unfinished sentence. I'm shocked at her bluntness and a whole lot embarrassed that she sees right through my immediate thoughts about her.

Trying to diffuse the uneasiness of the start of our conversation I immediately reply, "I was going to say awesome. But since you brought it up I'd like to compliment you on your accessorized wheels."

She looks around her body at the motorized chair she sits in, noticing all the stickers and painted graffiti covering the chair. I honestly have no clue the original color of her mode of transportation because every inch has some type of trinket plastered to it that screams 'Look at me'. "So you'd honk?"

"Absolutely," I manage between breaking out in laughter at her reference to the saying on her shirt.

"Callie, leave these poor people alone. Don't you have some work to finish?" Drew chides his sister who has joined me in a fit of giggles.

"Mind your own business, Drew. I'm meeting some new friends. Why don't you make yourself scarce and go in my office to call Beau back. We'll be fine out here alone for a few minutes," Callie says giving it right back to her brother with the same amount of snark. Drew shrugs realizing he is fighting a losing battle and escapes to the back to make his phone call. Callie composes herself in an effort to continue this strange conversation we have going on.

"So, Suzanna, I've heard about you from my dad and Drew. They both seem to think you have what it takes to make the tour. Better be glad my drunk ass friend decided to wrap us around a tree a few years back or else I'd be giving you a run for your money and fighting you tooth and nail for that coveted tour card," Callie says like she hasn't just shocked the shit out of both me and Flynn. No wonder Drew didn't want to leave us alone with her. The girl has no filter and just shoots straight from the hip. Suddenly, I start to fill in the blanks and I remember the story of a young promising golfer out the University of Florida whose career was abruptly ended due to a drunk driving car accident.

"Wait a minute, you're Callie Young? The University of Florida freshman who set golf records on the course that still exist today?" Any female who played the game of golf knew who Callie Young was. She dominated the SEC on the golf course and won the Most Valuable SEC player two years in a row. She was a shoe in to go pro after her sophomore year in college. Then tragedy struck one night after a fraternity party on campus when the young golfer was nearly killed in an automobile accident. After that, I never heard any more about the promising young golfer. That is until now, as she sits in front of me in all her blinged out colorful glory.

"Yep, Callie Young, the one and only," she replies answering the question I had already answered for myself.

"But Drew, his last name is Moore and yours is Young." Didn't Drew just introduce her as his sister?

"Ohhh, you're a smart one Suz. Same baby daddy, different whore for a mother. My last name is about the only thing my birth mother gave me," she states matter of fact. "Dad did more that hit it on the course, if you know what I mean. Seems he was quite the ladies man during his days on tour."

I spit out the sip of water I had just inhaled, choking as I try to keep from strangling. Flynn gasps then full belly laughs at this girl's blatant honesty of her life. Callie focuses on Flynn and begins to laugh with him while I try to catch my breath. "Hey, just being honest. Knowing my Dad all my life and being around the golf course from birth, I can spot a ladies man from a mile away. And looking at this hot piece of meat right here, I'd peg you Flynn as just that, a full fledged, card carrying ladies man!"

Now, I'm the one that's laughing while Flynn stares in shock at Callie's spot on appraisal of himself. "From your reaction and the reaction of your sister I'll assume that I'm right. Don't worry Flynn, my legs might not work but I can still feel everything in all the right places, stud," Callie says with a wink in Flynn's direction. "Maybe you can test things out Saturday night when Drew plays. Y'all are coming, right?" Callie asks like it's a normal day occurrence to come on to a complete stranger.

Both Flynn and I stare at Callie as she smirks, obviously proud that she has managed to stun us both into complete silence. Luckily, Drew walks back from Callie's office to the counter and saves us. "Oh no, what did you do Callie?" Drew asks when he sees the shock on our faces.

"Nothing, I just invited them to come watch you play Saturday night. You're in, right?"

"Yeah, just talked to Beau and it's a go. Looks like I'll be the opening act before they go on around ten. Suz and Flynn, you should definitely come. Beau's band is epic. I haven't seen them play since Kat, the old lead singer left. But Beau assures me that they are better than ever so the show goes on," Drew say excitedly.

"Beau's lead now?" Callie asks.

"Yep. Said he's replaced Kat so it's turned into an all male band," Drew answers.

"Hot Damn! Suz, you have to come now. And you'll probably *come* when you see and hear them on stage. Male hotness at its best. And don't worry Flynn. I'll be there to get you all hot and bothered," Callie says smiling at Flynn who is blushing with embarrassment.

"Callie, stop it! Get back to work now!" Drew says in a stronger voice which Callie seems to finally listen to.

"Fine," Callie says and whirls around in her chair heading behind the counter. But before she disappears behind the swinging doors she has some more parting words to her newest friends. "Suzanna, I'd be glad to help with any equipment adjustments you want or need to make. I'll see if Dad will let me go out on one of your lessons to see if I can tweak a few things to make your clubs easier to handle. Just let me know and I'm all yours. I really wish you luck at qualifying," Callie says with true sincerity. I realize how hard it must be for her to see me fulfilling my dreams when she came so close only to have it taken away because of one bad decision.

"Thanks, I'd appreciate that."

"Not a problem. So, I'll see you later. And you, mister hot pants," she says directing her attention at Flynn who is clearly uncomfortable with her forwardness, "I'll see you Saturday. I'll be the one riding in on her chariot. Can't wait!" Blowing Flynn as exaggerated kiss, Callie finally returns to the equipment room and the doors swing closed.

"I'm so sorry. She's a bit of a handful," Drew says shaking his head.

"Well, that's an understatement," Flynn mutters under his breath.

"I think she's refreshing and fun. And you, Drew Moore, could take some lessons from her about honesty. Really, you play and sing? In public? What else do I not know about you Drew?" I ask incredulously.

"You never asked. And I'm sure there's a lot you don't know about me but I'll have to keep some of my life secret. Else you may not want to be my friend. But seriously, y'all should come out to Dead Dog Saturday night. Not to hear me, but to hear my friend's band. They are incredible. So good that it won't be long before they are recording and playing to sold out stadiums. Really, they're that damn good!" Drew is so passionate about his friend's band I have to wonder if they aren't really the next big thing.

"Well, when you put it that way, how can we resist. Of course we'll be there. Just keep your sister in check, would you?" Flynn teases, although he might need some assistance when it comes to Callie.

"No worries. She's mostly talk, less action. Plus, Beau will be there performing and the girl has a serious fan crush on my friend. So you're safe, for now," Drew reassures my brother.

"Well, I'm looking forward to hearing you and your friend's band play. It'll be fun. I'll see if I can round up the entire gang and make a night of it. Hope you don't get stage fright!" I say realizing if everyone can go, we'll have at least a crowd of seven or more.

"Bring them all! The more the merrier. Hey, I've gotta get back to work so I'll catch y'all later. And Suzanna, please take Callie up on her offer for help. The girl is a genius with golf equipment and I think it'll do her good to focus her attention on you and your qualifying goals. She might not play anymore, but she still has the natural talent that only a few are given. Anything she offers to share can only help you."

"Of course. Like you said...the more the merrier. Plus, knowing what I know about Callie Young, I'd be an idiot to turn down any advice she has for me," I say loving the fact that someone with her golf talent would want to help me.

"Great! Okay, see you guys later," Drew says as we exit the pro shop to make our way home.

Chapter Eight

"That was interesting," Flynn comments as I drive us toward Garden City.

"Yeah? Are you referring to my exceptional golf skills today or the colorful fairy who floated in on her scooter and left us both at a loss for words?" I ask knowing Flynn isn't thinking one iota about our golf game.

"Um, that would be the latter. You think it's a façade? I mean, who just says whatever they think? Some of the stuff that came out of her mouth today would make even the most truthful person cringe. Talk about brutal honesty," Flynn says like he still can't believe how forward Callie came across.

"Could be she is using it as a coping mechanism. I mean, look what she has to live with. The fact that she got in the car with a friend who was as drunk as her and then crashes, taking away her ability to walk, has got to be something that you beat yourself up for everyday. The 'what ifs' would destroy you. What if we'd just called a cab? Or what if I had hitched a ride from someone else? Someone sober. And it's not just losing the ability to walk. She lost her dreams, goals and ultimately her career. Because, believe me, Callie Young was the hottest female golfer in the states when she was playing. Advertising companies were already lining up waiting for her to turn pro just so she'd endorse their products. She was that good!"

"Yeah, that's gotta suck. And it sounds like she didn't have the best family life to start off with, either. Did you hear her call not only her mother but also Drew's mother, a whore? Think there's some family tension?" Flynn asks sarcastically, because it was obvious.

"At least Callie has some sort of relationship with Drew and her dad now. They kind of have to be civil to each other since they all work together. And it looked like Drew knew how to handle her somewhat," I say remembering how Drew finally had to raise his voice for Callie to stop spilling any more family secrets. But let's face it, we've all got them. Of course I finally revealed my secret to Flynn just last weekend. It was hard, but it felt good to let him in and hopefully he can understand me better knowing all I've been through. I hope Drew's the type of brother in which Callie can confide in.

Wanting to change the subject from family, I ask Flynn to grab my phone and dial up Chloe. I haven't heard from her since her last text when we were in the middle of our golf game. I put Chloe on speaker while I drive. Flynn offered to drive, but he had a few beers during golf and I didn't want to risk it. Especially after meeting Callie. The phone rings several times and I think it might go to voicemail right before Chloe picks up.

"Hey Suz. Sorry I haven't called you back, but I've been kinda busy," Chloe says immediately when she answers. I can hear that she isn't alone. It sounds like she may be in a restaurant or bar with all the other voices I hear in the background.

"Where are you?" I ask point blank.

"Just getting ready to head back to your beach house. I have a ton to tell you, but don't want to do it over the phone. Are y'all done with golf?"

"Yeah, just finished and we are heading back now. Want us to pick up dinner?" I ask.

"Actually, I've got dinner taken care of. You two get some beer iced down and we'll eat out on the deck," Chloe says then she starts talking with someone else. I hear her saying goodbye and making plans to see them again this weekend. I wonder if Chloe has started seeing someone. Surely not. She just ended things with Brian, although she said that was a mutual decision on both their parts. They decided they were better suited as friends. But then there's this underlying thing with Flynn. Neither one of them will admit to the extent of their feelings for each other, but I'm smart enough to know it's more than friendship. I glance over at Flynn while we are stopped at a red light. His face is serious and there's a hint of a scowl as he listens to Chloe's conversation with an unidentified male blaring through my car speakers. He doesn't look happy. I'd venture he might actually be jealous. I need to talk to Flynn again about this Chloe thing before we are all back together at the house.

"We'll have the drinks ready. Drive safe. See you soon," I say and end the call. I glance back over at Flynn wondering how I'm going to bring this up again. He already said that Chloe was different than all his other conquests. But he didn't specify how. And I really need to know if there's hope for the two of them as a couple or if things should stay platonic.

"Flynn, what exactly are your_"

"Just pull over at the convenience store and I'll grab some more beer," Flynn interrupts. I'm sure there are more than enough alcoholic beverages at the house, but Flynn's insistence to stop and buy more is his way of avoiding this conversation. It won't hurt to take a few minutes to gather my thoughts, so I pull into the next gas station and wait while Flynn goes in for more beer. Something is bothering me and I can't quite put my finger on it. When I was apologizing to Chloe about the way I reacted to finding her and Flynn together, I never expected her response. She totally forgave me for calling her nasty, derogatory things but hinted that she had all heard them before. Now, I know how girls can be, exceptionally jealous girls. And believe me, if there is someone to be jealous of it is Chloe. She is exquisitely beautiful. Model facial features and a body of a goddess. But more than her outward appearance, Chloe is just as beautiful on the inside. She's always the glass half full one in the bunch. She never lets life get her down and runs around with a positive attitude. She's also the one who doesn't hold back when a little tough love is needed, however, she ends each of her lectures with an encouraging hug. So, Chloe, I'm sure has seen her share of snarky comments from the mean girls. But knowing the confident person she is, she'd never let them get to her.

So how odd is it that she told me this morning how she had been called a whore before and it truly meant something. Chloe is not one to sleep around. Sure, she's had her share of boyfriends. But she's never been much of the casual hook up type just to get an itch scratched. Whore would definitely not be the word to describe Chloe.

My thoughts are interrupted as Flynn climbs back in the car carrying a case of beer. A case? "Dude, you do realize we have plenty of beer back at the house, right? I thought you might just grab a six pack. You got plans I don't know about?" I ask.

"I might just feel like drinking tonight Suz. Is that a crime?"

"No, but just drinking and getting shit faced drunk are two completely different things. Come on, Flynn. Is something bothering you? Or someone?" I ask as I crank up the car.

"No. Yes. I don't know," he says confused. I realize Flynn has never had these feelings before concerning a girl. Sure, he dated Deanne Daughtery in high school during his sophomore and junior years. But I think that was more for something to do when he wasn't hanging with friends or playing sports. After Deanne, Flynn never had or wanted a serious girlfriend. Now that I think about it, I'm not really sure you could call his time with Deanne serious. So this thing with Chloe, not that they are in a serious relationship or anything, nevertheless the feelings are serious, scares Flynn. Since this is so hard for him I think I'll wait to have our Chloe/relationship conversation later. But I do want to let him know I'm there for him when he's ready to discuss things.

"Listen, just know you can talk to me whenever you feel ready, okay. I'm not gonna push. But I do have something to ask you. And it has to do with Chloe."

I hear him grunt as if my words meant nothing. But really this doesn't have to do with his feelings for her. This just has to do with her. "Did you hear or see anyone being mean to Chloe this weekend?" I ask.

"You mean other than you?" he says slicing me with his words. So if I didn't believe he liked Chloe before, I do now. You don't use that threatening tone unless you are defending or protecting someone. Good to know we are on the same page where Chloe is concerned.

"Okay, so I deserved that. And believe me, I've already had to beg for forgiveness. Not that she made me beg. She forgave me like the saint she is. But someone used the same disgusting word I called her at some point and for some reason she believes them. Someone actually thinks that Chloe is a whore. Whoever has that opinion of her couldn't be farther from the truth. But it has anchored into Chloe's conscious and she actually believes this person's false statement. I can tell it hurts her. And I hate for her to hurt," I say because it's true. When Chloe hurts, I hurt too. I wonder if she feels the same. Knowing I was hurting for years after I left Patrick, I hope I didn't inadvertently cause Chloe emotional pain. If I did, she sure hid it well and powered through with her college experience. "I mean Chloe's not innocent when it comes to sex, but a whore. No way!"

"I know..., I..., I, um, I mean, I assume Chloe isn't innocent. Just look at her. No twenty-two year old looking as smoking hot as she does could fight off the constant advances from the opposite sex. That would be a full time job!" Flynn declares.

"Yeah, yeah, I know. Chloe's always been the gorgeous one of the group," I respond with an eye roll.

"Aw, Sis, you fishing for a compliment? Now, now, Suz, don't sweat it. You're pretty too!" Flynn teases, which earns him another eye roll. "Seriously, Suz, you are beautiful. And I'm not just saying that because I'm your brother and I have to. I know, because as your brother, I see how other guys look at you. And believe me, the looks you were getting the other night said nothing other than 'Suzanna Caulder is absolutely, stunningly, beautiful'."

Well, wow. Not that I was fishing, but it never hurts to hear from someone that you're beautiful. Even if it is just your brother. I might actually be blushing. But enough of this flattery. I'm trying to get to the bottom of my concern over Chloe and her statement this morning. "Thanks, Flynn. It never hurts to hear such nice things said about my physical appearance. But enough with the whole looks conversation and let's get back to the question at hand. Did you see Chloe be upset by anyone this past weekend?" I ask.

"No, not really. I saw her talking to several people at the party. But she left every conversation being her happy go-lucky self. All but one, that is," Flynn says as he focuses to remember the events from that night.

"Which one, Flynn? Who was she talking to that maybe upset her?" I ask eager to get some explanation.

"Her parents," he deadpans. "Actually, she left quite abruptly once her mom joined the conversation. At first she was just chatting with Ashley and her soon to be husband. What's his name again?"

"Ben," I answer in a rush. Chloe's sister Ashley is engaged to Ben, a nice looking banker guy on the outside with just a little bit of edginess. Just the kind of guy to satisfy Ashley's appetite for non-ordinary, but also pleases the parental unit.

"Yeah, that's right. Cool dude. Anyway, at first it was just the three of them, Chloe's dad, sister, and soon to be brother-in-law chatting away and having a good time from the looks of it. But that all changed when Mrs. Ryder joined the group. I could tell Chloe's mom had had a few too many glasses of wine just from watching her walk or rather stumble toward her family. Then once she got there, her conversation skills obviously needed translating with all her exaggerated hand gestures. I could tell most of those hand gestures were aimed in Chloe's direction. Looked pretty heated toward the end, right up until Chloe hugged her sister and dad and walked away. She didn't look too happy on her way out of that family meeting."

"Huh?" Chloe's mom has always been a heavy drinker. She likes to have a good time, be the life of the party and all that. And sure, we've all seen our parents over indulge every now and again. But Chloe's mom makes it a habit. When we were younger it didn't seem to bother Chloe that her mom was the loud, obnoxious one of the group. But as we got older, Chloe became embarrassed of her mother's antics and drunken behavior. Can't say I blame her. Thank goodness my parents never put me through some of the public displays that Chloe had to endure. Most country club parties that we all attended usually ended with Mr. Ryder literally carrying his wife out to the car because she had long lost her ability to walk.

But regardless of her alcohol intake, I don't think Mrs. Ryder would ever resort to calling her daughter, her own flesh and blood, a whore. Especially not in front of Mr. Ryder and Ashley. You can say what you want about Mr. Ryder putting up with his drunk wife all of these years, but you don't ever have to question his love and devotion for his daughters. What Chloe lacks in fondness for her mother, is more than made up with how she feels about and views her dad. Chloe worships her dad because he has never shown her anything other than unconditional love.

"I seriously doubt Mrs. Ryder would degrade her own daughter. Especially in such a public place. You know how Chloe's mom relishes in the acceptance of others, especially the invited guests at that specific party. I mean, it was like the who's who of Florence and the greater Pee Dee area. She might embarrass herself with tipsy behavior and slurred words, but she would never disrupt her public image of having the perfect family and husband," I comment after thinking things through.

"Well, if it wasn't her parents who upset her, then maybe it was a friend. What about Landon?" Flynn asks.

"What? Landon? Why in the world would you think that Landon would say such a thing to Chloe? Besides, he was with Leslie all night," I reply flabbergasted.

"Whoa Suz, just hear me out. I realize Landon took Leslie to the party as his date, but I can assure you once they got there he barely paid her any attention. Seems to me he spent most of his time at the party looking out for you and Chloe. You two girls were never very far from his eye sight," Flynn says calmly.

"But why?" I ask.

"How should I know? I haven't talked to the guy in years because you apparently broke things off with the entire group, sans Chloe, when you left Patrick. But I swear, Suz, Landon was either in protection friend mode or he has a thing for you or Chloe. And I'll put money on Chloe."

This make me laugh. Hard. Like tears are coming out of my eyes making it hard for me to see the road in front of me. I slow the car down to almost ten miles per hour just to avoid a traffic accident. Flynn watches me from the passenger seat not one bit amused. After getting my giggles in check I realize he is completely serious about the make believe infatuation Landon supposedly has for me or Chloe, or both.

"Okay, sorry. But that's just plain stupid. And ludicrous! First of all, Landon is like one of our best friends." Flynn tries to interrupt but I continue before he can get a word in. "And before you bring up the fact that Patrick and I started off as just friends, well don't. Because that was different and a very long time ago. Plus, we all saw how that turned out. Now that we are older and wiser…"

Flynn chuckles at that statement. "Yeah, you all are so wise, now that you're what, like twenty-two, twenty-three years old."

"Shut up smartass and just listen. So maybe we don't know all the ways of the world but we have learned a lot in the last four years. So, no. Landon is not looking for a relationship with one or both of his best girl friends. You are so off base!" I say with conviction.

"Well, why would Landon take the time to tell me that Chloe is off limits and to not even think about making my move on her, huh?"

"He said that to you? Really?" I am stunned. What kind of game is Landon playing? Sure, he and Chloe are close. They've been friends forever, even as long as I and Chloe have been friends. And she did maintain relationships with the guys after my break up with Patrick. But never in a million years would I have pegged Landon as having any type of feelings toward Chloe other than friendship. "Are you absolutely, positively sure he said for you to stay away from Chloe? You don't think you were reading anything into the conversation you and Landon had?"

"Suz, I know what I witnessed that night and I certainly know exactly what I heard. For some reason, Landon doesn't want me any-where close to Chloe," Flynn says shaking his head like he still can't believe what went down at the party.

"Well, that's just weird. But with all this information you're tell-ing me it still doesn't solve the mystery of who insulted Chloe. Sounds like the last thing Landon would do is insult her if your read on things is accurate."

"Maybe it wasn't Landon. Maybe it was Leslie. While Landon was busy focusing all his attention on you and Chloe during the party, Leslie spent most of her time there huffing and puffing. I could almost see the invisible stem exploding from her ears. She was that mad! Instead of taking her frustration out on Landon, maybe she went straight to Chloe with a few choice words."

"Pfffft, Chloe could care less what Leslie thinks of her, or for that matter, calls her. And if Leslie did have the nerve to call Chloe a whore, well that would be like the pot calling the kettle black. Leslie has no room to pass judgment on someone else's sexual history. Everyone knows that girl wasn't very selective in high school. I think she has more notches on her bed posts than you do Flynn."

Flynn thinks about this for a few moments before giving me his opinion. "You girls are such bitches to each other. But yeah, you're probably right. Unless of course Landon was pissed that Chloe brought a date – what's his name?"

"Brian, and they are just friends," I reply.

"Brian, right. Well Landon could have been pissed that Brian *the friend* was in attendance and there's also the fact that Chloe was sending me some serious 'I want you' vibes."

Good grief, will my brother never think that any woman isn't immune to his charms and good looks? "Now, you really are being ridiculous! You just wish Chloe was sending any attention your way, bro." But I could tell from the night of my surprise party that there were some serious vibes between Chloe and Flynn. However, I'll never admit it to him. His head is already big enough.

"Believe what you want, Sis, but I know women. And Chloe definitely was digging my shit." Honestly, my brother never ceases to amaze me, but at least he has me laughing at his cockiness. Soon we are both laughing at this bizarre, yet entertaining, conversation and it just puts an exclamation point to the end of a great sister and brother bonding day. Under all his handsome exterior and cocky attitude,

Flynn Caulder is one hell of a guy and I'm so lucky to have him as my brother.

As we approach our beach home, Flynn's laughter stops but he still sports a soft, warm smile. "Suz, I'm glad we had today. And I know you're trying to solve the problems of your friends and butting into my love life. But I want you to try to enjoy this time you have getting ready to turn pro. Try not to worry about Chloe, Landon, or me too much and just concentrate on yourself. And promise me, when I'm an ocean away that you'll keep me updated. Call me whenever you need. Because I just want to know my sister is okay. You're okay, right?" Flynn asks.

Emotionally spent from his sweet words of affection, I have to try really hard to hold it together so that I don't cry. I don't want to end this special day with tears. Flynn will be leaving in a few weeks to play soccer in Europe for the summer. I know once he returns it'll be a long time before we can have another day like this again. With me hopefully playing professional tournaments and Flynn finishing his senior year at the University of Alabama, our schedules just won't permit us much time, if any, together. So I'm gonna suck it up and give him my best smile to reassure him that even though I'm not really okay, I'm working damn hard to get there. "No, I'm not okay Flynn. But today was the start of getting me back to being the Suzanna I was before Patrick and before Wyatt. So, thank you for today. It means more to me than you'll ever know," I say without breaking down, which is quite the accomplishment in my book.

"You'll get there Suzanna. You're strong and you're a fighter. So, no matter what happens with your love life, just know that you're my number one girl."

"It's nice to be number one in someone's eyes. Even if you are blood related."

"Hey now, I'm not just saying that because I'm your brother. Any man, related or not, should see how very special you are. And if they don't, then it's their loss," Flynn says sweetly.

"Would you stop being so sappy? God, you're gonna make me cry! I think I prefer cocky, conceited Flynn."

"You're gonna regret that preference. But Suz, last thing before we get home. I just want to leave for Europe knowing you're okay."

"I'll get there Flynn, I promise. It hurts a little too much right now. I just really, really miss him."

"I know, Sis. I know," Flynn says patting me on the shoulder. The remainder of the drive home we make in silence, each of us in our own thoughts. When we finally pull up to the beach house it occurs to me that Flynn never questioned which 'him' I was referring to. Did he think I was talking about Wyatt? Or was he thinking that I was still missing Patrick, a part of my past that I can't quite let go? If I'm being completely honest with myself, I guess I miss them both.

Chapter Nine

C hloe's VW bug convertible is parked under the raised beach house when we arrive. The top is still down and the driver's side door is open, but Chloe is nowhere to be found. We park behind her vehicle and Flynn starts unloading his clubs to store them in the downstairs part of the house. I usually just leave my clubs in the back of my BMW SUV. There's no real threat of anyone trying to steal my clubs. I mean we are in a pretty nice, affluent neighborhood. Plus, the back window of my SUV is tinted, so even if a thief came snooping around for something to steal, my clubs would be impossible to spot.

I go around to the passenger side of my car to grab the case of beer Flynn had to have and use all my upper body strength to lug it out of the car. "Hold up, Suz. I'll get that. Just let me finish putting my clubs away," Flynn yells from inside the downstairs apartment. He won't get any argument from me. That beer is damn heavy. I hear footsteps and turn just in time to see Chloe bouncing down the stairs.

"Hey Suz, great timing. I just got home and have dinner ready and waiting. Just let me put the top up on my car and get the last of the bags so we can go eat," Chloe informs me in her sing-song voice. Sounds like she's in a good mood. With the flick of a button, the top closes on her VW Bug and I hear the beep-beep sound of the security system automatically engaging when she locks her car for the night. Chloe comes back around to the foot of the stairs carrying a few to go bags from Dead Dog Saloon. It smells amazing and if what I think is actually inside that bag, then I can't wait to dig in.

"Hushpuppies? With sweet cream butter?" I ask taking a big sniff.

"Yep, and I got a couple pounds of boiled shrimp, potatoes and corn already upstairs. Just waiting for you guys to load up the cooler with some cold ones and we're ready to eat. I even set up everything outside on the back deck so we can enjoy the sunset."

"God, I love you! I'd kiss you right now, but it might make Flynn jealous," I tease but lean in and give her a hug and peck on the cheek. Upon hearing his name, Flynn walks our way with beer in tow. He definitely has his gaze pinned on Chloe. I just don't know if he's checking her out, or has his sight set on the bag of food she's carrying. Probably both. My brother lives for food and sex, and right know Chloe can provide both.

"Oh, hi Flynn. So who won today?" Chloe asks through a smirk, although she already knows what the answer is gonna be. Flynn hasn't won against me or Chloe in golf since he quit playing competitively in junior high. By then he was already a rising soccer player and putting in time with the football team as their long kicker. Chloe doesn't wait for an answer and starts ascending the stairs as both Flynn and I follow. "Regardless of the winner," Chloe says and gives me a wink, "I'm sure it was tons of fun. Hate that I couldn't make it a threesome this afternoon."

"There's always tonight, sweetheart," Flynn says as a matter of fact.

"Tonight? What are you talking about?" Chloe asks still climbing stairs and juggling the bags of food.

I hear Flynn clearing his throat behind us. "Well, I actually prefer to engage in my threesomes in private, not on a golf course. And definitely not with my sister! Wanna call up one of your *other* friends? 'Cause, yeah, we've got tonight, babe."

Chloe abruptly stops midstride causing me and Flynn to simultaneously bounce back like dominoes, me bumping into the back of Chloe and Flynn bumping into me. Once we all stabilize again, Chloe whips around with fire in her eyes. "You. Are. Sick! Honestly Flynn, is sex all you ever think about?"

Flynn brushes by me so he and Chloe are standing face to face, each one planting their feet getting ready for a stand off. "No, sex often enters my mind, but it's not the only thing I think about. Actually, I'm thinking about something else entirely right this second." Flynn leans down so that only an inch separates his face from Chloe's. With his free hand, the one not hoisting the case of beer, he brushes a stray hair off of Chloe's cheek, his touch lingering a little longer after completing the job. Chloe stares up into his eyes, her earlier gaze softening at his intimate touch and close proximity. "Wanna guess what I'm thinking right now, Chloe?"

"No, I'm not into playing your games or trying to guess what runs through your sex crazed mind. So why don't you just go ahead and inform me," Chloe says, trying to hang onto her stubbornness and anger. But the breathy tone in her voice indicates she is more affected by Flynn's touch and less angry at his earlier words.

Flynn leans down even closer, only a millimeter or so separating his lips from Chloe's. I stand back watching this interaction like a car wreck on the side of the highway. I know I should look away, but can't bring myself to miss one minute of this show. Flynn's hand is still lightly touching Chloe's cheek. It begins to slide down, oh so slowly, tracing her jaw line before inching its way down her neck and shoulder. "Okay, no games, just the brutal truth. You think you can handle that?" Flynn asks Chloe in a deep, seductive voice even I detect.

Chloe takes in a deep breath and briefly nods, not breaking eye contact with Flynn. The corners of Flynn's lips curve up just slightly. We all wait anxiously for whatever Flynn has to say. "Well, at this precise moment, the one and only thing I'm thinking about is..." he pauses before leaning down closing the gap and pressing a light, playful kiss to Chloe's lips. "Food!" he says while grabbing the bag from Chloe's hand and turning to walk into the house, laughing the entire way. "Come on girls, I'm fucking starving. Let's eat!" he commands through a chuckle.

Chloe is cemented to her spot, too stunned to move. She watches Flynn enter the house and disappear while I try to suppress my giggle. I fail, because, damn that was too funny. My giggles bring Chloe out of her stupor and she directs those angry glares from earlier in my direction. "I'm sorry, but that was..." I can't even finish before my giggles turn into uncontrolled laughter.

"That was what Suz? Funny? Cute?" she asks in a clipped tone. Oh no, she is pissed.

I rein in my laughter, but can't keep the smile off my face. "Actually, it was sweet. The kiss and all. Didn't you think that was sweet?"

"I thought it was disgusting and stupid. Just like your brother. Are you sure you're related?" Chloe is still fuming, but I'm guessing she's madder with herself than with what just happened with Flynn. It was quite obvious how affected she was by his words, touch and that quick kiss. She played right into his hands and then was made to look like a joke. I'm sure internally she's kicking herself for letting her guard down around my brother. However, she's in for a long fight if she's gonna try to hide the feelings she has for Flynn. I'll even bet it was harder for him to walk away, knowing he's harboring some serious feelings for her as well.

I wrap my arm around Chloe and physically drag her to the front door. "Come on, Chloe. Don't be mad. That was Flynn's way of showing he cares about you. I know, it's twisted. But he wouldn't pick on you if he didn't have an interest."

Chloe takes a few moments to collect herself and think about what I just said. "Whatever, Suz. Let's just go eat before your Neanderthal brother finishes it all." She follows me into the house and we head out back. Surprisingly, Flynn has set the table and laid out all the food Chloe bought. He appears up the back steps with a cooler in hand, which I suppose contains the now iced down beer.

"Hey girls, I've got everything out and ready. Here, grab a cold one and let's have dinner," he says like nothing just happened between him and Chloe. And I give Chloe credit. She plasters on her fabulous smile while she walks, or actually struts, toward Flynn and the cooler. Dramatically, she leans down to grab a beer, her flowy shirt hanging open as she bends over showing her abundant rack.

"Thanks, *sweetheart*! This looks amazing. I'm famished!" Chloe says before standing on her tiptoes and giving Flynn a peck on the cheek. Now Flynn is the one who is speechless. I roll my eyes at those two. They are too busy trying to one up the other they can't see that they both want the same thing. Each other.

Dinner conversation is pretty much nonexistent because we are all too busy filling our mouths with the scrumptious food. Half way into my food coma, I hear a car pulling into the driveway. Both Chloe and Flynn are too busy bantering back and forth with each other about something unimportant that they miss our arriving guests until we all hear the footsteps approaching. Landon bounds up the stairs first, wearing his typical outfit of a t-shirt and jeans. Tagging along closely behind him, Leslie appears dressed to impress. She sports full make-up, her hair is fixed, and she wears a dress with heels. Who wears heels at the beach? I guess they have plans later tonight that don't include our casual back deck dining.

"There're my favorite ladies," Landon greets us and moves in for hugs, leaving Leslie standing awkwardly alone.

"Hey, big guy. What are you doing here, in town?" I ask when he releases me from his bear hug.

"Well, Leslie's family is down for a couple of weeks on vacation and invited me to come for a visit. Plus, I have a job interview lined up for tomorrow that will take place at the beach. So, here I am. Miss me?" Landon asks. We just spent the weekend with our dear friend for Patrick's engagement party. Up until this weekend, I hadn't spent any time with Landon since high school. Once I left midway during my senior year, Landon and I didn't see each other until just recently. But the years apart felt like only a blur of time the minute we reunited. Our old friendship picked up like it never faltered and I am nothing but ecstatic to see him again so soon.

"Of course I missed you. I'm so glad you both came by. We were just in the middle of dinner and we have plenty. Please, please join us and help us eat all this food Chloe brought home from Dead Dog Saloon. It's delicious, but if I continue to eat, I'm gonna make myself sick." I make sure to direct my comments and my eyes to both Landon and his date, Leslie, who still stands alone a few feet away. I can tell she feels uncomfortable, but Landon doesn't seem to pick up on her uneasiness or he just doesn't care.

"Yeah, take a seat. Join us. We have plenty of food and drinks," Chloe says rising to pull up some extra chairs.

"Awesome. This shrimp looks amazing. Flynn, throw me a cold one_"

"Landon," Leslie whines, "I thought we were going out to dinner. Something private, just the two of us. I really wanted to spend some alone time together before you head back to Florence tomorrow after your interview."

An awkward silence settles on the deck as we wait to hear how Landon will respond to his date. I don't think she's going to like what he's getting ready to tell her.

"Leslie, I promise I'll take you to dinner another night while your family is at the beach. I can come back after I decide how this job possibility works out. But Flynn is leaving for Europe soon and Chloe is heading back to Columbia for summer school. Plus, Suz is gonna be too busy to see any of us once she starts the golf tour. Please, can't we just have dinner with my friends tonight?" Landon doesn't wait for her answer before he starts fixing his plate. Flynn slides him a beer and reaches into the cooler to grab another. He holds it out, offering it to Leslie. Leslie grabs the drink with more force than necessary, but tries to hide her frustration with a nod of thanks and a smile.

"Yeah, sure. Thanks for the invite guys. We would love to join y'all," she says in an overly sugary voice filled with fake sincerity. She slides in the chair closest to Landon and rubs his arm affectionately. "Honey, you should have told me you wanted to eat dinner with your friends tonight. I wouldn't have bothered to get all dressed up. I feel a little out of place." Leslie looks around the table and inspects our attire. I look exactly as I did when I left the house earlier today to head to the golf course. I'm still in my golfing clothes, hair pulled back in a pony and a visor on my head. Yeah, I look good. Chloe isn't looking much better. She has on a flowy shirt with cut off jean shorts.

Her hair is down, but due to the humidity and her convertible, it's wild and untamed. Leslie appraises our appearances with a look of disdain. It's as if she seeks some type of superiority over us girls while she's obviously fishing for a compliment. Too bad the boys are too busy stuffing their mouths with food and are basically ignoring this conversation. Chloe narrows her eyes at Leslie then shoots me a look like 'oh no, she just didn't'. Before Chloe has a chance to voice a nasty rebuttal, I immediately have to diffuse the situation. Although I'm not any happier with the way Leslie is conducting herself as a guest at my house, she is with my friend Landon. And honestly I really want him to stay so we can spend some more time together.

"Leslie, please don't feel uncomfortable or out of place here with us. I apologize for our dinner attire, but we weren't expecting guests. Plus, we just arrived home and Flynn wouldn't give us a chance to shower or change because quote "he was fucking hungry". By the way, you look beautiful tonight. Doesn't she look beautiful, Landon?" I ask trying to get the guys to break the unbearable tension amongst us girls.

"Huh?" Landon says through a mouth full of shrimp.

"I was just complimenting Leslie on how pretty she looks tonight."

"Yeah, you look beautiful Les," Landon says wiping his mouth with a napkin. He leans down and gives her a kiss on the top of her head. *The top of her head?* And there's a sure sign of platonic affection if I've ever seen one. He gave both me and Chloe hugs upon his arrival that were more affectionate than that gesture. Landon might as well be wearing a neon sign that says 'I'm just not that into you, Leslie'. Landon returns to his dinner while Leslie looks down at the table, either trying to hide her embarrassment or her frustration. I glance around the table to see if Flynn or Chloe have witnessed this exchange. Flynn continues to eat and picks up the sports conversation he and Landon were having earlier. Chloe pretends to stare at her plate, but I can see the corners of her lips curved up into a grin. I'm sure internally, she's laughing at Leslie's failed attempt to get all of Landon's attention, especially around his oldest girl friends. Chloe must sense me watching her and raises her head, grin still in place. I give her my best eye roll, but do it with a smile.

"So, what's with the interview tomorrow Landon?" Chloe asks.

"Oh, just something my dad set up. He wants me to work for him at his firm and has a potential client he'd like for me to meet with," Landon says seeming very disinterested. Landon's dad owns a security firm that is based in Florence, where we all grew up. Even though the home office is in a smaller South Carolina city, the firm is quite large. It has satellite offices all over the southeast and it's huge. Every politician, professional athlete, movie star, musician, or any other important person who needs security uses Landon's dad's firm when traveling in this area of the US. And if you met the owner, Landon's dad, you would understand why his firm has such a great reputation for top notch security. Colonel David Smith started his firm about fifteen years ago after serving as head of the South Carolina Highway Patrol. His career started after graduating from the University of Michigan with a criminal justice degree. He spent the next several years catching the bad guys and climbing the ranks of the police department in Detroit. He fell in love with Landon's mom, a South Carolina native and relocated to Florence to join its police department. After several promotions he found himself as lead commanding officer of the entire state's highway patrol. During his term, he met many important politicians in Columbia that asked him to provide private security. And this is how Smith Security was born. It's not just all his career accolades and honors that make Mr. Smith an intimidating man. Just his looks could scare someone into submission. The man is built like a linebacker, which isn't surprising since he played high school and collegiate football. His gruff demeanor and tough as nails persona add to his physical appearance telling anyone he meets he shouldn't be messed with. He has a tendency to demand perfection. All his employees go through rigorous physical training and psychological testing before the official hire. I figured Landon might follow in his dad's footsteps. I mean, he was sent to the Citadel, the military school of South Carolina. But Landon has never mentioned wanting to work for his dad or in any career that has to do with security or police work. I'm sure Landon's dad is strong arming him into this interview tomorrow.

When we were all younger, we thought Landon's dad had the coolest job. Landon got to meet some of Mr. Smith's clients. Whenever a professional athlete was playing close by, Landon always scored tickets to the sporting event. He also managed to get us sold out concert tickets because his dad's firm was hired as security. Landon has met a lot of very important and famous people. But he never bragged or thought it was that big of a deal. "Oh, who are you interviewing with tomorrow? Must be someone famous if they are calling on your dad's firm for security," Chloe says wanting to get the inside scoop.

"I'm not at liberty to say right now. Plus, I don't even know if I'll get the job or if he'll use my dad's firm. I'll let you know if things work out," Landon says again with little interest. I'm sure he realizes that his dad probably has a lot riding on this interview tomorrow, especially if it could be the deciding factor of whether or not Smith Security will get the business. I hope Landon can perk up before tomorrow or else it's a long shot.

"Well, poo! Come on, Landon, just a little hint would be nice," Chloe pleads.

"Believe me, it's not someone you would find very interesting. Some political figure that may be running in the Governor's race this year. He is about to announce his candidacy and needs security to start his tour of the state."

Chloe frowns. "Yeah, that's boring. I thought you might be interviewing with a movie or rock star. Politicians are just boring. But, good luck anyway."

"Thanks! Hey Runt, what did you do today? Rob a bank? This spread of food is incredible, but I'm sure it cost a fortune," Landon comments pushing his empty plate away and rubbing his full belly.

"I actually got an employee discount," Chloe says watching all of us as we digest not just our dinner, but her surprising words.

"What?" we all say practically in unison. All of us but Leslie, that is. She's still simmering in her anger at actually have to spend some time with Landon's friends.

"Well, I've been thinking. And it is my last summer before graduation. Next year I'll be in the real world, trying to find a real job. I just want to enjoy this last little bit of freedom. And what better way to do that than to get a part-time job and live at the beach. That is, if your offer still stands for a roommate this summer, Suz," Chloe says flashing her beautiful smile.

"Oh my gosh, of course the offer still stands. There's nothing more I'd love than for you to live with me this summer at the beach. But are you sure? You were adamant about taking classes this summer at the university."

"I was just gonna do that to lighten my load my senior year. But since you'll be traveling the world playing golf, I'll have plenty of uninterrupted time to study next year," Chloe informs me of her well thought out plan. I'm so excited that Chloe is spending the summer with me I can hardly stand it. I had begged her early on, from the moment I knew of my plans to move here this summer, to ditch school and come be my roommate one last time. Up until recently she had said no due to summer school. But now, she has suddenly changed her mind. My excitement slowly turns to guilt because I'm just figuring out why she had her sudden change of heart. She's worried about me. Since I returned from my break up with Wyatt, she's had to watch me live in a state depression for the past several days. No wonder she doesn't want to leave me alone all summer. Even with my little breakthrough today, getting back on the course for the first time in almost a week, she still feels like I could crumple at any given time. And she's sacrificing herself once again for my well being. Tears begin to well in my eyes when I think of Chloe's fierce loyalty and dedication to our friendship. I could demand that she continue with her plans for summer school and tell her that she would be better off sticking to her original plan. But, I truly do need her by my side these next coming months. Not only to kick my ass into gear to practice hard for qualifying. But also for moral support, especially, when I let my thoughts be consumed by Wyatt and our sudden break up. I know, I'm selfish and probably don't deserve her. But I'm taking her, any way I can.

I rise from my seat, run to her side of the table and almost hug the life out of her. Guilt seeps in one more time, so I have to give her this last chance to back out. "Are you sure, Chloe? I don't want you to sacrifice your plans just for me. And you can say all you want about wanting this last hooray before graduating, but I know what you're doing. You're staying because of me, right? Don't even try to deny it. Because I'm not gonna deny that I do need you. And I'm so happy you're gonna be here with me this summer," I say letting the words rush out. I'm on the verge of another crying fit just waiting for her answer.

"I need you, too. We're in this together, Suz. And it's gonna be a great summer. Almost epic!" Chloe says returning my hug. We release each other both with silly grins on our faces. "So, now the only thing left to do is tell the parents. My job as bartender at Dead Dog doesn't start until Friday, so I'm heading to Florence in the morning to grab some more of my things and tell Mom and Dad what I've decided about how I'm spending this summer."

"Your parents don't know yet?" Landon bellows, causing us both to jump at his gruff voice. Honestly, I had completely forgotten we weren't alone.

"No, not yet. I'll tell them in person tomorrow while I'm at home. Plus, Ashley is there and I'm sure she has some wedding stuff she wants to discuss with me. She hasn't told me which dreaded bridesmaid dress she has chosen for me. That should be interesting!" Chloe says with a chuckle.

Landon is way too serious, especially after Chloe's joke which involves her sister. We all used to joke about our siblings, Flynn excluded of course. But Landon doesn't even crack a smile. "I'll go with you tomorrow. What time are you planning to leave?" Landon asks.

"What?" we all say again, this time Leslie included.

"Landon, I'm fine to travel a little over an hour by myself. Besides, you've got that interview tomorrow," Chloe says with sigh.

"I'll reschedule. Just let me make some phone calls and work this out," Landon responds standing from his seated position and reaching in his pocket for his phone.

Leslie looks up at him with shock. "Landon, she says she'll be fine. You really don't want to disappoint your dad by cancelling this interview he set up for you. Plus, we are supposed to have dinner with my family tomorrow night while everyone is in town. I'm sure Chloe appreciates your offer to be her chaperone, but she looks like a big girl to me," Leslie says while placing her hand on Landon's arm which is holding the phone getting ready to dial. Landon shrugs off her touch and starts pacing the deck, running his hand through his dark hair. Landon has always had protective instincts when it comes to his friends. But this might be going a little too far. I look around the table and catch Flynn's gaze. I can see in his expression everything he can't say at the present moment. With the information he gave me earlier today about Landon's warning to him to stay away from Chloe, Flynn's look screams 'I told you so'.

Landon continues to pace with a tormented look on his face. We all wait anxiously to see what he is going to say next. "But what if you need me, Chloe? I can't get to you fast enough if I'm down here at the beach." Chloe looks at Landon and something unspoken transpires between the two of them. She slowly shakes her head, silently begging him to drop this protectiveness or possessiveness, or whatever it is that he feels toward Chloe.

"I'll go with her," Flynn says breaking the tense silence. "I actually want to get a few things from home before leaving the country. So this works out perfectly. Of course, if Chloe doesn't mind the company and will let me hitch a ride."

Chloe tries to protest, "Come on, guys. I think I'm capable..."

"No, Chloe. I would feel better if you didn't travel alone. If I can't accompany you home then I'm glad Flynn can. Please, just let Flynn ride with you home and back. It's just a day trip, right?" Landon asks not truly sold on the idea, but relieved that there is another option. I can tell Landon is not entirely thrilled that Flynn stepped up to the plate, but he can't really say anything since the problem is somewhat solved. Who knew Chloe going home for the day would turn into a problem?

"Fine. Flynn, I'm planning to take off pretty early in the morning so be ready or I'll leave your ass. Let's shoot for 7:00. I want to get home before Dad leaves for work so I can tell them both at the same time," Chloe says to Flynn but directs her comment to Landon. Landon nods his approval of her plan. This whole night just keeps getting more and more bizarre. As if on cue, our conversation is cut off by the sound of a boat motor. Sure enough, we all watch as a boat pulls up to our dock and the motor is shut off. The lights on the dock haven't been cut on, but the full moon's glow is enough that I immediately know another guest has arrived. I can identify that body anywhere. Patrick. His long, lean body steps out onto the dock and begins tying ropes to anchor the boat. I wish it wasn't so dark so that I could see his muscles flexing as he maneuvers the ropes around the stationary boat docking pegs. It was just a few nights ago that my body was pressed up against all those hard muscles, melting into his chest. I continue to stare, watching the moon illuminate his already very blonde hair, making it look almost white. I bet if he glances this way, the light from the moon would also enhance those baby blues that I continuously fall into whenever we are close enough. My heart skips a few beats as I watch Patrick finish anchoring the boat expecting him to start coming my way. But he pauses and then reaches back into the boat grabbing someone's hand to help them out of the boat and safely onto the dock. As soon as this person appears, I know exactly who she is too. Katelyn, Patrick's fiancée. Now my heart really speeds up. Up until now, I have only met Katelyn at their engagement party. Granted, Patrick and I haven't seen each other in years up until this past weekend. But he did visit me just the other night, proclaiming that he still loved me and then kissed me senseless. Now, he's bringing his fiancée to my beach house? Bizarre doesn't even accurately describe this night anymore.

As soon as Katelyn's feet hit dry land and she steadies herself, Patrick drops her hand and they walk side by side up the dock toward us. My heart rate approaches dangerous levels and I have to take deep breaths to calm my nerves. Chloe grabs my hand and gives it a squeeze sensing my uneasiness about their arrival. I practice my smile for Chloe. Although it's a shaky one, it'll have to do because Katelyn and Patrick are now walking up the stairs. I'm not ready for this. Yes, I've accepted the reality that Patrick and Katelyn are getting married. Even though he still has some unresolved feelings for me, as I do him, the fact still remains that he is engaged. I'm not crazy enough to think that will change just because I've resurfaced into his life. But what I haven't come to terms with yet, is that in order to maintain and salvage our friendship, I'm gonna have to get used to being around the both of them. As a couple. Reality sucks, but it's in my face right now as I look at the gorgeous couple standing on the landing of the stairs.

"Looks like I'm crashing another Caulder party," Patrick says lightheartedly. He seems a little nervous also, but maybe I'm the only one picking up on that vibe.

"Not at all, come on over and join us. I would offer you some food but it looks like Flynn and Landon finished it off just before you arrived. But there's beer in the cooler so grab a drink and sit," Chloe says ever the polite hostess. I narrow my eyes at her briefly before she whispers, "Hey, I live here too, now. Mi casa, su casa, right? I've got you, Suz. Everything will be fine."

Thank goodness she's here for the long haul. I've just been living at the beach a little less than two weeks. But with all that's happened, it seems like a lifetime. At this rate, it's gonna be a long summer.

"Thanks, Runt. Everyone, you remember Katelyn," Patrick says while Katelyn smiles and gives us all a shy wave. "Katelyn, to refresh your memory this is Flynn, Landon, Leslie, Runt or as she prefers to be called, Chloe and Suzanna." Patrick reintroduces us all leaving me for last. His gaze lingers on me just a tad bit longer than what's appropriate since he's standing beside his fiancée. Katelyn doesn't seem to notice.

"Hello, again everyone. Sorry for the reminder on names. I met you all the other night at the engagement party, but I apologize that I need a refresher. There were so many people at the party it was impossible to remember everyone. But now I think I'd pass the test!" Katelyn says seeming more at ease now than when they first arrived.

Flynn, taking his job as guardian of the cooler tonight seriously, reaches in and grabs two more beers for our guests. "So, what were you two out doing tonight?"

"We just wanted to get out on the water since it's such a beautiful night with the full moon. Plus, our dads are discussing business back at the house so it was kinda boring. We saw y'all from the boat and heard the laughter. Hope you don't mind that we stopped by," Patrick says to Flynn but continues to glance my way every so often.

"Not at all. We were just catching up. So, your dad, he's here at the beach? Doesn't he have a law firm to run in Florence?" Flynn asks trying to hide his hatred at the mention of Patrick's father. Plus, I guarantee he is scoping out the situation. If Mr. Miles is living at the beach, less than a mile from where I'm living this summer, Flynn will be none too happy. He might even hire security from Landon's family's firm.

Patrick goes tense at the mention of his dad and the law practice. Funny, since he's getting ready to spend the next three years of his life in school to become a lawyer. I just assumed he'd go to work for his dad once he graduated and passed the bar. But the scowl on his face says differently.

"He, um...he's working on a case for some clients here at the beach. Yeah, that's why he's still at our beach house," Patrick answers Flynn, but not very convincingly.

"Is it normal for him to spend so much time away from Florence? I mean, it must be hard to be away from his practice for long periods of time. Does he plan to return to Florence anytime soon?" Flynn asks again acting like a lawyer interrogating a witness. Flynn could never make it as a lawyer though, because his skills at subtlety are severely lacking.

"Dude, what's with the twenty questions? I know from the other night that my old man pissed you off about something. But really, where else does your interest lie in where or what my dad is doing?" Patrick says getting defensive. I shoot Flynn a look to stop this before he blurts out something that I really don't want anyone to know about, especially Patrick. Flynn could be a ticking time bomb now that he has the knowledge that Mr. Miles, Patrick's dad, attempted to rape me before I left midway through my senior year of high school. I just hope he has enough self control to rein it in and not spill my secrets.

Flynn grinds his teeth and clenches his fists by his sides. He stands but doesn't approach Patrick. His beef isn't with Patrick, but his dad. It's just Patrick is here and Flynn's taking out all his built up anger over this situation and directing it at him. "Honestly, I don't give a shit about your dad. I just find it odd that while all our parents work *at their offices,* your dad seems to be lounging around down here at the beach. I was just curious, that's all."

Patrick takes a small step toward Flynn, his muscles coiled tight with tension. "And I don't give a shit about your curiosity! Why can't you just mind your own damn business? I'm starting to think all those headers in soccer have caused some serious brain damage," Patrick says just riling up Flynn even more.

While everyone else watches this potential brawl with open mouths, I bow my head and try to hide under the rim of my visor. I wish I had taken out my pony tail earlier. Then I'd have my veil of my hair to hide beneath and shield me from this disaster taking place. Something has to be done before this escalates into an event we all will never recover from. Squeezing Chloe's hand to the point that I'm sure I've caused permanent damage, I whisper so that only she can hear. "Please, Chloe. You've gotta stop this. Please," I beg almost at the point of tears. Chloe gives me a nod and pries her hand free from my crushing grip. Giving me a pat on the thigh, she pops up beside me standing in the seat of her chair. She's turned her tiny self into something mighty and fierce and I'd be scared if I were Flynn or Patrick right now.

"Enough!" Chloe screams, her voice echoing through the night air. While everyone's attention is focused on Chloe, I slide from my seat and try to make a discreet exit into the house. I hear Chloe continue her rant. "What in the hell has gotten into you boys? Look, I'm all for a good testosterone fueled brawl between two hot, muscle clad guys. But you two? Come on, you two are friends. Or at least you were. Whatever is going on between you guys needs to be handled in a more adult way. So I suggest you both start acting your age and stop acting like you are ready to throw down like two bullies fighting on the playground in primary school." Leave it to Chloe to calm everyone down with her insulting, yet effective, lecture. I hear Landon chuckle at the two meatheads and it seems to break through some of the heavy tension from earlier. "I mean look what you've both done to our happy, little get together. Not to mention look what you've done to...," Chloe pauses but I know exactly what she's doing. Even though my back is turned away from everyone and my only focus in getting inside the house, I can practically see Chloe nodding in my direction, alerting everyone of my escape.

"Suz..."

"Sis..."

I hear both Patrick and Flynn call my attention at the exact same time. With one foot still on the deck and the other crossing the threshold of the door, I pause mid stride and wait for one of them to continue.

"I'm sorry, Sis. I guess I've had maybe one too many beers tonight," Flynn says using his moderate intake of alcohol as a lame excuse for his behavior. But hey, what else can he say? He surely can't tell his real reasons for the misplaced hostility toward Patrick.

"Yeah, sorry Suzanna. I didn't come to start up anything with Flynn. I just thought we could stop by and hang out like old times. Guess I was wrong," Patrick also apologizes still sounding perturbed with how the night has played out so far.

I turn and look at both of them. Flynn seems to find his flip flops very fascinating since he refuses to raise his head and look me in the face. I don't blame him because I'm angry he let the knowledge of my past secrets get him in such a confrontational state. If he even dared to meet my eyes he'd definitely be on the receiving end of one of my death glares. I'll deal with him later without an audience.

When I shift my attention to Patrick, he meets my hardened gaze head on. This is the first time I've seen Patrick since our kiss after his engagement party. If he regrets the kiss or is embarrassed by it, especially with Katelyn by his side, he sure doesn't show it. Our eyes lock onto each other and I am tempted to fall into the depths of his gorgeous baby blues. I try to read the emotions swirling in those hypnotic eyes, but can't pick up on just one. Anger, confusion, curiosity, they are all there just as I expected. What I didn't expect to see is the lustful and loving way he is looking at me. His gaze is doing some pretty intense things to my body at the moment, almost causing me to forget why I am mad at him and my brother in the first place. Before this moment becomes more awkward, because old lovers looking at each other with such intimacy in front of the new fiancée, friends and family, is definitely awkward, I silently beg my body to stop this nonsense reaction and break the spell I'm currently under. However, me, nor Patrick, looks away from each other voluntarily. It's only when Katelyn speaks that we are forced to turn our attention elsewhere.

"Patrick," Katelyn quietly says, "maybe it's best if we just go."

"No!" I blurt out. Now every eye, not just Patrick's, is focused on me. "Please, don't leave. God, my mother would kill me if you didn't feel like a welcomed guest in our home. I believe we all lost our manners momentarily. However, regardless of the trailer trash, redneck impression we just gave you," I say with pointed looks to both Flynn and Patrick, "we are actually very nice people. I would love to visit with you and get to know you better. Please, come and join me inside. I think I'm all beered out and I've got a bottle of chilled white wine waiting, I just need someone to share it with me."

I watch anxiously as Katelyn considers my invitation. She glances up at Patrick I guess wanting his opinion. He gives her a subtle nod which she returns with a small smile. Finally she walks over to where I'm still standing in the doorway. "Thanks, Suzanna. I'd love to join you for that glass of wine," Katelyn says as I move to let her enter our beach home.

I take one last look at the people on the deck. Leslie still thinks a gang fight is about to break out and is using the opportunity to sidle up to Landon's side and basically try to climb him. Ugh, the girl still acts like a slut in my book. Okay, maybe a reformed slut, but still. Well, who am I to break up her needy party and make her part ways with Landon. It's not like she would rather hang out with us girls anyway. Yay, more wine for me. Chloe is still perched on top of her chair taking her job as referee very seriously. "Chloe you good?" I ask.

"Yeah, but I think I'll continue to stay out here and manage the testosterone levels, just in case these knuckleheads try to get out of line again," Chloe says while flexing her itty bitty biceps. This only makes the guys chuckle, including Landon, who is oblivious to Leslie wanting to become an extra appendage. Since the biceps don't work in Chloe's favor, she gives them all the middle finger which only causes them to laugh harder. "I'll come join you girls when things completely cool down out here. Have fun!"

I give her a quick nod and finally leave the deck and my friends to walk into the house with Katelyn. The fiancée of my first true love. What the hell have I done? I can't get to that wine fast enough!

Chapter Ten

I stand frozen in place as Katelyn walks into the living area scanning her surroundings. "So, this is your family beach home?" she asks while taking inventory of the mismatched furniture and corny beach knickknacks decorating the home.

"Yeah, my grandparents built it when my dad was a child and it has stayed in my family for years. I've been coming here since I was a baby," I say nervously not really understanding why I want to impress this girl. I continue to watch Katelyn survey the living area, finding interest in the wall of photos my mom refuses to take down even though it highlights mine and Flynn's entire lives, especially the awkward teenage years. The smile on Katelyn's face says she has noticed those exact pictures that document that era of my life. I bet Katelyn, with her flawless olive skin, perfect dark, thick hair, and just overall exquisite beauty never had to suffer through acne, braces, and bangs. Yeah, my mother had a thing for bangs and I looked like the Quaker Oats page boy until late middle school when I refused to let her cut them again and went into, yet, a more awkward stage as they slowly grew out. Not only am I still nervous being in her company, but I'm also feeling a bit embarrassed and unworthy of Katelyn. Shaking out of my thoughts of inadequacy, I manage to unglue my feet and get moving to the kitchen. Wine is an excellent idea right about now. "You still up for that glass of wine?" I ask not really caring what her answer is because I'm not too proud to drink alone. Please, please say yes so I don't look and feel like an even bigger loser.

"Absolutely," Katelyn says briefly taking her attention from the photo gallery to look over at me in the kitchen. I let out a sigh of relief which seems to echo off the walls in the silence of the house. I'm sure she heard it and is probably thinking she should have stayed outside with the boys. I clumsily open the fridge door and pull out the closest bottle I can get my hands on. The door of the fridge slams shut causing the condiment jars and bottles to rattle in the door. *Get a grip, Suz. She's just another guest in your home. It's not like she's Miss America or something! But she could be...ugh!* I plunder around in the drawer until I find the electronic wine opener. Luckily, my mother likes her wine and bought an expensive wine opener that opens a bottle with ease. I've never been more thankful for wine technology than now, seeing how my shaking hands would most certainly have failed to open the bottle of wine with just a regular corkscrew. Failure and probably an injury. Once the wine is opened, I grab two acrylic, stem-less wine glasses from the cabinet. Yep, not even gonna attempt to use the real glass wine glasses. Don't really care if my acrylic versions are unimpressive. I'm just trying to have a drink with a *possible friend*, not cause bodily harm to myself or her by shattering a glass, which of course I'd do and cut myself, bleed profusely, and die a tragic death. Okay, so I'm being a little dramatic, but this girl has got my nerves in knots. I manage to successfully pour each of us a glass without spilling a drop. It's a miracle, but I think my subconscious knows I need all the alcohol I can intake without wasting any during the pour process.

Now comes the hard part. Taking a deep, deep breath to try to contain my nerves and stop my body tremors, I carefully pick up the glasses and walk at a slow pace toward Katelyn, who is still admiring my life in photos. I'm about to take pride in reaching her without spilling a drop of wine, but have to settle for an apology and some humility. My dumbass self was so eager to hand off the glass of rippling liquid that I might have thrust the glass toward Katelyn's hand a little too hard, causing the wine to slosh around and eventually spill over the rim. To make matters worse, Katelyn now stands holding a half full glass of wine while the remaining alcohol drips all over her hand and is making a small puddle on the floor. "Oh my gosh! I am so sorry," I mutter backing away from the mess I made. "Let me just get some paper towels to clean this up. I, uh, I can't believe I did that to you. I'm such an idiot!" I keep rambling on like the fool I am, frantically grabbing an entire roll of paper towels and a wet dish cloth. Running back over to Katelyn, I'm beyond shocked to find her licking, yes *licking*, the drops of liquid from her glass. This is such an unlady like thing to do, especially from the prim and proper upstate debutante and daughter of an affluent judge. Katelyn must see the shock that has registered on my face and starts laughing.

"What?" she asks like licking a glass is a normal every day occurrence to her. I'm still shocked stupid and mute so she continues. "Well, I figured since we're splitting a bottle and Chloe may join us, might as well drink all I can now. This is actually tasty. You might not know this about me, but I'm more of a beer and liquor girl. Wine is really not my thing. This may be a one hundred dollar bottle or a two buck chuck, I would never be able to tell the difference." She says all of this between licks and before I know it the glass is back to non-dripping. "See," she says holding the glass up so we can both take a look, "it's as good as new. Now, I do have some standards and I don't plan to lick up the puddle on the floor, so I could really use those paper towels now."

Katelyn is nothing like I presumed she would be. I mean, she seemed very pleasant and nice during our first meeting at the engagement party. However, I assumed from her family lineage that she would be a snobby prude. Guess that's what I get for passing judgment on appearances and affiliations alone. "Here," I say handing her the wet dish cloth, "use this to wipe the stickiness off your hand and I'll clean up the floor." I gingerly place my glass on the nearest table (no one needs any more spills to clean up) and fall to my knees to wipe up the mess on the floor. If only I could wipe away the last ten minutes of our interaction and start all over again. I pray Katelyn isn't as judgmental as I was earlier. If so, she has already pegged me as a freak!

Once the floor is spick and span, I stand beside Katelyn as she resumes looking at the photographs, eyeing one in particular. "Is that Patrick?" she asks pointing to a picture taken the summer before our senior year in high school. It's a photograph of the fab five on the beach. The guys, Patrick, James and Landon, are all on their hands and knees in the sand. Chloe and I are standing on their backs with our hands in the air. We are all smiling at the camera, which I'm sure was held by my mother or Aunt Betty. I remember not seconds after the picture was captured that the guys collapsed sending me and Chloe in a tailspin onto the ground and on top of them. Chloe screamed and complained only earning her more sand to the body and hair, thanks in part to Landon and James. Having enough, Chloe made her escape running to the ocean with Landon and James right on her heels. Meanwhile, I was left coughing up sand while Patrick laughed. Instead of picking a fight with more sand, he simply held out his hand to help me up. Then we strolled hand in hand to the water, ignoring the shenanigans of our other friends. Trying to be discreet knowing Aunt Betty or my mother could be watching, we waded out almost neck deep before all the sand wars were forgotten and it was just Patrick and me. Like magnets, our hands couldn't hold back from touching each other. Before either of us realized it, we were like a pretzel, my legs wrapped around his waist and his arms holding me securely under my ass and pressing me into his body. We were out far enough that the waves were forming, but not breaking so we floated over each one of them. The force of each wave gave us enough motion that our bodies slid up and down, my bare stomach and his bare chest rubbing against the other. Every time we rose to the crest of a wave, only to float back down, my core would hit his growing erection sending shivers throughout both our bodies, regardless that it was a sweltering mid July day and the water temperature was equivalent to a warm bath. Our lips crashed together in a breathless kiss causing us to forget that we were at a public beach. Thankfully, our hooligan friends swam over to crash our private party and lured us into their trivial water and sand fight. Good thing for Patrick. There was no way he would have immediately escaped the water without showing the tourist families the huge bulge in his swim trunks.

The memory still gives me goose bumps as I rub my arms, but it also brings a smile to my face. I'm still smiling at the photograph when I see Katelyn out of the corner of my eye waiting. Oh yes, she did ask a question and while I was off in la-la land has been curiously watching me. God, I hope the flush I feel from that intimate memory of Patrick and me isn't evident. Aw, who am I kidding? I can feel the heat of redness creeping up my neck and cheeks like someone is coloring me with a paintbrush. Clearing my throat, I try to sound as normal as possible. "Yes, that's Patrick," I say pointing to Patrick in the picture, wanting to touch his image with my fingertip just to have that connection. But I refrain and point out the other members of the photo. "There's Landon and James. And the goofballs on top of our makeshift pyramid, well that's Chloe and me. There you have it. Just one of the many candid shots of the fab five. I'm sure my mom has hundreds more of these embarrassing pictures around here somewhere."

"Why be embarrassed? I think it's sweet that you have memories with your closest friends," Katelyn says with all sincerity as I detect a wistful note in her tone. "You all must have been a real tight knit group for a long time to have your very own nickname, huh?"

"Yes, we've all known each other since grade school. Being from a fairly small town, we grew up together and our parents were all friends. I guess it was kinda inevitable that we would all become friends too. I'm very lucky to call them my friends. They're all really great people. But I guess you know that, especially about Patrick. I mean you are marrying him." Wow, did I just say that? How many glasses of wine did I drink? Looking down I realize that my glass is magically empty. I quickly walk back to the kitchen to get a refill. I'm so determined on my quest for another drink, I about jump out of my skin when Katelyn places her hand on my shoulder, alerting me that she followed me.

"Suzanna, I'm sorry I didn't mean to scare you. Look, I really do want to get to know you and the rest of Patrick's friends. Hopefully, you all will become my friends, too. Because I could really use some people in my corner." Katelyn, with all her exterior beauty, seems so lost and alone when she makes her plea for my friendship. I really do like her so far, beside the fact that she is the woman that will become Patrick's wife. But, with the way things have panned out the last few years, I realize I don't really have any say so where it concerns Patrick and his future. Our love relationship is in the past where it needs to stay so that we all can move on as friends. So, if the future holds a friendship with both Patrick and Katelyn, then that's not such a bad deal. Yes, I can definitely see Katelyn and me becoming friends. And who doesn't need more of those anyway, right? "Please, Suzanna. I feel like maybe we should just start over. Maybe not delve into the heavy stuff right away. I don't want to make you skittish, but obviously I already have. Are you nervous to be around me?" Katelyn asks. Now she's the nervous one while she bites her bottom lip, anxiously awaiting my answer.

"No!" I lie. Katelyn gives me a narrowed glare silently calling bullshit. "Okay, yes. Maybe a little. But you need to understand that it has nothing to do with you as a person. There's a little more history to mine and Patrick's story than just childhood friends," I say looking anywhere but at Katelyn. I busy myself with pouring wine to avoid eye contact.

"Suzanna," Katelyn says waiting for me to give her back my full attention. Slowly I meet her eyes and I'm surprised to see a smile on her face. "I know all about the romantic relationship between Patrick and you that took place in high school. I even know how you broke his heart during senior year, moving away to concentrate on your golf game." I open my mouth to defend myself, but Katelyn cuts me off with a hand gesture and continues. "Of course that's his side of the story. If you want to tell me your side, as your friend," she emphasizes the word and I can't help the corners of my lips lifting into a small smirk, "then I'm all ears. I'm a very good listener. Plus, even if I had no prior knowledge of your relationship with Patrick, I'd have guessed you two were an item at some point. It's so obvious that there are some unresolved feelings you two are harboring for each other."

"Oh. And you're okay with that?" I ask feeling suddenly very guilty.

"Of course. We all have our pasts. Lord knows I certainly do," Katelyn says with a bit of sad nostalgia. "Besides, since becoming engaged, Patrick and I have shared all of our past love and lust relationships with each other. We have no secrets between us."

"Isn't that something most people do before becoming engaged?" I ask finding it odd that their conversations about me and Katelyn's old boyfriends took place *after* Patrick placed the ring on her finger. I'm also a bit curious about all the details Patrick so willingly shared with his fiancée. However, I'm scared to find out. But I better get ready, because so far, Katelyn has been very forthcoming during our meet and greet.

"Yeah, well, I'll never claim to be anything close to normal. Normal is so boring!" Katelyn says trying to sound confident, but the way she is shifting on her feet I can tell I've hit a sensitive subject. However, Katelyn doesn't dwell on my question and quickly redirects the conversation. "Anyhow, with everything Patrick told me about your relationship and the way he talked about you, I thought it best that we meet before the wedding. I actually encouraged Patrick to send the personalized engagement party invitation."

"How noble of you," I say bitterly. What game is she playing here? Plus, I can't deny that it hurts a little to find out the personalized invite wasn't entirely Patrick's idea. "So Patrick and you decided to invite me to your shindig, what, like as a joke? Were you trying to size up the competition?"

"So you're entering this fight?" Katelyn asks not ruffled at all by my outburst. "Let's just keep calm and dial down the hostility, would ya? I have never and will never think of you in any way, shape or form as a joke. And I don't think of you as competition. I encouraged Patrick to send the note he had *already* written to you on his own, hoping that you'd accept the invite and come. The only reason I wanted to see you at the party was because of Patrick. Because I know that he has never gotten over you and he needs to find some closure. As do you."

"Sorry for jumping down your throat. And you're right. We both need to put a lid on our relationship of the past and focus on our futures. I'm trying to find that elusive closure, too."

"Any luck with that?" Katelyn asks. I must hesitate too long with my answer. "Suzanna, do you still love Patrick?"

"What? No!" I state with affirmation.

"You're lying," Katelyn says while I stare at her open mouthed and dumbfounded. "You love Chloe, yes?"

"Well, of course I do. She's my best friend."

"And you love James and Landon also, right?" Katelyn questions again while I start to catch on to her logic.

"Yes, most definitely," I answer.

"Then you've gotta love Patrick too. I mean, he is a part of the unbreakable group of friends you all refer to as the fab five."

This is total entrapment. And Katelyn, very innocently, has got me right between a rock and a hard place. Damn she's good. I'd venture to say she's picked up some tricks from her old man. "Well, when you put it that way, how can I say no? Of course I love Patrick like I love the rest of the fab five. As. A. Friend!"

Katelyn clicks her tongue against the roof of her mouth with an air of victory. "Uh huh, that's what I thought. Although I'm not quite convinced with your label of love."

"Believe what you want. You're not getting any more information from me, even using those sneaky tactics of yours," I say hoping it's my time to turn the tables. "You know, I can ask you the same thing. Do you love Patrick?"

"Well, duh. I am marrying the man. Of course I love him!" Katelyn says. But I notice all the signs of being in love are missing. There's no light in her eyes or flush to her skin when she talks about her love of Patrick. It's like me talking about the love I feel for James or Landon.

"How?" I ask, throwing it out there.

"Excuse me? What do you mean?"

"Well, since you brought up love labels, I'd enjoying hearing yours for Patrick." I could end up hating myself for this, but I have to know. Katelyn doesn't strike me as the mushy gushy type, but she's about to label her love for the man she plans to spend the rest of her life with. My mind is racing with her potential responses like 'unconditionally' or 'to the moon and back'. So I steel myself and wait to hear what she has to say.

"Sacrificially," Katelyn responds with no hesitation.

Chapter Eleven

Now wait a damn minute! *Sacrificially*, really? What the hell has she ever had to sacrifice? I mean, look at her...genetically donned the gorgeous genes from her former beauty queen mother. Yeah, guilty as charged. I happened to Google everything about the Bosticks and learned that Mrs. Bostick was once crowned Miss South Carolina. Not to mention, Google also told me of the life of privilege that Katelyn grew up in. Her father, the notorious ball busting attorney, took his small firm and turned it into a multi-million dollar fortune with offices not only in South Carolina but up and down the east coast. Unfortunately, I wasn't able to find a trace of dirt attached to the Bosticks or Katelyn. Looks like she is the perfect daughter, graduating with honors from her private high school and Clemson University. Other than finding out about her outstanding academic achievements, the only other source of info I found was the beautiful photographs of the happy family. In each and every photograph, Katelyn shines with her natural, exotic beauty. So sue me, but I'm having a really hard time believing she has ever sacrificed one measly thing in her entire life.

Internally, I'm fuming. How dare she love Patrick sacrificially when I'm the one who had to give up almost everything for him? I loved him so much that I was willing to leave my home, family and friends. I left during Christmas break of my high school senior year, forgoing senior prom and graduation with kids I attended school with since kindergarten. And most of all, I sacrificed the love of my life at the time, breaking both our hearts. As hard as it was, I'm pretty sure I'd do it all again. I loved Patrick enough that I chose to give up all of it, with the exception of golf, in order for him to continue to have Jim, his dad, in his life. Keeping the secret that Jim attempted to sexually assault me haunts me to this day. However, it was necessary so that no embarrassment came to Patrick and his family. Plus, since the passing of Patrick's mother, Marie, Jim was the only parent Patrick had left. A sorry excuse of a parent, but nonetheless, the only one. I just couldn't take that away from Patrick.

I'd like to scream at Katelyn "what did you give up to love Patrick sacrificially?" Then I'd have us both compile a list, which of course I'd totally win by a landslide. But the thing with secrets is that you have to keep your mouth shut and keep it a secret. There is no way I'm revealing my horrid past just to find some kind of justification with Patrick's fiancée. So I sit silently brooding. I'm so engrossed in my internal sacrifice battle with Katelyn I don't even hear my phone ringing. It's only when Katelyn thrust the cellular device my way that I release my thoughts and get out of my head and back to the present. With a shaking hand from the anger I'm still harboring over Katelyn's love revelation, I nod my appreciation and utter an almost incoherent thank you before answering the call.

"Hello," I say trying to sound normal.

"Susanna, hi, it's Drew. You okay?" I hear from the other end of the mobile phone. Guess my voice wasn't so normal sounding after all.

"Hi Drew. Yeah, I'm great. Just chatting with a friend," I say glancing in Katelyn's direction. She has retreated back to the kitchen for another glass of wine, graciously giving me a small bit of privacy to take this call.

"Oh, sorry to interrupt, but I wanted to get you that information you needed for the caddy forms you need to turn in before qualifying."

"Not a problem. I'm so glad you called because I need to get those forms mailed in like yesterday. Give me a second to grab a pen and I'll fill them out while I've got you on the phone." Drew agreed to accompany me to qualifying as my caddy for the tournament. Stupid me didn't even think about hiring a caddy since I never used one during college play. I was so caught up in the invitation to qualifying I neglected to think about all the changes that I needed to make in my transition from a college athlete to a career as a professional golfer. Luckily, my dad is staying on top of things, acting like a pseudo agent. Between fielding calls from future potential sponsors and endorsement deals, should I get my professional tour card, he also has handled the tons of paperwork that needs to be filled out for the United States Golfing Association. I've already turned in my online application for the qualifying tournament as well as all the notarized forms to the association and the tournament headquarters. The last piece of required documentation is Drew's personal identification information so that he can assist me on the course as my caddy. The caddy forms are due by the end of this week, which is cutting it close. Thank heavens Drew agreed and is calling me now with his info. The timing couldn't have been better, not because I'm closing in on a deadline, but because I really need a breather from my conversation with Katelyn.

Drew gives me all the information needed to complete the form. "Well, that should do it. I'll get these in the mail tomorrow morning, first thing," I say sealing the envelope.

"I'd send them priority mail just to make sure they arrive on time. Not sure you'll get a chance in the morning with our early tee time," Drew reminds me. Shit, he's right. I've got an 8:30 tee time in the morning with Coach Moore. Which means I need to arrive about thirty minutes early. Does the post office open before 8:00? Actually, Flynn is riding to Florence in the morning with Chloe. I'll just give it to him or Chloe before they leave and Flynn can hand it off to Dad, who will make sure it gets to the tournament headquarters on time, even if he has to drive it there himself. Whew, problem solved.

"Don't worry, I've got it all figured out. And I'll see you in the morning at eight sharp. Thanks again for doing this for me Drew. I know it was last minute and you're having to juggle some things around. But honestly, I can't think of a better person to have by my side during the tournament than you. I owe you one!" I say with all sincerity.

"The only thing you owe me is a first place finish," Drew says with all the confidence in the world in me. "I'll see you in the morning, Suzanna. Have a great night!"

"You too. Bye Drew," I say ending the call and getting my even kilter back. I might suck at relationships. I mean, that's fairly obvious seeing as how I messed up with Patrick years ago. And just recently, Wyatt basically threw me to the curb for some hot shot opportunity in New York. Not to mention, he made his point of not wanting a long distance relationship crystal clear with the butt naked skank he was hiding in his bed. Now, Katelyn probably thinks I'm a freak, asking her all about how she loves Patrick, the man she's going to marry. Then when she gives me an honest, yet confusing answer, I go off into a psychotic state of mind totally ignoring her and tuning her out. So let's just say my experience with relationships, be romantic or friendly, have all taken a turn for the worse. But the only relationship I need to care about right now is the one that involves a bag of clubs and tiny white ball...golf. It wasn't until I got the call from Drew and we talked about my golf that I started feeling somewhat normal. Yeah, golf just does that for me. No matter what else is going on in my crazy life, I can always center myself with the game I love.

Now that my phone call with Drew is finished and I have all the pertinent information I need, I prolong getting back to my conversation with Katelyn. I wish I hadn't been so hasty in sealing the envelope. At least then I would have all of Drew's paperwork to look over and double check. As it is now, I am engrossed in studying the address of the tournament headquarters which is preprinted on the outside of the envelope. Only an obsessed idiot would double check a preprinted envelope for correctness. Once I'm satisfied that an unnamed print shop hasn't goofed up, I then focus my attention on the return address I wrote very neatly. Yep, it's also correct since I've memorized my home address since preschool. What the hell am I doing? I'm sure if anyone was watching me thoroughly inspect the outside of this envelope they would immediately have me committed. I just don't want this golf euphoria to end just yet. Maybe I'll engage Katelyn in a conversation about golf. I wonder if she plays. Surely her parents are no strangers to the course. Most high profile professionals use the golf course as a second office. I'm certain Mr. Bostick has done some wheeling and dealing out on the links. Oh God, what if Katelyn is an excellent golfer? Not only would she have Patrick, but she'd also share my golfing talent. I am making myself crazy! Lucky for me, it doesn't look like I have to bore Katelyn with my golf achievements since Chloe busts through the door in a fit of giggles sparing me from another awkward encounter with Katelyn.

"Oh my, those boys out there are killing me," Chloe says almost doubled over in laughter.

"So I take it your referee gig is no longer needed," I ask just to make sure no one is shedding blood out on the deck.

"No, not at all. Once I told them there was no contest of whose balls were bigger, Patrick and Flynn both sat down and cooled off with some beer. Then slowly they started joking around and telling some outrageous college stories that had everyone hooting and hollering. Everyone that is except Leslie. She seems content to basically crawl up Landon's side, clawing his arm and smooching his neck."

"Ewww, gross," Katelyn and I both say in unison which has Chloe back in a fit of laughter.

"I know, it is gross. And y'all didn't even have to witness it. But I did. And when her claws weren't attached to those massive biceps, her hands were roaming up and down his body. She found his bulging thighs of particular interest. I swear, I saw her rub his cock a few times. I'll need a whole bottle of Clorox just to get that image out of my head," Chloe says followed by sticking her finger down her throat and exaggerating a gagging sound. "If they don't leave soon, I bet she'll hike up that pretty dress of hers to straddle him and go to town in front of everyone. That's why I had to make my escape inside!" This causes another chorus of 'ewwws' from me and Katelyn along with some shuddering.

"Does Landon like what Leslie is doing to him? Is he really into her?" Katelyn asks surprising both me and Chloe. I guess since just meeting all of us she's curious.

"No, he definitely isn't the PDA type of guy with anyone, especially Leslie. He looks at her like she's an annoying gnat and he's just waiting to take a swing and shoo her away. I just don't get why he keeps her around. It's so obvious that he's not into her like she is into him," Chloe says making me wonder the same thing.

"Seems like he's just protecting her feelings, maybe?" Katelyn offers as way of an explanation. "I don't know Landon very well, but he seems to be the protector of the group. I can see how he acts around you two, always making sure you're both okay. Maybe he's just trying to do the same for Leslie and he's waiting to let her down easy."

There Katelyn goes again with her labels. I wonder how she would label me. I'd put my money on freak or bitch. Although I'd rather she label me as a friend. I remember early on before our conversation got strange how she said she really needed some friends in her life. Other than her pissing me off earlier with her 'sacrificial love' quote, I like Katelyn. And maybe, just maybe, we can be friends.

Chloe breaks my train of thought commenting on Katelyn's description of Landon. "You pegged him perfectly! Yes, he is very protective of the ones he loves. You should see him around his momma!" Chloe says then immediately looks guilty. To avoid our curiosity, she busies herself in the kitchen looking for a drink. "Where's all the wine? Don't tell me you bitches finished it off."

"There's another bottle in the fridge door. Just need to open it. And yes, we finished off the first one. You should have escaped the porn show sooner if you wanted us to share," I say teasingly.

"Well look at you two, getting all chummy with each other," Chloe says with her exaggerated southern accent. "Now don't go getting any ideas Katelyn. Suzanna only has one BFF and that's me!"

"Oh, I'd never. Actually I'd love to get to know both of you a little better. I knew Suzanna was spending the summer here at the beach, but just found out that you are also. Since I'll be living down at Pawleys Island most of this summer, I'd love for all of us to hang out. I could really use some girl time," Katelyn says making that plea again for some type of friendship. I'm starting to feel sorry for her. Maybe she's just missing those close to her that she left behind in Greenville.

"Absolutely!" Chloe exclaims. "The more the merrier. And to be honest, I'm curious how you see me. I'm wondering if you'll be as close with your analysis of me as you were with Landon."

"That's an easy one." Katelyn takes a moment to ponder Chloe before spilling the beans. "You, my dear, are the encourager of the group. Nothing is ever half empty to you, always half full. You find the good in everyone, well everyone, except Leslie. Which by the way, one of you has got to tell me the back story on that girl. Anyway, you are always happy, at least on the outside. You can take any bad situation and find a positive. I think you're the go to girl when any of the rest of the fab five has a problem. Not only will you give great advice, but you'll make the problem seem not nearly as bad. Am I anywhere close?"

"Dead on," I agree while Chloe beams a brilliant smile our way.

"I was counting on being right. Cause I'd like Chloe to look at this god awful bridesmaid dress my mother picked out and find some redeeming quality," Katelyn says whipping out her phone and pressing buttons. Suddenly, a picture of the most hideous dress appears on her screen and both Chloe and I are speechless.

"Um, I, I don't know what to say. Let me look at that thing more closely," Chloe says grabbing the phone. "Wow, I've got my work cut out for me."

Katelyn is laughing now watching us try our best to find something remotely flattering about the chicken shit yellowish-brown dress that supposedly Katelyn's wedding attendants are so lucky to wear. "I know, it's just plain ugly. I don't know what my mother was thinking! I think her meds were screwing with her head that day."

"Or maybe she was off of her meds! There's just no other explanation," Chloe says still looking for something good to materialize from the picture.

For the next hour, Chloe, Katelyn and I talk about the wedding. Come to find out, Katelyn's mom is doing 99 percent of the planning. The only thing Katelyn would not hand over to her mother was the music for the ceremony. Seeing as Katelyn graduated with a degree in music and is classically trained on the piano, she insisted on picking out the wedding songs, using more contemporary pieces even though her mother urged for the traditional wedding march. When we questioned Katelyn about all the other details, specifying the awful bridesmaid dress choice, she just shrugged and told us that the music was the only thing she cared to butt heads with her mother about. All the other stuff is mainly for her parents anyway, citing that even though she and Patrick will be the ones at the altar, this really is a big party for her parents and their invited guests. Plus, her philosophy is that a wedding doesn't make a marriage. The wedding will take place one day, but the marriage will be built and last for years. I guess I can agree with her, but I'd really like to look back at my wedding photos and not cringe seeing all the bad decisions someone else made.

When Chloe still hadn't come up with one single good spin on the choice of bridesmaid dresses, Katelyn told her to quit trying. Frankly, she didn't really even care all that much what her attendants wore. Other than her sister-in-law, the other eight bridesmaids were first, second and even third cousins, which Katelyn hasn't seen in years. Chloe and I are shocked when Katelyn informed us that she didn't have one friend in her wedding. Her parents, who were fronting the whole lavish affair, didn't think too highly of Katelyn's friends from home or college, therefore dictating that only family members would be a part of the wedding party. Katelyn also sadly stated that most of her friends had been nixed from the guests list as well. Her parents, mainly her dad, explained that his only daughter's wedding would be the most sought after invite of the year and only the most influential people would be attending. There would not be wasted invitations to most of Katelyn's 'acquaintances', as he belittled her relationships with her friends. When Chloe and I both voiced our disgust and out-rage at the whole 'we're paying so we're in charge' parental attitude, Katelyn just shrugged it off and said it wasn't worth the fight. Now I'm really starting to understand Katelyn's need for some friends. And I'm thinking that maybe Katelyn is sacrificing something to marry Patrick. I think she's giving up her entire identity.

When the wedding talk gets gloom and doom, Chloe changes the subject and starts telling us about her new job. Which reminds me of the letter I need to send home with her and Flynn tomorrow. "Hey, Chloe, will you or Flynn take this letter home to Dad so he can send it priority mail to the tournament? It's got to be there later this week and I won't have a chance to mail it in the morning due to my early tee time."

"Yeah, sure. I've got a stack of mail I have to send to the university. I've gotta see if I can get my summer school money tacked on to the fall tuition. If not, my mom is gonna be pissed! Just stick it on the pile with my stuff and I'll take it to the post office with my things," Chloe says pointing in the direction of her purse.

"You sure? I can give it to Flynn to pass on to Dad and he'll get it done." I secretly hope that my dad can take care of it so I know it'll definitely get done. Not that I don't believe Chloe can handle the priority mail stuff, but sometimes she decides to just blow things off. Like she's doing with summer school this year. Plus, if she tells her parents about her living with me at the beach and working at a bar first thing in the morning, who knows what their reaction will be and what state of mind she'll spend the rest of the day in. I'm thinking it will not be good.

"I'd take Chloe up on her offer." We all turn to see that Leslie has entered the room leaving the boys on the deck. "The guys are really tying one on, Flynn especially. Whatever you tell him tonight he'll forget by the morning," Leslie says sounding disgusted at the entire situation.

"Oh, hi Leslie. Would you like to join us?" I ask being polite.

"No thanks. I just came in to use the restroom. I was hoping that I can convince Landon to leave soon. I can't believe I have spent an entire night sitting out on that deck listening to three men tell crude jokes while getting plastered. So much for my romantic dinner date with Landon," she says with a huff. Suffice to say, she has no desire to be here at all. Poor Landon will probably get an earful.

"Sorry, about your date. But I'm really glad y'all stopped by." Having enough of Leslie's bitter attitude I change the subject. "So Chloe, please, please don't forget to mail this letter tomorrow. It is extremely important and if it doesn't get there I won't be able to participate in the qualifying."

"Yeah, yeah I got it, okay! If Flynn is coherent in the morning I'll give it to him to pass along to your dad. Or I'll just mail it with my stuff. No biggie, it'll get done. I promise," Chloe says trying to ease my doubt. I walk over and place my very important letter on top of her pile then put them in her purse, just to make sure she doesn't drive away without them.

Leslie is still standing by the door, looking more irritated by the minute. She clears her throat drawing all our attention her way. "Flynn better be coherent enough in the morning to accompany you to Florence. Otherwise, Landon will feel obligated to take his place so he can make sure his precious Chloe arrives safely. Then I'll miss out on yet another chance for some alone time with Landon before my family packs up and heads back home from our beach vacation. Now, if someone could kindly tell me where the restroom is, I'd really appreciate it. And then maybe I can get out of here."

I hear Katelyn gasp. Chloe is breathing heavily trying hard to control her anger from Leslie's words. I'm sure Leslie is frustrated that tonight didn't go as planned, but does she have to be so rude. I feel Chloe getting close to retaliation and decide to take matters into my own hands. "Leslie, you're welcome to use the restroom in my bedroom. It's just this way."

I point Leslie in the direction of my bedroom and follow her inside to show her the restroom. From behind I hear a seething Chloe. "She is such a bitch!"

"True that!" Katelyn replies. I knew I liked that girl.

Chapter Twelve

After showing Leslie the facilities, I walk out to find the kitchen and living area empty. I guess everyone is on the deck and the night is coming to an end. I walk outside to join Katelyn, Chloe and the guys and to tell everyone goodnight. "Hi guys, what's going on?"

"We're just warning Landon of the ball of fury he's gonna have to contend with once he finally takes Leslie home," Chloe says.

"Why is she so mad? I mean it's not like I was ignoring her the entire night. Plus, she got food and drinks, thanks to you guys. What more could she want?" Landon asks basically clueless.

"From the vantage point I had, it looked like she wants your dick in her pussy," Flynn slurs.

"Gross Flynn! Do you have to be so vulgar?" Chloe chastises him with a playful slap to his chest. He grabs her hand and starts kissing and sucking her delicate fingers.

"I'd like to get vulgar with you baby," Flynn says between licks.

"Now who's starring in the porno?" Patrick says with a chuckle and a shake of his head.

"The only thing I'll be starring in is your dreams Flynn Caulder. Now get your drunk ass to bed so we can get an early start home in the morning. God forbid you back out and Landon rearranges his plans to drive home with me in your absence. Leslie may just kill him in his sleep. And I'll hold you personally responsible. Now come on and get up. I'll go tuck you in," Chloe demands pulling on Flynn's hand.

"Do I get a goodnight kiss?" A drunk Flynn is a quite persistent Flynn. No wonder he's got the man whore reputation. He just never gives up.

"If it'll get you in bed and to sleep, sure thing. It's not like you'll remember it in the morning anyway," Chloe says still trying to pull Flynn from his chair.

"I remember everything about you Chloe," Flynn says in a sudden moment of seriousness. He looks up at her face and their eyes lock. All the teasing of earlier has evaporated and Chloe is stunned into silence. She continues to hold Flynn's gaze, a look of longing on her face. An uncomfortable stall in surrounding conversations occurs and all eyes seem to settle on the intimacy passing between Chloe and Flynn. I feel like a voyeur, but can't seem to look away. Suddenly, I watch as Chloe's facial expression completely changes and she looks devastatingly sad.

"Yeah right, if only that were true," Chloe whispers, pulling her hand away from his hold. She slowly turns around and walks toward Patrick and Katelyn who are standing by the stairs getting ready to leave. "I think I'm calling it a night. 'Night y'all."

"We probably need to get going too," Katelyn says to Patrick. "Landon, good luck with your lady friend tonight. Chloe, you and Flynn have a safe trip home. And Suzanna, thanks again for having us over tonight. I really enjoyed getting to know you. Let's get together again soon and hang out."

"Hey wait, speaking of hanging out. I wanted to tell you that Drew is doing an acoustic set at Dead Dog this Saturday evening. He's the opening act for this band he knows that will follow later that night. I'm sure he'd appreciate it if you all would come and cheer him on," I say extending the invitation.

"Well, I have to work Saturday night so I'll definitely be there," Chloe says from the doorway.

"Drew's also a musician? Good grief, what else can that man do?" Patrick says in an irritated tone. I remember the first time Patrick met Drew. It was during my first paddle board lesson and Patrick drove up on the boat, causing my first and only attempt at paddle boarding to go awry. I recall the look on his face when he questioned the identity of Drew. At the time I thought it was silly for him to act and look a bit jealous, considering he was engaged. But now his tone suggests that he still harbors a bit of jealousy at the friendship that has developed between me and Drew.

"I know, that's exactly what I asked him. Apparently he's a man of many talents. And to add to his list, he graciously agreed to be my caddy during qualifying," I say looking at Chloe. Before I can remind her yet again about the importance of mailing that letter, she stops me with her hand.

"Don't worry Suz, I got it. For the thousandth time, I will not forget to mail that letter. Flynn? Since you commented on your stellar memory, how about remember that we need to go to the post office first thing when arriving in Florence to mail Suzanna's caddy info," Chloe says bitterly.

"Whatever Chloe," Flynn says opening yet another beer.

Chloe shoots Flynn a disgusted look that ends with an eye roll. I don't have a clue what's going on between those two. And I can't keep up with the constant changes of their relationship, switching from hot to cold in the blink of an eye.

"I love listening to live music. Count me in," Landon pipes up to break the tension.

"Oh, me too," Katelyn says glancing over in Landon's direction. "Patrick, can we go?"

"Sure Katelyn," Patrick says with no enthusiasm whatsoever. "Looks like we're all in, Suz."

"All in for what?" Leslie asks as she pushes her way out the door, giving Chloe a shoulder bump in the process. Never stopping to apologize, Leslie beelines in the direction of Landon, I'm sure in anticipation of getting her hands back on him. Chloe, acting so mature, sticks her tongue out at Leslie's retreating figure. Landon sees the entire thing and gives both me and Chloe a smirk.

"We're all going to hear what kinda finger talents Suzanna's caddy has on the guitar," Patrick answers Leslie with sarcasm.

"Oh," Leslie says waiting for an invitation to follow. But it never comes. It's obvious the rest of us don't want to include Leslie in our outing. Guess we all decide to leave that up to Landon as to whether or not he would like her to join the gang. Landon also remains silent and the atmosphere again becomes awkward. Not to be embarrassed further Leslie turns her attention to me. "Well, speaking of William, you just missed his call Suzanna."

"Who's William?" we all ask.

"Suzanna's caddy? Here," Leslie says shoving my phone toward me. "I tried to get to it before it stopped ringing but I wasn't fast enough." She pushes the button that lights up the display and says, "See, W. M. That's the abbreviation for William, right?"

With a trembling hand I reach out and take my phone. Staring back at me is the call I missed. W. M. isn't programmed in my phone for William, but the initials for Wyatt McCain. I stand rooted to my spot just looking at the screen of my cell phone. I don't know what I wish will happen. Maybe miraculously Wyatt will call again. Or even better, his initials will magically morph into a picture of him, that dark haired, brown eyed gorgeous creature who recently broke my heart. Better yet, maybe my phone will update to have futuristic powers and Wyatt will teleport through the screen and appear standing in front of me. How great would it be to see him in the flesh again? I know I wouldn't have the strength or willpower not to touch him. Just to wrap my arms around his broad shoulders and feel his hair at the nape of his neck with my fingers, would satisfy me. Wait, no it wouldn't. I won't be satisfied until my lips touched his in a kiss, that would start off slow and tender then build in intensity. His arms would support me, as the kiss would cause my knees to buckle. With little effort, he would pick me up in his strong arms and carry me inside to my bedroom. There, he would take his time undressing me, appreciating every inch of my bared skin. His tongue would find hidden crevices all over my body, leaving me breathless. I'd return the favor until we were both naked and pressed up against each other. With gentleness only ever shown to me by Wyatt, he'd lower me down atop my bed and cover me with his body. Our hands and mouths would roam until we both couldn't stand it any longer. Then Wyatt would make sweet love to me, taking his time to make sure I was completely sated until giving into his pleasure. Yeah, if only I had a special high tech phone. My desire filled thoughts are interrupted by the voices that I only now allow to recognize, being so caught up in my imaginary throes of passion.

"Suzanna's caddy's name is Drew, not William," Landon tells Leslie.

"So who is William?" This question is asked by Patrick who not only seems confused but is extremely curious.

Chloe shuffles up beside me and quietly ask, "Suz, was that Wyatt that called?"

I don't have the ability to speak so I just nod, confirming that indeed Wyatt tried to make contact. Chloe puts her arm around me in a sideways hug and whispers in my ear, "Are you okay?"

Before I have time to give her another nod, Leslie still clueless about the identity of W. M., says encouragingly, "Whoever this William character is, maybe he left a message."

A message? Oh dear, am I ready to hear Wyatt's voice? From the fantasy I just envisioned in my head, I'd say I'm ready for a lot more than just the sound of his voice. I know this isn't the first time Wyatt has tried to contact me since our break up. However, I refused to turn my phone on until just today, scared of what I would hear from past voicemails or see from his many texts. I think it's high time to bite the bullet and listen to whatever Wyatt has to tell me. Obviously, he hasn't given up trying to contact me since he just called tonight. Time to put on my big girl panties and face the many messages and texts waiting for me.

"Yeah, maybe Wy...I mean William left a message. I think I'll go check. Great to see you all. Have a good night!" I abruptly leave the deck and enter my house running into my bedroom for much needed privacy. I hear the sounds of footsteps outside, probably those of Katelyn, Patrick, Landon and Leslie leaving. Chloe and Flynn are puttering around on the deck, hopefully cleaning up from our last minute party. No doubt Chloe or Flynn will be knocking shortly to check on me, especially knowing what it is I'm doing. But I'll just ignore them because eventually I have to do this on my own. Just today I promised Flynn that if I gave into the temptation of torturing myself by listening to Wyatt's messages, I'd let Chloe or him be with me. After seeing me in my state of depression that lasted for days, I know they have every right to be concerned. However, these messages feel too personal to share with anyone else. I know it's gonna hurt and be painful, but at least it will be done. Maybe once I hear those final words, I can put mine and Wyatt's relationship to rest. I mean, there's got to be a point when I don't miss him so much. Nice try finding that happy place, but I'm not gonna fool myself. I'll miss Wyatt until the day I die.

Wyatt did leave a message tonight. I'm hopeful that he still wants to make contact and thankful that he was actually able to. I'm surprised that my voicemail box isn't full to capacity. When I turned my phone on this morning after having it off for days, it pinged with incoming texts and voicemails for a full two minutes. I quickly answered the calls and texts from my mom and dad, as well as my coach. All that's left are the numerous unanswered calls and texts from Wyatt. I decide to start at the beginning, that horrid Sunday morning when I last saw and spoke to Wyatt. The day my heart was shattered beyond repair. Gulping air, I press play and start listening to the first message, left just minutes after I drove away from Wyatt.

The first ten to twenty messages and texts were left during my drive from Columbia. In each and every one of them, Wyatt apologized and pleaded with me to call him just to let him know I was okay to drive. He begged me to contact him when I arrived back at the beach safely. I could hear the concern in voice. He was seriously worried for my safety. As well he should have been worried. Because of him, I was left in emotional distress and he's damn lucky I didn't end up lying in a ditch beside the road. The messages went on all day, basically saying the same things over and over. By Monday, Wyatt had finally talked with Chloe and found out that I indeed arrived home safely and physically unharmed. However, Wyatt mentioned that Chloe had clued him in on my agitated state and demanded to know what happened between us two. He assured me that he did not give Chloe any of the answers she was looking for, leaving me to spin the story any way I saw fit. Gee, how noble of you Wyatt. I didn't need to spin the story...the truth was terrible enough.

By late Monday, the messages focused on more apologies from Wyatt and him asking me to please consider calling so that he could explain. I would have loved to hear him explain away a very naked Bridgett which I found in his bed! His tone in most messages was soft, tender and pleading. However, there were a few when Wyatt, frustrated at my non-communication, would lose his cool, demanding that I call him back. He used a plethora of curse words, making even a sailor cringe. His anger at the entire situation was evident in his tone. Well, buddy, you only have yourself to blame. So no need to get angry with me!

I didn't expect to hear much from him on Tuesday, knowing that was to be his travel day flying to New York. However, the messages started coming in late Tuesday morning. On that day he stressed in each message how much he missed me and still loved me. He kept alluding to the fact that there was an explanation and that given the opportunity to tell it, he was sure I'd understand. As the day progressed, the messages became longer and longer. From the sound of Wyatt's voice in the latter messages, I'd venture to say he had been drinking. By the last message on Tuesday night, I had a hard time deciphering his slurred speech due to his definite inebriated state. Some of his messages were so long that the voicemail would cut him off. Minutes later, he'd call again only to leave more messages. His ramblings told of how he has loved me for years, even from afar. How he patiently waited until the timing was right to show and announce his love for me. He talked nonsense about making the right choice, referring to his choice in loving me. Then he would start questioning whether he was ever my final choice. Sometimes he sounded so deflated and down on himself, it actually brought tears to my eyes. Other times, he joked around, making light of our relationship. He made the asinine comment that at least he convinced me to love him long enough to enjoy some great romps in the hay. At least he complimented me on my bedroom talents, stating that I was the best sex he ever had. Making light of something so personal and intimate just pissed me off. Soon my tears of sadness over his sullen mood turned to tears of anger. How dare he belittle our most private moments together? Twisting the knife deeper, his last message Tuesday night, left in his most drunken state, applauded his tactics of having a naked Bridgett in his bed to help me get the message that we were done. Then he had the gall to ask me how it feels to see the person you love, with all your heart, choose someone else. "It fucking hurts doesn't it Suzanna!" he screamed through the phone. Then he told me to have a great life and hung up.

If I didn't think I could hurt anymore than I already did, I'd be wrong. Wow, wasn't it cruel enough to end things the way he did. Why did he have to say all those vicious things? Just to drive the point home. Well, point taken Wyatt. I hope you have a great life and good riddance! The tears are flowing down my face as I stare at the screen of my phone debating whether or not to listen to Wyatt's last message. The message he left tonight. I have a good mind to take my phone and chuck it as far out into the ocean as possible. I really don't think I can hear Wyatt berate me or our relationship again. But there's a part of me that knows I won't be able to live with myself if I ignore that last and final message. I guess I'm a masochist for wanting to listen to it, not knowing if it will be good or bad. Arming myself with a box of tissues and an unfettered determination, my finger hovers over the play button until I will it to press down. The message begins to play and I hear the only voice that still causes goose bumps to spring from my flesh.

"Hi Suzanna. It's me...again. I, um, I wanted to call and apologize. Seems like I've been doing that a lot lately. But really, about last night...I'm so sorry. I can vaguely remember some of the things I said to you. You have to know, I didn't mean any of them. I was drunk, which I'm sure was very obvious. But I was also frustrated, mad, sad, devastated... basically, I've been miserable without you. I miss you like crazy. But I don't need to make excuses for myself. Please know how very sorry I am. I don't deserve your forgiveness nor am I asking for it. I just hope that one day you can look back on our time together with fond memories. Because, with the exception of this past week, every hour, minute and second I spent with you was so valuable. Although our relationship as a couple was short, it was by far the best time of my life.

"Anyway, I just called to say that tomorrow I'm leaving for New York to start a brand new chapter of my life. You may think I've already left. I don't remember if I ever had the chance to tell you that my departure date was postponed for two days. God, when I got that news, I was so stoked to learn that I would have two extra days to spend with my girl. I couldn't wait to surprise you. But then I....well, never mind. It doesn't matter anymore.

"So, I guess this is goodbye. I promise I won't try to contact you again. You've made it pretty clear you don't ever want to speak with me again. I guess I don't blame you. I just wish you had returned at least one of my calls. I lie in bed at night praying I'll hear the sound of your voice just one more time. I don't care if you yell and scream at me or cuss me out. Just something... But I respect your decision and I won't bother you again. Good luck with your golf game this summer. I know you'll kill it at qualifying and soon be traveling the world racking up first place finishes. You will always be my first place finish and the prize of my life.

"Well, I better go before your voicemail cuts me off. Man, this is so hard. I don't want this to end. Just remember, I love you Suzanna Caulder. Always..."

I hear him sigh into the phone before the click that ends his call and our relationship. Uncontrollable sobs rack my body. I am in the most emotional and physical pain I have ever felt in my entire life. I listen to the message over and over again, torturing myself with his final words...I love you, always. I love you too, Wyatt. Always and forever, I say to myself in broken words. It's not until sometime in the middle of the night that my hopeless soul finally succumbs to sleep, gripping my cell phone to my heart.

Chapter Thirteen

The early morning light starts to make an appearance through my bedroom window. Not that I was asleep, having tossed and turned all night. Every time I did manage to get some shut eye, I would dream of Wyatt. Each dream started off wonderful, with Wyatt standing before me looking incredible. But when I'd reach out and touch him, his image would disappear. In some of the dreams, Wyatt's image would be so close, but then suddenly, he would turn around and walk away, never stopping to even glance back. The finality of his last phone call haunted me all night until I just gave up and stared into the darkness until sunrise. I don't even attempt to crawl out of bed. My eyes I'm sure are red and swollen. It's a miracle I was able to open them at all. My body physically hurts due to the sob fest I endured most of the night. However, it's my heart that sustained the most damage. Already broken, the remnants were shattered into a million pieces last night doubtful to ever be repaired. I must look horrendous. Add to that pathetic...as I lay in my bed surrounded by used tissues and an empty box. Still clutching the cell phone to my heart, I contemplate listening to his message again. But what good would it do? It'll only send me into another spiral of depression and start a crying fit all over again. Luckily, the battery went dead sometime during the night and saved me from more self inflicted torture.

I hear Chloe shrieking at Flynn to get a move on. Chloe's not the most sociable person in the early morning hours. I'd hate to be Flynn, on the receiving end of her demands to get his butt out of bed for their road trip home. "Dammit Chloe, I'm up. Give me a few minutes and I'll be ready to go," Flynn yells back.

"You're next Suzanna. Rise and shine sweetie. Don't want to be late for your tee time this morning," Chloe yells from the kitchen.

"Would you please shut the fuck up! Gah, my head is killing me," Flynn shouts from his room already in a terrible mood. Thank heavens I passed on that road trip. Sounds like it's gonna be a blast! Not!

"Well hurry up and I'll stop yelling," Chloe screams again, surely pissing off Flynn even more. "Suz, you better be out of that bed or I'll drag your bu....What the hell is wrong with you? Suz, you okay?" Chloe says having barged into my bedroom to witness the heap of distress lying on my bed.

"Just leave me alone, Chloe. I don't think I can muster enough energy to leave the confines of this bed, much less play a round of golf," I mumble with my face buried in the pillow.

"Oh, no way, Suz. We're not starting the pity party all over again. Now get your ass in gear or I'll get Mister Grouchy Pants in here," Chloe warns.

"Whatever, like I'm scared of Flynn, or you for that matter. Y'all just go ahead and leave and give me some time alone."

"Flynn!" Chloe shouts almost splitting my eardrums. "Get in Suzanna's room right now. It's an emergency."

"For the love of all that is holy woman, will you please turn the volume down?" Flynn says before he appears in my bedroom doorway. "Suz? What the hell happened to you?" he asks when his eyes take in my pitiful self.

"I found her like this. Now she's trying to get rid of us so she can spend the rest of the day wallowing," Chloe informs Wyatt.

"What changed? You were doing great yesterday and last night," Flynn says dumbfounded.

"It's that phone call from Wyatt, isn't it? Suz, did you talk to him last night? I'll drive all the way to New York and beat his ass for making you this miserable again," Chloe says. And I don't doubt for a second she wouldn't follow through with that threat.

"No, I didn't talk to him. I just listened to his messages...all his messages. Last night when he called, he left the final one and basically told me goodbye," I tell them hearing his last words run through my head. My tears start to flow again and I cover my face with my hands.

"Aw, Suz. Why didn't you get me or Chloe last night? You promised you wouldn't let him bring you down again without our support. Now look at you! Are you gonna spend the rest of the week hidden away in this room?" Flynn is upset that I took on the task of listening to the messages all alone and breaking my promise to him. He's also frustrated and at a loss at knowing how to deal with his sister's oncoming depression.

"Well what else can I do? I mean it's over, finished, done. He told me he wouldn't try to contact me again. Can't I just take some time for myself and grieve?"

"You just spent the last three days grieving. I think that's plenty of time," Flynn says exasperated. "And this is what you're gonna do. You're gonna get out of bed and go play golf. And you're gonna put this relationship with Wyatt to rest once and for all and get on with your life. Yeah, that's exactly what you're gonna do. Now get up, now!" Flynn has never been so demanding with me.

"I can't," I cry. "How can I go on existing knowing he's out there? Looking at the same stars I see at night. Breathing the same air I breathe. It hurts so much to feel him so close in my heart but know that he's so far away. I still love him, very, very much. And he loves me too. He told me so."

"I know it hurts, Suz. But if he really still loves you, do you think he'd want you to live like this?" Chloe asks gesturing to the snotty tissues strewn all around me.

"N-no," I say between sniffles.

"Of course he wouldn't. And as much as I'm sure he's hurting, I bet he's still getting up and going to work everyday at that fancy internship of his. Because, I'm sure he realizes that yes, he still loves you and you still love him and that will never stop. Just like life never stops, it just keeps going. So, Suz, you have to keep going too and hope that one day, if things are truly meant to be, then you and Wyatt will reconnect and live happily ever after," Chloe encourages.

"Yeah, Suz. Maybe this is just a timing thing. A bump in the road to real happiness later on," Flynn agrees. "I know a little bit about love and bad timing. But I never let it get in the way of following my dreams. Neither should you."

Chloe looks back at Flynn who is still standing at the doorway. "What do you know about love?" Chloe asks curiously.

"Enough to know that love should never leave someone looking like this," Flynn says pointing in my direction, again making me the show and tell part of this conversation.

"I'm not sure you'd know what love was if it hit you in the face! Do you even know how to spell it?" Chloe asks being a total bitch. And here they go again, hot and cold.

"What, do you think... I'm just a good looking dumb jock, with no feelings? You know what Chloe, don't even answer that. Your opinion of me isn't worth the pile of shit Darth Vader left in our yard that ended up on the bottom of my shoe," Flynn says angrily. "Suz, you better get your ass on that course today or you'll have to deal with me tonight when I return from hitting the road with Chloe. And believe me, all that time trapped in a car with that bitch, I promise to return in a very foul mood. I'm going to wait downstairs." Flynn abruptly leaves as Chloe and I watch slack jawed. Chloe sure is getting under his skin, because I've never seen Flynn be so rude and demanding. I guess my teeter totter emotional state isn't helping matters either.

"You better go before he slashes your tires or something," I urge Chloe.

"Yeah, I guess I need to apologize," she says looking down and defeated. "Suz, you're gonna be okay, right? I mean, you are going to get up and out of this bed today, yes?"

Taking in a gulp of air and exhaling slowly I tell her the truth, and only the truth. "I can't promise you anything, but I'll try. I'm sorry if that's not what you or Flynn want to hear, but it's all I can give you right now. Please try to understand and let me work this out my way. Please."

With disappointment written all over her face, Chloe can only manage to nod. She gives me a quick hug and walks toward the door.

"See you later tonight Suz." A final finger wave and she is out of the door. Minutes later I hear the sound of a car being cranked and pulling out of the driveway. Now, I'm left alone with only silence and my depressing thoughts of the former us, that was me and Wyatt.

I must have dozed off because I'm suddenly being roused from sleep. Light is now pouring into my bedroom as my make shift towel curtains are being torn from atop the window seal. Startled and now scared, I tense up when I realize someone is in my house, more terrifying, in my bedroom.

"Rise and shine, sweetie pie!"

That voice is so familiar. I'd know it anywhere. What the hell is Patrick doing in my room? Before I can ask he starts ripping the comforter and bed linens off my body, leaving me lying there speechless. I look down to make sure that I'm at least decent. Luckily I slept in a pair of boy shorts and a tank top that cover all my private parts. Thank God I didn't sleep in the buff last night.

"'Morning sunshine. We've got a busy day," Patrick says smugly. At this point I'm sitting ram rod straight up in the center of the bed, hugging my knees to my chest. My once almost swollen shut eyes are now as big as saucers. I rub them and refocus making sure I'm not dreaming. Patrick is for real, standing at the foot of my bed looking beautiful. I take a moment to appreciate his long lean physique, dressed in a pair of board shorts and tight fitting t-shirt. His blonde hair is wind blown, like he just stepped off his boat. His Maui Jims are hanging around his neck with a croakie. His blue eyes are twinkling and he has a devious smile plastered across his face. He gives me the once over, his eyes lingering a little too long on my skimpy attire before glancing down at his wrist watch. "Oh my, we are really pressed for time. Gotta get a move on, like now," he says walking into my bathroom and turning on the shower. I'm in a trance watching his graceful movements around my bedroom. It's not until I hear his voice again that I come back into the moment.

"Suz, chop, chop!" he exclaims with two quick claps of his hands. "Don't tempt me to drag you out of that bed and undress you for your shower. Because that just may be the highlight of my day," he says with a smirk.

"What...how...why the hell are you here Patrick?" I ask finding my voice.

"Because I want to be."

"And?" I ask, knowing there's a lot more to this story.

"I was asked and honored to comply," Patrick answers.

He was asked to come drag me out of bed and force me to shower and get ready? For what? And then it dawns on me. My tee time which is fast approaching. This has to be the doings of two suspects which I will personally ring both of their necks. "Chloe? Flynn?" I ask just for clarification.

"Both, actually. By the way, your egotistical brother is such a grouch in the mornings. I almost refused to help just to piss him off more. But then Chloe used her southern charm and well, who can resist Chloe's charm?" Patrick states like we are talking about the weather and not an ambush on my personal life. I am going to kill Chloe and my brother! Oh, and it's gonna be a slow torturous death. And then, when they take their last breath, I'm gonna cut up their bodies in hundreds of pieces and feed them to the sharks!

Patrick looks down at his watch again tapping the face with his index finger. "Time's a ticking, Suz. Come on, let's get you showered." He moves toward the bed and makes a move to grab me. But I'm too fast and swing off the mattress landing feet first on the other side of the bed, putting much needed space between us. Grabbing the sheet which he threw on the floor, I drape it in front of me so I don't feel so exposed in front of him.

"Fine, I'll shower. But you need to get out of my room, pronto," I say.

"Yeah sure. If you hurry you'll have time for breakfast before we leave. I'll make my specialty," Patrick says strolling toward my bedroom door.

"Wait!" I holler. "We? Where are *we* going?"

"Ah, Suz. *We* are spending the entire day together. First golf, then lunch, then maybe more golf. Or paddle boarding. That looked like fun."

Is this the twilight zone? There is no way I'm spending the entire day with Patrick so he can babysit me then report back to Chloe and Flynn that I didn't waste the day pining after Wyatt, my lost love. But I don't get to voice my opinion on the matter because Patrick has closed in behind me and is pushing my body toward the bathroom.

"Hurry up, Suz. You've got about twenty minutes to get ready. And don't look so annoyed. I happen to take my responsibility very seriously. But I promise, this will be fun," he says with a chuckle and a swat to my backside. I jump into action, moving at the speed of light into the bathroom and slam the door. I hear him laughing all the way out into the kitchen.

Fifteen minutes later, I'm putting on the finishing touches. I didn't do too much other than quickly shower, dress and brush through my hair. I'm wearing my daily uniform which includes a sleeveless collared polo shirt, a madras print golf skort, no show socks and a pair of athletic slides. I'll change into my golf shoes when I arrive at the course. I pulled my hair into a high ponytail and fastened a sun visor around my head. Skipping makeup, only because it will sweat off, I brush my teeth and viola...I'm ready for my chaperoned day. No thanks to Chloe and Flynn. The main culprit awaits me in the kitchen. God only knows what he's up to. As soon as I got out of the shower, all I heard was the clanging of pots and pans.

Taking a deep breath, I steady myself and open the door of my bedroom. Immediately, I'm concerned a bomb has exploded in the kitchen of the beach house. Pots and pans are scattered everywhere. The counters are littered with eggs shells and flour. The water is running from the sink faucet while smoke billows up from a frying pan left on the stove. Urgently, I sprint to the stove to prevent a fire from catching. Patrick is no where to be found. As soon as I take care of the fire hazard, the back door opens and here he comes, looking ridiculous. Patrick is wearing my mom's pink frilly apron covered in flour and an unidentified substance staining his cheek. "Were you trying to burn the house down?" I ask trying to sound serious. But I fail. Just watching him in that hideous get up, I can't help but smile.

"No, smart ass. I was trying to make you pancakes. But the burner got too hot and I ruined the first batch. I was outside throwing them in the garbage. How did the second batch turn out?" he asks looking toward the stove for the missing frying pan.

I hold up the frying pan which is now pretty much destroyed. The pan is covered in burnt butter and black fried pancake batter. "Oh shit! Sorry, Suz. I really wanted our day to start out with a good breakfast." Patrick looks around the kitchen in its state of disarray. "Man, I made a complete mess." No need to state the obvious. "Listen, I promise I'll clean it up and make this up to you by buying you lunch and dinner. Your choice. But I'll have to clean this up later because we're really gonna be late."

I pour some dishwashing liquid in the bottom of the frying pan and fill it with hot water. It can sit for a few hours to see if it is even salvageable. I walk in the pantry and grab two granola bars. Then I grab two bottles of water out of the fridge. "Did you make coffee?" I ask saying a silent prayer.

"Gesh, no, I'm sorry. I got so caught up in making breakfast I forgot to start it," Patrick says sounding way too defeated over simply forgetting to make coffee. Well, it is coffee and I can barely function without it.

"I guess your first make up purchase will start at Starbucks. Come on, let's get going. The sooner we start the faster it'll be over," I say not really dreading this day as much as I thought I would. "And Patrick... thanks for the attempt at breakfast. It's the thought that counts."

Patrick sheds his cooking attire and wipes off his face with a paper towel. He grabs my car keys from the table and informs me that he'll transfer my golf equipment to his car since that's what we will be driving today. I had hoped that we could take my car. That way at least I'd have a means of escape. But no, he wouldn't hear a thing about it, stating since he was the appointed chauffer today, he gets to choose which wheels we take. He still has his jeep so at least it will be fun riding with the top off. I hang back to straighten the kitchen where at least it looks somewhat presentable. Checking the stove to make sure all burners are off, I turn off the lights and lock up the house. Patrick is downstairs in the driveway, leaning down to pay Darth Vader some extra loving attention. He pats the dog's fat belly and rubs behind her ears all the while talking in an annoying baby voice. "Look at you Raquel. You get prettier and prettier everyday," Patrick says as I roll my eyes.

Not to be out done, the dog's owner, Mrs. Stokes comes strolling over and gives Patrick a big hug. "Not prettier than me I hope," Mrs. Stokes says batting her lashes and fishing for a compliment.

I stick my finger down my throat and actually gag. My gagging noises are loud enough to warrant the attention of both Patrick and Mrs. Stokes. Even Darth Vader lifts her big fat head to glance up before flopping in back down in her own puddle of slobber. "Well, there's our golfing princess now," Patrick says which earns a laugh from Mrs. Stokes.

"You kids going to play?" she asks.

"Actually, I'm just the driver. Under strict orders to deliver her safely to and from the course," Patrick clarifies. "Great to see you Mrs. Stokes. I'll just go grab your stuff Suz."

"What's this all about?" Mrs. Stokes asks once Patrick is busy loading my gear.

"Ask my ex best friend and disowned brother," I huff. I'm still going to kill them.

Mrs. Stokes barks out in her smokers laugh. "God, I love those two. You still moping around over that boy, huh? Serves you right. Especially if you're gonna waste all that God given talent because of a broken heart."

"Look, I'm going to practice. See! I'm fine and I wish you all would quit meddling in my business."

"Well, start acting normal and we'll stop meddling!" Mrs. Stokes declares, giving it right back to me. "Plus, if I had a play date that looked like that," Mrs. Stokes says nodding her head in Patrick's direction, "I'd have already forgotten about what's his name."

Not likely, I want to tell her. I want to fill her in on the heart felt last message I received from Wyatt. I want her nosey, but mature advice to tell me how to handle the end of what I thought was my future. I want her to tell me how to make the hurt go away. But I don't get the chance because both of our attention is drawn to Patrick who is looking at my golf bag like he's seen a ghost. The golf bag that once belonged to his dead mother.

Seconds turn into minutes as Mrs. Stokes and I continue to stand and watch Patrick. He stands rooted to his spot at the back of my car still staring inside. I can't imagine what he is feeling in this moment, seeing a tangible object that was once touched and held by his mother. Usually standing so tall and confident, Patrick's posture changes as his shoulders slump while I'm sure memories of his mother flash through his mind. The pain I feel watching him relive the loss of his mother is almost too much to watch. I can only sympathize with what he is experiencing right now. I'd like to turn away, run back upstairs and crawl back into my bed, ignoring the obvious pain Patrick is feeling. But it's my fault he's here. Well, technically, it's Chloe and Flynn's fault, having called him to be my babysitter for the day. Now, he's starting off his morning haunted by memories of his past and the wonderful mother he lost at such a young age. While I'm internally beating myself up, Mrs. Stokes nudges my arm and whispers, "Go on girl. Go to him. He needs you right now." She gives me a push in his direction. With narrowed eyes, I glance back over my shoulder at her. She's already turned to walk back to her house with Darth Vader at her heels. Some help she is!

I slowly approach Patrick and come to stand by his side. I don't want to startle him. Although, he's in such a trance, I don't believe a fireworks display could distract him. I timidly touch his forearm with my hand. "Hey," I say softly, leaving my hand on his skin.

"Hey," he returns still looking at the golf bag.

We stand closely, side by side, together a few moments longer until Patrick speaks. "I can't believe you still have this bag, Suz."

"I'm kinda attached."

"This thing has got to be at least a decade old. Surely, you've had the chance to replace this old thing with a newer, more high tech model," Patrick says still in a mild state of shock.

"Yes, I've had the chance to upgrade. During college play, every season I was given the option to use the uniform team bags, but always declined. I've had potential sponsors send me new models to use, hoping I'll be their next walking advertisement. But I always pass them along to other golfers or give them to a youth golf program. I love this golf bag. Since you gave it to me, I've used nothing else and I don't plan to either," I say.

"Why?" Patrick asks finally looking my way.

Oh boy, this is going to be hard. I can't tell him the main reason I continue to carry a golf bag that by professional standards is old, outdated and basically obsolete. I tried to convince myself years ago that I carry the bag out of respect to Marie. But really I still carry it so that I can still have some connection to Patrick and our time together. The bag represents the time in our relationship when we first started dating...when Marie was alive. It was happy, fun and new. We fell hard and fast into love while Marie watched, encouraging us and cheering us on. Things changed after the car accident that took Marie's life. Although, Patrick and I continued to date, our love still intact, other forces started to come into play. While Patrick handled his grief with maturity beyond his teenage years, his father turned to the bottle to numb the loss of his wife. Mr. Mile's drinking continued to spiral out of control until he turned into the monster who attempted to rape me, causing the demise of my relationship with Patrick. Patrick, although fully aware of his dad's drinking condition, never knew the man his dad became that awful night. And I hope he never will. From his aggressive behavior at the engagement party, it is apparent that Mr. Miles hasn't changed much. His excessive drinking continues to this day. I guess he never came to terms with the death of his wife.

I can feel Patrick's gaze on me still waiting for an answer. Taking a deep breath, I look into his eyes and try to explain. "Your mother was one of the kindest women I had the honor to know. I love her almost as much as I love my own mother. That bag," I say tilting my head toward the back of the car, but maintaining eye contact with Patrick, "isn't just a bag to me. It is a tangible representation of a person I miss everyday. I still carry it out of respect to her and the wonderful example of the perfect southern woman she inspires me to be. When I'm on the course, the bag constantly reminds me to play to the best of my abilities. She deserves nothing less. I guess the bag is my way of letting Marie's spirit live on through my golf game. I try extra hard on every swing, drive, putt, or chip knowing she's someplace watching over me. And I'll always try my best to make her proud."

Patrick turns to look away from me, trying to hide his now watery eyes. "Thank you, Suzanna," he manages to say through a clogged throat. Lifting his hand, his fingers trance the double M monogram stitched on the top of the bag. The letters, which stand for Marie Miles, are stitched in baby blue. She once told me that was her favorite color because it always reminded her of Patrick's eyes. "I miss her everyday," Patrick says still choked up.

"I'm sure anyone who had the pleasure of knowing your mother feels the exact same way. I don't imagine that will ever change," I say, because I will always miss that woman something terrible.

Patrick lifts his fingers from the golf bag to wipe his eyes that failed to hold his tears at bay. My own tears are trying to escape. Patrick takes that same hand and places it over mine, which is still lying on his forearm. "You know she loved you, right?"

I can only nod, my throat now thick with emotions.

Patrick removes his hand from mine, bringing it up to tilt my chin so that we are now face to face again. "You make it damn hard not to love you, Suzanna," he says. And I can see it. The love he still feels for me. Although he declared his love, the other night on the porch after that searing kiss, I chalked that up to him being caught up in the moment. But now, his eyes tell me all I need to know. He really loves me, still to this day. I want so much to tell him that I also still love him. But I can't. Not only because he's an engaged man, whose fiancée is a wonderful girl and we embarked on a friendship last night. But because that type of love, the kind I see reflected in Patrick's eyes, is tied up with a man states away, up the east coast.

I step back, putting some space between us. Comforting Patrick had been my goal, but now I'm the one feeling very uncomfortable. "Patrick, I don't think this is a very good idea. It's been an emotional morning for the both of us. So let's just forget about golf," I say backing away, ready to run and escape in my bedroom.

Patrick grabs my arm before I can make a getaway. "Oh no, you don't. You're going to golf and I'm driving you there. I'm taking this job responsibility very seriously. Plus, I have to answer to Flynn and I'd hate to think of what he'd do to me if I failed to get you to practice."

"Really, I don't feel like practicing today. I'll be sure to tell Flynn and Chloe you did exactly like they asked, but I didn't cooperate. I'll take all the blame."

"No!" Patrick says strongly. He removes my golf bag and the rest of the equipment and transfers everything to his jeep. Opening the passenger door, he waits for me to walk over and get into the car. I hesitate, knowing I'll be trapped in the close quarters of his vehicle with him if I concede. I've had enough closeness with Patrick this morning...more than I should have allowed. "Suzanna, I'm waiting. Don't think for a minute I won't sling you over my shoulder and deposit your ass on this seat should you try to make a run for it."

Yeah, he's crazy enough to do just that. Throwing my hands up in the air, I surrender to this madness. "Fine," I say and slowly walk his way. He waits patiently while I climb into the passenger seat and adjust my seatbelt across my body, pouting the entire time.

"Don't look so glum, Suz. Just remember, you're going to make my momma proud," Patrick says before shutting the door. That sneaky bastard! Bringing up his mother just to get me to practice. He knows he's won as I watch him walk around the front of the jeep wearing a smile. The first one I've seen since he discovered my golf bag. Honestly, how could I even argue with that? Besides, if Patrick's wearing a smile after discussing the loss of his mother, then I'll let him take me to every golf course on the planet. I'm sure Marie's looking down and laughing at my stubbornness. Patrick climbs in the jeep and shuts the door. "Ready?"

"Let's go," I say with a snarky tone. My comment only earns a laugh from Patrick as he cranks up the jeep and reverses out the driveway. I resign myself to the fact that although I don't agree with my transportation arrangements (I'm still gonna kill Chloe and Flynn), I'm touched by the support of Patrick. He genuinely wants to see me succeed. I turn my head and watch the houses fly by as I hide my smile. I realize in the mist of the crazy emotions that we still have to work through, at a least I've got my friend back. And that realization is enough to get me through this day.

Chapter Fourteen

The first part of our journey to the golf course is spent in silence. As we pass by familiar landmarks, I'm consumed with memories of Patrick and our time dating. Passing the Garden City pier, I remember strolling hand in hand watching the fishermen try their luck in the murky ocean waters. The arcade at Sam's Corner brings back our skee-ball battles, Patrick always letting me win. A certain putt putt course comes into view as I recall Patrick's frustration when I would always beat him with the lowest score. Unlike skee-ball, he always tried his hardest to beat me just one time. Now, I wish I had been as generous as he was at the arcade and let him have the glory of a win over me to gloat about. I wonder if he's made those same types of memories with other girlfriends. Surely, he's made new memories with Katelyn, his fiancée. Pangs of jealousy begin to emerge as I unsuccessfully try to squash them. I have no right to feel jealous. I'm the one that left Patrick. It still doesn't make it an easier pill to swallow.

As if sensing my thoughts, Patrick's cell phone rings. I catch a glimpse of the display before he picks it up to his ear. Katelyn is calling. Quickly my jealousy turns into guilt. "Hello," Patrick answers.

"No, I've been up since the crack of dawn. Dad and I went shrimping this morning. Now, I'm driving to Suz to golf practice," Patrick says into the phone. I cringe when he divulged his whereabouts and included my presence. Not that he'd hide anything from his fiancée. Well, he might hide some things. God, what if he tells her everything and she knows about the kiss? I want to just die now. Patrick looks over and sees the look of distress on my face. He mouths *you okay?*

while continuing to listen to Katelyn on the other end of the line. I silently answer with a nod.

"Katelyn says hi," Patrick says keeping his eyes on the road and the phone to his ear. I give him a finger wave that he catches from his peripheral vision. I'm such a dork! A finger wave...like Katelyn can see through the phone. Patrick interprets my hand gesture and tells Katelyn I said hi back.

"Okay, tell your mother good luck. So I'll see you in a couple of days?" Patrick continues his phone call while I eavesdrop. "Y'all have a safe trip. Just call me later. Bye Katelyn." He ends the call and places his phone back in the cup holder. No 'I love you', just a bye. Should I think it's odd that he confessed his love for me days ago with words and again just the morning silently, however he doesn't tell his fiancée? Sounds like she's going away for a few days. Surely, he'd want to tell her how he feels before she leaves. Maybe I should stop obsessing because it's none of my business. Besides, I've got better things to think about. Like how I'm supposed to get out of this mess of having Patrick be my personal chauffeur. I start scheming, searching for any excuse to get Patrick to turn his jeep around and take me home.

"Looks like it's getting cloudy," I say pointing to a big puffy white cloud in the otherwise blue sky.

"I've already checked the weather report. Other than some high temps and humidity to contend with, it's going to be a beautiful day. The only chance for rain will occur late this afternoon, and even that's unlikely. Unless a stray thunderstorm pops up," Patrick informs me.

Just my luck that today is another gorgeous sunny day. Normally, I pray for days like today, but I'd almost do a rain dance just so I can go home. I'll have to come up with another fabricated story. "Patrick, do you have any ibuprofen? I feel the start of a headache coming on," I say rubbing my temples for added effect.

"Oh shit, I forgot about your coffee. Hold on," Patrick says crossing lanes of traffic to pull into a McDonalds which is down the road. Pulling into the drive thru, having avoided a near fender bender, Patrick orders two large coffees and two breakfast sandwiches.

Handing me my drink and food he says, "There may be some Tylenol in the glove box, but I'm sure it's the lack of caffeine. Drink your coffee and eat your breakfast. Your headache will be gone before we get to the course."

The man has an answer for everything. I'm starting to think he may be catching on to my excuses. But the coffee is delicious once I've doctored it up with cream and sugar. It's no Starbucks mocha latte, but it'll have to do. And I'll have to come up with some other lie and fast. We're only about ten minutes from the course by now. Giving it one last shot, I throw it out there. "You know, we're so late I bet they gave my tee time away. This course is so busy, if you miss a tee time chances are you won't get playing time until the next day. I don't think..." I can't get another word out of my mouth because I'm concentrating on not being thrown from the jeep. Patrick abruptly steers the jeep over to the side of the highway, slamming the brakes so hard I have to hold on to the 'oh shit' handle bar to keep from face planting into the windshield. "Patrick!" I scream.

"Shut up, Suz!" Patrick yells back. "I'm sick and tired of hearing your lies to try and get out of golf today. You are going to practice, end of discussion."

I'm shaking I'm so mad. How dare he scare me to death and then yell at me. "What's it to you whether or not I practice?"

"You don't get it, do you?" Patrick asks. "Dammit Suz, you will not throw away your chance to make it big in golf on my watch. I don't know why Chloe felt the need to call me to fish your ass out of bed and babysit you all day. She didn't mention the reason, just said that you were depressed and she was worried about you. However, I have come to my own conclusions and I think this has to do with a man. An obviously very stupid man for breaking your heart and leaving you in this condition."

This is getting way too personal and I've got to find a way to stop this before I fall apart over Wyatt in front of Patrick. "I don't think this is any of your business."

"Oh, it's very much my business and I'm going to tell you exactly why. You told me the other night the reason you left so many years ago was because of golf. Golf was the end all, be all...the one thing you loved above all else, even me. So I'll be damned before I sit back and let you give up on your golfing dreams because of another man. Call me selfish and egotistical, but I will not watch another man become more important to you than golf. Especially, not when I wasn't." Patrick finishes his rant with a fist to the steering wheel for added emphasis.

I'm stunned silent. How could I even respond to that? I don't feel comfortable talking about my relationship with Wyatt, especially to Patrick. And I didn't leave Patrick because of golf. I loved Patrick more than anything. I loved him so much more than golf that I had to leave. I couldn't tell him my secret, so I lead him to believe that golf was so much more important to me than he was. That was definitely not the case. But he can never know the truth of why I left. So I've got to just suck it up and let him take me to practice. I'll continue to live the lies I created in order to save Patrick from the knowledge that his father is an attempted rapist.

"Suz, gosh, I'm sorry. I don't know where that came from. Listen if you want to go home..."

"No, you're right. I'm letting things get in the way of what's most important to me. Let's just go. I'm sure Coach Moore won't mind me being a few minutes late," I say not looking at Patrick, but instead staring straight ahead. Patrick puts the jeep back in drive and slowly pulls back onto the highway. Not another word is uttered between us for the remainder of the drive, both of us caught up in our own heads.

Patrick helps me unload my things in the parking lot when we arrive at the golf club. Standing together alone by his jeep, we both struggle with something to say. Finally, I break the uncomfortable silence. "Thanks for the ride."

"Any time, Suz. I'll be back in three hours to pick you up," he says walking backwards toward the driver's side door. I open my mouth to protest and offer to catch a ride from Drew or Coach Moore. But before the words leave my mouth Patrick stops me. "Don't! I said I'll see you later. End of story!" With that, he climbs into the jeep and drives away, leaving me more of a mess than when he found me this morning.

～o

My morning golf lesson was pathetic. I had too much on my mind to concentrate on the game. At least I was able to get out some pent up frustrations. Coach Moore even commented that he saw improvement in my distance. However, his concern centered around the fact that I couldn't hit a fairway this morning if my life depended on it. I think I even lost a few balls and I never lose balls during play. With my miserable performance, Coach Moore demanded I play another eighteen holes after lunch. I was hot, tired, and miserable but thought better than to argue with Coach. So I called Patrick to postpone my pick up until later. He sounded disappointed that we wouldn't be having lunch together, but assured me that he'd arrive later. I ate lunch with Coach, Drew and Callie. We discussed my game, or lack thereof, and focused on the things I needed to work on this afternoon. Although I tried to sound upbeat, my bad mood wasn't fooling anybody, especially Callie. After lunch she convinced me to come into her office, which was actually just the equipment room, telling her dad and brother that we were making some slight adjustments to my driver. Of course that was all a cover up because as soon as the door shut she started to drill me for information.

"Okay, Suzanna, go ahead and spill," Callie said using her no non-sense tone.

"I don't know what you're talking about," I said pretending her woman's intuition wasn't so sharp.

"Oh, stop lying. What bug crawled up your ass this morning? Wouldn't have to do with that hot body that dropped you off earlier, would it?"

"Were you spying on me?" I ask, not putting anything pass her.

"Of course. Between your brother yesterday and the gorgeous specimen of a man that I saw with you in the parking lot this morning, you've provided me with excellent material for my late night fantasies."

"TMI! And I forbid you to think about my brother or Patrick like that. That's just plain gross!" I'll never get used to Callie's blatant forwardness to express every detail of her life.

"Patrick. Now I have a name to scream out when my B.O.B. has done its job and gotten me to the point of orgasm," Callie informs me like we're talking about the weather and not her private night time rituals. I shake my head and try not to think about Callie in her moments of passion. "So, who is this Patrick to you? Boyfriend?"

"Ex-boyfriend." Callie starts to look excited. "But don't get your hopes up. He's taken, very taken. As in engaged."

"Well crap! All the good ones are taken. He'll just have to continue to exist in my dreams," Callie says sounding truly disappointed. "No wonder you're such a sour puss. I bet you're beating yourself up for letting that fine thing get away."

"Actually, I'm very happy for him," I say trying to sound convincing.

"Yeah, and I ran three miles this morning," Callie calls me out on my bullshit answer. This girl shocks me with her dry, in your face humor, which most of the time centers around her condition. I can't even laugh as I stare at the uniquely, beautiful girl in the wheelchair, her crippled legs dangling from her seated position. "Good grief, Suzanna. It was an effing joke. Stop looking at me like that. I don't want nor do I need your pity!" Callie is angry now. Seems I've been doing a great job at getting people angry today. They all feel the need to yell at me.

"Sorry," I say politely and focus my attention elsewhere.

"Well, if you're so happy for your ex, what's got you swinging balls all the way up into North Myrtle Beach?" Callie asks.

"I recently broke up with my most recent boyfriend. Or, to be more precise, he broke up with me."

"Ouch! Double whammy!" Callie comments. "That's really gotta suck, especially when your ex-ex, that blonde hot as sin creature, is tying the knot soon."

"You have no idea. Plus, it's very complicated. His fiancée, Katelyn, she's really a sweet girl. She came over..."

"Wait a minute. You're friends with the bride to be?" Now Callie's the one who's shocked. "You do realize they are probably doing it. Unless they are those people who believe in waiting until marriage. Personally, I'd require a test drive before committing to forever."

And here she goes again. "Really, Callie. I don't need you to paint that visual."

"Just saying," Callie shrugs as her way of an apology.

"Anyway, I've got so many things running through my brain right now that I'm finding it impossible to concentrate on golf. Which was extremely evident in my play this morning. I can't keep this up or I'll screw up qualifying."

"Okay, I'm gonna give you some advice, free of charge. Having some past golf experience, I know a little about the game. And it can be a cruel game if it feels neglected. You've got to push all that relationship crap somewhere else when you're on the course. Reality takes a backseat to your marriage to golf. When your mind feels too cluttered up, focus those images on that little white ball. Pretend that's Katelyn's face on the golf ball. I don't care how sweet she is, you've got to have some type of bad feelings for her. Use that anger and take a swing at her metaphorical face, sending her sailing away down the course. Next hole, picture Patrick as your golf ball. Knock the hell out of it, sending him down the fairway for not picking you to be his wife. Next hole, the golf ball is now the most recent ex...what's his name?"

"Wyatt."

"So you take a big, gigantic swing at Wyatt's head, connecting clean as you send him packing for breaking your heart. You getting the gist of this? Focus all that negative energy into your game with the sole purpose of burying those people in the hole on the green. The faster you do that, the faster they'll get out of your head. Makes for a fantastic low, low score card too!" Callie sounds confident is her advice. It's rather violent when you think about it. I can't imagine actually hitting anyone, enemy or not, with my golf club. But transferring my feelings to that little white ball, making it the real enemy, could bring me back to focus on the game.

"I think I get what you're saying. And I'll try it this afternoon. Want to come watch? I'd love your support on the course. Plus, you need to get a read on my equipment anyway, see if my clubs need any tweaking," I say hoping she'll ride along. I need her as a barrier should Coach Moore or Drew start asking questions about my erratic performance this morning.

"Nah, I'm really busy in here," Callie says avoiding eye contact.

"Please," I beg. "You can get to all this invisible work when we finish my round."

"Are you calling me a liar?" Callie asks angrily.

"Maybe. That or either a scaredy pants," I say pushing the issue. Drew told me that Callie hasn't been back out on the course since the accident. She basically hides in the equipment room all day. She could be a real asset to me if she'll let go of her fear to return to the game she can no longer play.

"Is that a dare?"

"It's a request. Look Callie, I really think I could learn so much from you. You are full of golfing knowledge. You were once the best in the game, even at such a young age. Just because you don't swing a club anymore doesn't mean you don't have anymore to offer to the golfing world. I think your talents are being wasted while you sit around inside this room all day."

"Just like your talents are being wasted pining over two guys who obviously don't want anything to do with you anymore," Callie says in retaliation. Her words cut like a knife. Obviously I've gone a little too far and pushed one of Callie's very sensitive buttons.

"Touché," I say and start making my way to exit her hideaway. I used to think that Callie and I were completely different creatures, sharing none of the same characteristics. But it was just this morning that I considered hiding away in my bedroom to avoid playing golf and wallow in my pain. Callie is doing the same, just at a different location. She hides away and marinates in the pain of losing her ability to play golf. I wish I could make her see she still has so much talent that could be used without her having to actually swing a club.

"Ah, screw it," Callie says, causing me to stop midstride in the doorway. "Fine, I'll go out on the course with you. Besides, you'll probably need me to remind you about all the free advice I gave you earlier. And it'd be a shame to let anything, your talents or mine, go to waste."

Callie maneuvers her wheelchair to the door where I'm still standing. It's hard to hide the smile I wear at her acceptance to help me get back on track. "Thank you," I say as she about runs over my foot.

"Don't thank me yet. I'm gonna ride your ass so hard you'll regret asking for my help. Better get your A game on in a hurry! Oh, and this was my idea, not yours. Just in case Dad or Drew asks. Lord knows they've been trying to get me back to the game since I lost the ability to walk. It'll hurt their macho egos to know all it took was some hotshot young woman who thinks she could even attempt to rival my game. Understand?" she demands.

"Understood!"

By the end of my afternoon round, I not only made a 180 degree turn in my golf game, but I posted a new low score record for the course. I used the advice Callie gave me and gave the golf ball a new name at each hole. Anyone who had ever hurt me, caused me pain, or simply just got on my nerves magically appeared in the form of a little golf ball. Wyatt, Patrick, Bridgett, Katelyn...and numerous others were with me today on the course getting their faces whacked off with each of my swings. Jim appeared at every par five hole, having to use all my strength and power in each swing to achieve the desired distance. And believe me, he got it the worst. I parred two of the par fives and birdied the other two. At some of the tee boxes, Callie asked me the call out the name of my golf ball. I thought it was silly to have a verbal conversation with an inanimate object, but Callie said that to funnel all my anger I had to make it believable. Of course, Coach Moore and Drew thought we were both crazy, but let it slide when they saw the numbers I was pulling on the course. I don't know what shocked them more, my low score, which was an unprecedented improvement since the morning round. Or the fact that their beloved daughter and sister had finally conquered her fear and returned to the golf course. Both Drew and Coach Moore were extremely appreciative and gave me hugs and thanks on finally getting Callie out of the equipment room. Just as promised, I told them both it was her idea to join us during play. They didn't care if it had been a psychic who persuaded Callie to make her glorious return to the game of golf. They were just happy it had finally happened.

I'm waiting for Patrick in the parking lot with Callie, while she waits for Drew to bring her car around. Even though I'm standing in a hot parking lot, exhausted from two grueling rounds of golf, I feel like I'm floating on cloud nine. "Wow, that felt amazing."

"Yeah, yeah," Callie comments not sharing in my enthusiasm.

"Come on, Callie. Even you have to admit that that was an epic round of golf I just finished."

"I still could have beaten you," Callie says with confidence.

"You wish. In your dreams, chicka!"

"Speaking of dreams, here comes the man who will be starring in mine later tonight," Callie says as we watch Patrick pull his jeep into the parking lot.

"Callie!" I scold. "I'm seriously starting to think you have a one track mind."

Patrick walks over and stands in front of us. "Hi Suz, how was golf?"

"Well, this morning's round was pretty rough, but I blew it out of the water this afternoon. I did so well I'm now the low score holder at this facility."

"Bravo!" Patrick applauds with both words and clapping.

"I can't take all the credit. If it wasn't for the advice of this golf genius I think I'd still be out there searching for lost balls. Patrick, I'd like you to meet my friend Callie..."

"Young," Patrick finishes my sentence. Then Patrick extends his hand in Callie's direction. "Hi, I'm Patrick Miles. It's a pleasure to meet you Miss Young."

"Please, call me Callie. Miss is reserved for the prim and proper girls, which I can assure you I'm far from being. And I'm afraid you have me at a disadvantage. Have we met before?" Callie asks curiously. "Because I can't imagine ever forgetting a gorgeous face like yours. That car accident must have done more than mangle my legs. I think the doctors overlooked some damage to my brain."

Patrick manages to laugh at Callie, while she continues to shock me with her forwardness. "No, I'm quite certain your brain remains in tact. This is our first meeting and I must say it's an honor. I'm a big fan."

"Why thank you, but I'm still at a loss," Callie says.

"During college, I majored in journalism. One of the assignments in my sports journalism class was to write a piece on an up and coming athlete. Since I followed the collegiate women's golf programs closely at the time," he says and looks my way, "I had a pretty good idea on who I would be writing about. But your name kept popping up in my searches and I had no other choice than to see what all the buzz was about. Curiosity won out and I ended up doing some extensive research on the future darling of golf. Turns out, it paid off and not only did I get an A plus on the assignment, my piece was published in the university paper. So, yeah, I would say I know a little about you, Callie Young," Patrick informs us.

"I'm flattered," Callie says while blushing. Wow, Callie Young blushing. I would never believe it had I not been present. "However, this isn't fair? Seems you know a lot about me and all I know about you is what Suzanna has shared."

Patrick looks over at me with a worried look. "Callie, stop making the man nervous. Patrick I assure you it was all good."

"Actually, you came up a few times on the course today," Callie chimes in.

"Shut up, Callie." I pray she doesn't open her big mouth and tell Patrick I imagined it was his head on the golf tee before taking a big swing at it. "You can get to know Patrick *and his lovely fiancée* at Dead Dog Saturday night. They are *both* coming to support Drew during his performance." As if on cue, Drew drives up in Callie's car. He parks and walks around to assist his sister.

"Looking forward to seeing you again, Patrick," Callie says with a sweetness I've yet to hear her portray until now. "And I can't wait to meet your fiancée." Now there's the sarcasm I'm used to hearing from Callie.

"Sounds like a plan. Again, it was nice to finally meet you, Callie." With a chuckle, Patrick starts loading my gear into the back of his jeep. I give Callie an eye roll and say goodbye to Drew. I'll see them both again tomorrow for another round of practice.

On the ride home, poor Patrick doesn't get a chance to get a word in. I monopolize the conversation with tales of golf and practice rounds. I tell him how miserable I played in the morning and compare it to the excellent round I played that afternoon. I tell how Callie made remarkable strides in confronting her demons, going out on the course for the first time since the accident. Patrick tells me that just weeks after his article about Callie was published in the university paper, the accident occurred taking her ability to walk and almost taking her life. The paper asked Patrick to write a follow up focusing on the details of the accident. Rumors ran rampant after the accident, most not portraying Callie as the talented golfer she was, but vilifying her into a wild party animal who threw caution to the wind by getting into the car with a drunk driver. Patrick refused to write falsehoods or even investigate the likeliness that any of the rumors were true. Rather, he published a story informing the student body of the basic details of the accident. Then he focused on how the golfing world suffered the loss of such a beautiful woman with extreme talent. He never did mention that he followed my college career, even though he alluded to that fact in his conversation with Callie. I didn't ask either, trying to keep our conversation away from the personal side of things. I just wanted us to have a friendly conversation and not get bogged down by the mistakes of our past.

When we finally turn onto Waccamaw Drive from Atlantic Avenue, I finally wind up my story. "Sorry to bore you the entire drive home with the details of my day," I say.

"Suzanna, you are never a bore. I'm just glad you didn't let me ruin your entire day," Patrick says sheepishly.

"Patrick, you could never...."

"Shit," Patrick mummers under his breath as we pass by his beach home.

"What's wrong?"

"Looks like we have guests. That's Ruth's car," Patrick says pointing to the driveway.

I met Ruth briefly at the engagement party. Apparently, she and Patrick's dad are an item, dating on and off the past several years. "Do you not like Ruth?" I ask.

"No, Ruth is fine. I'm grateful Dad found someone to spend some time with, especially since I was always away at school. It's just that almost each time she visits, she brings her five year old twin grandsons. Evidently, her daughter pawns them off on her every chance she gets," Patrick says, indicating his opinion of Ruth's daughter is low.

"They can't be that bad. Five year olds are cute and sweet and usually fun to be around. I'm sure you can find something to entertain them," I say trying to cheer him up. His good mood from earlier is on the brink of a disappearing act.

"Yeah, that's just it. I'm the one who has to be the twenty-four hour entertainment. Dad and Ruth are usually well into happy hour by this time of day. Which leaves me to watch the kids. There goes any chance of catching the game tonight," Patrick says totally bummed.

"What game?" I ask.

"Carolina is playing in the first round of the college World Series. They are trying to defend their title from last year," Patrick says.

"That's right. I just didn't know it started tonight. The boys aren't interested in baseball?" I ask.

"Those boys are only interested in causing havoc at each and every turn. I'm sure the television will be dialed in all night to continuous episodes of SpongeBob SquarePants or some other cartoon."

I have to laugh. I can't imagine Patrick sitting through just one episode of SpongeBob much less an entire night of it.

"Oh, you laugh now. But believe me it gets worse. Their idea of watching television consists of the volume up to an ear splitting decibel. Because in order for them to hear the cartoon they are supposedly watching, the volume has to be loud enough to drown out their screams at each other. Why are there screaming at each other, I'm sure you're about to ask? Well, while they take charge of the remote, and God forbid you try to change the channel, they also engage each other into wrestling matches on the couch. Usually, this ends with one or the other drawing blood. All of this goes on until, Ruth, in her drunken state by this time, has had enough and sends them to bed. Sounds fun, huh?" Patrick asks.

"It sounds like a nightmare." Poor Patrick, bless him. He can't even relax in his own home. I don't condone Ruth or Mr. Miles drinking themselves into a stupor, but in this case, who can blame them.

"Can't you escape and go watch the game at Katelyn's?" Katelyn's family has a beach home in Pawleys Island, which is just a short drive south of Garden City.

"Normally, yes. But she and her mother left today for Greenville. Her mom has to meet with her...." Patrick pauses before he continues. It sounds like he hesitated just in time before he revealed something private. "They are doing wedding stuff. They won't be home for a few days."

"Patrick, you don't have to get uncomfortable talking about your wedding plans. Actually, Katelyn was giving us a glimpse of the bridesmaid dresses last night." I almost bust out into giggles thinking of the hideous gowns her mother thinks are so lovely. "Listen, we're friends and I want you to be able to share details of the wedding with me just like you would with Chloe, Landon or James."

"Sure Suz, friends," Patrick comments dryly. A few moments of silence pass before we pull into my driveway. With a sneaky look, Patrick comes up with his brilliant idea. "Suz, since we're friends and all, I was thinking maybe I could hang out and watch the game here. Please!" he pleads with an exaggerated pout.

"I don't know, Patrick. This may not be the best idea. Plus, I'm bone tired and in desperate need of a shower."

"Come on, Suz. I owe you a meal anyway since you bailed on me for lunch. You can shower while I order and wait for the pizza. I'll even clean up the kitchen and the mess I left this morning," Patrick continues trying to persuade me.

I take a moment to think about it. I still think this has disaster written all over it. But that's the old Suzanna talking. The new Suzanna, who kicked some butt in golf today and said the hell with everybody else, wouldn't let her confused emotions get in the way of helping out a friend. And like I said, Patrick and I are just friends. And that's all we will ever be to each other again. Period.

"So what's it's gonna be Suz? You up for some company tonight? I mean, Flynn and Chloe aren't even home yet. And I know you don't want to go in that big empty house all by yourself," Patrick says laying it on thick.

He's right. I don't want to spend the night alone. And just where the hell are Chloe and Flynn? I thought for sure they would be back by now. Chloe starts her new job tomorrow afternoon. Plus, she's usually not one to spend a lot of time bonding with her parents, especially after telling them that she's dumping summer school to spend the summer at the beach working at a bar. I can only imagine how well that went over with the Ryders. Flynn is living the life of a king tonight. I'm sure my mother is pampering him with her delicious home cooked meals and 'don't lift a finger' service. He's probably thrilled they stayed into the evening. I'm just worried something may have gone wrong since they told me this morning it would be a short day trip. I haven't heard a word from either of them since I left my cell phone at home charging today. Hopefully Chloe or Flynn left me a message informing me about what is going on.

Thinking of cell phones and messages, I can't help but replay in my mind the final message from Wyatt. My exhilaration from golf today takes a nose dive and is suddenly replaced with sadness. A small light of hope flickers in my head that maybe he decided to call again today, one last time. But then I remember his decision to let me go, giving up on repairing our relationship and moving on with his new life in New York. I mean, who can blame him? I ignored his calls and texts for days. Granted, I didn't want to hear him try to explain away his reasons against our long distance relationship. And there was no way he could ever explain away why I found Bridgett in his bed, naked. But that nagging feeling keeps pulling at my heart telling me that maybe I should have tried. Our romantic relationship began with him convincing me to try. He broke my walls down and I finally conceded to his plea. Then the one time I don't try, not letting him explain or having any contact with him whatsoever, he gives up. Done. Finished. Adios! That thought causes a pain in my chest. So, no, I don't want to be alone tonight and replay that final message over and over again until I'm lying in a bed of snotty tissues again. Hanging out with Patrick is probably not the best idea, but at least he will provide the distraction I desperately need.

"Fine, you are more than welcome to stay here and watch the baseball game. But you have to feed me. I prefer Italian sausage, green peppers and onions on thin crust, please," I say answering a patiently waiting Patrick, while I've been lost in my head.

"Yes!" Patrick says punching the air with his fist. "Thank you, Suz."

"Don't thank me yet. I'm sure I'll be lousy company tonight. I can barely keep my eyes open." The humid temperatures and the hot sun are finally taking their toll on me. I feel drained and exhausted, not to mention disgusting. I really need to get out of these sweaty clothes and take a shower. "Let's get my stuff unloaded and..."

"I'll unload your gear while you go shower and change. By the time you finish, the pizza will be here and the game should have started," Patrick offers. Thank goodness because the air conditioned house is calling my name. I give Patrick a thumbs up and race inside to wash off the day.

Twenty minutes later, I'm clean as a whistle. I decide to throw on a pair of yoga pants and a tank top. Combing out my long hair, I leave it down to air dry. When I walk out of my bedroom, I find that Patrick has made himself comfortable on the couch, eating pizza and watching the game. "Hope you're saving some of that for me," I say in greeting.

"Absolutely, I've got you a plate right here. I didn't know what you wanted to drink though," Patrick says through a mouthful of yummy goodness.

"I'll grab a Diet Coke from the fridge. You need something?" Patrick holds up his Coke can, indicating he already helped himself to a beverage.

Plopping down next to Patrick on the couch, I grab a slice and begin to devour it. I didn't realize how hungry I actually was. I must have really worked up an appetite on the course today. While Patrick continues to consume his dinner and remain engrossed in the baseball game, my mind drifts back to the last time I ate pizza with a man. It was a magical night, the night I realized the very strong feelings I had for Wyatt. Earlier that same day, Wyatt had been on top of the world just receiving word that he had snagged one of the five coveted internship spots at a prestigious brokerage firm in New York. Me... well, I didn't share his enthusiasm. I was scared when he told me he would be spending the summer in New York. We had just started our whirlwind affair and I wasn't ready for the distance this opportunity would create. My child like tantrum and actions drove Wyatt away looking beaten and defeated. A complete opposite from when he had arrived to share his good fortune.

After crying myself to sleep and reliving the worst night of my life in dreamland, I woke with a new revelation. It didn't matter if Wyatt lived in New York. It wouldn't matter if he lived on the other side of the planet. No matter where his travels took him, as long as Wyatt remained in my life and in my heart, I could be happy. Why? Because I finally admitted to myself that I loved him. Suzanna Caulder was in love with Wyatt McCain. And I still am. In a rush to bare my soul, I showed up to Wyatt's apartment armed with an apology and to tell him of my true feelings. And I did. I can picture us standing there, facing each other as I blurted the words out in a rush. "I love you, Wyatt," I said, finally freeing myself of the barrier I erected around my heart. I had never allowed myself to love another after giving up on any type of romantic involvement since I left Patrick so many years ago. He was the only other man to hear those words from my mouth. And since we ended on a lie, devastating us both during our senior year of high school, I guarded myself of the possibility of ever finding that again. However, Wyatt was able to chip away at my armor and soon the hope of happiness and love flooded my heart like a tidal wave. Thank God my feelings were reciprocated. That night Wyatt loved me back, both with words and actions...and pizza... all night long.

Will my life always be this way? I ask myself as I look at the half eaten piece of pizza on my plate. Will something so mundane as eating a slice of Italian goodness bring back memories of Wyatt and the love we lost? Probably. Wyatt and I were so immersed in each other's lives during our short but intense time together, even the smallest everyday things seem to remind me of him and send me spiraling into a dismal state. I have got to move on. What kind of life will I lead if I continue to grieve the loss of a past relationship every time something triggers a memory? But how can I move on and focus on the future, when the person I thought was my future is gone?

"Suz?" Helllloooo...Earth to Suzanna!" I glance over and see that Patrick has turned his attention away from the game and is staring at me with concern. "Something wrong with the pizza?"

"Huh?" I ask looking down at my plate again.

"You haven't eaten but a couple of bites. I thought you were starving," Patrick comments pointing at the uneaten food.

"Yeah, seems I lost my appetite," I say avoiding his gaze and focusing on the television. "What's going on with the game?"

"Fuck the game," Patrick almost shouts. My head whips to the side to look at him. I'm surprised at his intensity that is solely directed at me now.

"What?" I question. "I'm just tired and don't feel like eatin..." My explanation is thwarted when Patrick raises his finger to my lips to shush me.

"I think it's time we have a little chat. Now, tell me what's going on with you. And don't bullshit me. I know something is bothering you. How? Well, my first clue was the fact that Flynn and Chloe called in their little favor this morning. Secondly, since seeing you this past weekend for the first time in years, your emotions have been all over the place. Maybe I'm reading you wrong, but this past weekend I felt you needed to tell me something but didn't know how. And today, you go from being on top of the world to looking like someone just kicked your puppy. You trance in and out and frankly, Suz, it's a little worrisome."

"I can't talk about it," I whisper.

"You can't or you won't. I mean, is it me? You won't talk about it with me?" Patrick asks.

"Well yeah, if you must know. Talking about this with you is just...weird."

"Why? We're friends, right? I mean, you've only told me that a million times since we met up again," Patrick reminds me with annoyance in his voice.

"Fine. If you really want to know," I say taking a deep breath. "I was dating someone."

"Was?" Patrick asks with a little too much interest in his tone.

"Yeah, but we recently, as in just under a week ago, broke up." The words still cause my heart to ache.

"You want me to go kick his ass?" Patrick says with all seriousness.

"No!" I shriek. "Besides, you'd have to go a long, long way to find him."

"Ahhh," Patrick mummers in understanding. "This douchebag is no longer in the picture because he moved away. Sounds familiar."

"He's not a douchebag," I protest in defense of Wyatt. "Besides, it was a mutual decision not to continue a long distance relationship," I lie.

"Lucky guy," Patrick comments dryly.

"Lucky? What on earth are you getting at Patrick?" I ask on the verge of anger. How dare he call Wyatt lucky for deciding to end our relationship? Am I that unwanted?

"Lucky in the fact that he actually got a say so in the decision process of your break up. Me, well, I was just left to wonder what the hell I did wrong," Patrick answers stopping my heart.

"Patrick...," I start, but I don't really have any words to refute his statement. And I really don't like where this conversation is going. As my friend, I thought he was going to console and give me some dude advice on how to get over a guy. However, he's twisting the knowledge of the end of my recent relationship and bringing it all back to our break up. I'm having a hard enough time dealing with the present state of my romantic life. Lord knows I don't need to delve into the past and conjure up all those feelings when I decided to let Patrick go and leave him behind. "Look, I'm sorry. For everything. And even though it's a battle to keep my emotions in check, every day is getting better. I'm just trying to move on."

"We're all trying to move on, Suz," Patrick says.

"Mission accomplished, Patrick."

"What do you mean by that?" Patrick asks as I turn the tables.

"Duh, you're engaged. Getting married. I'd say that qualifies as definitely moving on."

"You honestly think I've moved on?" Patrick has the gall to ask.

"I saw the ring on her finger!" I shout throwing my hands up in the air. "Your mother's ring," I add through clenched teeth.

"But that's all you see," he says like that will clear things up. "And all I see since the moment I walked in that back door over there," he pauses and points to the rear of the house but never takes his eyes from my face, "is you, Suz. After years of only seeing you in my memories, in my dreams, there you were...sitting at the table like a vision. I had to blink several times to make sure you were real. And then it was like there was some gravitational pull between us. I had to get physically closer to you. These last few days, knowing you are just a few blocks down the road, I painfully yearn to be near you. That's why when Chloe called this morning telling me you needed me I immediately dropped everything to show up in your bedroom." Patrick takes a moment to catch his breath and slides closer to me on the couch. "And now, sitting with you, sharing dinner, watching a game...just being alone together. I might have to literally use physical restraints not to engulf you in my arms, carry you into that bedroom and ravish you. I want to remove all barriers of clothing and press our bodies together, skin to skin. I want to kiss every square inch of the body I've committed to memory. I want to bring you pleasure multiple times over and over again before I give in to my own ecstasy, releasing a part of me inside you. Then I want to hold you close while we both fall asleep and wake the next morning with you in my arms, and do it all over again. I want to claim you, brand you, and make you mine. Once again, mine."

Our bodies are flush against each other, only a millimeter of space separating our sitting positions. Patrick's face has inched closer and closer to mine, until each of his words left his hot breath feathering across my skin. I'm too shocked to move, trying to replay his pleas in my head. We stare at each other in complete silence. The only sound is the ticking of the clock on the wall. "Now Suz, I wouldn't define that as moving on," Patrick says in a soft whisper. "For over four years I have wanted and wished for nothing more than to have one more chance with you. But...," Patrick hesitates.

I guess our reunion on the front porch the other night after the engagement party should have clued me in on Patrick's never ending feelings toward me. He did tell me he still loved me after all these years. And then there was that kiss. As if time stood still, it was just me and Patrick on that front porch, our lips melted together in a searing show of affection that still lives between us. How did I not connect the dots sooner? Oh yeah, I was so gung ho to get back to Wyatt and into his arms, I didn't give much thought to the confessions of Patrick. I guess I chalked it up to the sentimentality of seeing each other again after so many years. But now, with all that Patrick has just shared and the lustful look in his eyes, there is more than just unresolved feelings between two high school sweethearts. If I leaned in just a smidge, our lips would touch again. And this time I don't think I would be able to stop it, much less anything that would come after. How did we even get to this point? It's hard to concentrate with him so close. But I suddenly remember and I no longer want to get closer. His engagement. His impending marriage. Katelyn. Oh my gosh! Poor Katelyn. And she wants to be my friend? How could I even think to do something like this to her? Granted we just started to get to know each other last night. But still, what type of person would get close to someone then turn around and kiss their fiancé? I'm a dog!

I push away from Patrick and scoot all the way to the end of the couch burrowing my body into the corner. I have to maintain some distance before things happen that we will both regret. The look of rejection on Patrick's face is too much, so I turn away avoiding his face. "But you can't, Patrick," I say finishing his sentence. It's not a question but rather a statement of the facts surrounding our lives now.

"Yeah, I can't." Patrick turns his body away from mine and places his elbows on his knees, holding his head in his hands as if it weighs a ton. "Ugh! This sucks!" Patrick growls running his hands through his hair in frustration. "Listen, Suz. About the engagement..."

Our conversation is interrupted when the front door swings open. Landon rushes through into the house with Leslie on his heels. "Runt back?" Landon asks almost in a panic.

"Runt," Leslie parrots Landon with a cackle. Obviously, she finds Chloe's nickname very funny. But when all our eyes turn toward her in a seething glare, her laughter subsides.

I've never been so glad to see someone in my life. And Landon just provided the subject change that I need desperately. "Hi Landon. Leslie. Um, Chloe and Flynn haven't made it back yet," I say in greeting.

"But I thought it was supposed to be a quick day trip," Landon says irritated.

"Dude, calm down. I'm sure Chloe is fine. I mean she's either still at her parent's house or with Flynn, driving back as we speak," Patrick says trying to alleviate Landon's concern.

"Exactly what I told him," Leslie enters the conversation. "You'd think the way Landon worries, y'all let Chloe leave town with an escaped criminal." Leslie's sarcasm is clearly evident.

Before Landon has the chance to lash out at Leslie for her disregard to Chloe's safety, unnecessary as it may be, Patrick suggests that Landon give Chloe a call. "I know Florence isn't a metropolis, but last time I checked I remember them having cell service. Just give her a call, man."

"I have, several times. But my calls go directly to her voicemail," Landon admits, making Leslie none to happy that her date for the evening has been secretly trying to call another woman.

Leslie makes an effort to try and hide the anger that is boiling within, but miserably fails by scowling at us all. I make an attempt to soothe her hurt feelings. "So, looks like Landon made good on his promise and took you out on that romantic date you two missed last night."

"I wouldn't call the bar area at Dead Dog Saloon exactly romantic," Leslie replies.

"Hey, you got fed a great meal. Plus, the view of the inlet was excellent," Landon says in his defense.

"Well, thank you for the food. And yes, the view was amazing. I'm just lucky we had that because the conversation was nonexistent," Leslie complains. "Even though the place was packed and we got seated by the speaker of the band that wailed on and on, one song after another, Landon wouldn't dare consider going anywhere else. He just had to go to Dead Dog to fulfill a favor for Chloe."

"Since we were right there at the marsh walk, I figured I'd go ahead and pick up Chloe's work shirts since she starts tomorrow." Landon throws a plastic bag on the kitchen table. Chloe's uniform, which is none other than a couple of logo printed shirts and tank tops spill out. I think the gesture was sweet. However, Leslie seems to think it's ridiculous for a grown man to go out of his way for a friend. "Stop being so unappreciative...you got that one on one date you've been whining about all week."

"You call that a date? Chloe might as well have been sitting with us at the table. There was definitely no one else with you tonight Landon. You were way too preoccupied with Chloe's whereabouts," Leslie shouts no longer trying to hide her anger. Patrick and I watch them throw insults at each other like we are watching a tennis match.

Landon doesn't seem a bit concerned that his date for the evening is spitting nails. "Look, you got dinner and drinks, with a view. Plus, I actually enjoyed the entertainment. What more do you want, Leslie?"

Leslie is on the brink of tears now, having Landon call her out in front of me and Patrick. We wait, as Leslie takes a deep breath to try and control her trembling lip. She starts to answer Landon, but gets cut off.

"No, don't answer that right now," Landon says harshly. He then retrieves his phone from his pocket and starts dialing. "I'm gonna try to call Chloe one more time." I watch as Landon places the phone to his ear, glancing over at a stunned and hurt Leslie. I catch Landon's eye and he just shrugs, trying to hide a little smirk he is sending my way. I'm starting to figure out that Landon is playing some type of game with Leslie. I'm not sure what it is, or why he is even still with her. It's so obvious he wants nothing to do with her, while she is planning their future in her mind. "Shit!" Landon mummers. "Voicemail again."

"Let me go check my phone. I'm sure if their plans have changed either Chloe or Flynn would have called me." I walk to my bedroom to get my phone that was left charging all day. I should have checked it as soon as I arrived home. Then maybe we could have avoided the intense exchange between Leslie and Landon. But my avoidance at looking at any messages or texts kept me uninformed about Chloe and Flynn's schedule. It's not that I didn't want to know how their day was going. I was selfishly guarding my heart. Although Wyatt said in his last message yesterday that he will no longer try to contact me, I've had a sliver of hope all day that he would reconsider and call again. The thought that he didn't leave another message today will be another sign that we are completely finished. All hope of salvaging my relationship with Wyatt will die. But to ease Landon's mind, I have to check my phone. Maybe then he and Leslie will leave and I can go to bed and put this day behind me. Day one of no more Wyatt crossed off. At least that is one less day to contend with.

I'm so caught up in my thoughts of Wyatt and whether or not a message is waiting for me, I don't hear Patrick follow me into my bedroom until he closes the door. I turn around to find him doubled over in laughter, trying to catch his breath. "What's so funny?" I ask.

"Are you kidding me? Did you not just hear Landon? I swear the boy doesn't have a clue when it comes to romancing a woman. Did he really think a bar/restaurant was a good idea for his makeup date? I mean, he basically brushed her off last night to hang out with us and then takes Leslie to hear a band and see the view from a hopping place like Dead Dog." Patrick finds great amusement in Landon's attempt at dating.

"Yeah, I guess it's not the best atmosphere to wine and dine," I say through giggles of my own.

"Exactly! Maybe we need to enroll Landon in a Romance 101 course," Patrick suggests then busts out laughing again. I join him and before long the laughter escalates until all thoughts of un-left messages are forgotten. It takes a moment for us to collect ourselves. I unplug my phone, ready to check for any word from Chloe. I don't get the protective nature of Landon and Chloe's relationship. Sure, they've been friends forever and talked frequently over the years. However, it's strange how Landon babies Chloe more than the rest of us, me included. During my four years since leaving Patrick, Landon and I barely maintained a friendship. Occasionally, we'd happen to be at the same place and were always polite, but the closeness from before had evaporated. Landon always seemed too standoffish to be concerned about me at all. I'm feeling a little bitter about the whole thing. And jealous. I mean we were all friends, so why is Chloe so special?

"What's Landon's deal with Chloe? I mean, why is he so worried about her all of a sudden?" I ask Patrick hoping he can give me some insight.

"I don't know. But it's always been that way. He's just gotten over the top about her in recent years."

"Do you think he's interested in Chloe? Not just as a friend, but romantically," I ponder.

"We just discussed Landon's lack of romance. And knowing Chloe, Miss Dramatic, she's a little high maintenance in the romance department. I don't see her settling for anything other than over the top displays of affection. Obviously, our boy wouldn't come close to delivering. But honestly I don't think Landon sees Chloe as anything other than a friend," Patrick says.

"I just don't get it then. Why all the concern? It's not like he's sharing the love," I say under my breath.

"Awww, Suz...are you feeling a little left out?" Patrick asks in a baby voice.

"No," I reply immediately. Patrick looks at me with an arched brow. "Well, yeah, I guess." I hate admitting that I'm feeling jealous about Landon's undying concern for my best friend.

"Suz, Landon worries about you just as much as he does Chloe," Patrick consoles.

"He has a strange way of showing it," I remark snidely. "I mean I rarely spoke to Landon all during college. It was only this weekend that we reconnected."

"That's my fault, Suz. And I'm sorry. But with the bro code and all, Landon felt by continuing a friendship with you after our break up, he would somehow be betraying me. However, you have to believe me when I say Landon made sure you were okay from afar. He constantly received updates from Chloe about you. If at any point Landon had felt that you needed him, he wouldn't have hesitated to be right by your side. Just look at his attendance this weekend. Granted, he knew all along he would attend the engagement party. But as soon as he found out you were going he called Chloe immediately to make arrangements to stay here with you guys. Deep down he probably knew that it was going to be difficult for you to attend my engagement party." Patrick looks away at the mention of his engagement. Although his words about Landon make me feel better, I hate that he blames himself for my inadequate feelings.

I raise my hand and lightly touch his cheek, turning his head so that he has no choice but to look me in the eye. "Thank you, Patrick. And yes, it's hard to let go. But as long as you're happy, then I'm happy for you. And don't blame yourself for the distance I put between myself and Landon. Remember, I was the one to leave."

"Why did you leave me, Suz?" Patrick asks again.

"We've been over this before. I left to focus on golf," I reiterate the same thing I told him on the porch Saturday night.

Patrick shakes his head in wonder, causing me to drop my hand from his face. "When you're ready to get real, Suz, let me know. Until then, we can continue to be...

"Friends," we say in unison.

"Any word?" Landon asks as he opens my bedroom door. If he is surprised to find Patrick and me standing closely face to face, he doesn't show it. I grab my phone and locate several texts from Chloe.

"Oh, here it is," I say as I begin to read the texts out loud.

Hey, Suz. Please don't be mad...smiley face

"Why would you be mad at Chloe?" Landon asks puzzled. I point to Patrick as he points to himself, wearing a smug grin.

"Long story. Here's the next one," I say scrolling down to Chloe's second text.

So the parents now know of my change of plans for the summer. Went about as I expected. Dad okay, Mom not so much. As punishment I have to go wedding/bridesmaid dress shopping with Mom and Ashley this afternoon. Oh fun. Hopefully back in time to head back later tonight. See you soon

"I thought Chloe loved to shop," Patrick comments.

"Not with Ashley. Well, more specifically, not with Ashley when her mom is present. Bless her heart, Chloe is forever being compared to her perfect figured sister." Mrs. Ryder has never hidden the fact that Ashley, her first born daughter, is perfect in every way. Ashley is smart as a whip, getting scholarships to college and graduating with honors. Add that to her runway model looks and her Hollywood figure, Chloe never stood a chance to compete. Ashley loves Chloe in every way possible, as does Chloe's dad. However, her mother has never made apologies to criticize Chloe every chance available, from her average grades to her voluptuous curves.

"Why? Chloe's body is smoking hot. I bet she will put Ashley to shame, even if she is the bride," Patrick says kindly, not really understanding the Ryder family dynamics.

"Not in Mrs. Ryder's eyes," Landon says. Maybe Chloe has confided her feelings of being the unloved daughter to Landon. That would explain his need to protect her.

"Wait, there's one more text from Chloe. She must have just sent this about an hour ago," I say reading the last text aloud.

> Kill me now! We are still shopping and it's already past dinner. Mom insists I stay overnight instead of driving back. Don't know why since precious Ashley is staying the night. I'll only be ignored. Anyway, since so late gonna just leave first thing in morning. Flynn was more than happy to stay longer for more pampering from your mom. Have a great night, Suz. See u in morning! Hugs…

"Well, there you have it," I say to Landon. Although, he doesn't look relieved now knowing where Chloe is. Matter of fact, he looks pissed.

"Dammit!" Landon curses under his breath. "The thought of Chloe spending time with that vile woman infuriates me."

"Who, Ashley?" Patrick asks.

"No, her mother," Landon corrects.

"Landon, at least you know Chloe is safe." Landon gives an unconvinced look. "Chloe's strong. She's not the type to let words hurt her, even from her mother. Besides, I'm sure Mrs. Ryder is too busy doting on Ashley to even notice Chloe's presence. Chloe's probably enjoying spending some time with her dad."

"Yeah, I guess you're right. At least he loves Chloe for Chloe," Landon says sounding less angry but still concerned. "Please, if you hear from her again before tomorrow morning, have her call me. I just want to know she's okay."

"Will do. Hey, where's Leslie?" I realize our entire conversation has taken place in my bedroom while Leslie was left in the den.

"Probably sulking in the car waiting for me to apologize," Landon says with no regret whatsoever.

"Dude, you've got to up your game or else she's gonna dump your ass," Patrick teases.

"I wish," Landon says confirming my earlier suspicions that he isn't as into Leslie as she would hope.

"Why bother keeping her around, Landon? It's so obvious that you don't want to date her any longer."

"Long story," Landon says using my earlier words. "Listen, I've got to go. Sorry for the intrusion, again."

"What about the job interview? Did it go well? You get hired?" I say remembering his interview was scheduled earlier today.

"Yep, I got it," Landon says with boredom.

"That's great!" I say giving Landon a celebratory hug.

"Yeah, fucking great," Landon says sarcastically. "Adios, guys. See you tomorrow." And with that, Landon leaves Patrick and me alone again.

Chapter Fifteen

P atrick and I resume our positions on the couch, he on one end and me on the opposite end. Patrick returns his attention to the game, occasionally taking notes in an old notebook that apparently gets plenty of use from the looks of it. Every time he flips over a page, the sound of wrinkled paper grabs my attention. I try to sneak a peek at what he's writing, but the distance in our seated positions, which I insisted on, keeps me from reading his written words. "You know, they probably have a live feed on the internet that documents the stats of the game. So there's no need for you to keep up your detailed note taking," I say pointing toward his notebook.

"Thanks for the info, Sherlock. I'll have you know, I'm not taking notes of the individual player stats. Well, that's not all I'm doing," Patrick says still concentrating on the game and the players.

"Well, what exactly are you documenting?" I ask, totally curious.

"I'm telling a story," Patrick says jotting down something else he finds relevant. "See, it's not all about a person's performance on the field. Each one of these players has a life outside of baseball. I like to delve in and get the background story. It's usually the one that makes them the player they are."

"Who are you writing about in tonight's game?" I'm so interested in his perspective and would love a sample of his writing.

"See that guy," he says pointing toward the television. The camera is focused on the first baseman. "He's a cancer survivor. He had a rare form of cancer as a young boy. They thought at one time, he would lose his leg to the disease in order to save his life. But the doctors found a treatment that worked and he has been in remission ever since. Look at him now. He'll probably be a first round pick in the MLB draft this year. And to think, he came so close to losing a limb. He's the most determined player on that field. He's grateful for every opportunity he gets to play. He's also a frequent visitor to the children's cancer center at the University hospital."

"Wow, I would have never known had you not told me," I say. Just a few minutes earlier he was just a baseball player. "He sounds like a great guy."

"He's a great ball player *and* a great guy," Patrick says. We continue to watch the game. I find myself glued to the television in hopes of seeing the first baseman in action again. Knowing his back story makes me connect with him as a real person and not just as an athlete. I want to know more about Patrick's interest in writing the biographies of sports figures.

"Do you mind if I take a look?" I ask glancing at the notebook that lies in his lap.

"These are just scattered notes and thoughts. I don't think you'd be able to make sense of any of it. I do most of my writing on a word processor. I'll be glad to bring you my latest publication."

"You publish?" I ask stunned. I didn't realize his passion for writing was actually a paying job.

"Yeah, if a newspaper or magazine is interested. Mostly, I've just dealt with the university's newspaper and some small state magazines. Although I'd love to make this a career and write for *Sports Illustrated* or ESPN's online publication," Patrick says with conviction.

"Then why go to law school?"

"Oh, well, lawyers can write, too." The mention of law school takes all the excitement Patrick expressed when talking about his writing and flushes it down the toilet. "My dad really wants me to follow in his footsteps. I can still use my writing skills for contract law and other things." I'm not sure who Patrick is trying to convince, me or himself. But I can't understand three more years of schooling for a law degree he won't need to be a fantastic writer.

"That sounds boring compared to your passion for sports." Contract law compared to the inspiration of a once wounded athlete making it big time. There's just no comparison. Why bother with law school?

"Well, we can't all live the exciting life of a professional golfer, now can we?" Patrick says in a teasing manner.

"I guess not. But since you're so good at writing..."

"Let's just drop it, Suz. I've made my decision and law school it is." Patrick ends the discussion and focuses his attention back to the game. I wonder if Patrick's dad is forcing him to continue his studies to become a lawyer. I know Patrick, being an only child, is the only heir to his father's firm. I assume if Patrick didn't continue his father's legacy, the firm would be sold to a competitor. But could his father be that vain to want to continue the firm's namesake at the expense of his son's career dreams? Well, we are talking about the monster who attempted to sexually assault me. I'm not putting anything past that man.

Patrick closes his notebook and places it on the floor beside him thus closing the subject of his passion for writing. I decide not to push and try to watch the final innings of the baseball game. However, the long, exhausting day is catching up to me and I can barely keep my eyes open. After nodding off several times, I can no longer keep my head up. "Suz," Patrick says quietly with soft pats to my shoulder. "You're gonna get whiplash if you keep fighting sleep. It's obvious you're not very interested in this game."

"Is it still on?" I ask followed by a huge yawn.

"Extra innings. Why don't you go on to bed and I'll lock up after the game is over," Patrick suggests.

"You sure? I'm being an awful hostess."

"I'm sure, I just want to watch the game in its entirety and then I'll head home. Go on, now. You need your rest for another grueling day of golf tomorrow." Patrick stands extending his hand in my direction. I grab his offered hand and he pulls me up from the couch.

"Thanks for the company today. 'Night Patrick," I say and sleep-walk into my bedroom.

"Sweet dreams, Suz," Patrick says as he watches me walk away before turning his attention back to the television. After shredding my yoga pants, I do a face plant onto my bed. I'm asleep before my head actually touches the pillow. I don't even notice the message indicator blinking on my cell phone.

⌒〜⊙

Here we go again. Another night of sleep rudely interrupted by the ghosts of my past. Somehow, even in the slumbers of sleep, I prepare myself to relive that awful night. The dream begins with the events that took place on the golf course. Patrick and I involved in intense love making. But I know what lies ahead and I brace myself for this dream to take a turn for the worse. Images of the erotic display between Patrick and me are suddenly replaced with a dark shadow pushing my petite frame against the wall. His one arm securely holds my upper body in place while his other roughly feels and probes my breasts and lower regions. As with every other time I have had this nightmare, I hear my dress being torn away from my body. I watch in horror as his grip slips and I take the opportunity to bite him trying to make a desperate escape. That only refuels his brutality, giving me a hard slap across the face which leaves me stunned. Suddenly, he regains his hold while preparing himself to do the unthinkable. I hear his zipper slide down and the rustle of his suit pants being removed. Wait...never did the reality of that night get this far. He grabs my hand and directs it to his hardening cock, forcing me to touch him. Oh, no no no. This isn't how it happened. I should have been rescued by now. Where is Wyatt? His hand holds mine prisoner on his enlarged member making me stoke its length. All the while, he is kissing, licking and biting...yes biting, my neck and shoulders, his tongue travels leading to my now exposed breasts. He threatens bodily harm should I stop stroking before moving his hands to grab my underwear to rip them away from my body. "Please," I beg but my speech is thwarted when he stuffs my scrap of panties into my mouth as a gag. I squeeze my legs together trying my best to ward off his intrusion. He pinches my inner thighs to the point of drawing blood until I'm forced to relax my stance. "Wyatt, where the hell are you?" I cry silently through the material stuffed in my mouth. I feel the largeness of his hand on my mound searching for entry into my body. Trying my best not to hyperventilate or choke, I calm myself enough to use my tongue to dislodge my gag. Spitting the wet wad out of my mouth, I finally find my voice. "Help, please somebody help me!"

My attacker laughs maniacally before delivering a blow to my sporadically beating heart. "There's no one to save you this time, Suzanna. Wyatt's gone, for good. All the way up in New York. How will he ever be able to help you from there? He won't. He's finished with you, Suzanna. You two are done." Oh. My. God. He's right. Wyatt is finished with me. He told me so just last night. But this, this nightmare, happened years ago. Why isn't he here to come to my rescue? If it hadn't been for Wyatt's heroic actions four years ago this nightmare I'm having would be the reality of how things actually took place. But what really has the tears flowing is the fact that my life without Wyatt in it now is just as traumatic. A strong hand grips my chin, forcing me to look the monster in the eyes. He lines up his body with mine ready to complete the ultimate criminal act between a man and an unwilling woman. Rape. In a demonic voice I hear him declare, "This time, you're all mine!"

"Noooooooooooooooooooo," I scream over and over again.

"Suz, wake up. Oh God, Suz. Stop screaming! I'm right here, Suz. Please, just stop screaming." I hear the faint sound of someone's voice at the same time I am awakened with a gentle but firm shaking. I hesitate to open my eyes, scared of who I'll see in front of me. I hear the familiar voice again. "I thought someone was trying to kill you Suz." Patrick's hands skim my face, neck and shoulders looking for any signs of physical harm. "You scared me half to death!"

I open my eyes to find a terrified Patrick still taking inventory of my physical well being, holding me at arms length to get a good look. Why is Patrick here? Oh no. He knows? He can't. I left my entire life behind to keep Patrick safe from the awful truth of that horrendous night. I start to cry, knowing that I've done everything to hide my secrets, and yet, he still was able to find out.

"Shhhh, it's okay now, Suz. I've got you," Patrick says embracing me in a hug. I struggle to find my breath and continue to sob on his shoulder. "You want to talk about it?"

"N-no," I stammer, answering him immediately. In my foggy haze of sleepiness and terror, I realize that with Patrick's previous question, he maybe doesn't know the truth. Then I figure unless I let something slip while dreaming, there really is no way he knows the truth about that night. "It was just a nightmare," I squeak out between trying to take calming breaths.

"Well, that was some nightmare. Your screams had me so scared, I was afraid of what I'd find in this bedroom." Patrick takes in a heap of air before releasing it with a sigh and finally relaxing. He loosens his hold and goes to stand, but I tighten my embrace and keep him close. If that dream did one thing other than remind me of my past, it reiterated the fact that I am alone. There is no one to help me now. Well, no one except Patrick. "Hey, it's okay. Just try to go back to sleep. I'll be right here."

I slowly let go of Patrick and lie back down in my bed. Patrick remains in a seated position beside me, gently stroking my hair. I take one more look at Patrick's reassuring presence before squeezing my eyes shut. When all I see is darkness and not the demon – Jim Miles- I relax and try to slip back into sleep. Minutes pass before I'm about to succumb to fatigue when I feel the mattress rise slightly. Next thing I feel are the cool lips of Patrick against my cheek. "Good night, Suz."

Before he can escape I make a quick grab at his wrist. "Please don't leave me," I beg.

"You want me to stay the night? I guess I can sleep on the couch," Patrick offers.

"No, stay with me. Here," I say patting the bed beside me. "Please. I don't want to be alone." My fear that the nightmare will come back where I'll be forced to witness more horrors that could have occurred, overrides my rational thoughts. The fact that I'm asking Patrick for a sleepover is absurd, but I refuse to be left alone and pray he is willing to be my rock tonight.

"Are you sure?" Patrick sounds as surprised to be asked as I am surprised that I asked him.

"Yes." I try to sound confident in my request. Still holding tightly to Patrick's wrist, I wait anxiously for his decision.

"Um, okay." Patrick pries my fingers from his arm and walks to turn off the overhead light. I hear him shuffling around to the other side of the bed. A few moments later Patrick lies down beside me leaving enough distance that our bodies aren't touching.

"Thank you," I whisper.

"You're safe now, Suz. And you're welcome. Let's try to get some shuteye." I close my eyes and finally feel secure enough to fall back asleep. The sound of Patrick's even breathing lulls me over the edge into what I hope is a dreamless night of rest.

My internal alarm clock tells me it is morning, but I force myself to stay in the in-between state of sleep and awake. The blanket of warmth that surrounds me feels too good to get up. Actually, it's warmer than usual in my bed. Not quite uncomfortable, just different. Different in that I'm enjoying it so much I reach down to burrow further under the covers. As I begin to stir, a strong hand splays across my bare stomach stopping my sudden movement. My body stiffens at the human contact. When I try to pry my head from the pillow to look over my shoulder, the hand jerks me backwards, sliding me across the mattress until my shoulder blades connect with something hard. Each vertebrate from the top of my spine to the curve of my ass is pressed up against corded muscle. My panic elevates when a leg is thrown across my hip pinning me to the bed. I'm about to fight my way out of the stronghold until I feel feather light caresses on my belly. A finger is circling my navel singeing my skin and turning my insides to molten lava. So maybe I'm not quite to the point of waking up as I once thought. This has to be a dream, right? It's been so long since I've woken up in the arms of a man. Wyatt used to bathe me in his body heat every morning. Most of the time we set the sheets afire with our morning routine having to pry ourselves apart and out of bed. But Wyatt isn't around any longer so I know I must be living in dreamland right about now. If that's the case, what's it gonna hurt to let this fantasy exist just a little bit longer?

Pressing my body even closer, if possible, I snuggle up to every square inch of this manly body behind me. I relish the skin on skin contact. My rear involuntarily guts out until it touches the long, hard length of morning wood. Did I mention hard? Oh yeah. I wiggle just a bit feeling the smoothness rub against my rounded ass cheeks. "Mmmmmmmm," I moan out load.

My sounds of pleasure are met with a groan. A very male groan. "Awwww, it's a mighty fine morning, isn't it Suz?" The gruff voice is laced with lust and a hint of...teasing? I hear Patrick's familiar chuckle as he pulls me closer and his hot breath flows across my neck near my ear. "Know what would make it a perfect morning?" he asks in a sultry tone.

Like a bolt of lightning, I jump from the bed, stripping the bed sheets in my haste to cover my scantily clad body. I take a peek to find I at least still have on my underwear and a tank top, sans bra. Once I determine the barrier of the bed comforter and sheets are enough of a shield, I focus my attention back to the gorgeous specimen of a man lying on my bed. Wearing nothing but a pair of boxer briefs (his excitement still evident) and a smile. "Patrick? What are you....why are you? Ugh!" I'm too befuddled to form a coherent sentence. Gulping air like a fish out of water I try again, only after I take an appreciative look at Patrick from the tip of his toes to the top of his head. Trying to keep my focus on his face, but sneaking one last glance down his long frame, I return my heated stare to find the bastard wearing a smug grin. Oh, I'm so busted. "Why are you almost naked and lying in my bed?" I finally ask.

"Well, you took all the covers with you," he says still wearing that mesmerizing smile.

I throw him the bed sheet, but keep the comforter wrapped tightly around my body. He catches the ball of sheet in mid air and covers himself from waist down. Damn, that rock hard chest is still in view and making it difficult to think straight. What did I just ask him? Oh yeah... "Still doesn't answer why you're in *my* bed."

"You don't remember? I must be losing my touch," Patrick baits me still wearing that adorable grin.

"We didn't....I mean, you and me....No, I wouldn't." I glance under the comforter wrapped securely to my body to check again that I woke this morning with some clothes on. Yep, they are still there. I look at Patrick in confusion.

"No Suz, we didn't do anything other than sleep. Well, that and some morning cuddling. Although you act like it would be the end of the world if we had. You're hurting my feelings," Patrick pouts.

"You're engaged Patrick!" I shout. Why do I always have to keep reminding him of this?

"I'm well aware, Suz." With a frustrated sigh, Patrick sits up from his lounging position and the sheet falls down to his mid thigh. Dear Lord, help me. "Look, you asked me to stay with you, in your bed, even after I offered to sleep on the couch. You were terrified of being alone after having that nightmare. I didn't have the heart to say no to you," Patrick explains the situation. "I could never refuse you," he mummers under his breath but I hear every word anyway.

"The nightmare," I say quietly and then it all starts making sense. Flashbacks of the horrible dream from last night come back and my body starts to tremble from fear. It was the worst dream yet, going way farther than the previous ones. Wyatt never appeared in my dream and therefore wasn't around to rescue me. Somehow I managed to find the strength in my sleep to scream loudly enough for Patrick to wake me before the ultimate violation occurred. I might not appreciate his presence in my bed this morning, but I surely am glad he was here last night.

"Yeah, a nightmare. Obviously one of epic proportions. You remember now?" Patrick asks. I'm sure he doesn't need an answer as I cower against the wall turning pale and breathing heavily.

"Unfortunately," I say fright laced in my tone.

"Is this a reoccurring....." Patrick starts to ask but his speech is cut off as both our ears perk up from the opening and then slamming of the front door.

"Burrrrrrrr," I hear Flynn's over exaggerated sounds of being extremely cold.

"Did you grow a vagina last night or what? Stop acting like a girl and quit complaining. It was only a little air conditioning." Chloe chastises Flynn.

"A little air conditioning, my ass. The temp in that tiny car of yours was below freezing. Maybe if you'd dress like it's summertime instead of dressing like you're on your way to Antarctica for a ski trip, then I wouldn't complain so much." Flynn says as their voices get closer. "I swear my balls are so shriveled up they are about to disappear." This makes Patrick laugh until I shush him to be quiet. The last thing I need is for Chloe and Flynn to find us in my bedroom, both half naked.

"That's only possible if you actually had a pair," Chloe says always having to get in the last word. She's quick in her retort which makes me giggle. I try to cover my mouth with my hands in turn dropping the comforter to the floor, but it's no use. Patrick isn't bothering to conceal his laughter any longer, either. Before we can regain our silence, my bedroom door flies open and upon seeing us Chloe shrieks.

"Flynn!" she screams as her eyes dart from Patrick who is still on my bed to me leaning up against the opposite wall.

Flynn skids to an abrupt halt behind Chloe. "What's wron....Oh!" Flynn says as his eyes almost pop out of his head when he notices the unexpected guest. He looks my way with a slack jaw, but has obviously lost his ability of speech. We all just stand there in awkward silence while Chloe and Flynn continue to gape at me and Patrick. At least I get the chance to try to figure out what Flynn and Chloe were squabbling about when they arrived. Just as Flynn said Chloe is dressed for the wrong season. She wears a baggy hooded sweatshirt that hangs half way down her thighs, which are covered in a pair of sweatpants. I'm sure she realizes it must be at least ninety degrees outside by now. As Flynn shifts his gaze back and forth between me and Patrick, his arms are crossed over his chest while his hands rub up and down his biceps. He is obviously still trying to warm up from their car ride this morning. Finally, Flynn clears his throat. "Dude, you take your obligations of fulfilling a favor to a whole new level."

"I aim to please," Patrick comments not at all bothered by the fact that he was found in a somewhat compromising position.

"Well, you certainly have gone above and beyond the call of duty," Chloe adds still in a state of shock.

"I take my responsibilities very seriously. And I was gifted with a huge responsibility," Patrick say looking my way. "I would never take that lightly," he finishes with a flirtatious wink.

His behavior earns him an eye roll. I turn my attention to the two spectators still standing at the doorway of my bedroom. Working through my initial mortification, I summon the energy to give them my best death stare. "This is all your fault," I say pointing at Chloe and Flynn. Having enough of being looked at, I stumble over the comforter at my feet and walk ungracefully into the bathroom, locking the door behind me. I hear snorts of laughter at my expense.

"Job well done, man," Flynn compliments Patrick which earns him some type of physical pain from Chloe. "Ow, what was that for?" Flynn asks.

"Just go outside and warm up," Chloe commands Flynn. "And you, put some clothes on and get lost. I think your job here is done." She is obviously talking to Patrick now. I wait until I hear the bedroom door close before taking a peek from the bathroom. The coast is finally clear. I grab some clean clothes and return to the bathroom to shower and get ready for my day. At some point I'm gonna have to figure out exactly what the hell happened last night.

Chapter Sixteen

Dressed for another day of golf, I slowly make my way into the kitchen praying that Chloe and Flynn at least had the brains to make a pot of coffee. I'm sure I'm gonna be interrogated beyond reason and I can't answer any questions without some strong java coursing through my veins. I'm delighted to find the coffee pot full and hot.

"You might want to fix two cups because once you sit down, you're not going anywhere until you answer all of my questions," Chloe says taking a seat at the kitchen table. Just as I suspected, she's not wasting any time getting some answers about what she walked into this morning.

"I've got a couple of questions for you too," I say. With an expression that screams 'Oh really' Chloe raises one eyebrow. "What's with that get up?" I ask delaying her interrogation. She's still dressed like a freaking Eskimo. Just looking at her makes me almost break out into a sweat.

"I think I'm coming down with something. I must have caught your cold," she explains.

"Um, Chloe. I fabricated that story of being sick. My cold was fake."

"Well, it was still contagious," she says then abruptly changes the subject. "So why did I find a half naked Patrick in your bed this morning?"

"It's a long story," I say hoping to put her off just a few more minutes. I chug my coffee while she patiently sits and waits. "Okay, after his day of babysitting me, thanks a lot by the way, he wanted to watch the baseball game at my beach house. Ruth was visiting his dad and brought her grandchildren. Five year old twin boys that Patrick referred to as hell on Earth. Anyway, he asked if he could watch the game in peace at my house and we could share dinner. So of course I agreed. However, after an exhausting day of golf I couldn't keep my eyes open. Last thing I remember was leaving Patrick on the couch watching the game while I went to bed. Then this morning I woke up engulfed in his arms before realizing it was him and high tailing it out of bed. I was as confused as you before he told me that after hearing my blood curling screams he woke me last night and I refused to let him leave."

"Oh Suz, another nightmare?" Chloe asks. I nod. "I'm so sorry Suz. I should have been here. Same one?"

"Worse," I say. "Wyatt never rescued me so things escalated until I woke myself up screaming." Chloe lays her hand on top of mine on the table trying to soothe me. "I realized that since that last message from Wyatt, he's not coming back. Somehow that realization warped my dream into the most horrible one yet. Even though I know how things happened in reality, that dream was so vivid it seemed almost real. What if Wyatt wasn't there that night? I don't think I would have lived through it."

"But he was there, Suz. And I bet he'll continue to be there whenever you need him. Just because he left for New York and left some stupid final message, doesn't mean it's forever. I bet he thinks about you as much as you think about him. Maybe this is his way of letting you go, for now. Just until you both find your places in adult life."

"Maybe," I say, but am not as convinced as Chloe that a life with Wyatt in my future is even possible. I heard what he said and it still breaks my heart.

"But it wasn't Wyatt in your bed this morning," Chloe says steering the conversation back to Patrick.

"I know, I mean, I know that now. This is going to sound so pathetic, but in my half sleep induced brain I thought it was Wyatt in my bed with me this morning. I really did think I was dreaming, the good kind of dream for a change. I thought Wyatt had returned to me after not rescuing me in my nightmare last night. It's sick how my mind works, right?" I'm pretty disgusted with my thoughts.

"A little, yeah." Chloe holds nothing back with her brutal honesty. "So Suz, if you thought for a brief moment that you were dreaming of Wyatt...well, did anything happen? I mean, with you and Patrick?"

"Definitely not!" I respond immediately, but not with enough conviction to sway Chloe. She gives me that 'Oh really' look, again. "Just a tad bit of morning cuddling, but that's it. I swear."

"If that's it, why do you look so guilty?"

"I guess I kinda enjoyed it. I'm such a bad person. Guilty as charged. Lock me up and throw away the key," I say defeated and ready to surrender.

"So you enjoyed it. What's the big deal? Nothing to be guilty about," Chloe tries to persuade me.

"Yes, there is. I feel terrible, like by sleeping with Patrick, the platonic kind of sleeping, I somehow betrayed Wyatt."

"Last I checked, you two weren't dating. Remember, he broke up with you." Here she goes again with that honesty of hers that cuts like a knife.

"No reminder needed," I say close to tears.

"So what's the problem?" Chloe asks. Do I have to carry a flashing sign announcing to the world and my numbnut friends, Patrick included, that Patrick is engaged?

"He's engaged!" I say starting to sound like a broken record.

"Yeah, there's that. Where was Katelyn by the way?" Chloe nonchalantly asks even after finding Katelyn's fiancé in my bed this morning.

"Do you have to make me feel even worse by bringing up her name? And to think she wanted to be my friend just a few days ago. I don't have to bother wondering what she would think of our new-found friendship when she gets wind of this." No girl bonding trips with Katelyn in my future. I start to bang my head on the table, hoping the physical pain will replace my turbulent emotions.

"So she finds out Patrick stayed overnight at your place. Basically, he was helping out a friend in need. I think she would find his actions noble."

"I think you're all on crack!" I say serious as a heart attack.

Chloe busts out laughing which causes me to crack my first smile since hearing the constant bickering of Chloe and Flynn earlier this morning. When Chloe finishes her laugh attack she concludes, "Suz, she's not gonna find out unless Patrick decides to tell her. Besides, since nothing happened it's really not a big deal. And the morning cuddle, we'll just chalk that up to a friendly hug." Chloe looks off in the distance to contemplate her recent thoughts. "For your information, I trust you to make the right decision where Patrick is concerned. I know it's hard to be around him, especially alone. But you still seem to be wrapped up in your recent break up with Wyatt to let anything happen with you and Patrick. Now it's Patrick that I don't trust. I mean, I witnessed the flirting he was doing this morning. I have no doubt, had you been a willing participant, there would have been a lot more than snuggling involved this morning." I have to agree with Chloe on that. I definitely felt some serious vibes coming from Patrick this morning. Not to mention the way he looked at me like I was his favorite dessert. "Don't you think that's weird? I mean, it's not like Patrick ever had the reputation as a cheater when y'all were dating. So being engaged would make him even more straight laced. However, his actions are just the opposite."

If only Chloe knew the half of it. I think back on that kiss we shared. And his confession of still loving me, even to this day, over four years after I left him. Then last night's intimate conversation and our closeness on the couch. I remember him trying to tell me something pertaining to his engagement before Landon and Leslie showed up. Speaking of Landon...

"Hey, Landon stopped by last night," I tell Chloe.

"He did? Why?" she asks.

"He was looking for you. When he found out you weren't back yet he kinda freaked out. Oh, and he brought by some t-shirts for your work."

"Awww, that was sweet." Chloe ignores the fact that Landon was freaking out. As if our conversation has magical powers, Landon appears at the front door looking relived to see Chloe has arrived back safely.

"You're back," he says making a beeline in her direction. Chloe stands when he approaches waiting for her hug. He lightly grabs her upper arm to bring her in close. Chloe makes a sound deep in her throat, grimacing in pain. Landon immediately removes his hands from her arms and wraps her lightly in an embrace, bringing her head to bury in his chest. I watch the earlier pain that was etched in her beautiful features disappear as she relaxes in Landon's arms while he gently rubs her back. When she detects my witnessing their exchange, she pushes out of Landon's arms creating distance between them.

"Landon, I'm fine. You're so silly to worry about me." Landon is taken aback for about a half of a second before following Chloe's gaze. He realizes that they are not alone and turns to finally acknowledge my presence. "Hi, Suzanna."

"'Morning Landon." I say my greeting as I walk away from them trying to act like that strange interaction wasn't a big deal. Plus, the question and answer session I have for Chloe will have to wait. I'm due at the course soon and need to get a move on. "Sorry I can't stay and chat, but I've got to get to practice. Make yourself at home. I'm just gonna tell Flynn goodbye."

Landon places a tentative hand on Chloe's back. When she doesn't squirm away from his touch, he guides her to her bedroom. "Let's see if those uniforms fit before you have to go into work later," he tells Chloe. Chloe nods and they disappear behind her bedroom door. Something is going on between those two, I just know it. I'll make the time to find out exactly what it is later. Right now, I have to go.

I find Flynn lounging in the sun attempting to defrost. He is obviously working on his tan as well since he's ditched his shirt and wears only his shorts from earlier. "Hi, Flynn. I just wanted to tell you I'm leaving for practice. I should be home later this afternoon." I brace for the interrogation I received from Chloe earlier, but it never comes.

"Okay, Sis. I'll see you later," he says not bothering to open his eyes. I wonder if he's close to falling asleep. I guess he did get up quite early this morning to ride back with Chloe.

"See you later," I whisper not wanting to disturb him. I'm almost inside the door before Flynn's words stop me in my tracks.

"Suz, be careful. I don't want you to suffer another broken heart. You barely survived the last one." Flynn continues to lay flat, eyes shut. But I see the serious warning in his expression. Before I have time to thank him for his concern and warrant it unnecessary, he totally changes the direction of the conversation. "Where's Chloe?"

I hate to tell him that Chloe and Landon are closed up in her bedroom supposedly having a fashion show with her work shirts. As if! But I can't come up with a little white lie just off the cuff. "Um, she's in her room. With Landon. Bye." I turn to make a quick escape.

"Wait, did you just say that Landon is visiting Chloe, in her bedroom at," Flynn takes a moment to glance down at his wrist where there is no watch, "too early in the morning for a casual guest?" That sure did get him from his lounging position up on his feet standing at attention.

"Yep, that's what I said. Landon just popped in to see if you two made it back safely."

"What, so they had to go to her bedroom so he could personally inspect her for signs of bodily harm? Does he think for a minute I'd ever let anything happen to one strand of hair on Chloe's head, much less her gorgeous body?" Flynn's body is pulsing with anger. Or jealousy. Or both.

"It's not like that. He happened to be at Dead Dog last night and picked up her work attire for her. He was just making sure she got them before work. That's all."

"Whatever, Suz. You can go on being delusional that there is nothing going on between those two, but I'm not that stupid."

"Flynn," I say with compassion. I want to tell him he is way off base with his assessment of Chloe and Landon's relationship, but I can't. I don't quite understand it myself.

Flynn takes a moment to reel in his anger. "Anyway, it's none of my business. I made sure Chloe made it to Florence and back. My job is done. I think I'll work on my tan some more then go strolling on the beach for some hot babes to get into trouble with. Have fun at golf, Suz." Flynn pays me no more attention as he resumes his reclining position. He may think his words have me convinced that he doesn't care, but his actions speak volumes and I know that under his façade of being a player, he truly does have feelings for Chloe. But no time to confront him now, golf is waiting. It'll be a miracle if I make it through this summer with all the drama surrounding me. Let's just hope my game doesn't suffer.

I leave Flynn to stew in his anger/jealousy. I don't even say goodbye to Chloe or Landon. I don't want to interrupt their *fashion show*. Or whatever else they are doing behind closed doors. I bound down the fronts stairs with keys in hand. Opening my car door and throwing my purse into the passenger seat, I crank the car ready to make a speedy trip to the golf course. Glancing in my rearview mirror, ready to hit the gas, I instead slam the brakes so I don't go crashing into Patrick's jeep which has just pulled in and is blocking me in. Didn't he just leave? What in the world is he doing back so quickly, or at all? I put my car back in park, sling open the door, and jump out in a hurry. Standing beside my vehicle, which is still running, I put my hands on my hips to glare at Patrick.

"Well, don't just stand there. Come on, I've got to get you to practice," Patrick says still seated behind the steering wheel of his jeep.

"I'm more than capable to drive myself, thank you. Besides, unless Chloe or Flynn called in another favor, your work here is done."

Patrick shrugs before throwing his thumb over his shoulder. "I guess you could drive yourself, but I bet it's hard to practice without those." I look in the direction of his moving thumb to find my clubs and equipment still in the back of his jeep. "Sorry, I forgot to unload this stuff last night," he says, but doesn't sound even the tiniest bit apologetic.

I grab my purse from the inside of my car and shut off the engine, removing the keys with excessive force. I'm already short on time to get to the course and from the looks of it Patrick doesn't seem to be backing down. Why in the world he would want to cart me around all day I'll never understand. But before I concede to his demands of being my chauffeur once again, we're gonna get a few things straightened out. "Fine, you can drive me to golf again today. But let's get one thing clear. There will be no more sleepovers. At least not with me. You got it?"

"You're no fun, Suz," Patrick pouts.

"I'm serious, Patrick. If you insist on pestering me everyday from now until qualifying you have to play by my rules. Save all that cuddling for Katelyn, your-"

"Fiancée," Patrick finishes my sentence. "Yeah, I got it. Now can we just go." Patrick says nervously looking over his shoulder like someone may be following him. I hope his dad isn't out trying to track him down. After his warning at the engagement party for me to stay clear of Patrick, I'd hate for him to know how much time we have spent together since yesterday. I know first hand not to take a threat from Mr. Miles lightly. Now, I'm the nervous one.

I slide onto the passenger seat and buckle up. "Something wrong?" I ask trying to sound casual, but I'm suddenly very anxious. "Are you looking for someone?"

"Just trying to make a quick escape from the holy terrors who are probably in the process of wrecking the beach house," Patrick says referring to Ruth's grandkids. I'd be more inclined to escape the wrath of his father before two five year old boys.

"I'm starting to feel used," I say to lighten the mood. I need to get my thoughts away from Mr. Miles. Better yet, I need to stop thinking about any man with the last name Miles.

"Never," Patrick says accelerating onto the street. "Helping a friend will always come before being the punching bag to two boys whose sights are set on becoming the next WWF Tag Team Champions." I can't help but giggle. Patrick really has no desire to spend any time with those little ones. "All kidding aside, Suz, it's an honor to spend time with you."

I blush at his compliment. I feel the same way, loving every minute of the time that we have together. I feel we are making progress in our return to that bond of friendship we once shared. However, the looks, touches and kisses are going a bit too far. There's a line that doesn't need to be crossed for various reasons. Katelyn and Wyatt for starters. But is it possible for me and Patrick to revert back to just a relationship based on friendship? There's only one way to find out. "Let's go over those rules again."

It took the entire drive to the golf course for me to list my new friendship rules to Patrick. As I ticked them off one by one, he begrudgingly agreed to my conditions, as long as he could continue to drive me to and from golf each day. It's a slippery slope, being confined in the close proximity of Patrick's vehicle twice a day, but I relented and our quest to rebuild our friendship was born. Patrick dropped me off with the promise of returning in three hours to pick me up. I was only scheduled to play one round this morning, so I'd be finishing around lunchtime. Patrick insisted on buying me lunch. I didn't refuse, blaming him for my lack of breakfast this morning, forgetting to grab a granola bar. Well, I could divvy up the blame amongst Patrick, Chloe, Flynn and Landon. I figured Patrick owes me, so I'll let him pay for lunch. I'll make the others pay later.

Lunch was delicious and I found myself enjoying the conversation that easily flowed between Patrick and me. He told me all about his passion for writing. He gushed about an English professor he had his freshman year who, after reading Patrick's assignments, encouraged him to pursue a journalism degree. I heard about his time working for the college paper. He recited some of his stories about male and female college athletes. Their stories on the fields/courts were great, but the riveting parts came when Patrick revealed how they became the stars that they were today. Mostly, I enjoyed seeing the spark in Patrick's eyes when he talked about his passion for writing. Whenever the conversation turned to his future as a law student, that spark was extinguished. Patrick brushed off any conversation about law school changing the subject to focus on me.

I told Patrick of my years as a Lady Gamecock golfer. He was impressed with our multiple SEC championships, but didn't seem surprised. Later he admitted following my collegiate golf career using it as an excuse to write. Whether the writing excuse was true or not, it made me feel good that even though he had every reason to hate me for leaving him, he continued to follow my progress.

After lunch, we headed home. Patrick was happy to see Ruth's car gone from his house and his Aunt Betty's in its place. I told him how I had run into Aunt Betty when I first arrived at the beach. He begged me to let us stop by for a visit but I refused. It's not that I didn't want to see Aunt Betty again. She was more than welcome to come to my house for a visit. However, the fact that I might have to come face to face with Patrick's dad made me shudder. Sensing my uneasiness, Patrick dropped the subject and drove me home. While Patrick unloaded my golf gear into the back of my car (I guess he didn't need to hold them hostage since our agreement earlier) I got my purse and other belongings. "So what are you gonna do the rest of the day?" Patrick asks, climbing back into his vehicle.

"I guess I'll spend some time with Chloe before she takes off for work. Then maybe hang out with Flynn."

"You mean Flynn and his guest," Patrick says looking through his windshield toward the dock on the inlet. Sure enough, there was Flynn tangled up in the arms of some bikini clad playmate. I could hear her giggles travel across the yard while Flynn's head was buried in her neck. "Looks like Flynn will be too occupied with his company to hang out with his sister."

"So it appears," I say tearing my eyes off the unabashed PDA happening in broad daylight. "Guess maybe I'll go for a run later. I've been neglecting my cardio routine."

"Want some company? I could use the exercise myself," Patrick asks. I'm about to tell him no, but remember what strides we are making in our friendship. Besides, it's just a run. There's nothing even remotely romantic about that.

"Sure, but let's wait until it cools off a little and the tide goes out. I'd like to run the beach today." At least we have less of a chance of Patrick's dad spotting us running together if we take the beach instead of the sidewalk.

"Sounds like a plan. I'll see you about six?" he questions.

"It's a date...no, not a date. It's just a run. I just meant...."

"I know what you mean, Suz. See you at six. 'Bye," Patrick says and reverses out of my driveway. I walk upstairs trying to untie my tongue. I need to talk with Chloe anyway.

As soon as I walk through the door, Chloe appears from her bedroom with a towel wrapped around her head and her work uniform on. Well, her work t-shirt that she wears over a tight long sleeved undershirt. "Don't you think you're gonna be hot in that?"

"Don't be silly, Suz. I'm planning to dry and fix my hair before I leave for work," Chloe says dryly.

"Not the towel, stupid. The long sleeved shirt you're sporting."

"Oh, yeah, well the restaurant and bar blast the AC. I don't want to get chilly. You know, since I've got this cold," Chloe says avoiding eye contact.

"That's right, the fake cold you've come down with. How could I forget?" I reply sarcastically. "Okay, Chloe. What in the hell is going on with you and Land_"

"Who the hell is that?" Chloe interrupts staring out the kitchen window at the back of the house. No doubt she's spotted Flynn and his new friend.

"Flynn's entertainment for the afternoon, I assume." I watch Chloe's expression change from anger to hurt. Walking over to join Chloe, we watch as Flynn licks an unidentifiable substance off the flat stomach of his recent conquest while she laughs with delight. This is hard for me to watch, so I know it must be killing Chloe. I make to put my arm around Chloe's shoulder in consolation but she steps out of my reach before making contact. "Chloe...."

"I've got to finish getting ready for work. I'll talk to you later, Suz." Chloe closes herself in her bedroom ending our conversation. I guess I'll have to wait until another day for any answers pertaining to her and Landon's relationship. I just hope Flynn has the decency to keep his company entertained on the deck, at least until Chloe leaves. Come to think of it, I'd rather they stay outside myself. The last thing I need to listen to this afternoon is the sounds of pleasure from my brother and his plaything. I go to my room to change into my running clothes and wish time away. I can't wait until six o'clock gets here so I can escape the drama of this house and be with Patrick again. *Boundaries, boundaries, boundaries*...I have to keep reminding myself.

Chapter Seventeen

I wake the next morning to the sound of my cell phone ringing. Reaching over to grab it I grimace in pain. My muscles are so sore from my run yesterday afternoon with Patrick. Too proud to let Patrick know that I usually max out my runs at three miles, I tried keeping up as Patrick guided us at least more than five down the beach. The man has some serious cardio stamina. I bet his impressive stamina extends beyond just running. *Stop it Suzanna! Stop being a naughty girl and get your mind out of the gutter!* says my internal angelic voice. But the devil inside me urges my memories of Patrick's long strides and sweaty body as we ran together yesterday. As if running didn't make it hard to breathe, his presence exacerbated that fact. I definitely got my heart rate up. Shaking the naughty images and thoughts out of my head, I answer the call of an unrecognized number.

"Hello," I say groggily.

"Hi Suzanna, it's Katelyn." And that's why I didn't recognize the number. "I hope I didn't wake you."

"No," I lie and can't think of anything else to say. Well, that and the fact that I'm consumed with guilt at spending a lot of time with her fiancé while she's been out of town.

"So, I'm almost back in town and was thinking since you didn't have golf scheduled for today that maybe we could hang out," Katelyn initiates the conversation sounding hopeful.

"Um, wait, how did you know I wasn't playing today?" I ask slowly waking up.

"Patrick, of course. He told me how he's been taking you to golf each day. He said he didn't think you had plans to practice this weekend. Unless, you've changed your mind."

Are you freaking kidding me? She knows about Patrick's newly acquired non-paying job of chauffeuring me back and forth to the golf course. And from the sounds of it, she doesn't seem to mind. I'll never understand the dynamic between those two. Just add them to the other couples who totally confuse the hell out of me.

"No, I usually don't play on Saturdays because the course gets too crowded and I feel too rushed. It normally turns into a wasted attempt anyway."

"Well, you want to hang out? We can hang on the beach or go shopping or whatever," Katelyn suggests.

"Definitely beach. I'm not really the shopping kind of girl." Chloe has dragged me, usually kicking and screaming, numerous times to try to update my non-sexy athletic wardrobe with no real success. It's finally soaked through Chloe's head that it's more productive to go without me and just bring home things for me to try. She's done a great job so far. Maybe I'll hire her as my personal shopper once I hit the big time tour.

"Whew, you don't know how much I need to just chill out with a friend!" Katelyn sounds so relieved while I continue to drown in guilt. If she only knew some of the things that have transpired between me and Patrick, I'm sure her use of the word friend would be retracted. "These few days away with my mother have been horrible."

"Horrible? I thought Patrick said you two were meeting with the wedding planner. How can planning the most magical day of your life be horrible?" I ask seriously.

"Horribly overwhelming, I mean. Too many decisions to make. I would just let my mother make all the arrangements, but you've seen her choice in bridesmaid dresses. I don't want to even imagine her choices for the entire wedding and reception without my input." Katelyn talks a mile a minute rushing her explanation. Although the numerous decision making does sound like a tedious chore, I don't hear one thread of enthusiasm when Katelyn mentions getting married.

"So I'll see you in a couple of hours then, right?" Katelyn asks diverting the subject from her upcoming nuptials. The sound of a car horn distracts me from answering. Who the heck would be at my house on a Saturday morning honking a horn? "Suz, you still there?"

"Um, yeah, couple of hours sounds good. Listen, someone is in my driveway. I gotta go."

I end the call without a proper goodbye and toss it on my bed. As if timed by the gods, all three bedroom doors open to the living area simultaneously. "You'll call me?" Flynn's overnight guest asks in a pleading voice.

"I don't think so, hun. I told you I'd be going out of the country soon, so there's really no point," Flynn says as he pushes her toward the front door. The sound of a horn blares again.

"But we had so much fun last night," the nameless girl whines.

"And you'll just have to hold onto that memory. Your ride is waiting, so you need to run along. I bet your family will soon be checking out of their vacation home and are anxious for you to return." I walk to the window and look down to see a taxi in our driveway with the meter running.

Flynn walks his no-strings-attached lady friend to the door. "Just one more kiss to remember me?" she asks inching closer to Flynn's face for contact. He gives her a soft peck on the forehead before shutting the door.

"Who was that?" I ask.

"Brandi, no. Barbi. Wait, it's Barbara. Yeah, that's right, Barbara."

"You don't even know her name?" I'm shocked. I mean I knew Flynn had a reputation, but this is ridiculous.

"Don't act so surprised, Suz. Just go get your brother a knife," Chloe speaks from her bedroom door.

"A knife?" Flynn and I repeat back her words.

"He'll need it to carve the latest notch on his bedpost." Chloe reenters her room and slams the door.

Flynn takes off after her yelling, "How's it any business of yours?" I grab his arm and pull him to a stop before he barges into Chloe's bedroom to give her a piece of his mind.

"Flynn, don't!" I beg pulling him away from the door.

"You women, you're all infuriating." He pulls out of my grasp and goes back to his bedroom. I'm left alone in the living room to endure another ear splitting door slam. I love my brother, but I wish his departure for Europe would just hurry up and get here. This love feud he and Chloe have going on is grating on my nerves. I'm almost looking forward to spending some time with Katelyn and getting away from the crazy that resides in this house.

Katelyn arrived exactly two hours to the second after her phone call. I used the time to shower, shave, pluck, exfoliate, and all the other things a woman has to do before baring most of her body in a swimsuit. It's not like I had anything else to do. Flynn and Chloe stayed locked in their respective home territories the entire morning. When I heard Katelyn's car pull into the driveway, I grabbed my beach bag to meet her outside. God forbid she come inside and Flynn and Chloe make an appearance just to get into another shouting match. I watch Katelyn exit her vehicle and I think to myself, instead of all the self pampering I did earlier, I should have called in a plastic surgeon. It's really unfair for me to have to lay out beside this girl on the beach all day! I mean, does she possess a body flaw? I examine her closely, watching her long, toned legs stretch the length of her daisy duke cut off jean shorts. Her top half is covered, well barely covered, in a crocheted white tank top. Through the delicate holes of her shirt I can see the canary yellow string bikini top she is sporting today. Let's just say, the girl will have minimal tan lines.

I glance down at my own sunbathing attire and feel very inadequate. I chose my bandeau bikini top because I wanted no strap marks, but I second guess my decision. This top, although a vivid shade of aqua blue, flattens my chest, making me look like a fifth grade school girl. I'm already petite in overall size, only reaching Katelyn's shoulder in height, so I don't need a clothing choice to hide the little bit of curves I possess. I turn to sneak back into the house to change into my pushup bra top...yeah, I need all the help I can get. But before I can make it inside Katelyn spots me and calls for my attention.

"Hey Suzanna. Great, you're ready. I can't wait for a relaxing day on the beach," she says full of excitement. I wish some of that excitement would rub off on me. Well, who am I to keep her waiting? I've agreed to spend time with my ex-love's current fiancée. Add that to my insecurity about my body image next to her gorgeous physique and basically I'm screwed.

I put a smile on my face and turn around to greet her with perfect southern charm. "Katelyn, I'm so glad we can hang out today. Let's grab our chairs and stake our claim to a great spot on the beach." I wrangle two beach chairs from the storage closet while Katelyn takes our beach bags and cooler. We set out across the street for a day of fun in the sun. Thinking positive here!

Actually, the day is going better than expected. Of course, when we first got situated in our lounging positions, I ignored her comment of how cute, yes *cute*, my bathing suit was. I know she was just being complimentary, but coming from the girl who could take the cover of the *Sports Illustrated* swimsuit edition, cute was kinda hard to swallow. We spent most of the morning watching a group of toddlers play in one of the tide pools. They were adorable and very entertaining. Then we had a great laugh at the expense of a tourist who spent most of his time trying to secure an umbrella that kept falling over with the slightest gust of wind. We finally felt so sorry for the guy we decided to aid him during his twelfth attempt. Being both products of coastal living, Katelyn and I knew just what was needed to get that pesky umbrella to stay put. With much appreciation, and a few creepy glances at both me and Katelyn, the guy finally settled in to enjoy the beach with some shade.

I was prepared to head back across the street for lunch, but Katelyn informed me that she packed both lunch and snacks. When she handed me a sandwich, wrapped in wax paper and tied with twine, I assumed she had purchased lunch from a gourmet deli. Come to find out, Katelyn's maid/cook made the sandwiches as well as a fruit and cheese tray and homemade brownies for dessert. I was about to make a snide comment about having a live in staff at her disposable, but instead, I stuffed my mouth with a bite of the most delicious sandwich I had ever tasted. It was like an explosion of flavor in my mouth. Succulent chicken mixed with grapes and pecans and tossed in an herb and spice dressing, all layered with lettuce and tomato on thick slices of sourdough bread. It was scrumptious. I swear I'd scrape together my life savings to hire the woman who made this sandwich. Katelyn spoke fondly of Wanda, the live in maid and cook, who has been working for the Bostick family at their coastal home for years. And the list continues to grow of all the things I hate about Katelyn. Well, I don't really hate her. Maybe I'm just a tad bit jealous. Really, does she have to be sweet, beautiful and filthy rich enough to have hired help at her family's vacation home? Not to mention I keep getting blinded when the sun bounces off the radiant, huge diamond on her finger. It's a constant reminder that she is engaged to Patrick. My Patrick. Because I had him first. Before I become even more bitter, I excuse myself after lunch for a quick dip in the ocean. I need to cool off my body temperature as well as my raging jealousy.

When I return from my quick swim, Katelyn is fully reclined, ear buds in and eyes closed. I quietly settle in my chair next to her and pull out the latest Hollywood gossip rag. I want to immerse myself in the drama of famous people and not dwell on mine for a change. Plus, the lack of conversation is perfectly timed. Not that our time together has been strange. Actually, our conversations all morning have been relaxed and fun, not at all awkward or heavy like I thought they might turn out to be.

I'm halfway through my magazine, reading about the recent drug rehabilitation center a rising starlet just enrolled in, when I hear the melodic sound of someone singing. I look around to try and spot the chart topping recording voice that may be vacationing in South Carolina's coastal region. I swear it sounds just like a voice on the radio. When I don't spy anyone famous, I look over at Katelyn, still fully reclined singing her heart out to the song playing on her iPod. She still has her eyes closed so she doesn't see me gawking at her talent. This girl is just too good to be true. No wonder Patrick wants to marry her. Who wouldn't? I don't understand why she's sitting on a beach with me and isn't living the life in LA as an award winning solo artist. Katelyn must sense that she is being watched and opens one eyelid to find me staring at her in disbelief.

"What?" she asks. "Do I have something on my face?" she says while wiping her cheeks with her hands.

"You sing," I state.

"Oh, did I get too loud. It's hard to judge when I have my ear buds in and sometimes I get a little carried away, especially when listening to Rihanna and Pink. Damn, those girls can belt 'em out!"

"Um, so can you! I didn't know you could sing like that. You mentioned majoring in music. I just thought you played the piano or something. But, that voice. You sound like you could be on the radio."

"Awww, thanks Suz. But I think you're just being kind." Katelyn looks away almost embarrassed at her raw talent.

"I'm serious, you sound incredible. Have you ever sung for an audience?"

"I sang in a band back in high school and college. But it was really more of a hobby. I never wanted to make it a career," Katelyn says, but I hear the sound of loss in her voice. With a voice like hers, coupled with that body and face, she would be a music agent's and recording label's gold mine. And I don't believe for a minute she never considered a career in music. Hell, she even graduated with a major in the subject. "That's all in my past now. I'll focus on teaching music to elementary kids and hopefully hone their talents."

"Well, that would definitely be a missed opportunity for you. Plus, the world would certainly be missing out if they couldn't hear your angelic voice on the radio. You sure you don't want to pursue a singing career?"

"Yes, I'm sure. I'm happy with my life now." Katelyn avoids eye contact and focuses on the crashing waves of the ocean. When she finally thinks I'm convinced that she hasn't dreamed of becoming the next big thing in music, she glances my way seeing the magazine I'm still holding open. "Anything juicy in that issue?" she asks pointing to the open page.

I'm sensing Katelyn is very uncomfortable talking about her singing abilities. So I indulge her subject change and give her all the details of the happenings in Hollywood. Our conversation flows easily the rest of the day. Before long, it's time to head back to the house to shower. Tonight the entire gang is meeting up at Dead Dog Saloon to hear my caddy and friend, Drew, do an acoustic set during happy hour. Katelyn throws her beach bag and cooler in the back of her Mercedes sports coupe. Then she retrieves another bag from the trunk.

"Suzanna, I took the liberty of bringing my things to get ready at your place to go out tonight. Is that okay? I guess I should have checked with you first, but I didn't want to drive all the way back down south, just to turn around and drive here again."

"Katelyn, of course that's fine if you want to shower and get ready here. Go on up and make yourself at home. You are welcome to use my private bathroom to shower and my bedroom to change."

"Oh, thank you!" Katelyn squeals and starts emptying her trunk. I'm almost afraid to ask if she is moving in. That's a lot of outfits for just one night of going out. But then I remember when Chloe first arrived this summer, carrying enough clothes and accessories to last a lifetime. I'm sure Katelyn is prepared to change her outfit should the notion strike.

"No problem, just go on up while I hose off the sand on these chairs before I stick them back in the storage closet." I watch Katelyn skip up the stairs and walk into the house, just as happy as a lark. Speaking of happy, I wonder if Chloe's and Flynn's moods have improved. I'll have to wait to ask Chloe tonight, seeing as she has already left for work. I have no idea where Flynn is. I wash the chairs and start to put them away when I hear the deep breathing of my four-legged neighbor.

"Hello there, Darth Vader," I greet and giggle when the dog actually responds to his nickname. "What are you doing over here without your sidekick?" It's rare that you see Mrs. Stokes and Darth Vader without each other. As if I actually expect the dog to reply, I stand and wait. His only response is to come and drop a puddle of drool at my feet.

"Ugh, gross Darth. Come on, let's get you a treat," I say hoping my words register in her doggy brain. Yep, works every time. Darth Vader picks up her head and walks at an upbeat pace, which is that of a turtle, toward the downstairs apartment door. Mom and Dad always spoil this dog rotten, keeping dog treats in the apartment kitchenette. I open the door and follow the dog inside. I'm rummaging around the cabinets to find where Mom placed the treats when Darth Vader starts growling like a madman.

"Hold your horses, dog. I'm trying to find those doggie biscuits you like." Darth Vader continues to growl menacingly. Eventually, her growls turn into a full on bark. I turn around to reprimand the dog, but my words get lost in my throat. Standing in the doorway, blocking my passage of escape, is Patrick's dad, Jim. He's holding a golf club in one hand and a plastic bag in the other. He doesn't seem the slightest bit phased by Darth's aggressive barking. Instead he looks almost amused by the overweight, sluggish mutt trying to warn and protect me. I cower back against the counter tops to brace my trembling body. Jim makes a slow swing in front of his body with the club which has Darth Vader's barking transitioning to a whine. The dog slips behind my legs to hide. "Useless animal," I mutter.

"I have a feeling this belongs to you," Jim says still swinging the club with rhythm. "I just can't imagine how in the world it landed in the back of Patrick's jeep."

Oh no. I examine the club and sure enough, it belongs to me. It must have fallen out of my golf bag on our way home from practice yesterday. Now, Jim obviously knows that I've been spending time with Patrick. His threat from the engagement party rings in my ears. *Stay away from Patrick.* His demand was followed up with the warning of spilling my secrets, with an embellishment to make it look much worse for me. I don't acknowledge Jim because I can't. Fear has paralyzed my throat making it hard to breathe, much less talk.

"I come all this way to return your precious equipment just to find you cozying up to Katelyn. Isn't that her car parked out front?" Jim walks a step into the room and suddenly the air grows thick. I'm trying to concentrate on not hyperventilating, but I'm having a hard time as my body shakes with terror. "Tsk, Tsk," Jim says pointing a finger in my direction. "I'm not sure what your game is, Suzanna, but I need to remind you that should something go wrong with Patrick's and Katelyn's engagement, you will be held accountable. Do I need to help you recall the details of that December night some four years ago? Let's just say you'll look less like the good girl golfer and more like a high school whore who has an infatuation with much older men."

I gasp, not only because I need a gulp of much needed air, but also because of the ruthless lengths this man will go to make sure I'm completely out of Patrick's life. I watch as Jim tilts his head giving me the 'you-don't-want-to-test-me' look. I inch farther back into the cabinet door and countertops, almost stepping on Darth Vader's head. "Are you scared, Suzanna?" Jim has the gall to ask. "Take my advice. Stay away from Patrick and Katelyn. I don't need you worming your way back into his life and ruining all I have planned for him." Jim throws the club toward me where it lands with a rattling pang on the tile floor, causing me to jump and Darth Vader to bark.

"Raquel, where are you, Raquel?" I hear Mrs. Stokes' smoky rasp calling her dog. The sound has never been sweeter. Jim hears her too and changes his authoritative stance to one more casual.

"Mrs. Stokes," I call out, but it barely comes out as a whisper. Jim laughs at my attempt, knowing he has scared the bejesus out of me. I'm sure it pleases his psychotic self to see me so frightened. Plus, he probably believes his devious antics have worked and I'm gonna sever all ties with Patrick and Katelyn. Well, think again you cowardly bastard who takes pleasure preying on an innocent young lady. "Mrs. Stokes," I try again and luckily sound louder. I just hope it carries outside this room and she finds us soon.

"Jim?" Mrs. Stokes questions when she spots him in the doorway of the downstairs apartment. I sag against the counter in relief that I have been found. At the sound of Mrs. Stokes' voice, Darth Vader rises on his squatty legs and starts wagging his tail.

"Sylvia, it's always a pleasure to see you," Jim gushes with charm. "I was just dropping off some shrimp Patrick and I caught this morning. I thought Carol and Alan would be here, but I got extra lucky and ran into Suzanna." This guy has the Jekyll and Hyde act perfected. Too bad he's trying to use it on the bullshitter of all bullshitters, Mrs. Stokes. She can smell trouble from a mile away.

Mrs. Stokes ignores Jim's greeting pushing him out of the way to enter the crowded room. "Suzanna, are you okay? You look like you've seen a ghost!" Mrs. Stokes takes in my pale appearance and erratic breathing and knows something is wrong.

"She's fine, just a little flustered at not being able to find your dog the treat she promised. Poor thing...the dog has been whining since I arrived," Jim says playing on the affection Mrs. Stokes has for her pet. Sensing she's being used, Darth Vader leaves her hiding place behind my legs and prances to stand in front of Mrs. Stokes. She bares her teeth and lets out a deep growl aimed at Jim. My protector has returned.

Mrs. Stokes picks up the golf club and walks to the doorway, swinging it like Jim was earlier. "I'm sure Carol and Alan will appreciate the fresh shrimp. Now, Suz and I were just about to leave to take this bundle of preciousness," she pauses to point the club at Darth Vader before bringing it back between her and Jim's bodies, "to the vet. Suzanna will be sure to tell her parents you stopped by. Goodbye, Jim." Mrs. Stokes takes a step forward causing Jim to take a step back, out of the doorway. Mrs. Stokes shuts the door leaving us inside. The strength I maintained during his unannounced visit drains from my body and I slump to the ground.

"Mind telling me what that hell that was all about?" Mrs. Stokes asks lighting up a cigarette. My mom would kill me if she knew I let someone smoke inside the house. But I'm gonna give Mrs. Stokes a pass today for saving me from a potential disaster. "And before you try to say nothing, just know who you are talking to."

Okay, so no need to hide everything from Mrs. Stokes. She has just witnessed an almost meltdown at the hands of Jim's surprise visit. So I make a decision to spill my guts about everything that happened all those years ago that lead me to complete my senior year of high school at the beach. Once I finish the horrific story, I continue to tell her about the engagement party, the intimate moments with Patrick, the bonding time with Katelyn, and the ever present heartbreak I still feel for Wyatt. My mouth is like a broken faucet that won't turn off. After I finish with all the dramatic details of my life, Mrs. Stokes has almost finished an entire pack of cigarettes. We sit in a haze of smoke while she silently contemplates everything she just learned of what she once thought of as the boring golfer girl living next door.

"Well, I'll be. This is better than an episode of *Days of Our Lives,*" she finally says with a light chuckle. When I don't laugh at her light hearted joke she turns serious. "Sorry Suz, that was distasteful. I'm just trying to come to terms with all you've been through."

"Yeah, well, it's been a lot to deal with. Just promise me you won't say anything to my parents. They don't know."

"I won't. But it may be a good idea to tell them. I don't think they are very close with Jim, but they still run in the same social circles. I'd hate to know I was associated with the enemy who tried to do vile things to my daughter." Mrs. Stokes pauses a moment before lighting another smoke. "You know, I never liked that man. Not even when Marie was alive. God bless her soul. She was a saint to put up with his drinking."

"Wait, I didn't think his drinking was a problem until after Marie died."

"Well, I guess he didn't see it as a problem. But I'm sure Marie saw the amounts of alcohol he consumed during social settings. I'm not sure how he was at home, but he was always drunk by the time he left a party. Plus, he was just a slime ball. I never got the feeling he was ever being sincere. He came across as working every angle when talking to you, looking for that next big case or trying to get your legal business. I sure hope Patrick doesn't follow in his father's footsteps in his career as an attorney," Mrs. Stokes says between puffs. "He's way too good a person, inheriting his mother's qualities, to stoop to Jim's sleazy standards."

"I'm not even sure Patrick wants a legal career," I say, but then wish I could take it back. Patrick closed the lid to any conversation about that subject. He sure as heck doesn't need nosy Mrs. Stokes questioning him about his decision.

"Um, interesting. But let's talk about this problem you have with Jim. Are you gonna let him push you around, even after all these years?"

"I, I don't know. It's not like I have much of a choice." I sound defeated even to my own ears.

"Nonsense! You are a grown adult and you don't have to put up with his empty threats. You continue to surround yourself with friends, including Patrick and Katelyn. That man has already taken so much from you. Don't you dare let him take away anything else!"

"But what if..."

"He's not gonna do anything to you unless you're alone. And the coward that he is, he'll just probably continue to scare you into submission. You are not alone...you have Chloe and Flynn. You have James and Landon when they're around. Your parents will be visiting often. And it looks like you have Patrick at your beck and call. Not to mention the new friendship you've established with the fiancée. Which by the way, what's that all about?"

"She's nice?" I say as more a question than a statement.

"Whatever. We'll get to that later. Right now, focus on your relationships and surround yourself with friends. And Suz, don't forget, you always have me. I love you, like the daughter I never could have." Mrs. Stokes gives me a hug hiding her watering eyes from my view. I hug her back fiercely and realize how thankful I am to have this strong independent woman in my life. Having enough of the mushy, gushy display of affection, Mrs. Stokes pulls out of the hug. "Plus, I'm a legal card carrying member of the NRA. I got the licenses to several guns, all loaded and ready. That bastard comes back messing with my girl and he'll have the end of a shotgun barrel pressed right between his beady, ugly eyes," Mrs. Stokes promises.

"Good to know... I think." Oh my, just what my drama filled life needs. My elderly neighbor patrolling locked and loaded.

Mrs. Stokes finally leaves, only after Darth Vader gorges himself on half a box of dog biscuits. Upstairs, inside the house, I find Katelyn trying to decide on what to wear. Flynn is still locked in his room. I'm starting to worry that maybe Chloe snuck in there and killed him. I might need to go check. But before I can, Katelyn pulls me into my bedroom to seek my opinion on her clothing options. "Katelyn, I'm really not the best person to ask. Chloe is the fashion expert."

"Just choose something. I just want to fit in with you all," Katelyn says mirroring the insecurity I felt when I first saw her this morning. What a bunch a girls we are! Each one trying to please the other.

"Katelyn, it doesn't matter what you wear, how you fix your hair, what kind of makeup you use. All that matters is that you continue to be sweet and kind and you'll fit in just fine." Just to give her a little extra assurance I add, "But if I had to make a choice, I really like that strapless number over there."

"That's my favorite too," Katelyn says through a smile. "What time are we leaving?"

I'm sure she is concerned that I've yet to take a shower. "My friend goes on at six, but I'd like to get there early to get a table up close." I look at my cell phone for the time. Wow, it's already after four. I need to get ready in a hurry. "Katelyn, could you call Patrick and see if he'll pick us up. Also, go pound on Flynn's door. If he's riding with us, he better crawl out from his hiding place."

"Huh?" Katelyn looks confused.

"Just make sure he's awake. I'm gonna jump in the shower," I say as I toss my phone on the bedside table. I'm in such a rush I choose to ignore the flashing signal alerting me of a message. If it's that important, whoever it is will call back.

Chapter Eighteen

The bar is packed, as usual on a Saturday evening. It's mostly occupied with locals and the frequent weekenders, seeing as the tourists are just arriving and settling into their vacation homes for a week. Unfortunately, we were not able to secure a table close to the stage. We had to settle for one back toward the bar, but close enough to a speaker so we could still hear Drew sing. Plus, we were close by to Chloe who barely had enough time to acknowledge our arrival since she was busy filling drink orders. Hopefully, she'll get a break at some point and come join us for a few minutes. Patrick picked up me, Katelyn and Flynn at the house earlier. When we drove by his house, I had the urge to slump down in the seat just in case his father was watching us from the porch. But I suppressed that urge and stood tall. As scary as it may be, I have to agree with Mrs. Stokes. I'm a grown woman and I'm sick of being bullied by a drunk criminal. I pray I'm not taking his threats too lightly. I'd die if he followed through and told the secrets of that night. Of course his version would be completely untrue, but it would lead to some major questions that I'm not ready to answer.

Patrick orders the first round just as Landon arrives, thankfully alone. I guess Leslie didn't get that invite after all. That, or her family's vacation has come to an end and she's headed back home. I hope it's the first option and Landon has finally cut loose from a relationship that was already one-sided. Drew appears on stage as we all stretch in our seats for a view. He seems so relaxed in front of the big crowd. After an introduction, he goes straight to the music, playing classics from James Taylor to Journey to

Eric Clapton. The crowd sings along to the lyrics, most knowing them by heart. Drew's smooth voice carries over the crowd and through the speakers. He is really good. Not as good as Katelyn on the beach today, but he can hold his own. The bar patrons banter back and forth with him between songs while he entertains with his personality. He takes requests and encourages his fans to accompany him on the dance floor. When he belts out some beach music, the dance floor becomes a blur of bodies doing the shag, the state dance of South Carolina. Flynn pulls me up from my seat and pushes me on the dance floor so we can join the fun. If you live in South Carolina, you better know how to shag, or at least be able to fake the basic eight step dance. Flynn and I learned at an early age, watching my parents for years. Plus, we were both forced to take cotillion classes each year from fifth grade through middle school. And it wouldn't be a successful cotillion class without proper shag lessons.

After cutting the rug for a few songs, we make it back to our table to find our pitchers of beer empty. Well crap, I'd really worked up a thirst. I grab an empty while Flynn grabs the other and we walk up to the bar to try and flag down Chloe. It takes us a good five minutes to get right up to the bar for service. Flynn leans down to talk in my ear over the bar crowd. "I know I've got a fine ass, but you grabbing it is kinda bordering on incest."

"Gross Flynn, I'm not grabbing your ass! You are a pompous jerk!"

"But you love me," Flynn says with a grin.

"You're my brother. I have to," I say and grin back. I look around to find the culprit of Flynn's ass grabbing. "Callie! Stop feeling up my brother!" Callie has somehow managed to conspicuously maneuver her blinged out electric wheelchair on the other side of Flynn.

"Cool it, Suz. I just needed something to grab onto to hoist myself up so someone would serve me a cold beverage. What does it take to get a drink in this place?"

"Glad to be of service, Callie," Flynn says and then gives her his signature wink. "If you need something a little longer, but just as sturdy_"

"Don't encourage her Flynn. She'll take you up on that offer." Flynn collapses against the bar in laugher while Callie giggles. I roll my eyes at them both.

"Yo, blondie. You think I might could get a drink any time this century?" Callie yells as Chloe walks by with a tray of freshly made cocktails. She hands the tray off to a waitress before turning blazing eyes in our direction.

Both Flynn and I hold up our hands and lean back slightly. Simultaneously our gazes shift sideways and down alerting Chloe to her offender. Chloe strides up to the bar, leans over, giving Flynn an unobstructed view of her cleavage. Not bothering to watch Flynn drool, Chloe goes straight to business with Callie. "You think just because you ride in here encased in some tacky, fake jewels and sporting that obnoxious hair color, you're gonna get a drink before the men and women who have been waiting patiently down there. I mean, you've got the whole crippled thing going for you, but your attitude sucks. Wait. Your. Turn!"

"Damn that was hot!" Flynn says while I gasp in shock. While Flynn continues to ogle Chloe from across the bar, I push him aside to check on Callie. Had anyone talked to me that way, I'd be in a puddle of tears. But Callie seems amused by the whole thing.

"Callie, I'm so sorry. Chloe's probably just stressed out with this new job. And it's so busy and_"

"Wait, you know that bitch?" Callie asks.

"Um, yeah. See, that's Chloe. She's my, well, Chloe's my best friend." I can't believe I'm embarrassed to say that. But after those rude comments, especially the crippled reference...is crippled even the socially acceptable term to use?

"I like that girl," Callie says shocking me even more.

"*What?*"

"She's got some spunk. It takes guts to put a girl like me in my place. I can't wait to get to know her." Callie laughs off the incident like Chloe just did a stand up routine, not told her off.

We wait a few minutes longer, then Chloe finally comes to take our order. "Okay, folks what's your pleasure?"

"Why don't you find out during your next break?" Flynn says full of sexual innuendo.

"Yeah, like that's gonna happen. Does it look like I'll get a break tonight?"

"I'll wait 'til you get off," Flynn offers.

"Hey, enough with the flirting. I'm thirsty," I say breaking up the love fest. "Here, fill these up with Blue Moon. Callie, what do you want?"

"Hi, I'm Callie. I know Suzanna from the golf course where she practices. And Drew," she gestures toward the stage, "he's my brother. Sorry about earlier."

"Yeah, me too," Chloe says in agreement. "So, what are you having?"

"Give me a vodka water with a slice of lime, light on the water."

"You got it." Chloe goes off to fix our drinks. I invite Callie to join us at the table. She agrees, but only until the next band comes on. She really has the hots for the lead singer and wants to get as up close and personal as her wheelchair will allow.

"Here you go," Chloe says as she brings back our drinks. Flynn and I grab a pitcher each and start to walk away. Chloe leans over the bar to hand Callie her drink. I overhear her say, "I'll put this one on Flynn's tab as long as you keep your hands off his ass."

Callie cackles with laughter drawing the attention of half the bar. "It's a deal, blondie."

Callie joins our table and the party goes into full swing. After I introduce her to everyone, Callie makes herself right at home, like she's been friends with us forever. During the introductions, Callie took an intense interest in Katelyn. She swore they had met before. But Katelyn assured her that she'd certainly remember a character as lively as Callie had they met in the past. However, that didn't stop Callie's interrogation, bombarding Katelyn with questions about where she was from, where she went to college, who she dated, etc. This only made Katelyn more jittery than she had been most of the night. Which was the complete opposite of Katelyn's behavior during our day together. Katelyn skirted most questions with vague answers to pacify Callie. I did find it strange that she said she was from Pawleys Island, when I knew she grew up in Greenville. Even odder, when she described her beach house in one of our earlier conversations, she alluded to the fact that it was far from a home. Much more a showplace her parents used to entertain guests. But between the joking around and trying to listen to Drew's last set, I found it impossible to dwell on Katelyn's reasoning for her little white lie.

Callie also found Landon entertaining. Of course, she didn't refer to Landon as Landon, always having the need to give everyone her very own nickname. Thus Landon became "Big Guy". While Landon listened to the music, he constantly was thumping a beat on the table or strumming an imaginary guitar mimicking the notes Drew was playing live. Callie was relentless is her teasing, telling Landon that he needed to uncage the rock god underneath all those hard muscles. She even offered to help, starting with the shedding of his clothes. Good natured Landon took Callie's suggestive comments by laughing along with everyone else. The only person not laughing was Katelyn. She seemed mesmerized with Landon's silent musical movements. I knew Landon may have inherited some musical genes. His mother could have been a concert pianist before marrying Mr. Smith and raising a family. Mrs. Smith was the go to music teacher in Florence if you wanted your child to learn to play piano. But I had never heard Landon play a musical instrument in my life, since he spent the majority of his time on the football field or the golf course.

Once Drew strummed the last note and bid farewell to his audience, he came to join us at our table. I immediately drew him into a hug, congratulating him on a job well done. "Drew, you were amazing!"

"Thanks, but the real treat is coming on in about an hour. Y'all gonna stick around to hear my buddies play?" Drew asks shying away from all the attention.

"Of course. Hey, let me reintroduce you to everyone." I go around the table reminding Drew of my friends which he met while giving me my first paddle board lesson.

"Hey Drew, I've got a cold one waiting for you at the bar," Chloe yells over the crowd.

"And you remember Chloe." Drew nods and tries to walk away, but I want to finish my introductions before he gets swallowed by the crowd. "Hold up, just a few more. That's Patrick, who you met and his lovely fiancée hey, where's Katelyn?" She was just there a few minutes ago sitting back in her corner seat like she has been doing all night.

"I think she went to the bathroom," Patrick says then directs his attention back to Drew. "Good to see you again. I enjoyed your performance." Although Patrick's words sound sincere, he keeps looking down at where I still have a firm hold on Drew's arm. I can't read his facial expression, but his demeanor tells me he doesn't like the fact that I'm touching another man. I slowly release Drew and watch Patrick relax back in his seat. I'll never understand the man. I mean, he's the one who's engaged yet he acts like he has some claim on me.

"I'm going to get that beer now," Drew says as he walks away with a wave. "I'll catch you guys later."

"I'm coming with you," Callie swirls her chair around and chases after him.

"Thank God," Landon mutters and we all break out into hysterics.

After refilling our drinks and putting in an appetizer order, Katelyn still hasn't returned from the restroom. I know the place is packed and I'm sure there is an extremely long line for the women's bathroom. When will the bar/restaurant owners get a clue that women take longer to piss than men and go more frequently, usually in groups? Would it be too terribly expensive to give us a few more bathroom stalls? This whole bathroom dilemma has me feeling the urge to go. "Excuse me guys, I'm gonna head to the little girls' room," I say sliding my chair from the table.

"I've gotta take a leak too. I'll walk with you," Landon says and stands to join me.

"Big Guy's going to the little girls' room," Flynn teases as Patrick laughs. This earns them both the flip off from Landon as we walk away. We have to hold on tight to each other as we migrate through the maze of people crowding the bar and restaurant.

226

"Damn, this band must be extremely popular to bring in these numbers," Landon says as he tries to clear a passage to the restroom.

"Drew swears they are really good. Says they are on the cusp of stardom, just waiting to get signed by a label." We finally make it to the bathroom line and wouldn't you know, the women's line is wrapped around the corner while the men's line has no wait at all. "Ugh!"

Landon chuckles as he strolls to the men's room to relieve himself while I stand crossed legged holding my pee and my space in line. I look around to try and take my mind off my screaming bladder. I don't see Katelyn at all in the line so hopefully she's made it inside the bathroom by now. I glance around to people watch when something catches my eye. I see Katelyn standing outside the building in the shadows of the old oak tree on the front lawn. And she's not alone. I let the person behind me in line cut ahead so I can keep my spot at the window to spy. Katelyn is very animated in the heated conversation she is having with some...guy? What? I watch as he steps closer into Katelyn's personal space causing her to step back until she is trapped against the trunk of the big oak. If this was some random guy and Katelyn felt threatened, I'm sure she would be putting up more of a fight than what I'm witnessing. All she would have to do is scream bloody murder and someone would come to her rescue. But she does neither, which leads me to believe the hot, hunky guy is far from a stranger to Katelyn. The closeness between them suggests that they know each other very, very well.

"Eek," I squeal when Landon taps me on the shoulder distracting me from my spying. "You scared me."

"I don't think you've moved an inch since I left you here," Landon complains and looks in the front and the back of the line.

"I haven't," I admit and direct Landon's attention to the window. "I've been watching Katelyn."

Landon leans in and all but presses his head to the window to get a look. "Who's the guy?"

"I don't know but I think they might know_" Wait, did that guy just grab Katelyn's upper arms and try to shake some sense into her.

"Oh, hell no! Come on, let's go," Landon commands dragging me from the line causing me to lose my space. I'll use the men's room before I wait in that line again. I might go all country girl and make my own bathroom by that big oak tree as soon as we rescue Katelyn. Landon drags me out the front ready to confront the unknown guy. Confront my ass, he'll probably take his head off first and ask questions later. To keep Landon out of jail I need to take control of the situation.

"Landon, calm down. Just follow my lead. Let's not go all Rambo on the guy before we hear from Katelyn what's going on." Landon huffs an okay and follows me toward the tree. The leaves crunch under our feet alerting Katelyn and unknown guy of our approach.

"Hey Katelyn, are you okay?" I ask. Katelyn looks at me and Landon with eyes the size of saucers. Her panic stricken face tells me she either is surprised she got busted or is in some serious trouble.

"Um, yeah. I'm fine. I'm just catching up with an old friend."

Unknown guy releases his hold on Katelyn's arms, but still stands close. He shifts his stance to angle his body toward me and Landon. Leaning slightly, he whispers in Katelyn's ear, "It's *Katelyn* now?" Katelyn ignores his question and goes right into her introductions.

"Suzanna and Landon, this is Henry_"

"Cut all that fancy shit, *Katelyn*. You know I go by Beau."

"If you'd have let me finish, I was going to introduce you as Henry Beaugard, otherwise known as Beau," Katelyn snaps back.

Well, wouldn't you know his sexy name is befitting to his sexy appearance. Even though it's a balmy eighty five degrees tonight, Beau is dressed in a black leather jacket which covers a tight plain white t-shirt. His jeans fit loosely around his hips, but mold perfectly to his ass and thighs. Taking my inspection lower, his bad boy ensemble is completed with a pair of unlaced combat boots.

"Hello," Beau says as he extends his hand in my direction. I snap my head up hoping he didn't notice my perusal of his entire body. I accept his hand and focus on the rough texture of his fingertips against my skin. Redirecting my focus to his face only one word comes to mind...Wowza! This man is sex on a stick. His sharp facial features look like they have been carved by an award winning sculptor. His black as night hair, I'm guessing, must be at least shoulder length or longer, but is pulled back in a slick pony tail. His jaw is covered in a sprinkling of dark black stubble, the kind that would provide just enough sting to cause immense pleasure. Oh, and those eyes, so dark and dangerous, they make you want to run for your life, are softened by a fan of thick dark lashes that makes you want to stay. This joker has got it all, from his bad boy looks to his yes-I'm-a-rebel facial and ear piercings. He could push me up against a tree and put his hands on me anytime he wanted. Wait, what? Good grief, I've been hanging out with Callie too much!

The sound of Landon clearing his throat brings me back from fantasy land and the reason I just met this sexual creature. "Hi, I'm Suzanna," I say in a squeaky tone so far from my normal voice it's embarrassing.

"Nice to meet you," Beau says finally letting go of my hand. How long were we touching? And I already miss it? "And you," Beau says looking toward Landon, "you must be the lucky bastard who convinced Ka, um *Katelyn*, to marry you. Beau drags out each syllable of Katelyn's name before extending his hand to Landon.

"Beau, Landon's just a fr_"

"A freaking lucky bastard. Yes, I'm the fiancé, Landon says as he pulls Katelyn's hand until she stumbles into his side so unnatural and stiff any idiot would realize that Landon and Katelyn are by no means romantically involved. What kinda game is Landon playing anyway? Landon wraps his arm across Katelyn's shoulder until she has no other choice but to melt into his side. As if some miracle occurs, Katelyn relaxes in his arms and goes the extra mile by wrapping her arms around his waist, solidifying the lie that the two of them are heading to the altar. Watching them, it's hard to decide if this is pretend or real. They do make a beautiful couple.

From across the parking lot a guy screams at Beau, "Dude, get your ass in here and help with the set up. We are supposed to go on in less than an hour."

Beau rakes his hand across his slicked back do causing a few strands to loosen and fall around his face. I have to force myself to look away, scared I'll never look at anyone again if I take even the slightest peek. With a frustrated huff, Beau shuffles his feet almost in a war as whether to leave or stay and continue talking with us. "I've gotta go. The band has problems to solve before we can entertain the idea of performing tonight." His comments are directed straight at Katelyn as he trains those sexy eyes on her and her alone.

"You'll figure something out. You always do," Katelyn says with an unflappable resolve.

"Wait, you're in the band," I say when it finally registers.

"What's the problem, man?" Landon says at the exactly the same time.

Beau does that thing with his hair again, thinking carefully of how to answer us both. Finally he says, "Yes, I'm the lead singer of The Gardians. Well, I'm the lead now. We've just recently had to readjust our duties and set lists due to an integral band member leaving us... high and dry." Beau should sound angry. I'd be angry if my band was about to make it big and a band member just up and left. But his tone suggests that of disappointment and sadness. "And to top things off, our lead guitarist had to rush home because his girlfriend went into labor, two weeks early."

"Josie's in labor?" Katelyn squeals with a smile on her face. "Roger must be ecstatic." Her brows bunch together with a look of sudden worry. "You think he was okay to drive? I hope he's being careful. What if he doesn't get there in time?"

"Relax, he's fine. Something about centimeters and dilation. Oh, and he mentioned the time between construction_"

"Contractions," I help out.

"Yeah, that. Anyway, with all that medical jargon the baby won't make an appearance until much later tonight, or tomorrow morning. He said he had plenty of time to get there and assured me he'd text once he arrived."

"Whew, that's a relief," Katelyn exhales.

"You sure you can't help_" Beau starts but looks at the pleading eyes of Katelyn before continuing. "Never mind." With a wave of his hand Beau walks away. He glances back over his shoulder, "Nice to meet you folks." And then he disappears into the night. I would be sad, but I remember I'll get to see him again on stage and a surge of excitement runs through my body. No wonder Callie is goo-goo crazy about the man.

I turn to see Landon and Katelyn still in their *fake?* embrace. When they both notice me watching, they reluctantly pull away from each other. "What's with the big fat lie about being Katelyn's fiancé?" I ask Landon in an accusatory tone. But I don't give him time to answer before I direct my questions toward Katelyn. "And why didn't you say anything about knowing the band members of tonight's headliners?"

While Landon looks sheepish and is trying to form a coherent sentence to explain himself, Katelyn ignores my question all together. "I never made it to the bathroom before getting sidetracked. Excuse me," she says before walking away toward the restroom.

"Wait, I'm coming with you. I really, really have to go," I yell after her. I give Landon one last scornful look before following Katelyn to the restroom.

"I'll wait for you girls right here," Landon says. When I look back I don't dare to question him. His over protectiveness is at full throttle. I give him the thumbs up and pray the bathroom line has dwindled.

Fortunately, I'm able to walk right into the bathroom and find an empty stall. Now, with a grateful bladder, I wash my hands and check my makeup while waiting for Katelyn. A few people come in and out and still Katelyn hasn't emerged. When I know we are alone I call out, "Katelyn, are you okay in there?" fearing she has gotten sick or something.

Through a sniffle Katelyn replies, "Um, no."

I rush to the stall door, luckily the one reserved for the handicapped and knock. "Katelyn open the door, I'm worried about you." After a few tense moments, I hear the click of the lock and walk inside relocking the door. Katelyn is sitting on the toilet seat, fully clothed-thank goodness-, wiping at her face. The smeared mascara and wet cheeks are a dead give away that she has been crying. "Hey, what's the matter?"

"I...I...I just need to go home. Like now."

"Are you sick?" I ask with concern.

"Yeah, sick in the head. Sick of my life," Katelyn says sarcastically. "I'm just gonna call a cab. Can you tell Patrick I wasn't feeling well? I don't want to keep him from having a good time tonight."

"Not until you tell me what, or should I say who, this is all about?" I know physically Katelyn is fine, but emotionally she is a wreck. This is where that new friendship we've been working on will come in handy. She obviously needs to unload some heavy stuff or she's going to continue to be miserable. "Does this have to do with Beau?"

"Yes," Katelyn says through a sigh.

"He'd be hard to give up, that's for sure. I had a hard time trying not to look at him."

Katelyn giggles which eases some of her tension. "We're not like that. Sure, we fooled around in the past, but he couldn't keep his hands off his adoring groupies to form any type of committed relationship. Plus, I didn't want that with him. We were just having fun."

"So, what's bothering you?" Here I thought she was pining over an ex-flame. *That's what you do, Suzanna.* Shut up, I tell that annoying inner voice.

"I can't tell you, Suz. Not because I don't want to. It's just, complicated." Katelyn hangs her head in her hands with a defeated posture. "Will you just please, please let Patrick know I needed to get home? And don't mention Beau or our conversation or anything about me knowing the band, okay."

"Well, sure, okay. But you don't want to stay to hear your friends play?" I ask incredulously. "Drew said they are awesome."

"God no," Katelyn says before the tears start to leak from her eyes again. Wiping away the evidence, Katelyn looks at me forcing a half hearted smile. "They are awesome. Fantastic. Great. You're gonna love their sound. And you can say you saw them before they made it big. Because believe me, they are gonna be huge!" She says this all with conviction but her words are laced with loss. Behind that fake smile, I can see the pain etched into her features. I have nothing to say to make her feel any better. Hell, I don't even know what's wrong. So the only thing I know to do is give her a hug. Katelyn at first is caught off guard by my affection but soon gives in and uses my shoulder to cry those tears she held back earlier. I let her get it all out and compose herself before we decide to leave the confines of the ladies room.

Right before we exit, I remember Landon. Flashes of Katelyn and Landon together and how natural they both looked in each other's arms cause questions to enter my mind that need to be asked. But seeing Katelyn so devastated, I know now is not the time. But I have to warn her that Landon is waiting to safely escort us back to the table. "Um, Katelyn?"

"Yeah?"

"Landon is waiting for us. He's right outside. He wouldn't take no for an answer when I tried to tell him we would be fine. I just wanted you to know before you got caught off guard."

"Do I look upset? Can you tell I've been crying?" Katelyn asks flustered. We just did a whole make over in the bathroom with the products Katelyn carries in her purse. She could start a cosmetics shop with all her loot.

"You look beautiful. Not a trace of evidence that you were the slightest bit upset."

"Thank you, Suzanna. You are truly a dear friend," Katelyn says as her eyes get watery. I have to blink a few times to get my emotions under control. I'm not sure exactly what Katelyn is battling, but I'm glad I could be there to lend my support. "Why don't you go on to the table and I'll take care of Landon?" I'm sure he'll insist on waiting with me while my cab arrives and I don't want to take anymore of your time tonight than I already have. I've probably ruined your night."

"Nonsense. Text me when you get home so I don't worry, okay?"

"Okay, thanks again Suz. I'll see you soon." With a quick hug, Katelyn floats out the front door of the restaurant while uneasiness settles deep within me as I prepare to lie to Patrick. Again. Something I should be used to by now. However, it never gets any easier.

After assuring him that Katelyn didn't have the plague and wasn't on death's door, Patrick relented his cell phone assault from calling her every thirty seconds. His concern was touching, as it should be considering they were engaged. A feeling of jealousy bubbled up, but I forced it down and focused on returning to a fun night with friends. We were anxiously waiting for The Gardians to take the stage. I saw glimpses of Beau setting up and tuning equipment. I hope he figured out a solution to his problem so the band could still perform to impatient fans who crowded the stage, bar and restaurant ready to be entertained. If not, I fear there might be a riot.

Our table now consisted of me, Patrick, Flynn, Callie and Drew. Landon still hadn't returned from the front of the restaurant where he was making sure Katelyn got safely into a cab. With the large weekend crowd tonight along the Marsh Walk, I figured the cab services were stretched thin and they probably had to wait a little longer for a car to arrive. After the incident in the bathroom, I should have felt tense with worry. And I did, Katelyn was never far from my mind. But I also wanted to forget all the escalating drama in my life. So like the mature twenty-two year old I am, I ordered shots. Tequila shots. Now, I know I have sworn off tequila more times than I can count, but tonight I needed that blissful feeling of numbness. I wanted the beat of the music to course through my veins and feel nothing else.

I was starting to give up on the music and just concentrate on getting drunk. The band was already an hour behind their advertised start time. Chloe slipped in beside me with an exhausted sigh. "What a night!" she comments propping her legs on top of the table. "My feet are killing me. If this band doesn't hurry up and start I fear we might run out of alcohol. We can only keep the fans satisfied for so long."

"I think an emergency popped up with one of the band members and they were scrambling to find a quick replacement."

"Figures," Chloe grumbles rubbing her sore calves.

As if they could sense us talking about them, the band emerged on stage taking up their instruments. With natural swag, Beau walked up to the microphone, "Are you ready to rock?" His question was met with screams and hollers so loud I swear the walls shook. Of course I was sitting next to Callie, whose screams were at least a few decibels louder than anyone else in the bar. I had to cover my ears to protect against hearing damage. "Sorry for the delay. But believe me it was for a good cause. Roger, our lead guitarist is about to become a father. And as soon as he texts me the good news, you all will be the first to welcome the newest little member of The Gardians." Raucous cheers followed until Beau silenced them again. "And while we are introducing new members, let's give a round of applause for the guy who stepped in for Roger at the last minute to save this show. Everyone give it up for Landon!"

Landon. Landon? *Our* Landon? The occupants of our entire table stand on their tip toes to get a view of Landon on stage. Sure enough, it's our Landon. Landon Smith. Who I believed didn't have a clue how to play a guitar until now. But the way he handles the six string with confidence, strumming a few notes while he walks up to the front of the stage to give the crowd a salute, I do believe our Landon has been holding out on us.

Beau shoos Landon back to his place whispering in the mic, "Show off." He glances around to all his band members checking their readiness. With a slight nod to the drummer Beau stirs the crowd. "Since we don't want to make you guys wait a minute longer...let's get this party started! Let's show our newest little rocker or rockette how it's done. One, two, three..." The drummer sets a beat and the bassist joins in with a sensual rhythm. Then Landon strums the melody of a song that's a crowd favorite. Finally, Beau begins singing the lyrics and I swear I feel like I've been transported to a live concert in a twenty thousand seat stadium. Wow, these boys are even better than Drew or Katelyn said. And Landon...he's like a natural on stage, never missing a beat. One song blends into the next as my friends and I watch in awe as Landon transforms from the serious straight laced security guy to a rock god.

After an incredible show, Landon is awarded with high fives from the rest of the band. Then we bombard him with hugs from the girls and back slaps from the guys, not to mention the numerous questions being thrown his way. "Dude, how'd you learn to do that?" "Landon, how long have you been playing?" "Where the hell did that come from?"

"Whoa, guys...give me a minute to catch my breath." Landon chugs a bottle of water trying to cool down from the exhilarating high and physical exertion he just displayed.

Chloe wraps Landon in a hug, squeezing the life out of him. "I'm so proud of you!" she beams.

"You knew he could do that?" we all ask.

"Well, I knew he possessed the talent to do that. I didn't know he'd be that good."

It shouldn't surprise me that Chloe knew about Landon's hidden musical talent. He has a closer bond with Chloe than he does with the rest of us. It's no wonder he shared his talent with her. I'm just curious why he hid it for so long. If I had the ability to perform on stage for adoring fans night after night, I'd give up everything else and run with it. Kinda like I do with my golf.

Beau breaks up our friend fest. "Here's your cut of tonight's earnings," he says handing Landon a wad of cash. Landon tries to refuse the payment, but Beau is persistent. "Man, you earned every penny of this money. We couldn't have performed without you. It was an honor and I'd be happy to play with you again anytime." Landon blushes at the compliments and accepts the money. "Let me get your number. I'm sure Roger will be busy with the baby for a while and we may need a replacement for some shows."

Landon passes his phone over while Beau keys in his contact information. "I can't make any promises with my new job. As long as there isn't a conflict, I'd be happy to fill in."

"You might want to rethink the nine to five gig. You've got some serious talent," Beau says. Landon nods, but doesn't comment. "Thanks again for saving our asses tonight. I'll be in touch." He and Landon exchange a fist bump before he leaves to help tear down and load the equipment.

From behind us, a group of fan girls have gathered waiting their turns to talk to the newest musical heartthrob. Landon ignores them and gestures all of us closer until we've formed a tight circle. "Look guys, I'd appreciate it if we can all keep this on the down low." We all look at Landon like he has lost his mind. "Music is a very personal thing that I don't normally share with just anyone. But the band needed my help tonight so I decided to come out of the shadows. That doesn't change the fact that I have a responsibility to my dad's company to provide security to his clients. God, if he knew I was out tonight playing rock star, he'd kill me. Anyway, let's not make a big deal out of this. Really, it's just a hobby."

"We love you Landon," the fan girl group screams vying for his attention.

"This gig comes with much better perks than your security job," Flynn teases thumbing over his shoulder at the girls who wave, bat their lashes and stick out their chests.

"Don't remind me, man," Landon says shaking his head. "Come on, let's get out of here. I want to hear your critiques of my performance."

"You just really want us to inflate your ego, right? Awww, man. One night on stage and you're already an attention whore," Patrick ribs Landon good naturedly as we all walk out on one of the most interesting nights I've ever had.

Chapter Nineteen

The month of May flies by so fast I find myself making plans for the Memorial Day weekend, which is just a few days away. Well, I'm not making the plans. I'm just going along with whatever my parents have cooked up. My parents are coming in on Friday afternoon for the long weekend. They've only visited one other time since I moved down to the beach. And that was just for a night to check on me and Flynn and make sure we hadn't burned down the house or something. I've practiced almost everyday this month, with the exception of the weekends. And yes, Patrick is still acting as my personal chauffeur, driving me to and from practice. We have eased into a comfortable friendship and can talk about almost anything. The topics we steer away from are that of his engagement and my recent failed relationship. I never told Patrick all the details about me and Wyatt. Actually, Patrick doesn't know that it was Wyatt I was involved with. I also never mentioned the unexpected visit I received from Patrick's dad. He hasn't bothered to come around unannounced again and hasn't tried to reach me with any more threats. I can only assume he has no idea the amount of time Patrick and I still spend together.

Katelyn and I are also still spending time together. Mainly she comes over and keeps me company when Chloe is working at night. Sometimes Patrick joins us. If I thought it would be awkward to spend time alone with the both of them, I was mistaken. They act more like friends than lovers. I wonder if they are just putting on a show for my benefit. But when I rack my brain, I can't think of one time I've ever seen anything intimate transpire between the two. Not even as much as a kiss.

Chloe is loving her job and her co-workers. And the bar patrons are loving her...especially the male ones. She is making bank with her tips. Doesn't surprise me that her special southern charm is helping her bring in the dough. Flynn hangs around sometimes, mostly when Chloe has a night off. When Chloe's working, he always makes plans to go out. They still bicker with each other nonstop. But occasionally I'll catch them giving each other a smile or a wink when they think no one is watching. I don't know what exactly is going on with those two, but I don't understand the secrecy. Certainly they don't think I would disapprove of them starting a relationship. I would be their biggest cheerleader. I just hope they know what they are doing, especially since Flynn will soon be half a world away. I hope Chloe can handle his absence when he finally leaves. I'd hate to see her broken hearted. I know from experience, it's not a fun place to be.

We see Landon a lot less now that he has started his security detail for his father's company. He still won't tell us who he is protecting, but so far his travels have been limited to places in South Carolina. I'm guessing he's acting as a secret service agent for some big wig politian. We all kept his promise not to dramatize his stage debut on one condition...he had to tell us if and when he was ever asked to play again with The Gardians. He agreed, but so far we haven't been informed of another gig. I assume Beau hasn't contacted Landon, or if he has, Landon's job interfered and he couldn't perform as their fill in guitarist. Since we haven't seen much of Landon, that means we haven't had to see any of Leslie. Thank goodness! Landon will neither confirm nor deny if they are still together. As long as she keeps her distance, I'm fine with his nonchalant attitude toward the situation. It's not that I don't like Leslie...well, maybe I don't like her just a little bit...but she never quite fit into our close group of friends.

It's one of those nights when Chloe had to work the late shift. Katelyn and Patrick just left after we all watched a movie. I'm getting ready to lock up when I hear a car pull in the drive. I look through the window surprised to find Chloe already at home. It's only half past ten and usually when she works at night, she normally doesn't get home until the wee hours of morning. Sometimes it's after three a. m. before she gets home, after waiting for everyone to leave the bar and closing out her shift. I unlock the door and wait for Chloe to come up the stairs.

"Hey, you're home early," I state when I see her shadow rising.

"Yeah, it was a slow night. I've been working late this entire week so they let me leave early," Chloe says sounding exhausted. Once we enter the light of the living room, I can see the wear and tear this late night job has taken on Chloe. Dark circles are visible under her eyes and she walks at a sluggish pace, completely drained of energy. What I don't expect to see is the redness in her eyes and salt dried liquid in their creases and down her cheeks.

"Chloe, have you been crying?" I ask seriously concerned for her physical and emotional well-being.

"Nah, my eyes are just watery because I'm trying so hard to keep them open. I just need a decent night's sleep and I'll be fine. 'Night Suz," Chloe says as she sleep walks into her bedroom.

"Goodnight Chloe," I reply, but I don't think she heard me. I bet as soon as she entered her bedroom and shut the door she collapsed into a state of unconsciousness.

I go back to lock up, leaving the porch lights on for Flynn to return. I've almost made it to my bedroom when I hear a knock at the door. Who would be coming by at this hour? Maybe Flynn forgot his house keys. I open the door and am surprised to see Landon and *Leslie?* standing on the other side.

"Sorry to bother you so late, but I was hoping to talk to Chloe," Landon says pushing his way into the living area.

"Landon, she's wiped out. She just went to bed and I don't think you should wake her. She really needs to sleep so she can re-energize. This job is really draining her."

"This will only take a minute," Landon says as he walks toward her bedroom, Leslie on his heels. Landon turns around causing Leslie to crash into his wall of steel chest, projecting her backwards. Had he not grabbed her by the shoulders, her backwards momentum and loss of balance surely would have landed her on her ass. I have to suppress a giggle just thinking about it. "Leslie," Landon says in his best appeasing tone, "I need a moment *alone* with Chloe."

"But you're just checking on her. I'm sure she's fine now that she's home. Why can't I come in with you?" Leslie whines.

"Please," Landon begs for understanding. To sweeten the deal he pulls Leslie in for a hug. More of a friendly embrace, but it seems to pacify her. Landon looks my way and gives me the can-you-help-me-out-here look. Now I've been reduced to entertaining Leslie, an unwanted guest. But how can I resist that imploring look Landon keeps shooting me?

"Leslie, would you like something to drink?" I ask as Landon tries to untangle himself from Leslie's arms.

"Yeah, sure." Leslie finally releases her vice grip on Landon. As soon as he is free, he slips into Chloe's bedroom and shuts the door.

After telling Leslie the menu of drink choices available, I pour us each a glass of white wine. If I'm gonna have to occupy Leslie while Landon does whatever he is doing with Chloe in her bedroom, I'm allowed an alcoholic beverage. We sit on the couch and sip our drinks in an uncomfortable silence. When I can't take it anymore I try for some polite conversation. "So, you're in town again."

"I came to visit a college friend who is vacationing on the coast. I was so excited that Landon's job kept him in town tonight so we could spend some time together." From Leslie's tone you'd never guess she was excited at all. "So when he offered to take me to din-ner, I shouldn't have gotten my hopes up. Big f-ing surprise we would end up back at Dead Dog."

I fail to hold in my amusement at the situation which earns me a glare from Leslie. I zip my lips and tighten my facial muscles to keep the smirk from curving my mouth. "Anyway, at least we were seated in the restau-rant part this time and could actually enjoy a pleasant conversation. But that was only when Landon's focus returned to me. He constantly kept an eye on the happenings in the bar area through the window to watch out for his precious Chloe." The malice in Leslie's voice is unmistakable.

"He couldn't have seen much. Chloe said the bar was slow tonight and that's why she came home early," I comment.

"The bar was packed. Chloe came home because someone from a bachelorette party rattled her so badly she was almost in tears."

"What?" Chloe never mentioned being upset. However, there was the evidence that she had been crying. I shouldn't have let her off the hook so easily when I questioned her earlier. But she looked so tired I didn't have the heart to keep her from the much needed sleep she was so desperate for. "Who was it that upset Chloe?"

"I don't know. It was a huge group and they kept moving back and forth from the dance floor to their table. I didn't recognize anyone I knew. Maybe it was one of Flynn's former flames."

"Flynn? What does he have to do with this?"

"He was at the bar tonight. Several of the girls talked with him. I think they were playing one of those stupid bachelorette games and were trying to convince Flynn to join the fun. By this time, I was already beyond the point of caring and just wanted to continue my date with Landon. But noooo. Of course Landon would pick up on Chloe's distress and follow her to the ends of the earth to console her. I swear I don't know why I even bother to fight for his attention. It's obvious I'm the last person he wants anything to do with." Well at least Leslie has finally figured out how one-sided their relationship is. I do feel a tinge of sympathy for her. She sounds so sad and looks like she is seconds away from bursting into tears.

"I'm sure that's not entirely true," I lie. "He's just got a lot going on with his new job and all. As far as Chloe is concerned, I assure you it's strictly platonic. Landon is loyal to a fault with his friendships. I think he just needs to make sure Chloe is okay before he can concentrate on you and your happiness. He knows you deserve his undivided attention and he's trying to get to that point. He obviously cares about you." *Or else he'd have cut you loose a long time ago,* I think, but don't dare say.

"You really believe that? That he cares about me?" Leslie asks with hope.

No, I don't believe that at all. I'm just trying to make you feel better so you don't break down into a puddle sitting on my couch. I also have no idea why Landon continues to string you along. He no more wants a relationship with you than I want to become an astronaut. All I care about right now is whether or not Chloe is okay. And if Landon can soothe her bruised ego then I'll dish out whatever you want to hear. "Um huh, absolutely."

Landon saves me from fabricating any more lies when he finally emerges from Chloe's bedroom. I jump to my feet and run to meet him as he closes the bedroom door. He puts his finger to his lips telling me to keep my voice low. "Is she okay?" I whisper.

Landon pulls me away from the door and into the living room before he answers. "She's asleep. And she's fine now. Some drunk guy got a little aggressive at the bar tonight and downright belligerent when Chloe refused to serve him any more alcohol. It frightened her."

"But Leslie said it was a group of girls_"

"Leslie was mistaken." Landon gives Leslie a look that screams mind your own business. She opens her mouth to defend her earlier comments, but thinks twice when Landon continues to stare her down. "Chloe should be back to her normal tough as nails self by morning. It'd probably be a good idea not to bring this up with her. The faster she can forget this ever happened, the faster she can get back to work. And she really loves that job, drunks and all." I nod my affirmation, but Landon needs more. "Please Suz, just don't make her relive tonight. Promise me you'll act like you have no idea I ever stopped by."

"Fine, I promise," I relent, although with the two conflicting stories from Landon and Leslie I don't know who to believe. And the only person who can tell me the truth of what really happened tonight I can't ask because of the promise I just made Landon.

"I don't guess Flynn has made it home yet?" Landon asks as he leads Leslie toward the front door.

"Haven't seen him yet."

I hear Landon mumble under his breath, "That bastard." I take offense at Landon's derogatory remark about my brother and I'm about to go into full on defend Flynn mode. But I don't get the chance. Landon and Leslie make a hasty exit. "Sorry to bother you Suz. Good night," Landon says from halfway down the stairs. He sure was in a hurry to leave. I'm sure his purposeful exit was to keep me from asking anymore questions. Damn these people. All they seem to do is make the drama exponentially increase until I think my head is going to explode!

Bang, Bang Bang! "Suzanna!" *Bang, Bang, Bang.* "Suzanna, open the fucking door!" I startle awake to the sounds of someone trying frantically to get inside my house. "Please, Suz, please come open the door." The familiar pleading voice belongs to Patrick. He sounds so impatient. Oh God, I hope nothing has happened. Visions of his father, pissed off and drunk fill my mind as I fight to untangle myself from the bed sheets. *Please let Patrick be okay* I repeat silently as I stumble from my bedroom into the living area to open the front door. Before I can swing the door fully open, Patrick's arms engulf me in an embrace so tight I struggle to breathe. My face lands on his bare, slick chest right below his erratically beating heart. His sweaty male scent mingled with the salt air makes me forget why I was suddenly wrangled out of bed. I take a deep breath and let his delicious aroma fill my senses, eliciting thoughts I shouldn't be having this early in the morning. Or not at all! Patrick slowly releases his tight hold, but doesn't stop touching me. He leans me back, his hands securely gripping my shoulders and inspects me from head to toe. "Thank God!" he breathes out in relief.

"Patrick?" I don't understand what's going on.

"When I came up from the beach on my morning run and saw all the destruction downstairs, I thought...I thought..." Patrick shutters then pulls me back into his arms like he never wants to let me go. He kisses the top of my messy hair while stroking my back. I'm bewildered as to why he needs to offer me comfort. "I didn't know what I'd find inside the house. I believed for a moment you might be dead," Patrick chokes out overwhelmed with emotion.

"Dead? Patrick what's going on?" His close body proximity and his alluring scent make it very difficult to concentrate on the reason he showed up here in the first place. I try to piece together a coherent thought from Patrick's earlier phrases and words. Beach, morning run, destruction, downstairs, dead... Still nothing is making any sense. I try to pull out of Patrick's hold to take a look downstairs, hoping a visual will help. He shifts his body to block my view each time I attempt a turn or angle to peek downstairs. "Come on Patrick, why are you acting like a lunatic so early in the morning? And what do you not want me to see?"

"Suz, just stay put upstairs until we know it's safe. Landon and the police are on their way."

"The *police*?" Now I'm scared to find out, much less witness, what lies beneath the structure of the house.

"It's just a precaution. Plus, they will have to file a report so you can turn it into your insurance company for compensation for the damages." Patrick guides me inside the house.

My head is swimming with all the possibilities of what I will find once the police and Landon give us the all clear. Something serious happened last night while we were sleeping. We...Chloe. Oh, I've got to check on Chloe. What if someone did get inside the house and go into her room first? Trembling with fear, I squeeze Patrick's hand and point toward Chloe's closed door. "Ch-Chloe," I stutter, my throat clogged with unknown fear. Patrick interprets my unspoken request. He goes to check on Chloe, trying to pry my hand from his, but I won't relinquish his limb. He leads the way, while I shuffle closely behind him. He slowly opens the door while I cover my eyes with the hand that's not permanently attached to Patrick. When I hear Patrick release a sigh of relief, I chance a glance through my fingers to find Chloe curled in a ball on the middle of the bed softly snoring. Before it registers to not wake her, I spring from the doorway and jump onto her bed. We bounce with the sudden weight applied to the mattress before I get a chance to hug the daylights out of my best friend.

"If this is some kind of joke, I'm going to kill you Suz. And you too, Patrick." Chloe huffs with annoyance at being awakened so early and in such a crazy way.

"I love you Chloe, so much. Thank goodness you're okay," I say while I can because the relief I feel at finding a healthy, unharmed Chloe hits me instantly and I began to cry tears of joy.

"Suz, what's all this?" Chloe says trying to sit up in her bed.

"It looks like someone attempted to break in last night," Patrick answers. Good thing he still has his wits about him. At this point, I'm a complete mess. "There is evidence of vandalism to both yours and Suzanna's cars. Also, some items were destroyed. I'm not sure yet if anything was stolen."

"What about Flynn's vehicle?" Chloe asks. I just realized I haven't thought about Flynn once this morning. I guess I know Flynn is more than capable of taking care of himself had there been an intruder in the house. Still, the thought of his safety should have at least crossed my mind.

"Um, well," Patrick starts looking around the room, anywhere but at Chloe, "I don't know for certain if his vehicle sustained any damages because it's not here. Considering the early hour of the morning I suspect it wasn't here at all last night."

"That son of a bitch," Chloe says furiously ripping the covers from her body. She makes a beeline toward the ensuite bathroom that joins her bedroom with Flynn's. Slinging doors open so fast, she tests the limits of the hinges, Chloe storms into Flynn's room yelling his name. "Flynn Caulder!" But her verbal assault is met with silence. I follow Chloe into Flynn's room to find the bed made and empty. Flynn never came home last night.

With our nerves on edge, all three of us jump at the sudden constant rapping at the front door. "That must be Landon. Or the police," Patrick says. "I'll go get the door." Patrick walks out of Flynn's bedroom leaving me alone with Chloe. Now, I'm really, really glad I found Chloe safe and sound this morning. However, the fury that is radiating off her body tells me I don't want to be anywhere near her at the moment. I'm torn between giving her a sympathetic hug or running far, far away. Taking the coward's way out, I quietly ease my way to the door.

"What a fan-fucking-tastic way to start the morning," Chloe says through clenched teeth. Good thing, otherwise she'd be spitting nails. "Well let's go see the extent of the mess we've got to clean up." Stomping mad, Chloe goes into the living room to confer with Patrick, Landon and the police. Guess I'll finally get to see what all the fuss is about. Oh joy!

Following everyone downstairs and taking in the first view of last night's/this morning's criminal events, I swear I've entered a war zone. Small pieces of glass litter the ground where both mine and Chloe's front and back windshields were busted out. Bent and damaged golf clubs are strewn all around the yard, driveway and into the street. Someone went to town on our vehicles using my clubs as their weapons of choice. Papers, that I can only assume are documentation of vehicle registrations and proofs of insurance, are trapped in the bushes or either lost for good traveling down the street with the ocean breeze. Our thieves were nothing if not efficient in searching every nook and cranny of our cars, even the glove boxes. I have to keep reminding myself that it could have been so much worse. At least Chloe and I are unharmed. Our cars, having seen better days, can at least be repaired. My clubs, although expensive and especially made for me, can be reconstructed if salvageable. If not, I'll be spending some extra time with Callie to get a new set to fit just right.

As one policeman walks with Chloe around her car asking questions and making a list of stolen items, the other police officer does the same with me. Other than the sheer lack of respect for another person's belonging, I can't find anything of importance missing. This only spurs my positive attitude about the intrusion. For once I feel like I'm acting like an adult, handling the situation with maturity. Mom and Dad would be proud. The optimistic view of this bad situation takes a nose dive when I notice the gray flaps of material lying in the road as cars run over them flattening them like pancakes. "Oh no, no, no, no," I scream as I take off into the street.

"Ma'am, just a few more questions," the officer calls from behind me, but I ignore him.

"Suz?" Patrick questions, but doesn't keep me from getting to my destination. However, he does follow me keeping a watchful eye on the object in the road that has my full attention. I reach the remains of one of my most treasured possessions. My golf bag. Gifted to me years ago by Patrick. It belonged to his mother and he wanted me to have it after she passed away from injuries sustained in a one vehicle car accident.

I collapse to my knees in the middle of the street gathering the remains of my golf bag. The soft gray leather has been ripped away from the inner casing like someone peeled a banana. The flaps of leather are hanging on by threads to the bottom of what is left of the bag's structure. A pile of broken rods and shattered plastic is all that is left of the casing. Scooping up the ruins and holding them to my chest, I openly sob causing a traffic jam. I'm barely aware of the honking horns or the officer's insistence that I move from the road. My concentration is focused solely on the destruction of a tangible piece of my heart.

The feel of Patrick's arm sliding around my shoulders breaks my spell. He pulls me to his side, his face leaning in toward my ear. I can't bear to look at him because I'm scared his pain will mirror my own. My acceptance of his mother's bag, and the fact that I have used it for years, means as much to him as the bag itself means to me. "Suz," Patrick whispers and I feel his breath fanning my face. He tries to sound strong, but I hear the loss we both are suffering in this moment. Without another word, Patrick helps me gather the remaining pieces then pulls me to my feet. He continues to hold me closely by his side as he walks me to the foot of the beach house stairs. Taking the golf bag remnants from my hands and adding them to his pile, he gently sits me on the bottom step and kneels in front of me, his hands on my knees. Chloe, Landon and the officers circle around standing behind Patrick with looks of sympathy on their faces.

"I know it's silly, right? It's just a golf bag. I can get a new one. Probably needed to upgrade anyway. But, but...I don't want a new one. I want that one," I say pointing to the pile of rubble. "It was my golf bag. Mine. And because it belonged to your mother it was so, so special." I cry as the words rattle out quickly.

"I understand," Patrick says softly looking me in the eyes.

"No! You don't understand. You can't. You have all of Marie's things surrounding you all the time. Her pictures, letters, her life's belongings. Me? I just had this golf bag. And that's it. I don't even have you anymore. Sure, I have her memories. But this was something she touched and felt at one time in her life. It was like a connection between us even though I know she is no longer physically with me. And now...now, it's gone. Ruined," I get out before another sob escapes.

"Shhh, baby," Patrick tries consoling me as he wipes the overflowing tears from my face. "I'll fix it," he declares.

I let out a joyless laugh. "Fix it? Fix it! Are you crazy? Just look... look at what's left. It can't be fixed. It's destroyed. Gone, forever. Oh God," I shriek. "This hurts so much. What am I gonna_"

My one hundred mile per hour rampage comes to a screeching halt as Patrick crashes his lips into mine. I'm so stunned at first I sit there motionless. Patrick eases into the kiss, nibbling my bottom lip and probing my mouth's entrance with his tongue. The sensations soon take over and I relent, letting Patrick take control. His kiss is soft, sweet, comforting. Soon I relax and the tension of the morning dissipates. The longer the kiss continues the more turned on I become until I find myself wrapping my arms around Patrick's neck and pulling him closer. When his tongue strokes every crevice inside my mouth, I suppress a moan.

"Well, that's a sure way to shut her up." Landon and Chloe burst into laughter at Patrick's distraction tactics. I can feel the slide of Patrick's lips against my own, forming a smile. He ends the kiss, far too soon for me, but places his forehead against mine maintaining our connection.

"I'll fix it," Patrick says looking deep into my eyes. And I believe he will. He may have to work some voodoo magic to make what's left resemble anything close to a golf bag. But his determination and unwavering declaration convince me that it might be possible.

"Okay," I say softly and give him a sad smile. He gives me a friendly peck to the end of my nose before pushing back to a kneeling position. One last inspection of my overall emotional state convinces him that I'm not gonna go off the deep end anytime soon. He stands and walks over to the police officers to wrap up the report. Landon and Chloe still stand there mouths agape at the intimate moment they just witnessed. I should be embarrassed about my audience, but I'm not. I should feel guilty for enjoying the kiss, but I don't. I feel... loved, cared for, comforted. All thanks to Patrick.

"What?" I question Landon and Chloe with sternness in my voice. A far cry from the fragile girl Patrick carried from the middle of the road moments earlier. Landon and Chloe have the decency to leave well enough alone, for now. They move quickly and start the clean up process. I'm left sitting alone with my thoughts. All I want is to remember all the details of that kiss with Patrick. However, my head refuses to cooperate and churns with uneasy speculations about the criminal events. The police officers said this was probably just a random act of violence. Maybe some bored, drunk, belligerent teenagers looking for a cheap thrill. But the shredding of my golf bag, something of no value to anyone else but me, seems too personal. Almost like the vindictive act was aimed directly at me where it would hurt the most. And I have good reason to believe it wasn't random at all. The threats from Patrick's dad replay in my mind. Guess they weren't so empty after all. Internally, I've already convicted him of the crime, no need for a trial or jury. But I can't voice my suspicions, especially not to Patrick. I'll have to act like Jim didn't even enter my mind as a possible suspect. Then there's the dilemma with the cars. Both Chloe and I will have to depend on Landon and Patrick for transportation since both of our vehicles will be out of commission until all the repairs have been made. Of course, Patrick would expect to continue taking me to and from golf practice regardless of the condition of my car. But with the recent events, I'm not sure that's such a good idea. Maybe some distance from Patrick will convince Jim that I've received his discreet, yet destructive message loud and clear. However, I'd have to explain to Patrick why I'm suddenly pulling away. That's certainly not gonna happen. Once my parents arrive for the weekend, I'll just have Mom or Dad cart me around. Patrick can't argue about me wanting to spend some time with my parents.

"Miss Caulder, we've got all the paperwork finished. I just need your signature," the office interrupts my thoughts.

"Yeah, sure." I stand and listen as the officer goes over the details of the police report with me and Chloe. Once we've signed and been given a copy for our insurance claims, the officers say their goodbyes and go to leave. Landon is still sweeping up the glass littering the concrete. I hear snippets of Patrick talking on his cell phone. Sounds like he is arranging tow trucks to come collect mine and Chloe's cars to haul them away to the dealership body shop for repairs. Since I can't stand around any longer and do nothing I pull out my own cell phone to make the call to my parents. I dread the conversation ahead of me, telling them the news of the attempted break in. My fingers dial and I'm just about to press send when I hear the screeching of tires next door in Mrs. Stokes' driveway. All heads turn and watch as a frantic Flynn exits his car and runs straight to Chloe. She doesn't have a second to prepare herself before Flynn has trapped her in his arms. He pulls away moments later leaving his hands securely on her shoulders. Giving her a slow perusal with his eyes, from the top of her head to the tips of her toes, he lets out a sigh of relief before pulling her back into his chest.

"You're okay," he breathes out in obvious assuagement.

Chloe pushes against his chest with enough force to send Flynn back a couple of steps breaking their connection. "Get away from me," Chloe demands.

"Come on, Chloe, I was worried. The thoughts swirling through my head at the sight of the cop cars at the house...." Flynn can't even finish his sentence with the images of Chloe being hurt, or worse.

"Worried. Worried? If you were so freaking worried, where the hell have you been all night, huh?" Chloe is fuming.

Flynn stuffs his hands in his jeans pockets and looks down at his feet. The look of guilt is written all over him. Composing himself, he looks back up at Chloe and starts to explain his whereabouts.

"Stop! Never mind. I don't even want to know," Chloe starts in again. "This," she says pointing to the mangled cars and piles of glass, "is probably all your fault anyway."

"My fault?" Flynn yells. "How in the hell do you figure that?"

"I'm sure one or more of your scorned sluts tried to take revenge. They just took it out on the wrong people."

Now Flynn is the one fuming. He takes a couple of steps closer invading Chloe's personal space. Getting right up in her face he says, "For your information, my so called scorned sluts don't need to take revenge. When they leave me after a night of mind blowing sex, they are more than grateful, feeling sated and satisfied. No need for revenge, sweetie." He smirks with arrogance. "How dare you blame me for this mess? You might want to take a closer look at all the cock blocks you've been dishing out after flirting shamelessly with your bar customers. Maybe then you'll have the right guy."

Chloe pushes away from Flynn again, but the fight has left her. She has tried to stay strong, but Flynn's words affect her to the point of tears. "You're...you're...I hate you, Flynn Caulder!" she screams before running up the stairs and into the house. Flynn lets out a frustrated growl before stomping after her. He doesn't get far in his pursuit. Landon grabs hold of Flynn's arm stopping him in his tracks.

"Leave her alone," Landon commands.

"Hands off rock star. Last I checked I actually live here. You... you just continue to show up. Uninvited," Flynn spits in anger. They continue to stare each other down coming close to blows until Patrick intervenes.

"Calm down. Both of you. The girls have had a stressful morning as it is. Let's not add to it." Patrick eases in between the two hulking bodies until they both back away from each other.

"Come on Suz, tell me what happened," Flynn gestures for me to follow him inside.

"Thanks for asking, and yes I'm fine," I say sarcastically. I've just realized he hasn't even bothered to check on my well-being.

"Don't start now, Sis." Flynn gives me the 'I'm-not-in-the-fucking-mood' look. I immediately zip my lips. "You coming or what?"

"We'll finish up down here and I'll let you know when the tow trucks arrive," Patrick says encouraging me to go talk with Flynn. Giving him a nod of appreciation I follow Flynn inside the house. *Oh what a beautiful morning* dances in my head and I laugh at the audacious song lyrics. I'll have to save that musical tune for another day.

Rather than having to repeat myself, I call Mom and Dad and put my phone on speaker. Recapping the events of the night and what we found this morning I shutter to think how the situation could have been so much worse. What if someone had actually tried to get into the house? What if they succeeded and found two vulnerable sleeping women to prey on? The thoughts unnerve me and the fear is evident in my voice. Flynn gives me a hug while Mom and Dad voice their concerns, asking over and over if I'm okay. Dad immediately starts making calls to local security companies. He tells Flynn that a representative will be at the house this afternoon to install both outside surveillance cameras and an alarm system for the inside. Flynn assures my dad that he will take care of it and meet the person responsible for the installation. Once I've calmed my parents down enough that they aren't ready to jump in the car and make an early visit to the beach, I end the conversation promising to check in first thing in the morning.

Flynn and I sit on the couch in silence for a few minutes both of us deep in our own thoughts. At the exactly the same time, Flynn says, "I'll go help with the clean up." While I ask, "Where were you last night?"

"Honestly, Suz, I had a few too many drinks and crashed at Mark's house on the couch. Seriously, that's all I did last night," he says in such a way like I might think he's lying.

"I believe you."

"I'm so sorry I wasn't here. If anything had happened to you or Chloe...," Flynn sounds truly upset for his absence.

"We're both fine, Flynn. This wasn't your fault."

"Not how Chloe sees things," Flynn says with a huff. He looks so pained and defeated when he glances at Chloe's closed bedroom door.

"I'll talk to her. She hasn't been acting like herself since she came home early from work last night. You wouldn't know anything about that, would you?" I ask remembering Leslie's mention of Flynn being at the bar.

"I'm going down to help out Patrick and Landon. Need to talk to Landon anyway," Flynn says avoiding answering my question.

"Flynn," I pressure him to stay, but he's already halfway out the door. "No fighting," I yell to his retreating back. Lord, the last thing we need is a brawl between Landon and Flynn.

I'm about to check on Chloe when I hear the loud roar of an engine downstairs. Patrick sticks his head in the door. "Tow truck is here," he announces.

"Be there in a sec." I walk over to Chloe's closed door and softly knock. "Chloe, the cars are ready to be towed."

I hear the sounds of sniffling before Chloe speaks through the still closed door. I have to press my ear to the wood to hear her say, "Suz, will you ask Landon to handle it? He can bring the paperwork up to me once they leave. I'm on the phone with my dad."

"Oh yeah, sure thing. Tell your dad I said hello." I wait for a reply but it never comes. So I go downstairs to fetch my own paperwork and give Landon Chloe's message.

As soon as the tow truck drives away, Landon takes the stairs two at a time to go check on Chloe. Patrick, Flynn and I follow him inside the house. After thirty minutes, Landon and Chloe are still shut up in Chloe's bedroom and Flynn has had enough. "I'm going out," he says angrily. He stomps into his bedroom and returns a minute later wearing workout clothes. Grabbing his keys from the console table, he leaves without another word slamming the door on his way out. Patrick and I both jump at the noise.

"I sure hope he works out some of that sexual frustration," Patrick deadpans.

"Sexual frustration? Pfff, the boy gets some whenever he wants it."

"Not from Chloe he doesn't. And it's obviously driving him mad," Patrick states his observation. "If those two don't do something about the abundance of sexual tension between them they are liable to end up killing each other."

"If you say so," I comment but don't share his theory. I don't think it's just sex they need to work on. It's all the other emotional stuff between them which neither will own up to.

"So, what's the plan? You need a ride to golf?" Patrick asks changing the subject.

"And play with what? My broken clubs."

"I'm sure there's a loaner set at the club you could use. Or you can borrow mine," Patrick offers.

"Actually, Callie is picking me up soon to go get fitted for a new pair. Then we'll go back to her office so she can start tweaking them where adjustments are needed."

"Oh," Patrick says and I hear the disappointment in his voice.

"Come on, Patrick, you've earned a day off from lugging me back and forth to the course. Especially after this morning. Go on and enjoy the rest of your day," I encourage trying to make light of the situation.

"Well, I guess I can find something to do." Patrick walks toward me and pulls me in for a hug. I tense up immediately and squirm out of his hold. "Suz, what's this?" he asks noticing my tension.

"Nothing," I lie. "I just have a lot to do before Callie gets here."

"Don't do this, Suzanna."

"Do what?" I ask innocently.

"Start pulling away from me when we've gotten so close," Patrick answers.

"Too close. What was up with that kiss downstairs? And in front of Landon and Chloe? Have you lost your mind?" I say throwing my hands in the air for added emphasis.

"I'm sorry, I know I crossed that friendship line," Patrick looks away sheepishly.

"Crossed it? You practically erased it!" I whisper scream in exasperation.

"Look, it was the only thing I could think of at the time to keep you from rambling on and working yourself into a frenzy."

"So you kissed me?" I ask incredulously.

"Well, I didn't have any duct tape on hand. So, MacGyver style, I improvised, using my lips instead," Patrick says in all seriousness.

"Duct tape? Really?" I ask through a smile.

"Hey, whatever is needed to keep those tears at bay," Patrick says more relaxed. "From now on, I'll keep a roll of duct tape on hand, you know, so we can avoid any more accidental lip locks."

"Accidental, my ass," I retort in laughter. Patrick laughs with me until we're back to our comfortable friendship.

"So, are we good?" Patrick asks as he begins to walk toward the door to leave.

"As long as you stop kissing me. Then yes, we're good."

"Where's the fun in that?"

"Patrick," I admonish.

"Fine, fine. I'll keep my lips to myself." I narrow my eyes and glare at Patrick coercing more from him. "I promise."

"Goodbye, Patrick."

"'Bye Suz," Patrick says walking backwards. When he finally turns around, I notice the crossed fingers he hid behind his back. Sneaky ass!

Chapter Twenty

After the criminal events that took place, my parents couldn't wait any longer and arrived a day early for the Memorial Day weekend. Although, I was a bit perturbed that they disregarded my assurance that we were adults and could handle things, I was more than thrilled to see them. Even though we talk daily, I haven't had any face to face time with Mom and Dad in a while. With Dad's busy work schedule and Mom's busy social life, their visits have been close to nonexistent until now. Upon arrival, Mom made a big fuss over me, Flynn and Chloe. She was so busy inspecting us from head to toe, she didn't notice the lack of interaction between Chloe and Flynn. They haven't spoken since their explosive scene outside yesterday. Dad was too busy checking out the new security system to notice much of anything else.

The majority of the weekend was spent lounging on the beach, boat rides on the inlet and eating. Good grief, when Mom cooks, she cooks for an army. Nothing beats her home cooked meals. I'll definitely have to ramp up my cardio routine to work off all the calories I consumed. Dad and I fit in a round of golf on Saturday. He liked how my game has improved under the direction of Coach Moore. Coach Moore assured Dad I would be more than ready come August for qualifying and encouraged him to go ahead and line up a manager/agent for me. Dad agreed, informing Coach Moore that he already had a few prospects. He also surprised me with news for several sponsors who are ready to get on board as soon as I give up my amateur status and turn pro. Wow, I'm flattered!

On Sunday, we all rise and attend the church service at Garden City Chapel. The non-denomination church offers tourists and second home owners a place to worship while in town. My family has been coming here since I was a child. I'm sure the reverend delivered a spectacular message, as he always does. However, I wasn't able to concentrate because Jim Miles and his family, Patrick included, were sitting a few pews ahead of us. When my mind would stray, calling Jim every bad name in the book and thinking of all the terrible ways I could take my revenge, I would snap back and remember I was in church. Saying one prayer after another, asking for forgiveness, not only for myself but for Jim as well, I finally was able to sit and listen to the end of the sermon in peace. When the reverend dismissed the congregation I said one last prayer asking that my family exit the church and leave before the Miles clan spotted us. That one went unanswered. Jim and Ruth sneak up and reach my parents before they can leave the building. Luckily, Chloe and Flynn had already spotted the weasel and they dragged me down the aisle ahead of Mom and Dad. We hurriedly left the church, foregoing shaking the reverend's hand to wait at the car. It must have been five to ten minutes before my parents joined us. "You kids in a rush to get somewhere?" Dad asks.

Mom doesn't let us answer as we all pile into the car. She immediately starts chatting. "It was wonderful seeing Patrick and his dad at the church service. And Ruth, too. I didn't realize they were still seeing each other. Oh, and I finally got to meet Katelyn. What a lovely young woman." Mom is still carrying on while Chloe, Flynn and I do a simultaneous eye roll. When Chloe starts making fake gagging noises, we can't contain our laughter and explode in the back seat. "What's so funny?" Mom asks.

"We were just discussing the reverend's opening sermon joke," Flynn says on the fly. Man, he's quick on his feet today. Mom gushes over Flynn's rapt attention during church and starts discussing the sermon in more detail. I'm glad someone was paying attention this morning. I tune out the conversation and stare out the window watching as we pass by familiar homes. When we get close to our house and Dad has yet to slow down, I lean up and poke him in the shoulder.

"Hey, old man, you're gonna miss your turn," I say jokingly.

"Old yes. Senile, not just yet. We're going to the Sunday brunch at the Gulf Stream Café. Meeting Jim, Ruth and the kids for lunch." Dad continues driving past our house toward the restaurant.

Panic grips me as I lean back against the seat. From my position in the middle, both my hands reach out and grip the thighs of both Chloe and Flynn. I look back and forth between them with fear in my eyes, silently pleading for help. "Awww, I was hoping we could heat up the leftovers of that delicious meal Mrs. Caulder cooked last night. All during church my mouth was watering just thinking about it." I hope Chloe's complimentary statement about Mom's cooking is enough to turn this car around.

"Thanks, Chloe. You're a sweetheart. But I've packed up the leftovers for you kids to eat after we leave. Plus, we've had all our meals at home since we arrived. I think we deserve a treat today. So let's dine out," Mom says as we pull into the parking lot of the restaurant.

"I'm really not that hungry," Flynn explains. Both Mom and Dad whip around and look at Flynn like he's crazy.

"Since when are you never hungry, son?" Dad asks while Mom reaches to feel Flynn's forehead.

"You feeling okay?" Mom asks looking concerned. "You don't feel warm or feverish." Flynn swats her hand away with embarrassment. Mom will never see Flynn as a grown man. He'll always be her little boy.

Dad parks the car and he and Mom open their doors. He notices that none of the back seat occupants have made a move to exit the vehicle. "Y'all coming? We've got a large group and I want to go ahead and get a table before it gets too busy."

"We'll be there in just a few minutes, Dad," Flynn says.

"Oh, Suz...I wasn't even thinking when we accepted the invitation to join the Miles for brunch," Mom starts in looking at me through her opened car door. "Is this hard for you? I thought you and Patrick were back to being friends. Plus, since you're dating Wyatt now_"

"Mom, she's fine," Flynn barks.

"Don't take that tone with me son. And I'd like to hear from my daughter if you don't mind." Mom waits patiently until I feel I can talk without breaking down in tears. The fact that I'm going to have to endure lunch with a man I despise is quite the predicament. And then there's Patrick, who I have to watch doting over his fiancée Katelyn. Then to top off this disaster, Mom had to bring up Wyatt. It's not her fault she doesn't know we broke up. I didn't want to tell her or Dad and have to hear the 'I told you so' lecture. But hearing his name is like a stab through my heart. I actually bring my hand to my chest to try to ease the ache. Mom clears her throat to get my attention.

I force a smile. "Flynn's right, I'm fine. Let's go eat." Yeah, like that's gonna happen. I've suddenly lost my appetite.

"Mr. Caulder? You know I have some experience in the restaurant industry," Chloe chimes in with her sugary sweet voice. "If you don't want to wait, maybe you should request two tables. One for the adults and one for the kids?"

"Aren't we all adults?" Dad chuckles.

Chloe shifts her gaze to Flynn and adds, "That's questionable. But splitting up a big party usually gets you seated and served faster than dining as a large group. Just a suggestion."

"Not a bad idea," Dad considers. "I'll go see what's available. You sure you're not trying to avoid the parental figures because we bore you, right?"

"Absolutely not!" Chloe says with a wink. She could charm the skin off a snake. I'm sure there's some validity in her restaurant knowledge, but I know she made the suggestion for my benefit. I give her thigh a squeeze in appreciation.

"Come on Carol, let's go get *two* tables. Wouldn't want to embarrass the kids." Dad leads Mom away from the car and into the restaurant.

"Whew, we just dodged that bullet," Chloe exhales.

"This is bullshit!" Flynn says angrily. "I hate the fact that Mom and Dad hang out and socialize with that sleaze ball Jim. Suz, please_"

"No, don't even think about asking me to tell our parents what happened. It would kill them." Flynn just shakes his head in frustration. Chloe grabs my hand linking our fingers together.

"Let's go get this over with. The faster we eat, the faster we can get out of here."

"Amen to that," Flynn agrees opening the car door. That church service must have really sunk in. I know my quota of prayers has probably reached its limit, but I ask the good Lord one last thing. Please, please help me survive the potential disaster today, camouflaged as Sunday Brunch.

Well, I survived...just barely. We ended up sitting at the "kids' table". Never thought I would ever want to do that again. However, today reminded me that growing up sucks. The majority of the time the conversation focused on the annual Memorial Day barbecue hosted by the Bosticks. This year we were all invited. Yay us! With our association to Katelyn via Patrick the entire gang would be heading over to Pawleys Island tomorrow to celebrate. Katelyn was so excited that we accepted her invitation. She said in years past she had to endure the barbecue as the only person under the age of fifty. Most of the attendees were her parents' friends and colleagues, leaving Katelyn to play the role of obedient daughter, kissing up to her parents' snobby friends. This year, she promised we could have our very own party down by the beach once she completed her obligatory hand shaking, cheek kissing and hugging act under the watchful eyes of her parents. I no more wanted to attend the party than I wanted to dye my hair purple. But bursting Katelyn's bubble when we had already told her we would come was something I couldn't bring myself to do. It's not that I didn't want to spend time with Katelyn and check out the monster sized mansion she vacationed in every year. My hang up revolved around the fact that Jim Miles would be in attendance as well. And let's just say I didn't want to spend another day in his presence. Yuck!

Things were going smoothly right up until we were paying the check. The adults walked over engaging us in conversation. Dad mentioned a round of golf which Jim immediately accepted. When Jim asked if any of the youngsters wanted to join them you could hear crickets chirp. The silence should have been a resounding 'NO', but Jim wouldn't let up. He snaked his way around the table coming to stand right behind my chair. His closeness caused my muscles to tense and my skin to crawl. The sound of his voice gave me the hibbie jibbies. "No takers? Not even you, Suzanna? Gee, I was looking forward to seeing your game so I could figure out for myself what all the fuss was about." He then placed his large filthy hand on my shoulder and leaned in. "What's wrong Suz...you scared?" I trembled in my chair with fear, not scared of the competition, but scared of the man. Flynn who was sitting beside me jumped to his feet, accidentally (not) brushing into Jim, causing his hand to fall from my shoulder.

"Whoops, sorry," Flynn said but didn't sound the least bit apologetic. "Suz and I actually have plans for the afternoon, so we'll both pass on the golf outing. But y'all have fun." Flynn grabbed my arm and jerked me up from the chair leading me out of the restaurant without so much as a wave goodbye. He kept a strong hold on me until we reached the car. Good thing, because my shaking legs continued to wobble from Jim's touch. Pulling me into a hug Flynn whispered in my ear.

"You're safe Suz, now and forever. I'll never let him touch you again," he growls. I burrow my head against his chest listening to his rapidly beating heart.

"Thank you."

"Don't thank me yet. If I see his face again today I can't be blamed for messing it up. I'd like to make him unrecognizable," Flynn says still pulsing with anger. We hear the click clack of heels pacing across the pavement.

"Warning...get ready for a lecture from the 'rents. Your rude and hasty exit didn't sit too well with them," Chloe informs us. Flynn and I both grumble as he releases me from his arms.

We did get that lecture. Mom and Dad were none too happy with us both. Flynn took most of the brunt of their verbal attack. Mom told us over and over how she raised us better than our earlier actions and reminded us to be more respectful to our elders. When Flynn finally could get a word in edgewise, citing his dislike at Jim's statements about my golf game, Dad finally told Mom to give it a rest. Evidently, Dad wasn't happy either with Jim's attempt to get me out on the golf course just to prove my ability.

Back at the house, the subject of brunch was finally put to rest and I could breathe easier. Chloe got ready to go to work, going in early to help out the late lunch shift. She wasn't scheduled until this evening. Although, she and Flynn rallied together to help me out earlier, back home they returned to ignoring each other. Flynn and I had to come up with something to do giving truth to his statement at lunch that we had plans. So we paddle boarded in the inlet while Dad and Mom watched with amusement. An hour later, Flynn finally got the hang of it and was able to paddle up and down the canal without falling off. It was a good brother/sister bonding day. I'm really gonna miss him while he's overseas.

I wake up Memorial Day with the smell of coffee and bacon floating through the air. After a bathroom break, I walk out to the kitchen to see Mom standing over the stove. It must be her favorite part of the house because she's spent the majority of her visit cooking. "'Morning Mom," I say sliding up beside her to see what she's stirring. Yummy cheese grits, my favorite.

"Good morning, doll," Mom says kissing me on the cheek. "I hope you're hungry."

"Starving," I mumble through a mouth full of bacon. Mom swats at me to stay away from the food until she officially announces it is breakfast time. Dad walks in already breaking a sweat. He grabs some bags from the floor and starts to leave again.

"Hey Dad," I call out.

"Oh, hi honey. I didn't know you were up. Sleep good?"

"Yep. What are you doing?" I ask going over to offer my help.

"Packing the car. Mom and I decided to leave straight from the Bostick's barbecue and head home. I've got an early meeting in the morning I need to get back and prepare for. Mind grabbing the last bag?"

"Yeah, no prob." I help Dad finish loading the car. By the time all the bags are packed Flynn is awake. Go figure, I do all the heavy lifting while my brother enjoys his beauty sleep. "Mom, you need any help?"

"No, it's all ready. Should you wake Chloe?"

"Nah, let her sleep. She got in pretty late last night from work," Flynn says scooting up to the table to be served. Men!

"Well, okay then...breakfast is served." My family sits around the table scoffing down the delicious grits, eggs, bacon and toast. Only after our plates are cleaned and Flynn and Dad dive in for seconds does the conversation start to flow.

"So Suzanna, how's Wyatt enjoying New York?" Mom asks.

I choke on my last bite of eggs. Flynn pats my back while Dad shoves my glass of juice in front of me. I take the juice and chug it down, spewing and coughing in between sips. Wiping my watery eyes, I see my family staring at me. "Um, I don't know."

"Well, he's started his job right?" Dad says around a mouthful of eggs.

"I don't know," I answer again looking at my empty plate.

"Suzanna?" Mom questions.

"I don't know because, um because, we broke up." There I said it.

"Oh Suzanna, we're so sorry," Mom says with sympathy glancing at Dad.

"Really? You're sorry? I thought I'd get the big 'I told you so' lecture." Dad looks guilty but keeps his mouth shut. Mom sighs loudly.

"I know, I know...we weren't exactly thrilled to hear about you starting a romantic relationship with golf qualifying so close. We thought he would be a distraction," Mom says with contriteness. "But, we saw how happy he made you. And a mom can tell when her child's in love. You loved him, right?"

"Yes," I sniffle.

"Oh baby, I'm so sorry. Maybe the distance thing was too much on your new relationship. If things are meant to be, they'll work out once he returns. If that's what you want." Mom is patting my hand in comfort.

"We'll have to wait and see," I say forcing a sad smile. Dad and Flynn quickly change the subject, having listened to too much mushy love talk. Dad goes over Flynn's itinerary for his European soccer schedule while I help Mom clear the table and do the dishes. Mom gushes with excitement about the barbecue. She's been dying to see the inside of the Bostick mansion. While she chatters on, my mind flips back and forth between Wyatt and Katelyn. I remember Katelyn's first visit to my beach home and her comments about how welcoming and cozy it seemed. She made the drastic comparison to her large beach house, never once calling it a home, but instead a show place. She referenced how cold and empty her house was, likening it to that of a mausoleum. I didn't get it then, but I get it now. Katelyn is lonely. Spending night after night in an almost empty mansion with not another human close by. She mentioned her dad rarely stays at the beach working from different cities across the state. And her mom is frequently making extended trips back to Greenville. Having spent an entire weekend with my family and enjoying breakfast together just this morning, I feel sorry for Katelyn. As much as I'd like to back out of going to the party today, my realization of how much Katelyn needs some companionship squashes the idea.

And Wyatt? Well, he's all alone in a new strange city with not one familiar face. I'm sure he's made friends at work. He's such a likable guy. But going home to an empty apartment, night after night has got to be lonely. I don't know what I'd do if Flynn or Chloe wasn't home to greet me after golfing all day. I'm going out on a limb for Katelyn by attending her parents' get-together. Maybe I should do something for Wyatt. Call him? Text him? I just want him to know that although we are through romantically, I still haven't forgotten about him. Of course, I won't tell him how I still think of him every single day and my heart still aches. Just a friendly text message to let him know I care. Hell, if I've managed to be friends with Patrick, can't I do the same with Wyatt?

"All done," Mom says interrupting my thoughts. "I'm going to get ready. You should do the same. The party starts at noon and I hear parking can be a nightmare. Might want to arrive early."

"Yeah, okay," I agree and head into my bedroom. "Hey, Flynn. Wake Chloe up, will you? We've got to leave soon." Flynn nods his head still listening to Dad's conversation about his and Mom's plans to visit Flynn while he's in Europe.

I don't immediately shower. Instead I grab my phone and pull up Wyatt's contact. There's a light indicating a message. I press play to listen. The sound of Wyatt's voice has my heart singing. "Hey Suz, I just wanted you to know I made it to New York safely today. Moving in this weekend before starting work on Monday. It's a cool place. Wish you were here to see it. Anyway, hope you're doing well. I...I... um, never mind. Just thought you'd like to know I made it. Have a great summer. 'Bye."

How long has this message been here? I look at my phone and check the date. Thursday, May 8. Wait, wasn't he supposed to leave on Tuesday? Yes, because I was going to take him to the airport that morning. He did say he arrived *today*, the same day he left the message. I guess his plans were delayed. But why didn't he tell me? Oh yeah, that's right. He did mention his plans being postponed when he called leaving what I now refer to as "the final message". But with my heart too busy breaking into more pieces than I could count, I must have ignored that bit of info. Bitterness and hurt try to bubble up to the surface, but I push them back down. I'm reaching for something positive. At least he made contact even after he said he wouldn't call me again. That's something, right? Maybe he thinks about me as much as I think about him. Doubtful. I think about him constantly. So, should I still reach out and text him? His message was left almost three weeks ago. He probably thinks I've forgotten about him, wiped him from my memory. Ouch, that's gotta hurt. Yes, I'll text him. If not for any other reason than to let him know I got his message.

> Wyatt, hey, its me, Suz. Glad you made it to NY. Hope you are adjusting well to big city life. Happy Memorial Day. Bet the fireworks in NY are spectacular. Good luck with the job.

My finger hovers over the send button. Taking a deep breath I press down. There, done. I texted Wyatt. I don't know why I'm suddenly so nervous. I guess I don't know how Wyatt will receive the contact from me. The first contact since our break up. Will he text me back? Will he call me? Do I want him to do either? I don't know. I'm finally at a good place. Yes, I still mourn his loss. But I'm moving forward, concentrating on golf. I need to stay focused. Too many questions to answer and not enough time, especially today. I power off my phone and throw it on the bed. I've got to worry about Katelyn today. I'll deal with Wyatt later.

Chapter Twenty One

M om and Dad drive their car to the Bostick house, which leaves me and Chloe to cram into Flynn's sports car. Now is the one and only time I'm thankful that Flynn and Chloe are on non-speaking terms. At least I don't have to listen to them bicker the entire drive to Pawleys Island. Pulling up to the beach front home, my first observation is that this isn't just a backyard barbecue. The catering trucks and hired help decked out in formal full service uniforms give me the first clue that this is some party. And Mom need not have worried about parking because there is valet service. I kid you not! I'm so glad I opted to wear a sundress instead of my bathing suit and cover up. I have those items packed in a bag for later.

We exit the car and Flynn passes the keys to the valet attendant before turning around and letting out a low whistle. Chloe and I stand beside him as we all look up at the impressive three story structure with awe. I knew Katelyn's dad was very successful, but this is like something out of *Lifestyles of the Rich and Famous*. Chloe voices my sentiments, "You sure we're at the correct address? This looks more like a hotel than a family residence!" Flynn nods in agreement. We make our way down the paved walkway taking in the freshly manicured lawn, flowers and shrubbery. When we get to the bottom steps that will take us up and onto the veranda and eventually into the house, we are stopped at a check point. A woman dressed in a black skirt and matching blazer greets us.

"Hello and welcome to the annual Bostick Memorial Day barbecue. Could I get your names and invitation, please?" We give her our names and continue to stand in her presence as she waits patiently for our invitation. This could get sticky because our invite was only delivered by word of mouth. Katelyn never gave us anything formal. "Invitation?" she asks again holding her hand out in our direction.

"Um, well, Katelyn invited us, but never gave us a printed invitation," I tell her while Chloe and Landon shuffle beside me looking anywhere but at the party planner/security.

"Ah, yes. Katelyn did give me a list of friends who she invited this year. I'm so glad you could make it. Poor girl, she never has anyone her age to hang out with at events like this," the woman comments flipping the pages on the clipboard she is holding. "There you all are... Suzanna and Flynn Caulder and Chloe Ryder," she says checking off our names. "Will Mr. Landon Smith be joining you later?"

"No, Landon isn't able to make it. He had to work today," Chloe informs the woman. Flynn scowls at the mention of Landon's name and Chloe's knowledge of his whereabouts. I nudge Flynn and mouth *Stop* before Chloe or the gatekeeper can pick up on his angst.

"Well, okay then. Looks like all of Katelyn's invites are now accounted for. Please proceed this way," she says gesturing toward the front entrance where two men dressed in black suits and sunglasses guard the door. More security? Exactly how important is Mr. Bostick? And how prestigious is that secretly held guest list? "Katelyn should be inside. I'll get a message to her that you've arrived. Have a wonderful time." The party planner goes back to checking her papers and waiting for more guests to arrive.

We walk into the massive foyer and are greeted by the hosts of this elaborate party. Judge and Mrs. Bostick welcome and thank us for coming. Then we are shooed away to the back of the house, which opens up to a patio and pool that overlooks the Atlantic Ocean. The view is breathtaking. A buffet of southern barbecue, corn, cole slaw, shrimp, oysters,...you name it, it's here and prepared to perfection for everyone to enjoy. Across the pool there's a stage occupied by a band playing classic beach music. A number of bars are set up sporadically around the yard so that guests don't have to wait in line to be served. Chloe, Flynn and I gravitate to the buffet and fix our plates. Scouting out an unoccupied table, we stake our claim. Flynn offers to get our drinks while we save our spot. "This is freaking incredible," Chloe exclaims taking a bite of her shrimp and grits appetizer. I'm sure she's referring not just to the delicious food, but the entire atmosphere.

With drinks in hand, Flynn returns along with Katelyn and Patrick. "Hey, everyone. I'm so glad you all could come," Katelyn says with excitement and sincerity. I remember her very short list of guests, just us minus Landon, and I think how sad. All this hoopla and extravagance with no one to share it with, until now, must be lonely. I'm glad we could be here to support Katelyn today. For the next hour, we eat, drink and listen to the music from the band. A few of Katelyn's parents' friends drop by and speak, but otherwise we are left alone to enjoy each other's company and the amazing view. The band takes a quick break and I need to do the same.

"Excuse me, but I need to use the restroom," I stand and announce.

"The main house is crowded and I'm sure a line has formed already. Go through the kitchen and down the north hall. There's a small guest bath at the end you can use," Katelyn offers.

"Thanks Katelyn. I'll be back in a few." I give them a wave and navigate through the throng of guests in search of the kitchen. It's buzzing with cooks and catering staff when I enter so no one even notices me. I find the door that leads down the hallway to the secret bathroom Katelyn told me to use. Luckily, it has remained a secret because the hallway is deserted. Walking slowly down the dimly lit passageway, I search for the correct door. Almost to the end, I hear voices coming from a room to the right. I stop, frozen to my spot against the wall when I recognize one of the voices belongs to Jim Miles, Patrick's dad.

"I don't know, Jonathan. Katelyn isn't gonna be too happy with your announcement," Jim says. Who's Jonathan and why are they talking about Katelyn?

"Katelyn will be fine. I promised to cut back my hours to tend to her mother and I've held up my end of the bargain. Nancy is recovering and her treatments are effective. Soon she'll be cancer free," this Jonathan man replies. "I'll have Nancy campaigning with me throughout the state. How much closer could I get to her when she'll be with me practically every day? Katelyn will have no reason to be upset since her mother will be by my side and her medical condition closely monitored." So Jonathan must be Katelyn's dad, Judge Bostick. And Nancy is Katelyn's mother. And she has cancer? Who campaigns while trying to battle cancer?

"Jonathan, you'd really drag Nancy all over the state in her condition? Maybe you should set your political ambitions aside and focus more on the well-being of your wife." Well, what do you know? Jim Miles and I are thinking on the same wavelength.

A menacing laugh follows that makes me shiver. This time it's not Jim giving me the creepy chills. "That's classic coming from you Jim. Tell me again about how focused you were with the well-being of your wife when you wrapped your car around a tree."

"Jonathan," Jim admonishes, but he is ignored.

"Did you consider Marie's safety after that first, second or third drink? How about the fourth or fifth one, huh? Did you think maybe you should have laid off the liquor so you could drive her home without killing her?" Judge Bostick rants loudly making his point. Oh my God! I press my hand to my mouth to silence my shock. If I heard correctly, Judge Bostick basically just inferred that Jim's car accident was no accident at all. He killed Marie by driving drunk that night all those years ago. How did he manage to get away with it? Surely, he would have been arrested at the scene had he been that intoxicated.

"Don't forget, I know all about your little secret. The one I helped cover up. And a secret it will stay as long as you hold up your end of our agreement. Patrick and Katelyn will get married. Just an added bonus to my family values political platform...my one and only daughter, marrying your clean cut, law school bound, son. And all this taking place during my campaign for governor. This is priceless," Judge Bostick exclaims happily. "Now, let's go round up the kids and take the stage. The real show is about to begin." I hear what sounds like Jonathan giving Jim a good 'ole boy slap on the back.

"Jonathan, you sure about this? You know better than anyone how Katelyn can rebel." Katelyn a rebel? No way. The beautiful, sweet girl who has recently befriended me and the rest of the fab five? I just can't see Katelyn ever being rebellious. However, remembering the bad boy Beau and his rock and roll friends, I think maybe Katelyn does have a liking to walk on the wild side. Maybe her lack of friends isn't a lack at all, but that her friends just don't fit into the stereotypical southern belle or beau her family accepts.

"Jim, let me worry about Katelyn. You just make sure this wedding goes as planned and I'll guarantee your firm is safe, as well as your stellar reputation," the judge says with sarcasm. My head is spinning from the information I just gathered while eavesdropping. And there are still so many unanswered questions. Are Patrick and Katelyn being forced to marry? If so, why? This isn't the middle ages and arranged marriages cease to exist. Don't they? Then there's all the incriminating evidence or lack there of surrounding Marie's death. If any of it is true, it's no wonder Jim went off the deep end and straight to the bottom of the bottle after the accident. Who could live with that guilt? The sound of approaching footsteps kicks me in gear as I search for a place to hide. As quietly as possible I stay close to the wall, continuing down the hall. I need to find that bathroom, now! The first door I get to I open and make my way inside to keep from being seen. Two steps over the threshold, I walk right into the hard chest of someone leaving the room.

"Ow," I whisper scream bouncing back and rubbing my forehead.

"Suz?" I look up and I'm surprised and relieved to see one of my best friends. Landon. He's dressed exactly like the two men guarding the front entrance and the rest of the security detail scattered throughout the house and grounds.

"Landon," I say as realization dawns on me. Judge Bostick is Landon's new client. Landon is working for possibly our next state governor. A man who is more calculating and manipulative than Jim Miles. And that's saying a lot.

"What are you doing back here, Suz? This is a restricted area."

"Katelyn gave me permission to use the restroom in this wing of the house. But I seem to have gotten lost," I say with a smile.

"Easy to do in this fortress of a house. Come on, I'll show you where it is," Landon offers. I hear the sound of another person's voice coming through the earpiece that is attached to Landon's ear. He continues to guide me down the hall while giving orders to his team members. "Roger that. I'm headed that way now. I'll meet you on the south side of the stage. Make sure all men are in place before the governor and the Bostick family takes the stage."

I feel safe under Landon's watchful eye. However, the information from earlier still has me rattled and tense. "I've got to go, Suz. Are you sure you're okay?" Landon asks with concern. I really want to tell someone everything I just overheard and Landon would have been the perfect person to share it with. But I can't now, especially since Landon's job is to serve and protect Judge Bostick. How do you tell your friend he's working for a slick, conniving bastard?

"I'm fine," I say trying to sound convincing. "I'll find my way back out. Go on, I know you are needed." Landon gives me a nod and walks toward the room where I left Jim and Judge Bostick talking. I watch until Landon disappears into the room before closing myself inside the bathroom. I wish I could stay in here until the barbecue ended. But I'm curious and anxious about the judge's upcoming announcement and how it will be received. So I stay until I know the coast is clear, only then leaving to join the others at our table.

By the time I make it back to our table, Judge Bostick is at the podium thanking everyone for coming today. After introducing his family, he announces his special guest. "Please give a warm welcome to our South Carolina governor," he beams and claps excitedly. The governor takes Judge Bostick's place at the podium and waits patiently to speak while the crowd roars their approval.

"I can't believe the governor is here," Chloe has to almost shout in my ear to be heard. Just wait, I think to myself. It's only gonna get more interesting.

"Thank you, thank you," the governor begins. "I'm thrilled to be here today with you all. As some of you may have heard, I was on the short list to replace the retiring secretary of state. Well, this morning I received the news that I had been granted the nomination." Loud cheers interrupt the governor. "Thanks, it is quite the honor and I am humbled. The congressional hearing will begin as early as next week. My political advisees tell me that's just a technicality. With my distinguished political service record and unblemished personal life I've been guaranteed the job. It's bitter sweet, leaving my loyal South Carolina constituents. The state will require a special election this fall to vote in a new governor. Now, I have some say in the matter. I get to endorse the republican who will hopefully take my place. So today, I'm asking you all to help me convince the Honorable Judge Jonathan Bostick to accept my endorsement and make a run for the governor's office to continue to lead this state into the future. Judge Bostick," the governor says and waves him back to the podium. Judge Bostick and his wife walk hand in hand to stand beside the governor. "Will you accept my endorsement and serve the great people of the state of South Carolina as our next governor?"

"Absolutely," the judge responds. The crowd erupts again in heavy applause. As every eye is on the governor, the judge and his wife, I watch Katelyn. Her normally olive complexion has turned pale. She sways into Patrick, on the brink of fainting, before he catches her and holds her upright. He quickly whispers something in her ear to calm her down. She no longer looks ready to hit the deck, but the scowl she's directing at her father is evident. Unhappy doesn't touch what Katelyn's feeling in this moment.

"I am honored to have the opportunity to serve you all. Thank you governor for your service to our great state. I will continue your good works. In addition to job growth and expansion, I have several items on my agenda that I will work tirelessly toward, if elected. My top priority is more awareness and research for cancer, specifically breast cancer. As some of you know, my beautiful wife Nancy was diagnosed months ago with this horrible disease. She's fought with a strength few possess and she's now a survivor. With her help, I'd like for women all across this state to get the medical treatments needed to survive this deadly disease and hopefully one day eradicate it." The judge places a tender kiss on his wife's lips and the crowd ohhhhs and ahhhhhs. I too believe in helping all women struck with cancer, however, it seems such a personal story to use as campaign propaganda. By the look on Katelyn's face, she agrees.

"Continuing this family affair, I will implement state supported preschool programs for our little ones. My son Rodney and his lovely wife Stephanie are expecting my first grandchild in just a few months. I believe it's my duty to provide that grandson or granddaughter, as well as all the other children in this state, with every educational opportunity I can." Katelyn's brother and his wife step forward to smile and wave at the crowd. "And while we are on the topic of education, our schools have seen an increase in budget cuts, especially in the arts programs. Come here Katelyn, you too Patrick." Katelyn and Patrick walk hand in hand to stand on the other side of the podium beside Judge Bostick. "This beautiful young woman is my daughter. And this," he says pointing to Patrick, "is her soon to be husband. As a young girl, Katelyn was extremely musically talented. Under the encouragement of her school music teacher, Katelyn focused on her abilities and became musically educated and gifted. She has the voice of an angel and her fingers can fly over the keys of a piano creating enchanted melodies. With her help, I will fight for more funding in the public education system, designating them specially to go toward art programs, like music and drama." Chloe claps with enthusiasm beside me with the mention of anything to do with drama. Katelyn stands by her father's side as he waits for her to reply. She forces her lips to curve into an almost smile and just nods. The crowd, interpreting Katelyn's behavior as shyness, claps encouragingly. Katelyn shrugs out of her father's embrace and goes to stand a few feet away putting distance between them. The judge continues his speech.

"Thank you all again for coming today and accepting me as your republican candidate in November's special election. With the support of my family and you all, I know I can win. South Carolinians are the greatest people on the planet. It will be my honor to work and serve each and every one of them. Enjoy the rest of the afternoon and let's get this party started!" The judge finally finishes his speech to hoots and hollers from the now rowdy and restless crowd. People rush to the front of the stage to congratulate and shake the now governor's and possible new governor's hands. Katelyn and Patrick are trapped on stage having to endure press and media questions and photographs. I know Landon is somewhere among all the security people guarding the stage, although I haven't seen him since we were inside the house.

"Wow, never expected that," Flynn says bringing us another round of refreshing drinks.

"I know, me either. Can you believe Katelyn's dad and Patrick's future father in law could be governor?" Chloe giggles just thinking about it.

"I'm not sure everyone is as excited about this as you two are," I mumble.

"What? Who's not excited to be partying with the governor and his possible successor?" Flynn asks dumbfounded.

"I'm just worried about Katelyn. Trying to plan a wedding while her mother recovers from cancer treatments. And now, having to deal with her dad's intense and fast campaign. It might be too much for her to handle."

"Okay, mother hen. Yeah, it's gonna be busy. But the governor? Really? I'd be thrilled if my dad was asked to run. Hey, do you think we'll get invited to the governor's mansion?" Chloe asks suddenly all serious. I burst out laughing.

"Probably not," I reply. Chloe looks like I just told her her beloved pet died. Which only makes me laugh harder.

Chapter Twenty Two

"**G**ood grief, Chloe," I yell as she speeds down the winding roads that lead us to Folly Beach. I'm scared I might die before we actually get there. Her multitasking...eating French fries, talking to Katelyn in the back seat, changing radio stations, and breaking every traffic law while driving...well, it's making me just a little nervous. Fortunately we are just a few minutes out and should be arriving soon, I hope, to her Aunt Tina's beach cottage. We decided to get away from Garden City for the weekend. Since the Memorial Day barbecue at Katelyn's parents' house, things have been weird. I still play golf everyday and yes, Patrick is still carting me back and forth from the course. Even though Chloe and I both got our cars back from the body shops, Patrick still insisted on playing chauffeur. But our easy conversations of the past have become tense again. It's not Patrick, it's me. With all the information I learned eavesdropping on Judge Bostick and Jim Miles...possible arranged marriage, accusations of involuntary manslaughter, Katelyn's so called rebellious ways, Landon working for Katelyn's dad...I'm just keeping my mouth shut. I really want to ask Patrick questions, especially concerning his engagement. But I'm scared that will open up a whole can of worms I'm not yet ready to deal with. I'd hoped to talk to Chloe about everything I overheard. She's been so busy with work and me with golf, we've hardly found time to have a decent conversation, much less something so heavy. That's why when Chloe found out she had the weekend off, I suggested this out of town trip to visit her aunt. I was so excited with my brilliant idea for a girls' weekend, I blurted it out in front of the guys and Katelyn. Although I really, really needed some quality time with my bestie, the look of exuberance on Katelyn's face prompted me to ask her to join us. I mean, I couldn't just take it back.

So here we are, all three of us, pulling into the gravel drive of Aunt Tina's Folly Beach home. I breathe a sigh of relief that we made it in one piece. I'll be the one driving back on Sunday. "There you are," Aunt Tina yells from the covered porch. Chloe rushes out of the car and runs to meet her aunt halfway. They both throw their arms around each other in a touching embrace. Chloe and her aunt have had a special bond for as long as I can remember. Chloe seems much more attached to her aunt than to her own mother. "I'm so glad you girls came to visit," Aunt Tina exclaims with Chloe still in her arms.

"Thanks for having us. It's good to get away," I say and walk over to share in the love. Aunt Tina gifts me with one of her motherly hugs. When she finally releases me and gives me a good looking over, she glances over my shoulder. "Oh, and this is our friend Katelyn. Patrick's fiancée". I don't miss the look of astonishment at my introduction. Aunt Tina knows that Patrick and I dated in high school. I'm sure she's more than shocked that I'm now friends with his soon to be wife. Regardless, she still extends her open arms wide for Katelyn to walk into. The woman sure knows how to give some hugs.

"Well, welcome Katelyn. It's a pleasure to meet you," Aunt Tina says. "I hope you girls haven't eaten lunch yet. I've got everything prepared and it's ready."

"Yum, I'm starving," Chloe says giving her aunt a quick kiss on the cheek before grabbing her bags out of the car. I guess her breakfast of French fries wasn't all that satisfying. She complained on the drive down that I rushed her so much this morning she forget to pack her daily intake of sugar, having to forego her standard breakfast... a Pop-Tart and Diet Coke. Chloe's choice of meals certainly lacks nutritional value. Maybe Aunt Tina's lunch will remedy that, at least for today.

After a delicious lunch of shrimp salad croissants and homemade potato chips, we change into our swimsuits and head out to the beach.

For a while we each just do our own thing. I'm reading a magazine, Katelyn is listening to music and Chloe is watching the surfers. After a couple of hours of sun and a few dips in the ocean, Chloe finally asks what we want to do this evening.

"I'm hoping to see Lisa and James while we are in Charleston. Any word from either of them?" I ask.

"Lisa really wanted to join us on the beach today, but had to work a shift at the hospital. James is studying, as usual. But they promise to meet us for drinks and maybe dinner later."

"Happy hour? If that's the case, we need to go ahead and get ready. I'm guessing they want to meet somewhere downtown." The ride from Folly Beach to downtown Charleston is about twenty to thirty minutes depending on traffic.

"Katelyn, you up for a night on the town?" Chloe asks.

"Sure, as long as we don't step foot inside the Omni Hotel."

"O-kay...you got something against that establishment?" Chloe probes.

"My dad is campaigning in the lower state. Chances are he's booked a room at the Omni if he's anywhere near Charleston. That's where he always stays while on business." Katelyn puckers her lips, just the mention of her dad and his campaign leaving a bad taste in her mouth. I'll be sure to steer clear of that topic tonight.

"Actually, James mentioned a great place for drinks. The Palace Hotel just opened a few months ago. A buddy of his from medical school knows the owner. And it's not even within a comfortable walking distance to the Omni," Chloe offers.

"Then it sounds perfect. Let's go get glam. Can't wait for a night out with you girls!" Katelyn's mood drastically improves. I'm pretty psyched myself for a girls' night out. It's been a while since I tore one on. Tonight, I'm looking forward to forgetting everything and having some fun with my friends.

Katelyn's worry about running into her father flies out the window as the cab takes us west of Calhoun Street. We are far away from King and Meeting Streets which travel east and end at the Battery. That's where you'll find the expensive shopping district, fancy restaurants and multimillion dollar homes. That's also the direction of the infamous Omni Hotel and shops. No, we are nowhere near those places. The cab pulls to a stop in front of a nondescript building on Hanover Street. I'm thinking James must have given us the wrong address. "You sure this is it?" I say looking at my surroundings. Most of the buildings lining the streets are old and in desperate need of some fresh paint. Some actually look vacant. The windows of the building we are parked in front of has iron bars on them. The only clue that we have stumbled upon the right place is the lighted beer signs flashing in the windows. However, there's nothing indicating the bar/restaurant's name.

"Yep, this is it. James said the outside might look like a dump, but inside it's spectacular. Come on," Chloe says throwing some cash at our cab driver. We are greeted by a huge African American man just outside the door.

"Evening ladies," he acknowledges us while opening the heavy wooden door. Although my surroundings scream 'run', this man's presence makes me feel safe. The contrast between outside and inside is unbelievable. I feel like I just walked into a posh big city night club. Scanning the room, I see a polished wooden bar to the right with chrome barstools lining the floor. Tables are scattered around the remaining area lit by crystal chandeliers draped across the ceiling. In the corner to the left are stairs that rise to a platform which I assume is used as a stage. Down the hall, there is a sign indicating the directions to the restrooms and to the outdoor patio area in the back. This is actually a very nice place.

"Yay, you're here," Lisa screeches from the bar. She swings her legs around and hops down before breaking out into a full run. Her little arms stretch wide pulling all three of us into a group hug. "We just got here a few minutes ago and ordered a round of drinks. So what do you think?" she asks gesturing with a hand around the bar.

"Now that I'm off the street and safe from being mugged, I think I really like this place."

Lisa laughs. "You have nothing to fear. This part of town is being revitalized. The property values in this neighborhood are starting to increase. Before long, it'll look just like the part of downtown you're used to visiting." Yeah, maybe my grandchildren can enjoy it. It'll take a long time before this area resembles anything from the historical district around the Battery.

"Hey, where's the love?" James shouts holding up a tray of drinks. "Come this way, I've got us a table." We follow James to a table in the back corner farthest from the stage. After grabbing our drinks and showering James with hugs and kisses, we take our seats. "So, tell me what kinds of trouble you girls are causing in GC?"

"Trouble free in GC, but tonight..."Chloe teases.

"So you come to my stomping grounds to raise a little hell?"

"If the opportunity arises tonight, absolutely," Chloe confirms with a smile.

"Great," James says shaking his head.

"Oh my gosh, Katelyn, we heard about your dad's run for office. That must be so exciting!" Lisa says enthusiastically. I lean back as not to be seen by Katelyn and discreetly shake my head. Lisa doesn't take the hint. "Wow, I can't believe I'm sitting with the daughter of the future governor."

"I wouldn't really know. Mom and Dad are both traveling for the campaign. I'm not really involved," Katelyn replies politely.

"Well, of course it's a busy time for you all. I'm sure you're overwhelmed with the news of the special election right smack dab in the middle of trying to plan your wedding," Lisa continues clueless. I'm gonna have to up my game. I lean back even further out of Katelyn's sight and scrape my finger across my neck. Lisa finally looks my way, recognizing my impromptu sign language to cut this line of questioning.

Katelyn never one to be inconsiderate answers Lisa anyway. "I guess, but Mom took care of a lot of the wedding details while she was recuperating from chemo treatments. I'm just handling a few last minute things." I don't know if it's the mention of her mother's cancer battle or the wedding that makes Katelyn sound so sad. I think it may be both.

"How is your future hubby? I haven't called him in a while." James takes over the conversation.

"Patrick is fine. He is finalizing his class schedule for law school in the fall. We are still looking for a place to live in Columbia. A realtor has some prospects lined up for us to come see next time we make the trip. Other than that he keeps busy driving Suzanna back and forth to golf everyday." Although Katelyn's statement was said matter of factly with not a trace of jealousy or maliciousness, both Lisa and James look to me with raised eyebrows. I'm sure they are curious as to why Patrick and I are spending so much time together.

"I was without a car for weeks so he offered me a ride," I defend his actions and mine.

"Yeah, Mom told me about the vandalism and attempted break in. That sucks! Did they ever catch 'em?" James asks.

"Not that I'm aware of." I doubt they are looking in the right place. They would never suspect Jim Miles, attorney at law, to trash mine and Chloe's cars. Secretly I'm adding that to his long list of crimes. Destruction of personal property, attempted sexual assault, involuntary manslaughter...wow, his rap sheet rivals that of one on *America's Most Wanted.*

"What about Landon? What's he up to?" James inquires.

"We haven't seen much of Landon lately. He's got this new *secret* client that's keeping him really busy. I've talked to him a few times, but every time he's been out of town. I miss the big guy," Chloe says wistfully. I want to share with Chloe what I know about Landon's new client, but I don't think it's my place. When Landon never showed up at the barbecue to say hello to the rest of the gang, I had the sneaky suspicion that he wanted his job title to remain a secret. I never asked Katelyn if she and Patrick ever ran into Landon after the announcement. Surely, with all the media and press they had to do after Judge Bostick's endorsement, they would have seen Landon at some point. I glance over at Katelyn and see the frown on her face. I bet she knows about Landon's job of protecting her dad. She's just not ready to share that information either.

"Boring. Come on, you guys have got to have some juicy gossip. Tell me what Lover Boy is up to. I bet there's at least a few entertaining stories involving Flynn," James pries.

"Flynn leaves for Europe next week," I say sadly.

"No, no, no, no," Chloe stands abruptly and says with authority, shaking her head. "We are not going there tonight. We're supposed to be having fun not trying to depress Suz." Sure, I'm sad at the thought of my brother traveling to another country for at least a year, but I wasn't gonna let it ruin my night. I'm thankful to Chloe for the sudden subject change. However, I think she's protecting herself more than me. Although their relationship remains turbulent, she and Flynn share something between them that is more than lust. Next week will be hard for Chloe. I make a mental note to be extra attentive to her feelings. "Hey, bartender, could you get us a round of shots over here? Don't care what it is, just make it strong."

The bartender arrives shortly after Chloe shouts her order with a tray of small glasses rimmed in sugar and filled with vodka and a bowl of lemons. "Strong and sweet, just the way I like my customers. James excluded, of course," the bartender flirts as he delivers our drinks. "This round is on the house."

"Thanks man. Ladies, this is Taylor, the owner of this dump. Taylor meet Suzanna, Chloe and Katelyn," James introduces us.

"It's a pleasure to meet you all. And thanks for enhancing the scenery around here." Chloe and Katelyn giggle while I roll my eyes. "What are we waiting for, girls? Bottoms up!" Taylor grabs his shot glass and waits for us to join him.

"Dude, lay off my friends," James threatens in a joking manner. When Taylor pushes the only remaining shot glass James' way, James throws up his hand to stop it. "You guys will have to drink one for me. I've still got a ton of studying to do before classes start up again on Monday. I've got to cut our visit short." James was always the most studious of the bunch. He is so intelligent I don't know why he feels the need to study so hard. He was always an overachiever striving for perfection. I guess old habits never die.

"Ah, come on James. Just one more drink," I plead.

"No can do. But I'll let Lisa join you girls for the rest of the night if you promise to get her home safely."

"You sure, baby? I haven't seen you in days."

"You two live together, for pete's sake. You've seen him. Party with us tonight Lisa. You don't get to see us that often," Chloe begs. Lisa pulls her bottom lip between her teeth torn to make a decision. James pulls on her lip until she releases it and smoothes the bite mark with his thumb.

"I have to study anyway so we really wouldn't be spending any time together tonight. Hang with the girls and have fun. You work so damn hard. You need to let loose," James reasons with Lisa and tops it off with a quick kiss. That's not enough convincing for Lisa because she pulls his lips back to her and kisses him hungrily until I have to look away. It's not until Taylor clears his throat that they unlock their lips and their mouths separate.

"Okay," Lisa says breathlessly. "But study until I get home then we'll have our own party."

"It's a date," James says through a smile. Laying one last kiss on Lisa's lips he tells us all goodbye. "Taylor, watch out for my girls."

"Will do, man."

As soon as James walks out the door, Lisa's eyes fill with unshed tears. "Lisa, you okay? You can leave with James if you want."

"No, I want to stay and hang with y'all. It's just, I don't know. I feel like I never get to see James." She looks at Chloe to direct her next statement. "Yes, we do live together, but my work schedule and his school schedule are complete opposites. When he's walking into the door I'm walking out, or vise versa."

"Lisa, the first few years of medical school are always the hardest. But it'll get better," Chloe encourages.

"Yeah, if we can make it that long. I love that man more than anything. But our limited time together usually ends up with us bickering at each over something stupid. Both our stress levels are through the roof," Lisa sniffles wiping at her nose.

"That's gotta be tough on a relationship," I comment.

"And in the bedroom," Chloe adds.

"Chloe," I chide. Lisa's and James' sex life is none of our business.

"No, she's right. And I've been dying to talk to someone about it." Poor Lisa. I'm not getting any on a regular basis, or not at all.

But heck, I'm not living with my boyfriend either. "Half the time our sleep schedules are just as whacked out as our school and work schedules. But the few times we actually land in the bed at the same time, we're asleep before even the heavy petting gets started. We're both running on fumes and by the end of the day we're exhausted."

"Who says you have to have sex at the end of the day? That's not a rule, Lisa." Here Chloe goes doing her best impersonation of Dr. Ruth. "Morning, noon, or night you go seduce that boy. I guarantee if he has just a thread of energy to keep his eyes open long enough to see you sashay your sexy ass toward him, his brain won't care that he's tired, or has to study, or go to class. His lower regions will be making the decisions for him. And I think we know how those lower regions think," Chloe says with a wink. Lisa cracks the first smile since James left twenty minutes ago.

"I know something about strained marriages. God knows my dad put work ahead of his wife and family for a long time," Katelyn joins the conversation. "Still does," she mumbles under her breath. "That's why it's so important to make the time to show that someone special how much you love them. Life is short, so take advantage of each and every moment while you can. I'm with Chloe...doesn't matter the time of day it's done, just that it's done."

"Amen, sista!" Chloe raises her glass for a toast. "Here's to spontaneous, hot, sweaty, wild, toe-curling, scream to the top of your lungs, satisfying sex. The kind Lisa is gonna have tonight when we get her home at some ungodly morning hour."

"Here, here," Lisa says as we clink our glasses and down the shots.

"Hope you ladies wore your dancing shoes. The band is about to start up," Taylor says as he delivers us yet more drinks. He never lets our glasses get empty before providing a replacement. To say we are all feeling no pain, would be putting it mildly.

"Hot damn, I love a man with talented fingers," Katelyn swoons.

"Oh me, too. And I'm not referring to just guitar playing talent," Chloe slurs. They both giggle while Lisa, Taylor and I watch in amusement.

"So, who's playing tonight? You don't normally have live entertainment," Lisa asks Taylor.

"I'm not sure they even have a band name. Just a few Citadel graduates who are all back in town on the same weekend. They wanted to jam so I offered the space. Figured the customers would enjoy it, so it's a win win."

We are all so drunk we didn't notice the band members setting up earlier. The strumming of guitar chords and the beat of the drums direct our attention to the stage up front. The lights have been lowered so it's kinda hard to see clearly. The only thing I can make out is four silhouette figures getting ready to rock. "Good evening everyone. We're so happy to be here tonight...thanks again Taylor. It's been awhile since we played together so please bare with us. Okay, you ready? One, two, one, two, three..." The drums start a heavy beat followed by the base guitar. Once the rhythm is set, the lead guitar joins in with a fast paced tempo. The lead singer begins singing in a smooth sexy voice and the crowd goes wild. A crowd which has doubled in size since we first arrived. Right now the place is packed.

"Let's go get our groove on, girls," Chloe shouts to be heard over the band. We walk, or more like stumble, out to the small dance floor and try to squeeze out some floor room for the four of us. We bump and grind to the band's covers of Daughtry, Nickelback, and Maroon 5. They even put their rock and roll touch on Blake Shelton's country song "Boys 'Round Here", which the southern patrons loved. The band was a little rusty in parts due to their lack of practice but it was barely noticeable. When the lead singer sang the wrong lyrics and the drummer missed a beat, the crowd continued dancing and singing encouraging the band to just go on. The only spotless performance of the night was given by the lead guitarist who never missed a note and shredded his guitar solos like a pro.

Given the small dance space, I frequently kept bumping into strangers with my arms or legs. On one such occasion, I'm flailing my arms to the rhythm of the beat when my hand connects with a hard, cold and wet surface. Seconds later the dance floor around my feet is covered in liquor, ice and small pieces of glass from the drink I accidentally knocked out of someone's grip. I turn around quickly to apologize, but the apology gets stuck in my throat. Standing before me, at least wearing more clothing now than when I saw her last, is the one woman I never, ever wanted to lay eyes on again.

"Bridgett?" I question. Surely my body heat from dancing is frying my brain. And the copious amounts of alcohol I consumed tonight are making my eyes deceive me. This can't be Bridgett. She's supposed to be back in Florida.

"Hi Suzanna, what a small world," she says in greeting. I stand frozen in a sea of bodies dancing around me still trying to decide if I'm hallucinating.

"Um...hey?" What else do you say to the woman you found naked in your boyfriend's bed. If I was quick with my tongue like Chloe, I'm sure I could think of unlimited insults to hurl her way. But I'm not a confrontational person. I'd rather just walk away than rehash the horrible day when I last saw Bridgett. So I begin to back up ready to flee to our table.

"Wait Suzanna," Bridgett starts, but I put up a hand to quickly cut her off.

"I...I, I don't want to talk to you."

"Then just listen, because I really need to talk to you," Bridgett almost begs. She waits anxiously for me to respond. What in the world could she possibly want to tell me? What a great lover Wyatt is? How good it feels being in his arms? How attentive he is to a woman's every need? Hell, maybe we can sit down for a chat and swap stories about our between the sheets experiences with him. Holy moly, this is pure torture. I can't have a conversation with Bridgett. I can't even stand looking at her. The pain she caused and continues to cause is unbearable. Not offering to lend my ear, I turn around hoping for a quick escape.

"Suzanna," Bridgett pleads as she grabs my arm to keep me from leaving. "Please."

"Get your grubby, back stabbing hands off her, you bitch," Chloe screams in Bridgett's face as she pushes her back to stand between us. People around us notice the commotion and stop dancing to watch.

I'm sure some of the guys are secretly hoping to witness a cat fight. Ugh, men!

"This is between me and Suzanna. I really need to explain things to her." Bridgett remains calm even under Chloe's fury. Although she is responding to Chloe's demands, she never breaks eye contact with me.

"Explain? Explain! How the hell do you manage to explain the fact that Suzanna found your naked ass in her boyfriend's bed? Huh? This has got to be a real good one," Chloe laughs but there is no trace of humor.

"Suzanna," Bridgett addresses me again, ignoring Chloe and taking a step forward in my direction. The tone of her voice breaks through my earlier resolve. The conceitedness I thought I'd hear from stealing my man is absent. And the guilt that should be present because of her betrayal of our friendship isn't apparent either. The only thing I hear is the weight of something Bridgett has been carrying around and needs to get off her chest desperately.

However, Chloe's read on Bridgett is entirely different. A few seconds after Bridgett's forward motion, Chloe is back in her face. She shoves Bridgett backwards causing her to stumble into the surrounding onlookers. "Leave her alone, you slut!" Chloe doesn't stop there. With clenched fists, she continues in Bridgett's direction. I swear, if she starts a brawl in this place I'm gonna kill her.

"Chloe, stop it!" I grab her and pull her back. Strong male arms secure Chloe around her waist as she kicks and screams to get loose.

"Put me down, you Neanderthal," Chloe screams. When I just stand there gawking in surprise, for the second time in the last five minutes, instead of helping Chloe escape, she realizes something else is up. She turns her head to the side and looks up, a smile lighting up her face. "Landon," Chloe says much more calmly than seconds earlier. Simultaneously I question, "Landon?" Is everyone I know from my present and past gonna show up tonight in this bar?

"What seems to be the trouble, ladies?" Landon asks.

"That leg spreading, that boyfriend stealing, that...that whore," Chloe begins pointing at Bridgett. I slap my hand over Chloe's mouth to shut her up.

"Landon, would you take Chloe to the bar for a drink and make her stop talking? I'm going back to our table to listen to what Bridgett has to say."

"You're doing *what*?" Chloe asks in shock.

"Landon, please." Landon keeps his arms securely around Chloe's waist.

"You sure about this Suz?" Landon knows nothing about my break up with Wyatt. I never even told him we were dating. Unless, Chloe spilled the beans, I'm not sure Landon knows anything about what's going on at the moment. But he definitely feels the tension and immediately goes into protection mode. I'm lucky his protectiveness is not exclusive to Chloe. Tonight, he's truly concerned about my well-being.

"Yeah, I'm sure. This should only take a few minutes. Come join me soon?" I don't want to be with Bridgett by myself for too long. I don't have a clue what she's about to tell me. Good or bad, I know I'll need my friends regardless. Landon gives me a nod then carries a very non-complacent Chloe to the bar. I walk to our table in the back not bothering to see if Bridgett is following. Giving her the chance to speak her mind, it's her call now whether or not she'll actually follow through.

Arriving at the table I find a fresh drink has been placed at my seat. Lifting my arm with drink in hand I sign my appreciation. Taylor acknowledges my gesture of gratitude with a flirtatious wink. Downing half the drink in one gulp I quench my thirst. More so, I use the alcoholic beverage to ease my nerves about the conversation that is about to take place. When I place my glass down on the table, Bridgett is occupying the seat across from me. "So...," Bridgett starts but then finds it difficult to continue.

"Look, you wanted to talk, so talk. I don't know how long Landon can subdue Chloe at the bar and keep her from storming over here to claw out your eyes. Plus, I'm sure Katelyn's and Lisa's curiosity is at an all time high. If you want to do this without an audience I suggest you get started."

"I didn't sleep with Wyatt," Bridgett blurts out.

"Come again." I'm not sure I heard her right.

"I know how it looked, but Wyatt and I didn't sleep together. Other than having to drag me from the car and up into his apartment, he never even touched me."

"But, you were naked. In. His. Bed!" I might not be the smartest chick on the block, but I know what I saw. Does she take me for a fool?

"Just let me explain. I attended Wyatt's going away party that night. He was there for maybe thirty minutes until he bolted. Me and the rest of the bartenders and some regular customers continued partying into the night. When we shut down the Blue Marlin we headed over to some seedy bar where the guys sometimes go after work to play pool. I had an awful lot to drink by that time. While the guys were engaged in their pool game, some douchebag was putting the moves on me. At first it was fun to flirt with him and yank his chain. But when he started getting hands on and wouldn't take no for an answer, I became afraid. No one was paying me any attention except that sleazy guy. Then suddenly Wyatt appeared and he was in a piss poor mood. It must have been at least four or more hours since he left his party. Anyway, he realized how drunk I was and the distress I was in and came to my rescue. I'm embarrassed to say how drunk I was, Suz. I couldn't even give Wyatt directions to get me home. So he took me to his place to let me sleep it off. He offered me his bed and he took the couch."

"Then why were your clothes off?" I ask trying to make sense of everything Bridgett just divulged.

"I guess I took them off sometime during the night. Wyatt said I all but face planted on his bed and passed out before he could even turn off the light. He said I was fully clothed when he left to sleep on the couch. I'm thinking I got hot and threw them off sometime in the middle of the night while I was still half asleep. Next thing I know, you're standing at the door. My brain was still very fuzzy, especially waking up in strange surroundings. Seeing you there, the first thing that popped in my head was your living at the beach. That's why I said something about I thought you would be there. Looking back,

I'm sure my comment only made you think the worst." Bridgett's sincerity and apologetic look sways me into maybe believing her.

"So you didn't sleep with Wyatt? After your major crush on him you can't blame me for thinking you didn't at least try to use some of your seduction tactics that night."

Bridgett laughs. "Suz, I could barely say my name much less try and seduce someone. Plus, as soon as I realized how much Wyatt loved you the night I found you two together at the Blue Marlin, I knew I never stood a chance with him."

"Oh," is all I can manage.

"By the time I dressed and walked out of Wyatt's bedroom you were gone. Wyatt sat on the couch all mopey acting. Stringing together the events that must have taken place after you found me, I begged Wyatt to let's go after you. I was ready to explain the misunderstood situation. But Wyatt said to just leave it alone. The entire drive to my house I pleaded with Wyatt to let me call you, but he asked me not to. I figured he wanted to tell you himself. The last I've seen of Wyatt is when he dropped me off. I believed you two were back together. However, with the icy reception I received from you and Chloe tonight, I assume he never told you the truth. I'm so sorry, Suzanna."

"Me too. Thanks for telling me." I'm more than relieved to hear that Wyatt didn't cheat on me. But the relief is quickly replaced with the never ending pain I feel since my break up with Wyatt. If he didn't cheat, then why did he end things? Cheating, as awful as it is, did give me a conclusive reason as to why our relationship didn't continue. Now, I can only assume he just didn't want to be with me anymore. And I think that hurts even more.

"Suzanna, I know we aren't friends and will probably never be. I'm sure any advice I give you'll ignore. But Wyatt is such a good guy. And he and you were great together. Whatever is going on between you two, please, please try to fix it." Bridgett stands from the table getting ready to leave. "Well, good luck with...well, with everything. Goodbye Suzanna." After giving me her last apologetic expression she turns to walk off.

"Hey, Bridgett?" She stops and glances back over her shoulder. "Thank you. I'm not sure if it'll change anything, but I really needed to hear that. Good luck to you as well." She gives me a smile before disappearing into the crowd.

I sit alone at the table replaying every word Bridgett just said. She didn't sleep with Wyatt. I'm still having a hard time wrapping my head around the reality of the situation. Why would Wyatt make me think he cheated on me? To be fair, he did tell me he no longer wanted a long distance relationship before I discovered Bridgett in his bed. I was already reeling from that statement. Why the need to pour salt in the wound making me think he slept with Bridgett? Seems downright cruel. Something I would have never thought Wyatt could be. Maybe it was his cowardly way to rely on my untrue assumptions rather than tell me he just didn't want me anymore. This new feeling of being unwanted really, really hurts.

I'm so consumed in my depressing thoughts I don't realize the band has started back up. From the crowd of people around the stage, looks like they've been back at it for a while. Which means Landon is no longer guarding Chloe at the bar. Then where the hell is she? Oh no. I hope she didn't run into Bridgett before she came to talk with me. I wonder where Katelyn and Lisa are. I thought for sure they'd be at the table firing questions at me after witnessing the yelling and almost cat fight that ensued earlier. But they are MIA as well. While I look around the bar for my missing friends the band finishes their current song. Although the stage lighting is still dim, I recognize the familiar voice speaking through the microphone.

"Thank you guys. You've been great tonight." The crowd claps with enthusiasm at Landon's praise. "I'd like to slow things down a bit. This next song means a lot to me. But I need some help to perform it." Girls on the front row line up waving their arms in hopes of being picked. "Katelyn, you mind accompanying me tonight?" A shy Katelyn is pushed toward the front of the stage. Landon extends his hand and hoists her up on the platform. The other band members take a breather while Landon exchanges his electric guitar for an acoustic. He situates himself on a stool in front of the one microphone and Katelyn sits on the empty one beside his. He whispers something in her ear before striking a slow melodic chord. When he begins singing, I recognize the song as a folksy love ballad that was made famous by a movie years ago. His voice, smooth, crisp and soft adds to the tenderness of the song. When Katelyn joins in, their voices harmonizing perfectly, I think I might cry. They sing about wanting each other and falling slowly in love. Words about making a choice and still having time fill the chorus. The lyrics trigger my memory and I place the song as the one in the international film about two musicians making beautiful music together and developing feelings for each other. But the woman's husband and the guy's ex-girlfriend are barriers that can't be overcome halting their budding relationship. The parallels of the storyline and Katelyn's and Landon's lives do not go unnoticed. I've had the feeling since that night at Dead Dog that Katelyn and Landon share a bond. Whether it's just musically or more, I can't say for sure. But the passion between them when they sing together is obvious, not just to me but to everyone here tonight. When the song finally ends, Katelyn and Landon rest on the stools, sitting closely, their foreheads pressed together. Not one person makes a sound and the bar is eerily quiet. We are all speechless at the tender moment we just witnessed. Moments pass before people erupt in applause. Katelyn quickly snaps out of her trance, pulling away from Landon and hopping off the stage. I watch as patrons congratulate her on a job well done. She really did perform like a professional tonight. Leads me to believe she is no stranger to the stage. She graciously and politely accepts her accolades, but never stops until she arrives at our table. I stand to give her a congratulatory hug as she approaches. "That was amazing...hey, what's all this?"

From her forced smile, no one could tell Katelyn was feeling anything other than elation. However, her watery eyes tell me differently. She falls into my arms, burying her face in the crook of my neck to hide the onslaught of tears. I hold her and let the emotions of her performance wash over her. She doesn't have too much time to pull it together. Lisa and Chloe make a beeline through the crowd rushing to the table. "Katelyn, wow, just wow. You're like a star," Chloe gushes. Katelyn peels herself from my embrace, discreetly wiping at her eyes.

"I didn't know you could sing," Lisa pipes in. Both Lisa and Chloe are bouncing on their toes with excitement. Katelyn has the newest members of her fan club, no doubt.

"Thank you," Katelyn replies hiding her previous emotional state with a beaming smile. "I haven't performed live in a long time. It felt really good."

"You've been holding out on us, chicka. What other secrets do you have?" Chloe asks. Although she is teasing, Katelyn looks startled by the question. "Suz, you okay? Where's Bridgett? I'm ready to take that bitch out!"

Yeah, Chloe's had enough to drink tonight. "That won't be necessary, but thanks. Hey, y'all ready to call it a night and get out of here?"

"But what about Landon?" Chloe asks glancing back at the stage. We all watch as the band continues to play. Landon pays no attention to his screaming female fans that have pushed their way in front of him. His intense gaze is directed only at our table, mainly focusing on one particular individual. Katelyn. Hmmmmm.

"What's Landon doing in Charleston anyway? I thought he had to work this weekend." Of course I know that Landon is working since finding out that Katelyn's dad has been campaigning in the area. I'm just wondering how much Chloe is aware of.

"Guess he didn't have to work after all. Once he heard some of his college buddies were getting together, I assume he planned to make the trip. I'm so glad we got to hear him play again." Smiling like silly fan girls, we continue to watch Landon play on stage with the band. Well, all of us except Katelyn. Deep in thought, obviously making the connection about Landon's so called impromptu visit to Charleston, she scowls at his performance. I don't think she is very happy about the working relationship Landon has with her dad. "I'll give a message to Taylor for Landon to stop by Aunt Tina's later once he wraps up things here," Chloe says as we make our way to the bar to settle our tabs. Taylor wouldn't let us pay a dime for our drinks so we pooled together our money and gave him a big fat tip. He walked us outside to our waiting cab and watched us pile in. Waving goodbye, he shuts the door ending a night packed full of new revelations.

Chapter Twenty Three

T he next day, I arrived back in Garden City tired and cranky. I even let Chloe behind the wheel again, figuring her reckless driving was the safer option than my exhaustion. Our conversations on the trip home were minimal. I tried dozing a few times to no avail. Just like last night, my mind kept replaying every word of my discussion with Bridgett, keeping me awake. Of course, not only did I have to retell all the details to Chloe, Katelyn and Lisa during the cab ride, my brain kept the entire episode on a loop. Play, rewind. Play, rewind. All night long.

The realization that my break up with Wyatt had nothing to do with his cheating left me with a dilemma. If he didn't seek the warm, willing body of Bridgett, then why make me think he did? He would have known how that would destroy me. He had seen first hand my insecurities and jealous tendencies where Bridgett was concerned. Surely, he knew there would be no future path toward reconciliation if he had slept with Bridgett. Which leads me to believe that he never had any intentions of us getting back together. But then, why all the texts and phone calls? The first week after our break up, he flooded my phone trying to make contact. Was he finally going to own up to the lie and man up...tell me that he just doesn't love me anymore? If that's the case, I'm sure glad I avoided his calls. It was hard enough thinking I was cheated on, but to have him be so brutally honest telling me I'm no longer wanted...yeah, that would have been a hard pill to swallow. Then and now. I can't quit thinking that there is a missing piece to this puzzle. I really hope there is something I'm missing because being the dumpee sucks.

We drop Katelyn off at her Pawleys Island beach home. Or rather mansion. I'm sure she doesn't appreciate the pitiful look I gift her as she walks into the empty, cold monstrosity. Of course, she dished out her own look of pity toward me during our goodbyes. No doubt she was thinking of the mess that has become of my romantic life. Well, what used to be my romantic life. And since we're being fair, seems Katelyn's feelings of love are just as convoluted as mine.

As soon as we are alone, Chloe wastes no time sharing her assumptions about why Wyatt suddenly ended things. "So, you really believe what Bridgett told you last night?" she starts off.

"Yes," I say definitively. Chloe takes her eyes off the road and turns them toward me. Her raised eyebrows tell me she's not quite as convinced about Bridgett's confession. "Look, Bridgett never tried to hide her attraction for Wyatt even after she found out we were dating. It's not like we're buddy-buddy and share some close friendship. She could have let me continue to think that she and Wyatt slept together. But she didn't. She fessed up to the truth. I don't have any reason to not believe her."

"Okay, I can understand that. But why do you think Wyatt didn't set you straight from the beginning? It's kinda a shitty thing to do, making you believe the worst."

"Yeah, it's pretty uncharacteristic for Wyatt to be so cruel. But I'm starting to believe that letting me think he cheated was Wyatt's way of protecting me," I offer. Wow, the way that sounds out loud is just weird.

"Um, *what*?" Chloe screeches, sharing in my weirdness factor. "Where in the world did you come up with an idea like that?"

I sigh heavily trying to wrap my head around the statement I just voiced. How can I make Chloe understand if I can't make sense of it myself? "Wyatt broke up with me upon arrival, stating he no longer wanted to do the whole long distance thing. Even though I was shocked, I didn't believe him. I mean, we had talked in length about the distance and how we'd make it work. He even gave me those two round trip plane tickets for graduation, remember?" Chloe nods. "I was getting ready to call bullshit on his explanation when I heard movement from the bedroom. That's when I found Bridgett."

"Oh, I see. Wyatt broke up with you blaming the long distance thing. You didn't believe him and were getting ready to push for answers. But then you found Bridgett in his bedroom and bolted. Right?"

"Exactly, yes."

"But now, with this newfound evidence, you think Wyatt lead you to believe he cheated because..." Chloe prompts.

"I don't know," I say throwing my hands in the air exacerbated.

"Well, maybe he just wasn't that into you."

"Ouch!" I grimace. I don't know if I'll ever get used to Chloe's honest direct approach.

"Wait, let me finish. As I was saying, there is the small, teeny weeny, itty bitty, miniscule chance that Wyatt just wanted to end things. But honestly, I don't believe that for a minute. I saw you two together. That boy was head over heels in love with you. It wouldn't have mattered how many miles were between you, he loved you enough to endure that short span of separation. I'm sure he was planning on your future, not dwelling on the three or four months you had to be apart. So, I agree, I'm calling bullshit on his break up having anything at all to do with the long distance relationship."

"Thank you. But there is still that chance, as you pointed out, no matter how small you try to make it." My permanent frown is in place just thinking about the probability of Wyatt no longer wanting a relationship. More precisely, no longer wanting *me*.

"Pfft, impossible. Besides, I failed my statistics class so I don't really know what I'm talking about." Chloe nudges me with her elbow causing the corners of my mouth to slide upward just slightly. "Seriously though, something must have happened to trigger Wyatt's about face ending your relationship." Chloe takes a few moments to think while I search my memory for any clue I might have missed concerning Wyatt's happiness.

"Things were fine when you left Columbia to move to the beach?" Chloe starts her interrogation.

"Yes, they were perfect."

"And the time you were away, you didn't have any fights or anything?"

"No, all our phone calls and texts were pleasant. All we could talk about was how excited we were to see each other again. Well, that and how much we missed each other." Oh how I still miss that man.

"And just to cover all my bases here, Wyatt was okay with you attending Patrick's engagement party, correct?" Chloe asks.

"He wasn't thrilled about it, but he said he understood how I needed to go, and needed to go alone." Having to tell Wyatt about me attending my high school sweetheart's engagement party was one of the hardest things I have ever had to do. He begged me to let him accompany me to the party, knowing how hard it would be to see Patrick again after all these years. Plus, he didn't want me anywhere near Patrick's dad, Mr. Miles. Wyatt hates the man, having seen first hand what the monster tried to do to me one night during my senior year. Wyatt was the one to save me from the hands of Jim Miles. Even if Wyatt and I never reconcile, I'll always be grateful to him.

"You don't think someone said something to Wyatt, do you?" Chloe asks interrupting my thoughts.

"About?"

"You and Patrick. I mean, I'm sure I'm not the only one to notice the sparks that still fly between you two whenever you're together. Maybe someone at the party saw it too and it got back to Wyatt." Chloe has a point. There were a ton of people at that party. However, most of the people were either classmates of Patrick's or much older people, mostly friends and business associates of Mr. Miles and Judge Bostick. I highly doubt any of those people would even remember Wyatt McCain other than as the bartender at the country club some years ago.

"I guess it's possible, but highly unlikely. Hey, do you know if Landon or James or even Patrick still communicates with Wyatt?" Even though Wyatt never mentioned still being friendly with my high school buddies, it's worth asking.

"That's a definite negative. Especially with all those rumors floating around after you vanished midway senior year. People were certain you left after breaking poor Patrick's heart to go continue your so-called fling with Wyatt."

"But that's not true at all," I yell defending myself. Wyatt may have crushed on me for years, but we didn't start anything until I was in my last year of college. Do people not have anything else to do than to make shit up?

"Of course we knew it wasn't true, even back then. But as the saying goes 'bros before hos'…"

"Did you just call me a ho?" I could strangle Chloe right this instance. I don't care if she's driving or not.

"Chill out, Suz. I'm not calling you anything. I'm just explaining the loyalty between male friends. So you can rule out the possibility of Landon or James or Patrick spying on you and reporting back to Wyatt. The whole idea is ludicrous!" Chloe continues to concentrate on the road, never glancing my way. Good thing, cause if looks could kill… How about that saying, huh?

Chloe doesn't initiate more conversation until she knows I've cooled off. Which means she's waiting for me to break the ice. "Okay, I guess I was grasping straws with that one. But please, please don't mention those rumors again. It just brings up a terrible period in my life. One I'd rather just forget."

"Yeah, okay. I'm sorry about that," Chloe apologizes with a shrug. "But stop coming up with stupid scenarios that make no sense. Come on, we've gotta think. What could have happened to cause Wyatt to break up with you?"

I can't come up with anything. Nothing. Nada. Sure, Patrick and I have been spending a lot of time together. But just as friends. Except there are those moments when he's crossed that friendship boundary. A few times we've held hands. Friends hold hands, don't they? And then there were those times he might have mentioned still loving me. Hey, I love my friends. Who doesn't? Okay, so a few times he might have kissed me. He. Kissed. Me. What's the big deal? A peck on the cheek is a friendly gesture. Europeans do it all the time. What am I doing? I'll never explain the tongue action. Friends don't do tongue kissing. Plus, I'm guilty for maybe enjoying those kisses. However, in my defense all of this happened after Wyatt broke my heart into a million pieces. A stolen kiss to aid in my recovery isn't so bad. Is it? Who am I kidding? I blamed Wyatt for cheating and he was innocent. Meanwhile, I'm spending my spare time kissing an engaged man. Maybe Chloe wasn't so far off the mark calling me a ho.

"Suz? Earth to Suzanna," Chloe says waving her arm in front of my face. I've been so busy trying to justify my guilt that I didn't notice we had made it home. "That is some intense brainstorming you're doing. Come up with anything else?"

"No, I have no clue what could have made Wyatt change his mind about us." My guilt doesn't compare to the pain of having to face the reality that Wyatt was just ready to be done with me. "I guess he just didn't love me anymore."

"I know that's not true. And if I'm this adamant about it, you've gotta know in your heart that Wyatt still loves you. You can't believe Wyatt just up and fell out of love with you overnight, do you?"

"I don't want to believe that. But what else could it be?" I ask defeated, not really looking for an answer. "Guess I'll never know."

"So you give up. Let it consume you day and night making you miserable. Sound fun?"

"Nooooo," I stress. "But what other option is there? We've come up with nothing solid."

"You could call him. Ask him to tell you the truth," Chloe suggests.

A humorless laugh escapes me. "Oh, that would be classic. I can hear it now... 'Hey, Wyatt, this is Suzanna. Look I know you didn't cheat. So I was just wondering why you broke up with me. And please be honest, don't use the excuse of a long distance relationship this time.' How pathetic does that all sound? He'd probably laugh in my face before hanging up on me."

"Hey, don't let your pride get in the way. You want to know, right?" I nod slightly. "I've got it! I'll call him. That way I'll do all the digging and get the scoop. And I won't even need my superior acting skills. I'll dutifully be looking out for my friend." I can see Chloe getting all excited about her fact finding mission. I need to put a stop to this fast.

"Absolutely not! I don't need you to fight my battles for me. Plus, I think this might be a conversation best had face to face, not over the phone."

"Aw, Suz. Don't make me wait until the end of the summer before solving this mystery. The curiosity will kill me," Chloe says dramatically. "Oh, and I'll be so worried about you." Chloe changes her expression to one of concern in less than half a second. Damn, she's a really good actress.

"Right...your concern is touching," I remark with sarcasm. "Anyway, who said anything about waiting until the end of the summer? I thought you always wanted to visit New York."

"I do, but what does...wait a minute. Are you saying what I think you're saying?" Chloe looks to me for affirmation, her excitement bubbling.

"Figuring as I have these plane tickets just lying around, why not use them. You game?"

"Hell yeah! Whoo hoo...we're going to New York City, baby!" Chloe screams and hugs me fiercely. Chloe's excitement is contagious as we bounce in each other's arms. I'm sure once the reality of going to New York to confront Wyatt settles in, I'll be less than enthused. For now though, I'm just going to enjoy this moment and look forward to the trip that I'll be sharing with my best friend.

"We 'bout ready to take off for the airport?" No, Chloe and I are not yet traveling to New York. We're a little over a week out from that trip. Chloe made sure that the minute we entered our beach house I was planted in front of my computer making our airline reservations. She had her reasons of persistency, knowing I'd probably chicken out once I had a chance to think things through. Rightfully so, since each day I get a little more nervous as our departure date gets closer. Yeah, I'm excited to visit one of America's greatest cities. It's just remembering my reason for going that causes me to break out in a cold sweat. Pushing all thoughts of my impending confrontation with Wyatt aside, today I focus on my brother Flynn. We are minutes away from taking him to catch his international flight.

"As soon as Mom double checks her list. She's currently in my bedroom rifling through my luggage one last time," Flynn says.

"Ha! She checking to make sure you packed enough clean underwear?" I ask through a snort.

"Probably." Flynn shrugs shaking his head.

"It's nice of you to give her this moment. You know, you'll always be her baby boy," I say giving Flynn a pat on his cheek. "Let's just hope she hasn't divided your clothes into individual daily outfits and placed each one in a labeled Ziploc bag." Mom used to pack both Flynn and me for summer camp each year. We'd open our suitcases to find a week's worth of clothes organized for the duration of camp. It was great as a child. We didn't have to think about what to wear when. It was all laid out for us. But as an adult, well that could be embarrassing.

"Oh, don't think she didn't mention it. But that's where I put my foot down. Besides, we'd have to own stock in Ziploc to have enough storage bags for each outfit with the amount of time I'll be away."

"Don't remind me," I say sadly.

"What's with the frown? You admit you might miss me a little?" Flynn teases.

"Of course, I'm gonna miss you. You're my brother." My eyes get watery just thinking about not being able to see Flynn on a daily basis. Pain in the ass or not, I love him. "I'm so glad we had this time together before you left," I manage to choke out.

"Come here, Sis," Flynn motions me over. And I gladly obey. He wraps me up in a hug. "I'm gonna miss you, too." He kisses the top my head showing his brotherly affection. We stand embracing each other in silence, knowing it'll be the last hug for a long, long time. "I hate that I'll miss your annihilation of the qualifying competition and your rise to superstar on tour."

"You'll be there in spirit. And, thanks for the confidence. I'll keep you posted. Besides, you won't have time to worry about my career.

Won't be long before you're a bona fide soccer star and an international household name."

"You think?" Flynn asks.

"I know. But don't let it go to your head," I warn with a smile.

"Me?" Flynn asks incredulously. "Never." We both burst out in laughter ending our mopey moment.

"Well isn't this sweet," Chloe comments from her bedroom doorway. She obviously just woke up still sporting her pjs and a bad case of bed head. Mom reappears seconds later from Flynn's room.

"Looks like you have everything packed. Dad is taking down your things now and loading the car." She nervously looks at her watch then glances at Chloe. "Honey, you better get dressed fast if you're going with us. We've got to get a move on to make it to the international terminal for Flynn to catch his flight."

"Oh, you all go ahead and do the family send off. I've got to get ready for work anyway. I'm scheduled for the lunch shift today." Chloe addresses my mother, but never takes her eyes off Flynn.

"Okay then. Now where did I put that bag with all the paperwork?" Mom asks no one in particular as she searches the living area.

"Flynn, Suz, Carol," Dad calls from outside. "We've got to go. Now!"

"Coming dear," Mom yells back having found her misplaced items. "Let's go kids."

"Chloe," Flynn says in such a reverent tone. He shifts away from me and proceeds in her direction. He doesn't stop until only an inch separates him from Chloe's body. Chloe shuffles nervously before taking a deep calming breath.

"Flynn, good luck to you," she whispers and forces a smile. "Have a safe trip."

"Um, thanks," Flynn returns with disappointment and confusion.

"Okay, um, well...goodbye, I guess," Chloe stutters before giving Flynn an awkward hug. Flynn remains stiff even while placing his arms around Chloe's waist.

"Yeah, goodbye to you too, Chloe." Flynn loosens his hold and gingerly places a light kiss on Chloe's forehead. Their eyes meet one last time before he bids her a final farewell with a head nod. Then he turns away and we follow our mother out the door.

"You okay?" I whisper as we descend the stairs.

"Why wouldn't I be?" Though his words are meant to show nonchalance, his tone suggests the opposite.

"This is hard on her Flynn. She's hurting having to see you leave," I try to assure him.

"She has a funny way of showing it," Flynn comments dryly.

"It's not like you acted any differently. Maybe she was waiting on you to show your true feelings first." Both Flynn and Chloe are so darn hard headed, especially when it comes to their feelings toward each other. God forbid, one actually let the other know how much they care!

"Doesn't matter now, does it?" Flynn states as we pile into the backseat of the car. Bless my dad's heart. He had the forethought to have the car running and the air conditioner jacked up. The confines of the vehicle are nice and comfortable as we enter and begin to buckle up.

"You got everything?" Dad turns from his position in the driver's seat to ask Flynn. Flynn is so deep in thought gazing up at the house before us that he doesn't respond.

"Son?" Dad questions again.

"Um, wait. There's one thing I forgot to get. I'll be right back." Flynn bolts out of the car and up the stairs disappearing into the house. I smile thinking of Flynn and Chloe having their proper goodbye.

We make it as far as the airport security check before our time with Flynn comes to an end. Mom has made a valiant effort of keeping on her happy face. Eventually, she loses the emotional battle and sobs like a baby as she hugs her son goodbye. Dad gives Flynn a fatherly hug repeating over and over how very proud he is of Flynn's soccer success. He finishes his farewell with an encouraging pat on the back and a firm handshake. Quickly, he sidles up to my mom wrapping his arm around her shoulder in comfort. He steers them toward the exit doors no doubt trying to hide his own emotions.

"So, this is it," I say making a poor attempt at conversation.

"I guess it is," Flynn says looking around for the entrance to the security check line. I throw myself into Flynn's arms unexpectedly causing him to stumble backwards a few steps.

"Whoa!"

"I love you, little bro. And I'm really, really going to miss you," I manage between gulps of air. I faired about as well as Mom, letting the tears run rampant down my face.

"Hey," Flynn says prying me off of him. He gently wipes my wet face with his hands. "I love you, too, Sis. So much." His eyes are misty as well, but he continues to hold it together.

"'Bye, Flynn."

"Bye, Suz." I let go of my brother and begin to walk away. My progress is hindered when Flynn grabs my arm swinging me to face him one last time.

"Do me a favor?" Flynn asks. I nod because words are impossible right now. "Look out for Chloe for me?" The affection with which he speaks her name sends my tear ducts working in overtime. The fact that his last request involves my best friend and his secret love is extremely touching.

"Of course I will," I assure. His smile is all I need in way of his appreciation. "Now go kick some soccer butt!"

"Yes ma'am," Flynn obliges and takes his place in line. I give him a finger wave and walk out to meet my parents. The respect I have for my brother to follow his dream, even moving to a foreign country, fills my heart with pride. Holding onto that sentiment will get me through the many months of not being able to see him.

Chapter Twenty Four

The week following Flynn's departure was one of the hottest on record. There were several days the temps reached the triple digits. The air conditioner ran constantly in a futile attempt to cool the inside of the house. Outside, there was no relief to be found. Not even on the beach. The sand was so hot it scorched the bottom of your feet sending you in a high speed sprint toward the shoreline. The ocean could have passed as a humongous hot tub, minus the jets and bubbles. And the little breeze that existed was like a heater blowing hot air. Basically, everyone was miserable.

Despite the heat, I continued to play golf, scheduling my tee times for the early mornings. By the end of each round, I was melting. Dragging myself into the comfort of the clubhouse, I headed straight for Callie's equipment room to try and cool off. Collapsing in the tattered leather chair, I slipped and slid. My sweat soaked clothing and body made a squishy sound when I landed. I know, very ladylike, right? Exhaustion kept me from caring about my outward appearance as I righted myself and found some traction before falling on my butt on the floor. Securely seated, I reclined back closing my eyes and let the air conditioning wash over my overheated body. Ah, that felt good!

"Hot out there?" Callie asks from somewhere in the room. I wouldn't know exactly where because I didn't have the energy to open my eyes.

"That's an understatement. It's brutal! I'm sweating in my panties." Dealing with the heat was torture enough, but today the humidity had climbed making the air muggy and thick. I swear it was actually hard to breathe.

Callie snorts with laughter and starts singing, "Suz has got swamp ass, Suz has got swamp ass."

"I suppose I do," I say with a chuckle. No use in denying it. I'm wet with sweat from head to toe.

"Well, don't bother getting up any time soon. Patrick called and said he was gonna be late picking you up," Callie informed me. Now, that got my attention. Normally, Patrick was here waiting well before I entered the clubhouse. His punctuality was never in question. So of course I began to worry what his hold up was today.

"Did he say why?" I ask locating Callie behind her desk. She was sitting on the floor working with the head of a driver.

"No, not that he was real chatty. Actually, he was kinda rude."

"Rude?" That doesn't sound like my Patrick.

"Maybe rude isn't the right word to use. I don't know, he just wasn't his normal jovial, charming self. Sounded preoccupied and more than a little pissed. Yeah, that's it...he definitely was pissed about something," Callie says describing Patrick's mood on the phone.

"Oh," I reply as my mind races back to our little spat earlier this morning.

"Oh? That's all you got? Sounds to me like you might know something about Patrick's uncharacteristic disposition today." Callie scoots her butt across the floor so that she is no longer hiding behind her desk. She's abandoned her work on the set of clubs and is now focusing all her attention on me.

"I don't know why Patrick would be angry. Or why he is late picking me up," I lie.

"Suzanna, don't give me that bologna. Don't think I didn't notice him not walking you inside this morning. I had to give up my daily dose of morning eye candy because you obviously ticked him off and sent him running. Now, what did you do?"

"Me? Why do you assume I did something? Maybe he's the one to blame for our fight."

"Ah ha, you did have a lover's squabble this morning," Callie says beaming with self righteousness. Shit, I hate that she flustered me so, I admitted to my disagreement with Patrick.

"Fine. You're right. We argued on the car ride over. You happy now?" I ask hoping to close the subject.

"Nope. Won't be happy until I hear details." Callie scoots closer taking a front row seat for story time.

"Okay, but just to clarify, Patrick and I are not lovers."

Callie dismisses her early statement with a flick of her hand. "Yeah, yeah, whatever. Just get on with it."

"Ugh," I groan, delaying the inevitable. Callie waits none too patiently. "Well, our conversation started off fine, just discussing normal things. Then Patrick asks about my plans for the upcoming July Fourth holiday. He's concocting plans...a beach day, a cookout, late night fireworks. Before he could get too carried away I had to tell him about my trip."

"Going to New York with Chloe," Callie adds. She is aware that I'll be out of town for a couple days. I had to clear my golf schedule with her, Drew and Coach Moore.

"Yes, that trip. Anyway, as soon as I mentioned New York, Patrick got all pissy. I thought he'd be excited for me and Chloe to go explore the big city. But nooooo, excited he was not. When I questioned him about his disdain toward my traveling destination he declared through gritted teeth he knew my reasons for going to New York. And he also knew they had nothing to do with catching a Broadway show or checking out all the tourist attractions. He knows I'm going to see Wyatt."

"Patrick's mad because you're going to see your ex? Doesn't make sense. He's your ex too and y'all see each other all the time. I'd venture to say he spends more time with you than his fiancée". Callie's attempt to make any sense out of this mess is a wasted effort.

"I don't think it's all about the trip itself. Or that I'm going to talk with Wyatt. I think his anger is based on the fact that I didn't tell him about my relationship with Wyatt in the first place."

"Wait...he didn't know you dated Wyatt?"

"No, I only told him I just broke up with someone recently. Never mentioned who I was dating." Callie looks at me with what can only be read as a big silent 'Why?'. "Believe me, I had my reasons for keeping Wyatt's identity in the dark. There's some bad blood between Patrick and Wyatt," I try to explain.

"Ohhhh, the plot thickens," Callie says rubbing her hands together. She's having too much fun at my expense. "Go on," she demands.

"Years ago, when Patrick and I broke up, there were unsubstantiated rumors flying around about me leaving Patrick to continue an affair I had begun with Wyatt. Totally untrue! Wyatt and I were just friends at the time. We only started dating a month before I graduated from college. I guess my omission that Wyatt was the guy who just recently broke my heart brought back all those memories of a time where Patrick chose to believe I was unfaithful. Even though I swore on the Bible that Wyatt and I had nothing remotely romantic until just recently, the doubt that those rumors caused still resides within Patrick." Granted, had I been in the same situation, I'd find it hard to let go of those doubts as well. Can't fault him since I never gave him any other excuse about our break up other than focusing on my golf dreams. Sounds lame even to my ears.

"I see," Callie comments seriously thinking about all that I just told her. "Not that it's important, but if you didn't let Patrick in on your recent romantic relationship with Wyatt, then who did?"

"Flynn," I say with a scowl. Guess while the girls were away for the weekend in Charleston, Flynn and Patrick had some bonding time. After a twelve pack or more of beer, Flynn developed a bad case of loose lips. He revealed to Patrick how devastated I had been with how my relationship with Wyatt suddenly ended. I'm sure Patrick didn't once goad my drunk brother into providing details. Um, yeah ri-i-ight! "Flynn better be thankful there's the Atlantic Ocean between us now, or else I'd kick his ass!"

"I've a got few things I'd like to do to his ass...all less violent," Callie says in a dreamy state. Even in a foreign country Flynn still manages to mesmerize women. If I got my hands on him today, he wouldn't look so appealing to the opposite sex.

"Callie, gross. That's my brother you're violating in your mind," I yell in admonishment.

"You're no fun. No Patrick and no Flynn...where am I supposed to get my thrills?" Callie asks with all seriousness.

Luckily I'm saved from answering her ridiculous question when my phone buzzes. Patrick's short, curt text states nothing but the facts. I'm here, Waiting in car, P. Alrighty then.

"Gotta go, Patrick's here," I say prying my butt off the leather. The sweat has long since dried making my skin stick to the chair. Ouch!

"He's not coming in to say hello?" I shake my head signaling no. Since knowing Callie not once have I ever seen the look of pure disappointment cross her face. Until now. Patrick and Callie have developed a companionship of sorts, spending time together while I golf. I hate that I may be the cause that ends their friendship. Callie, having never asked anything of me pleads, "Fix this, Suz."

"How? I've already told him the truth. I can't make him believe it. Plus, he has no right to tell me where I can go or who I can see. Especially when it comes to men. How many times do I have to keep reminding people? He's engaged!" I breathe heavily after my rant. "If he doesn't love Katelyn or is being coaxed into this marriage for other reasons, then that's his fault. He's the only one who can fix that."

"What? His engagement to Katelyn is a sham?" Callie doesn't look as distraught as she did moments ago. Oops, did I just say all that out loud? Like my brother, I have contracted the loose lips disease. "Suzanna?" Callie probes.

"Forget I said anything about that." Like that will ever happen. Callie is like a dog hunting for a bone. She'll never let this go. "Gotta go. 'Bye Callie." I run, yes run, out of her office. Grabbing my golfing stuff I make it outside in record time. The thick hot air nearly knocks me off my feet. I search through the haze to find Patrick waiting in his car, just like his text read. Huffing and puffing across the parking lot, I've already broken into a sweat by the time I reach his vehicle.

"Hi," I say climbing into the passenger side door. He grunts his greeting. Nice... the silent treatment. This should be a fun ride home. I ignore his nonverbal communication and fiddle with the air vents, pointing the majority of them right toward me. Ah, cool air. I'm basking in the refreshment avoiding another confrontation with Patrick. Finally once my body temp is back to a normal level I decide to strike up some conversation.

"Callie gave me your message. About you picking me up late. Everything okay?" I ask.

"It is now," Patrick answers coolly.

"That's good. What was the hold up?" Now my curiosity is peaked.

"Something with my dad, not that you'd care."

"Patrick, of course I care. He's your dad." He doesn't need to know how much I despise the man. My caring revolves around how this affects Patrick.

Patrick focuses on the road and we drive a few miles in silence. I'm about to give up that he'll expand on today's issue with his dad. But surprisingly he begins speaking. "I had to go fetch my dad from one of his favorite watering holes. Apparently, he'd been there since they opened at ten this morning. What bar opens at ten a.m.?" He asks not really expecting me to answer. So I don't. I let him continue to get it all out without judgment. "By the time I arrived at lunch, Dad could barely hold his head up, he was so intoxicated. Man, is he a sloppy drunk! I had a hard time understanding his slurred speech, but apparently the other drunks at the bar could decipher his every syllable. And from what I learned he didn't have a lot of nice things to say. I got there just in time before a fight was about to break out." Patrick lets out a diabolical laugh. "Never thought I'd find myself breaking up a fight my fifty some year old dad tried to start because he was too blitzed out of his mind to care if he got hurt or not. It's bad enough I have to be on call as his sober ride. Thank goodness I had the foresight to give the bartenders my cell number. Otherwise, I know I'd be picking his ass up from jail instead." Seems jail might be the exact place he needs to be. I keep that thought to myself.

"I'm so sorry, Patrick." He nods his appreciation, but doesn't respond. "Have you talked to him about getting professional help? Rehab or something?"

"Yeah, he promised he'd get treatment after the wedding," Patrick confirms. Alarm bells start blaring in my head at his statement. If Patrick wanted his dad sober, why wait until after his wedding? Unless, this was the one condition Patrick was allowed when his engagement was negotiated. But I'm missing the piece that Patrick's dad hung over his head to convince him to enter into such a permanent agreement like marriage.

"You do know that alcoholism is a disease. Just like cancer or MS or diabetes. Delayed treatment will only make the condition worse."

"My dad's not an alcoholic!" Patrick yells this like the idea is just crazy. "He drinks a lot, yes. But he can control his urges. He just needs the liquor to numb the ache he still feels daily over the loss of my mother. He misses her so much."

"Well, so do you and a lot of other people, yet I don't see you or anyone else drowning their sorrows on a daily basis," I yell right back. Patrick's laser beam death glare tells me he doesn't appreciate my loudness or tone. Taking a calm breath, I try to speak with more civility. "Patrick, I'm not refuting your dad's love or longing for your deceased mother. But you have to know that his drinking only escalated after the accident. His heavy intake of alcohol has been going on since long before your mother died."

"What are you getting at Suz? You telling me my dad had a problem even while mother was still alive? I don't believe you. I would have noticed. And I know my mother would have never put up with it," Patrick says still in denial. "Honestly, I don't know why I'm even talking to you about this."

"Yeah, me either," I mutter under my breath. My muffled comment is loud enough for Patrick to hear me.

"What was that? Am I bothering you with my problems? Forgive me...I'll just shut up now." Whoa, I just pushed Patrick's button that takes him from mildly pissed to full blown anger. But why drag me into this mess?

"All I meant was that maybe there is someone else you should be having these very personal conversations with. I don't know, maybe like you fiancée, Katelyn," I stress her name. "This problem your dad has isn't going away overnight, especially if you remain in denial and don't seek help for him immediately. You and Katelyn will start your life together soon having to deal with your dad's treatment options. I guess it's just fair you let her know now the serious nature of the family life she's marrying into."

"Ah, here you go again. I don't need the constant reminder of my soon to be marital status. And Katelyn does know how Dad struggles with alcohol. But Suz, she wasn't there to witness his transformation after Mom passed. You were. You saw first hand how he turned to the bottle to cope with his grief."

"I saw him turn to the bottle more frequently than he did prior to the accident. Don't forget I was there before your mom died also. And I saw your dad indulge in alcohol way before you claim it started as his coping mechanism." If he chose me to discuss all his dad's alcohol issues with, well, I'm not gonna hold anything back. Patrick has to understand that although his dad's drinking escalated after losing his mother, the problem most definitely didn't start there.

"Back to that again, huh?" I nod my affirmation while Patrick shakes his head in disbelief. "Whatever, we'll just have to agree to disagree on that point. Besides, I lived with the man my entire life. I would have noticed if there was a problem early on."

"No, you wouldn't have noticed. Because he was your dad. But you managed to notice how sloshed Chloe's mom became after her endless glass of wine." I remember all of us, Chloe included, talking about the embarrassing stunts Chloe's mother would pull at social gatherings. Although, Mrs. Ryder never remembered them the next day. And bless Chloe's heart, she'd rather forget than bring them up with her mother. Patrick's dad was the same. However, he managed to slide under the radar, holding his liquor like a man. Up until he became gruff and belligerent, at which point no one risked calling him out.

"That's different. Chloe's mom enjoyed being the life of the party. My dad lingered at the bar and pretty much kept to himself."

"Yeah, kept to himself *at the bar*. What do you think he was doing there, huh?" I'm getting quite bold with my questions. Why not? He's already angry at me for suggesting his dad might have a problem. I know for a fact his dad has more than just one problem...he's hiding quite a few. Guess now's as good a time as any to test the waters on how much Patrick knows about the accident. "Patrick, was the car accident your dad and mom were involved in ever investigated?" I throw it out there.

"No, not that I'm aw_" Patrick stops abruptly turning his gaze from the road to me. "Whoa, what are you implying Suzanna?"

"N-nothing," my voice trembles with fear.

"Don't fucking 'nothing' me now. You brought it up. You better damn well finish it!" Patrick angrily demands.

"I...um, I was just curious. I don't remember ever hearing what caused the accident," I say with hesitation.

"Careful, careful. Making false accusations is a punishable offense," Patrick spits through gritted teeth. His knuckles have turned white from his death grip on the steering wheel and I'm afraid he's liable to dislodge it from the dashboard. I'm focusing on his hands because I'm too much of a coward to look him in the eye. "If you ever, ever loved me, you'd never ask the question implying my dad could have been responsible for my mother's death. Guess I know now how you really felt about me."

"Patrick..."

"Shut up and get the hell out of my car!" He yells at me as he burns rubber into my driveway. I didn't even know we were this close to home yet. I obey immediately opening the door to escape. I've never seen Patrick this furious and it scares me. *He* scares me. I quickly grab my things from the backseat as Patrick continues to seethe behind the wheel. I don't want him to leave being this angry with me, so I try once more.

"Please, Patrick. Just let me explain."

"You know, you've had years to explain. Yet you never did. You just left, no excuse other than that fabricated story about focusing on your precious golf game. What a joke! Even after all those nasty rumors about you cheating, I still defended you. Still put you on a pedestal because you were the great Suzanna Caulder, the love of my life. Now, to find out that you probably were with Wyatt...well, that sucks and hurts my pride."

"But I wasn't with Wyatt. The rumors were not true," I interject but am quickly dismissed.

"Whatever, Suz. I don't even care now. Because after today...we are so done. Done!" He yells throwing his hands to the sky to emphasize his point. "You basically just accused my dad of murdering my mother. Murder, Suzanna. Do you have any idea how serious that is?" He shakes his head and re-gathers his thoughts. "I don't want anything else to do with you from now until the day I die. You hear me? Don't call me, text me, contact me in any way, shape or form. And stay away from Katelyn."

"Patrick, don't do this," I sob openly.

"You did this all on your own," he says in parting, reversing out onto the roadway and driving right out of my life. I watch with blurry vision until his taillights disappear from sight. Using the last molecule of energy left in my body I make my way into the house and collapse on my bed in a heap of tears. Losing Patrick for the second time in my life hurts so much more. Because this time, there's no one to blame but myself. My only hope is that once he calms down and thinks about what I said, maybe then he can focus on helping his dad get clean. Why I bother to continue to protect Mr. Miles, pushing

Patrick away from me and closer to him, I'll never understand. Once again I find myself keeping secrets to salvage the father-son relationship. And once again, I'm the one paying the price for my honorable effort.

Chapter Twenty Five

*T*hump, thump, thump. The repetitive noise rouses me from sleep. Not that I was in a deep state. After Patrick dumped me out of his car to get far, far away from me, I've done nothing but think constantly about our argument. The cold shower did nothing to cool my emotions. With Chloe at work and Katelyn no longer an option (per Patrick's demand), I ate dinner alone. Even the channel surfing couldn't keep my mind from replaying Patrick's harsh words, dismissing me from his life. Giving up on finding a television program that would occupy my mind, keeping me from thoughts of Patrick, I finally decided to call it a night. I tossed and turned until evidently I faded into a restless sleep. *Thump, thump.* I hear again. My body rises from my bed along with my hope. Maybe enough time has transpired for Patrick to calm down. Maybe he's here now to smooth things over and get back to us being friends. I rush to the front door ready to take him back.

However, it's not Patrick that I see as I throw the door open. A big burly dude stands on the other side of the threshold looking relived that I answered his knocking. "Oh, thank goodness you're home. I drove straight from the ER before realizing Chloe left her purse and keys at the restaurant."

ER? Chloe? Who is this guy? "And you are?"

"Sorry, I'm a little shaken up. I'm Sam. I work with Chloe at Dead Dog. Could you hold that door open while I carry her up the stairs and inside house? She's still out of it given the pain meds she received at the hospital." The guy leaves me more than confused as he dashes down the stairs. Moments later he returns with a limp Chloe in his arms. Seeing her droopy eyes and slack mouth, I think Chloe may be drunk. But the white gauze bandage wrapped around her head tells me differently. Now Sam's earlier words about the ER and hospital send me in a panic.

"Is she alright? What happened?" I ask as I direct Sam to Chloe's room. He gently deposits her on the bed. She makes to roll over adjusting her body to get horizontal. But Sam repositions her body to a seated upright position with pillows propped behind her back.

"Not time to go to sleep yet Chloe. You've got another," he pauses to look at his watch, "four to five hours to go before it's safe. Doctor's orders, remember?"

Chloe moans and reaches back behind her head. "Ouch, it hurts," she slurs.

"What's going on? Why can't she go to sleep? What happened?" I bombard both Chloe and Sam with multiple questions. Chloe's condition frightens me.

"We're not exactly sure. A customer found Chloe on the bathroom floor, knocked out and bleeding. Our guess is that she slipped on a wet spot, lost her balance and hit and cut her head on the hand dryer attached to the wall. She has a pretty big gash that required ten stitches. Also, she has a giant sized goose egg above the cut where her head hit the tile floor knocking her unconscious."

"Oh my God," I whisper my hand flying to cover my mouth in shock. Poor Chloe. "Is she, um, is she going to be okay?" My voice is shaking with fear.

"Doctor said she will make a full recovery. But he did diagnose her with a severe concussion. That's why she can't go to sleep for the next few hours. He wants to make sure that she doesn't slip back into unconsciousness. Also said to call him immediately if she gets nauseated and starts vomiting. Said they'd have to admit her if that happens."

"Oh," I manage still standing shell shocked.

"You're Suzanna, right? Chloe mentioned you were her roommate. She babbled about you tonight after receiving her pain meds. Wouldn't let me take her anywhere else but here. Said you'd take real good care of her."

"Yes, I'm Suzanna. Nice to meet you Sam. Sorry it's under these conditions. But thank you so much for getting her home. And I'll definitely take good care of her," I promise.

"Hey, wake up sleepy head," Sam redirects his attention to Chloe as she attempts to close her eyes. How I'll ever keep her awake for the duration of the night is beyond me. "Suzanna, I really need to get back to work. We left the bar shorthanded to get Chloe immediate medical attention."

"Sure, sure. Go ahead. I've got this." Sam reaches in his pocket and produces a bottle of pills.

"Doctor gave me these. Said Chloe could have another dose of pain meds in a couple of hours. And believe me, she's going to need them." I grimace at the pain Chloe has suffered tonight. Sounds like she'll still be feeling the effects of her injury for some time. "You got someone you can call to help? I hate to bail on you, but..."

"You've done more than enough Sam. Thanks again. And I'll call in reinforcements if needed."

Sam walks over and gives Chloe a gingerly peck on the cheek. "'Night Chloe. Get well soon." He makes his way to the door and I go to follow him out. "No, please stay here with Chloe and make sure she stays awake. I'll see myself out and lock the door behind me." I'm reminded of the seriousness of Chloe's condition and the strict doctor's orders to keep her awake.

"Good idea," I say extending my hand in Sam's direction. He takes it and gives it a firm shake. "Chloe's lucky to have such a caring co-worker."

"It's nothing. Just want her to get better. Need her back at work to pretty up the place. Plus, she's fun to be around," Sam says and I hear the fondness he has for Chloe in his voice. I'd venture to say he might have a slight crush on my friend. Not surprising in the least. I bet every male coworker feels the exact same way. Chloe is hard not to love. "Here's my number in case you need anything. I'll be glad to bring her things by tomorrow," Sam offers. What a nice guy!

"I'll call you with an update. Goodnight Sam," I say my farewell and focus my attention back to Chloe making sure she's awake. Sam does the same before walking out the door. I slowly climb in bed beside Chloe, as not to jostle her too much, and set in for a long night.

Two hours later, I've exhausted every conversational topic under the sun to keep Chloe awake. I booted up my laptop and searched all things related to New York. We decided which Broadway show we'd see, what restaurants we'd dine at, and which tourist attractions we were going to visit. Soon, we had our itinerary set. Of course when Chloe mumbled Wyatt's name, I looked over all the things we had planned and he wasn't on the list. "Oh, I'll call him at some point," I commented. I wanted to push that to the end of our trip. How could I enjoy our time in New York if the first thing I did was contact Wyatt? I was still scared that the reality of the situation was that Wyatt just no longer loved me, thus breaking up with me on that principle alone.

"Chicken," Chloe starts name calling.

"Am not! Really, I'm going to call him. Here, I'll pencil him in during our shopping time."

"Nooooooo!" Chloe whisper shouts. That'll shut her up. She's not letting anything deter her from the mega shopping New York has to offer.

"Thought that would get you off my back. Don't worry, I definitely plan to call him and get some answers about our break up. But I really want to enjoy our time together first. Understand?" Chloe nods because speaking makes her head hurt.

With our trip organized, I talk to Chloe about my golf practice round this morning. But after Chloe nods off several times, I realize detailing my every shot is boring to even the biggest golf enthusiast. Changing subjects, I tell Chloe about my fight with Patrick. Chloe, even drug induced, can't tune out this drama filled piece of info. Knowing she'll probably not remember much of what we discuss given her head injury and pain meds, I don't hold back. I tell her everything, from how I think Patrick's engagement is arranged to accusing Patrick's dad of involuntarily murdering his mother. As I listen to myself tell the story, the plots and turns sound like the makings of a good novel. Only this is no fictional piece. Sadly, this is my life and I'm smack dab in the middle of it all. Normally Chloe would have at least a hundred opinions about all I've just thrown at her, but she's being very nonresponsive. The only sounds she makes are frequent groans and moans. Although she's still awake, I can tell her pain is intensifying. Luckily, enough time has passed that she can take another dose of medication. Turning the television on and increasing the volume to a decibel level that could wake the neighbors, only then do I leave her room to brew a pot of coffee and get her a drink to wash down her pills. In the dimly lit kitchen, I stretch and yawn, battling my own exhaustion. Maybe I should call in back up. I'd hate to accidentally fall asleep risking Chloe's health. Once this latest dose of pain meds kicks in, it'll be even harder to keep Chloe awake.

I hurry back in the bedroom with Chloe's glass of water only to find she has drifted off during the few minutes I was away. "Chloe, Chloe! Wake up!" I yell over the obnoxious volume of the television. If she fell asleep with that thing on, no amount of my yelling will wake her. Setting the glass down, I grab her shoulders and gently shake her careful not to move her head.

"No, Mom. It hurts," Chloe talks through her sleep. Bless her heart, she's longing for her mother's comfort. Why didn't I think about this sooner? Of course she'd want her mom. And luckily her parents have been in town all week on vacation. Though I haven't seen them at all. Come to think of it, neither has Chloe. She's taken every extra shift offered to her this week, so she basically has been living at her job. I assumed she was working so much lately in an effort to make some extra spending money for our New York trip. In the process, she's ignored her family's presence spending no time with them at all. I imagine that hasn't set well with her folks. Well, now's the perfect time to correct that and give Chloe the motherly comfort she deserves.

"Chloe, wake up sweetie. Time for that feel good medicine," I say coercing her to take the pills. She winces as she sits up straighter popping the pills in her mouth and swallowing them with a drink of water. "There now, won't be long 'til you feel no pain. Plus, I'll call your mom like you asked, see if she'll come over."

Despite her severe injury, Chloe thrashes her head from side to side. "No, don't tell Mom. I don't want her here," she grimaces through the pain.

"But you just called out for her when you dozed off. You sure you don't want me to call? I'm sure she'd come right over to take care of you. Plus, I might need the help. I'm running on fumes as it is and I'm worried I won't be able to keep you awake all by myself."

"No, please, just let them enjoy their vacation without having to worry about me." It takes all her strength to beg me not to alert her parents about the accident. "If you need help call Patrick or Landon." Just as I assumed, she remembers nothing of our prior conversations. Since Patrick isn't an option, I guess I'll try Landon. If he's available, I have no doubt he'll come running to help take care of Chloe.

The coffee pot dings letting me know it is done brewing. "Fine, I'll leave your parents out of this for now and call Landon. Hey, can you stay awake until I fix me a cup of coffee? I really need the caffeine." All I get is subtle nod. Hurriedly, I go fix my cup of java and make the call to Landon.

As expected, Landon arrives in record time. Unexpected, is who accompanies him. Patrick strolls in behind Landon as they enter Chloe's bedroom. Keeping Chloe awake was becoming harder and harder so I had to resort to extreme silliness. So both Landon and Patrick find me acting like a loon, dancing to the loud music I'm playing to keep both me and Chloe awake. I'm only alerted of their presence when I'm laughed off my makeshift stage in front of Chloe's bed. "Hey, my moves aren't that bad!"

"Yeah, Suz, they are," Landon replies biting back laughter.

"Well you try keeping this semi-comatose girl awake for hours. It's harder than it looks," I defend my actions. At the mention of Chloe both guys walk further into the room ignoring me and focusing all their attention on the patient.

"Good thing you have a hard head, Runt," Patrick teases. Meanwhile Landon looks grief stricken seeing Chloe all bandaged up and droopy eyed.

"You flatter me, Patrick. I'm making a fashion statement. Like the new look?" Chloe rubs at the white gauze. Even her light touch triggers pain as her face contorts in agony. "Damn, that hurts!"

"Easy there," Landon pulls her hand away from the injury intertwining their fingers. He gets comfortable beside her as her eyes grow heavier. "How much longer before she can sleep?"

"Another two hours at least," I say through a yawn.

"We've got this Suz. Why don't you go on to bed?" Landon offers. Patrick has yet to speak one word to me. And with his back turned I doubt he plans to now.

"Okay. But I'll sleep on the couch in case you need me during the night. Oh, and I made a pot of coffee if you're interested." I give Chloe a brief hug and whisper, "Hang in there, just a little longer and you can finally get some rest." She gives me a small smile. "'Night boys." Landon gives me a chin tip while Patrick continues avoidance. Such childish behavior. But at this point I'm really too tired to care.

Chapter Twenty Six

Light is filtering in through the windows as I wake. I blink several times adjusting to the brightness and take in my surroundings. Why did I sleep on the couch last night instead of my bed?

"'Morning sleeping beauty," I hear from a male voice across the room. Panic momentarily sets in while I still try to wake fully. I look around the room to find my good friend Landon seated at the kitchen table drinking a cup of coffee and playing with his phone.

"Landon?" I question rubbing the sleep from my eyes.

"I thought I'd have to call in your prince charming for that magical kiss to wake you up. You really were exhausted from last night, yeah?" Ah, last night. Finally my brain starts working and I remember Chloe and her accident.

"How is she this morning?" I ask immediately.

"She's still asleep, but I imagine she'll be waking up soon. It's almost time for another dose of pain meds. She had a rough time last night getting comfortable without the medication. Don't think she slept more than an hour at a time without waking in pain. But I couldn't give her more than prescribed."

"Sounds like it wasn't so great for you either," I say noticing how tired Landon looks.

"I'm fine, Suz. Don't worry about me. Let's just hope Patrick gets back soon with that breakfast so I can give Chloe her meds with some food in her tummy." Landon looks down at his phone again while I fully register what he just said. Not only did Patrick come by *my* house last night with Landon to see about Chloe, but apparently he's coming back. To *my* house. And all this after our big blow up. Huh.

"Looks like we don't have to wait long. Patrick just texted saying he and Katelyn are on the way."

"Katelyn? But he... Why is she...," Patrick's parting words were that he never wanted to see or hear from me again. He also added that I stay away from Katelyn. Now he's suddenly a frequent visitor *and* he's bringing Katelyn. For crying out loud, I just woke up and he's already making my head spin. Landon waits for me to continue but I'm at a loss for words. "Never mind."

"What's with the arctic chill blowing between you and Patrick?" Landon asks. I look at him like I have no idea what he's referring to. "Come on, Suz. My attention was solely focused on Chloe and her condition. But even with that, I still noticed the freeze out Patrick directed toward you. And, you, you received his behavior like it was expected. So don't act like you are in the dark here."

Painful moans from Chloe's bedroom keep me from answering Landon. I hate what she's experiencing, but her timing couldn't be better. Landon forgets that he asked me anything and rushes in to check on her, me close on his heels. "Runt, how you feeling this morning?" he asks.

"Like my head is gonna explode," Chloe answers with a grimace. "Can I get something to drink and some more of those feel good pills?"

"I can get that drink for you, but Landon's making you eat something before taking more medication," I say alerting her to my presence. She gives Landon the evil eye, but he refuses to back down. "Don't give Landon all your grief. I happen to agree with him. You need something in your stomach so you don't get nauseated. The doctor warned against that." She turns her glare toward me. I'm not as tough as Landon and I'll give in if she asks. Time to make my escape. "Let me get you that drink...and the door. Sounds like your breakfast has arrived." Great, this should be fun. Can't wait to see Patrick and Katelyn first thing this morning. Oh yay!

Only it's not Patrick and Katelyn I'm ready to greet when I open the door. It's the Ryders. Chloe's parents. Shit, this can't be good. They will be furious when they see Chloe in her condition and know we didn't call to tell them. "G-good morning, Mr. and Mrs. Ryder," I stutter. "This is a surprise."

"Surprise? Hardly, Suzanna. It's our last day on vacation and we've yet to spend any time with our baby girl. Figured that bar establishment she's so fond of working at can't be open this early. So why not pay her a morning visit?" Mrs. Ryder tells me all this as she pushes her way inside not waiting for an invitation.

"Good morning, Suzanna. How are you?" Mr. Ryder asks giving me a hug and kiss on the head.

"I'm good, thanks. It's great to see you," I answer. It's easy to see how Chloe adores her father. He's really a kind man.

"So sorry to barge in like this. We are leaving today and wanted a chance to see Chloe before heading back to Florence. I hope it's not a bad time."

Two screams from Chloe's room send us running that way. I recognize one as belonging to Chloe. The other, more high pitched shrill has to belong to her mom. "Would you look at your daughter? Lying in bed with that...that man," Mrs. Ryder says with disgust.

"Chloe, baby...what happened?" Mr. Ryder asks sidestepping his wife to stand closer to Chloe. Obviously he's the only one of them to notice her bandage.

"Hi Daddy," Chloe says with watery eyes. She extends her arms and he leans down for an embrace. "Uh, Daddy...careful."

"I'm sorry baby," Mr. Ryder says releasing his hold. "What in the world happened to you?"

Chloe begins to tell her father all about the accident. She explains that Landon, Patrick and I have had to be with her around the clock, first to keep her awake and then to administer her meds. Mr. Ryder sits at her bedside and listens patiently until she finishes. Just retelling the story takes a good amount of Chloe's energy.

"You should have called us young lady. We'd have taken care of you." Mr. Ryder notices Chloe's tired state and helps to ease her back on the pillows behind her. Right next to Landon's body on the bed. Guess he's not as pissed off as Mrs. Ryder about finding Landon in Chloe's bedroom.

"She didn't want to bother you on your vacation," I add to smooth things over.

"We had it taken care of anyway," Landon assures Mr. Ryder. He doesn't bother speaking to Chloe's mother. The mother who has yet to acknowledge Chloe's condition or ask how she is feeling.

"I bet you did take care of her, Landon," Mrs. Ryder says with sarcasm.

Mr. Ryder doesn't appreciate his wife's snide remark. "Good grief, woman. Your daughter is hurt. She's laid up in a bed fully clothed with a bandaged wrapped around her injured head. Her male friend, who is also fully clothed, is helping her recover. What's your problem here?"

"It's very inappropriate! And it doesn't look right. That's my problem. I don't like seeing my unwed baby daughter in a bed with a man regardless of the situation," Mrs. Ryder fires back at her husband. "You young people these days....no morals."

"Morals? You want to discuss morals?" Landon's voice is calm but threatening.

"Landon, let me handle this," Chloe states as she pats his arm, which is corded with tense muscles. "Mom, thanks for asking and yes, I'm feeling better already. In a couple of days, I'll be back to normal. Just a stupid head injury. No need for you to worry about my *health* or anything. As for my morality, it should ease your mind to know I haven't spread my legs for anyone since the accident. I'm taking the whole 'I've got a headache' excuse very seriously," she says pointing to her injury and shocking us all.

"You ungrateful little who_"

"Hey, that's my daughter you're getting ready to insult." Mr. Ryder scolds his wife. "And you, young lady, that's no way to speak to your mother. I've had enough of the constant bickering between you two."

"Sorry Daddy," Chloe is quick to offer.

"Don't apologize to me, apologize to your mother."

"Um, yeah, sorry about that Mom. Must be all the drugs I'm taking." I hear no sincerity in Chloe's apology to her mother. Her dad levels her with his look that says neither did he. "What? I said I was sorry." Mr. Ryder sighs heavily and gives up.

"Of course it's the drugs talking. No daughter of mine would ever be so vulgar. You must be picking up some real bad habits from that bar you're working at. I mean, who wants to be a barmaid? Thank goodness this is just temporary. Even so, it's still embarrassing. I hate telling my friends you're spending your summer working at a *bar*." Snotty much, Mrs. Ryder? She really knows how to kick Chloe when she's down. The lack of motherly concern and derogatory remarks aimed at her job, it's no wonder Chloe never wants to go home. Had Chloe been up for it, I'm sure she'd have come back with fighting words. But in her current state all she manages is an eye roll.

"Chloe, darlin', you sure you're gonna be okay?" Mr. Ryder asks ignoring his wife.

"In a few days, yes, I'll be fine. Thanks for stopping by to check on me." Chloe leans in and gives her dad a kiss. "Next time, can you leave her at home?"

"For you kiddo....maybe I can arrange that," her dad whispers as not to be overheard by mommy dearest. "Take care, sweetie. I love you."

"Love you too, Dad," Chloe sniffs and I can see she's struggling with emotions. "Bye Mom, it was a pleasure, as always."

"Chloe, girl. You know I love you. You just worry me so," Mrs. Ryder steps in touching Chloe's shoulder. "You take care of yourself," she adds with a few pats to said shoulder. Then she leaves. No kiss, no hug, she just leaves. That was the bare minimal of touching between a mother and daughter I have ever seen. I've seen friends be more affectionate with Chloe than what I just witnessed with her mother. Maybe she hadn't had enough wine this morning to show her touchy/feely side. *Ohhhh, that's mean Suzanna.* Well, she deserved it.

Mr. Ryder goes to follow his wife. "I'll see you out," I say and he nods his appreciation.

"Take care of her, Suzanna. She needs you," Mr. Ryder says in a normal voice, his wife long out of earshot. She made a hasty exit and is probably already waiting in the car. "And you have her call me. I want to know she's fully recovered before you two head off to New York."

"Of course," I assure him. He gives me a farewell hug and walks out the door passing by my next unexpected guest. Gee, am I running a Garden City welcome center?

"Leslie," I say, as if bored. I don't have the time or patience to deal with her this morning. "What can I do for you?"

"I was looking for Landon," she says getting right to the point. No pleasantries offered.

"Why?"

"Look, I know he probably told you we are no longer dating. And I don't expect you or the rest of your friends to be too broken up about it. It was obvious you never liked me or wanted to include me."

"Then why are you here?" I ask again. Landon hasn't mention Leslie in a while. Not that we've talked often lately. His job has been keeping him quite busy. But I'm playing along.

"I wanted to return some of his things." Leslie motions to the bag of items she's holding with one arm. "I stopped by James' parents' place, but no one was there. I didn't want to leave these things just sitting outside. I took a chance that he might be at your place. And lo and behold, his truck is parked in the driveway just as I suspected." Irritated doesn't begin to describe her tone. She hates the fact that she had to track down Landon at my house, knowing all along he'd more than likely be here.

"Fine, come on in. Landon's with Chloe. And before you start, it's not what you think. Chloe had an accident last night at work and we've all been helping to take care of her. As a matter of fact, it's been such a long night and busy morning I've yet to brush my teeth." Gross, did I just admit that? I run my tongue over my grimy choppers and shudder with disgust. "Gotta take care of this pronto," I say holding my hand over my mouth to cage my offending breath.

"Maybe I should just leave his things with you," Leslie hesitates.

"Suit yourself, but I'm sure both Landon and Chloe would want to say hello." I don't have a clue if Landon's and Leslie's break up was a mutual decision or if she's trying to win him back. Regardless, I have to at least make her feel welcome in my home. "Listen, I really need to freshen up. Go on and say hello. Or don't. The choice is yours. See ya, Leslie." I retreat to my bathroom for my overdue hygiene morning ritual, leaving Leslie in contemplation.

Washed face, brushed teeth, minty breath and tamed hair, I reenter Chloe's bedroom a new woman. Katelyn is fussing over Chloe, fluffing her pillows and rearranging her covers. Relishing in the attention, Chloe is playing the dutiful patient, asking for an adjustment here and there. She's telling Katelyn the awful story of how the accident occurred. And Katelyn is riveted to her every word. Meanwhile, across the room, Patrick and Landon are hovering over an almost empty box of doughnuts. "Leave any for me?"

"You're just in time. A couple of more minutes and I'd have eaten the last one," Landon says looking hungrily at the lone doughnut in the box.

"Go ahead, Landon. You eat it. I'm really not that hungry." Landon goes to swipe the doughnut from the box, but Patrick catches his wrist just in time.

"No, that's Suzanna's. You've had like five already." Landon pulls his arm out of Patrick's grip and pouts. Patrick grabs a napkin from the dresser, picks up the doughnut and hands them both to me. "Here, this is for you."

"Thanks," I say shyly accepting the food. What a difference a day makes. Yesterday Patrick wasn't even speaking to me. Today, he's thrusting food in my face. Hey, it's a start. I nibble on the glazed dough, the sweet flavor filling my mouth. The yummy goodness causes an involuntary moan to escape. At the sound, Patrick whips his head in my direction. He stares at me, his eyes hungry with lust. Quick to cover it up, he breaks our gaze, engaging Landon in conversation. The moment is over so fast I convince myself that I imagined it.

"They're good, aren't they Suz?" Chloe asks licking her fingers. "Better than a Pop-Tart!"

"Now I know you've hit your head. You're talking crazy," I tease. Chloe loves her Pop-Tarts. Religiously, she has one every morning for breakfast. She'll fight you if you even get near her stash of sugary, frosted, unhealthy breakfast food.

"You're right. What I am thinking?" We all laugh, glad to see Chloe returning to her normal charming self.

"So what's the plan today? I know we all have things to get done, but I don't think Chloe should be left alone just yet," Landon initiates an action plan. "I've got to report to work, but luckily I'm close by. Only have to be at the north end of the beach today. I can be back by mid afternoon."

"I've got a tee time in about an hour. But I can cancel and play later. Although, the afternoon heat will be a bitch."

"No need to cancel, I can take the morning shift," Patrick offers. "And Katelyn will stay and help Chloe with her bathroom and showering needs. That is, unless, Chloe, you want me to help you with those things? Which of course I'd be more than happy," Patrick says with a wink in Chloe's direction.

"Patrick! Leave the poor girl alone. She's already been through enough without you traumatizing her," Katelyn admonishes her fiancé. "Chloe, I'll be glad to stay and help you with whatever."

"Ah, baby, you know I'm just kidding. No need to get all jealous on me. The only naked goods I want to see are yours, sweetheart." Patrick walks up to Katelyn and lays a big fat, sloppy wet kiss on her lips. His hands grope her hips and ass in this overly avert attempt at PDA. This is the first time I have seen the two get remotely intimate. Katelyn seems as shocked as the rest of us at Patrick's sudden affection. Her eyes remain wide open, even while kissing, and her body tenses at his touches.

She pulls back from him stopping the onslaught of his hands and lips. "Patrick, stop. This is embarrassing. Especially in front of your friends," she says in a small voice.

"They all know how much I love you, K. I just can't wait to marry you. Speaking of which...we have an announcement to make." Patrick gets grabby again pulling Katelyn into his chest and nuzzling her neck. "I'll tell you all, but I've got to get one more kiss." He slurps, licks and smacks up her neck and across her jaw line until he reaches her lips. He nibbles her bottom lip before going in for the plunge. Finally, Katelyn yields and opens her mouth to what can only be described as a porno worthy kiss. Tongues, teeth and lips all clashing together for what seems to me like an eternity. I have to look away. This is too much for just a bystander to witness. But me, the ex who still has unresolved feelings? Yeah, just too much. "God you taste sweet," Patrick whispers and I hope that means that the kiss is over.

"Y'all gonna get a room or tell us this big announcement?" Chloe asks. Thank God her pain medicated brain still has enough wits to get this show on the road. Cause one more second of this out of nowhere romantic affection Patrick suddenly feels the need to share and I might throw up.

"Well, since we love each other so, so, soooooo much. And we can barely wait another day to be husband and wife. Katelyn and I, and also our parents, decided to move the wedding up. So we'll be getting married the first weekend in August."

"*What?*" Both Landon and I question in unison. Not the elated response Patrick was hoping for from the scowl on his face.

"OMG! You're pregnant!" Chloe screams.

"Hell no, I'm not pregnant!" Katelyn affirms and we all let out a collective sigh of relief.

"Not yet, but we're gonna have a lot of fun trying, aren't we baby?" Patrick coos in Katelyn's ear.

"Gonna? You mean you haven't had sex yet?" Chloe so bluntly asks.

"Chloe!" I say with reproach. I so don't need to know the details of Patrick's sex life.

"That's actually none of your business, Runt!" Patrick scolds. "Besides, it's a very *personal* matter. And I was recently told by a friend my *personal* matters should only be discussed with Katelyn, since she's the one I'll be spending the rest of my life with. The one I'll be making future decisions with. So, sorry guys. Any *personal* things that affect me will no longer be on the table for discussion. Right Suz?"

Oh, I see now. All this talk about pushing the wedding up, declaring his love for Katelyn, and the rest of the bullshit Patrick's shoveling is his way of making a point. Everything I said during our fight, he's twisted and taken to the extreme. Well, fuck him. I don't need to be called out this morning. He's got a problem with me, he needs to take it up with me. Not involve Katelyn, Landon and Chloe. "Yep, you're exactly right, Patrick. Which is why I'm so confused. You come in here announcing your change in wedding plans. Um...*personal.* You make an over exaggerated display of how in love you are with Katelyn. Yeah, quite *personal.* Then you allude to your plans to make babies in the future. Doesn't get any more *personal* than that! So what's your game here, huh? Cause you can't have it both ways!" My voice rises with anger. Take that you little dipshit!

"Suzanna, I'm sorry if we've upset you," Katelyn makes the attempt to calm me down.

"I'm not upset. Actually, I couldn't be happier for you both. Let me offer my marriage congratulations now, since I won't be there to do it at the wedding."

"You're not coming?" Patrick has the nerve to ask.

"No, that's the same weekend as the LPGA qualifying." Their wedding is just something else to think about while I'm trying to get that tour card. Great!

"The wedding is on Saturday. There's always the chance you won't make the cut which would free up your weekend," Patrick states. Damn, he's nasty today. Everyone in the room looks at him with an opened mouth.

"Shut your mouth! What's wrong with you, Patrick? We all know Suz is gonna win the whole damn thing. Katelyn, go ahead and cross her off the guest list. She will NOT be at the wedding." Chloe sticks up for me and my golf skills. I love that girl. She gives me a fist bump then adds, "My money is on you, Suz. Always!"

"Me too, Suz. Me too," Landon decides to participate in the conversation. "Besides, this wedding business has your dad's doing written all over it. You're pushing the date up because of the campaign, right?" Landon ignores Patrick and directs his comments to Katelyn.

"No, um, I mean yes..." Katelyn struggles to finish her sentence.

"Well, which is it?" Landon demands. He seems as put off about all this as I do.

"What's with you all? Can't you just accept that Katelyn and I really, really want to get married? It's because of our wishes alone that the wedding date is earlier. Sure, Judge Bostick's campaign schedule benefited from the adjustment, but that's not the reason we decided to speed things along," Patrick says unnerved by Landon's accusation.

"R-i-ight! So it's a win-win for everyone. How convenient!" Landon says incredulously, leaving no doubt that he believes nothing Patrick just said.

"And I thought you were my friends?" Patrick says shaking his head. "Come on, Katelyn. Let's go be with the people who are actually happy for us. Those that don't question our motives."

"But what about helping out with Chloe?" Katelyn asks truly torn. She really is a sweet girl. Despite the secrets that she keeps hidden surrounding this engagement and upcoming marriage, underneath it all, she's a good girl. I hate to see her in turmoil.

"I can stick around until Landon gets back from work. You go ahead with Patrick," I offer. Hopefully she can talk some sense into him. Not only is he about to make a huge commitment for unknown reasons. But he's also turning away from his friends, trying to shut us out. With all he's got going on, now is certainly not the time to exile himself from the people who love him the most.

"Landon?" Katelyn takes one last look in his direction. I don't know what it is she's hoping for. Maybe that he'll ask her to stay. Maybe that he'll keep probing until Katelyn has no other choice than to tell him the truth. Maybe that Landon will confess that he sees Katelyn as something other than his friend's fiancée. However, she gets none of those things. Landon gifts her with a head tilt toward the door. His silent command to follow her fiancé and leave. Katelyn deflates with his dismissal. "Feel better Chloe," she says in parting with a squeaky voice. Head hung low she leaves the bedroom in search of Patrick.

"You guys give me a headache," Chloe pronounces, reclining back ready to succumb to the effects of another drug induced coma. I can relate. Although, the dull throbbing between my ears has nothing to do with a head injury. Between the Ryders, Leslie, and finally Patrick and Katelyn, I'm scared to think who else might show up. All that excitement and it's not even noon. Man, I hope this isn't a sign for how the rest of my day will pan out. If it is, I'll be consuming some of Chloe's happy pills and slip into my own la-la land.

Chapter Twenty Seven

S tanding in front of the mirror in the bathroom of our hotel suite, I finish applying the last touches of my makeup. Taking a glance at myself in the full length mirror, I'm still uncertain about the outfit Chloe insisted I wear. The silver and black material barely covers my ass cheeks. "Are you sure this isn't a shirt?" I ask tugging at the hemline.

"For the last time, yes, I'm sure it's a dress. Not a shirt, silly." Chloe acts like I'm crazy for even thinking such a thing. "Stop being so self-conscious and show some skin, Suz. Besides, your legs look amazing in that get-up. Here, put these on." She tosses me some shoes that are at least four inches in heel height.

"Not only are you trying to humiliate me with wearing this dress... the strong potential of my junk being exposed, but now you're trying to kill me too? Chloe, I'll break an ankle in these heels."

"That's why you're putting them on now. So you can practice walking around the hotel room. It's not like you have any other options. People would laugh you out of the state if you showed up wearing that fabulous dress with your flip flops," Chloe warns. "Come on, Suz. We're in freaking New York City. While in the Big Apple, getting dressed up in fancy clothes and shoes are a requirement for going out on the town."

"I don't remember reading that in the tourist guide," I quip.

"Oh, it's in there. You just didn't read the fine print." Fine, not like I have a choice. Chloe and I spent our entire afternoon shopping on Park Avenue for the perfect night-on-the- town ensembles. Let me rephrase, Chloe did most of the shopping...browsing through endless clothing racks at every store. I just stood there and tried on whatever she picked out for me to. This shirt/dress (I still think it's a shirt) was Chloe's top choice for me to wear out dancing. She wouldn't let me leave the store until I had made the purchase. At that point, I was sick and tired of shopping and just wanted to head back to the hotel. So I didn't put up much of a fight. Now, I'm regretting that decision.

Strapping on the skyscraper shoes, I test out my balance, only wobbling a little. I slowly start walking around the room while Chloe continues getting dressed in the bathroom. "So, did you call him yet?" Chloe yells from the other room. Her question startles me, almost sending me in a face plant. Luckily, I catch the wall with my hands, bracing myself from an epic fall.

"No, not yet," I reply.

"Suzanna.... What are you waiting for, huh?" Chloe asks. "You're not planning to chicken out, are you?"

"Gesh, Chloe, give it a rest, will you? I'm going to call Wyatt. Probably tomorrow. We've only been here for two days. Plus, it's not like we've had time for much else except being the typical tourists." That's actually an understatement. From the time our plane touched down, Chloe and I have been going nonstop. Yesterday, we visited the Statue of Liberty, the Empire State Building, and Rockefeller Center. Last night, we watched the Broadway show *Wicked* and had a late dinner at a highly recommended Italian restaurant. This morning, we hit the ground running, literally. I convinced Chloe to join me for a morning jog through Central Park. Of course she only agreed after I bribed her with treating us to breakfast at The Loeb Boathouse. After our meal, we went out on the row boats on the lake adjacent to the restaurant. Soon, the sun was high in the sky, heating up the afternoon, so we decided to head somewhere indoors to escape the heat. We strolled through the New York Metropolitan Museum of Art where we studied the classic works of European masters as well as the modern collection of American artists. Cutting our time short at the museum, Chloe insisted we go shopping for new outfits for our night out on the town. She dragged me up and down Park Avenue, into stores way, way above my price range. Luckily, we found a reasonably priced boutique that catered to the trends and styles of our age group. Now, I'm carefully navigating the perimeter of our hotel room wearing the fruits of our labor. "Stop nagging...I promise I'll call him tomorrow. Let's drop it for now and enjoy the night."

"Okay, okay. But tomorrow, first thing. I'm holding you to it," Chloe says appearing from the bathroom. Whoa, she looks amazing. She's styled her golden dirty blonde locks in big spiral curls that hit her shoulders. Heavy eye makeup gives her a sultry look. And her lips are perfectly plumped and glossed with a touch of subtle color. The coral strapless dress accentuates her ample bosom and the fitted bodice shows off her tiny waist. It's rich, vibrant color compliments her sun-kissed skin tone. Starting at the hips, the silky fabricate flows loosely, hitting her mid thigh. The gold strappy heels are at least as high as mine, making her bare, toned legs look a mile long. She's definitely gonna turn some heads tonight. I let out a low whistle. She answers by doing a full body spin. "Whatcha think?"

"Looking good, Chloe, looking good. How about me?" I ask and start my own 360 degree turn, only faltering in my shoes once.

"A+ on your overall appearance. But we're gonna have to work on your moves," she teases and giggles. We grab our clutches and key cards and head out the door in anticipation of a fun filled night.

The cab pulls to a stop in front of the high-end sports bar Ainsworth. We decided on this place for two reasons. First, it came highly recommended for its atmosphere and food, not typical of the majority of sports themed establishments. Secondly, it promised to show the Real Madrid soccer match in which my brother, Flynn, will make his La Liga League debut. The regular midfielder for Real Madrid was injured earlier in the week, and the team pulled Flynn up from his position on the minor league squad to take his place. It's his first time in the big leagues and I can't wait to watch him in action. Having called earlier today to make our reservations, the hostess assured me one of the bazillion TVs in the bar would be carrying the game.

While our table is being prepared, Chloe and I take some open spots at the bar and order a drink. The place is very classy. Were it not for the television screens mounted throughout the restaurant, broadcasting live action of baseball, tennis and soccer, you'd never guess it was a sports bar. "Incoming, incoming...three o'clock," Chloe whispers looking over my shoulder. I whip my head around, my sleek, high ponytail taking flight and slapping Chloe in the face. I watch as three very attractive men, all dressed in power suits from a day of business, approach us. Chloe sputters, swiping at her face from my hair assault. "Smooth, Suz. Real smooth."

"Hello, ladies. Mind if we join you?" the blonde haired man who looks more like he belongs on a surf board at the beach rather than in a boardroom asks.

"Not at all," Chloe says extending her hand. "Hi, I'm Chloe and this is my friend Suzanna."

"Sweet Jesus, say that again," the biggest of the three says with a drawl. "Better yet, just say anything. As long as you keep talking so I can hear that adorable accent. Makes me miss home."

"Big Jon here is a sucker for your southern twang," the surfer confirms nudging the man I assume is 'Big Jon' in the ribs.

"I apologize for my friends and their rudeness. Please let me introduce myself. I'm Brice," the most polished of the three says. He certainly seems comfortable in his three piece suit. Fills it quite nicely as well. He sounds like most of the people we have encountered since arriving in the city. I'd bet he is originally from around the area. "And these degenerates are Jon," he points to the big guy, "and Matt," he then points to surfer dude.

"It's nice to meet you all," Chloe says with her charming smile that doesn't go unnoticed by any of the men. "So what brings you out tonight? Hard day at work?"

"Work, it's slavery, I tell you," surfer dude, or rather Matt, complains. "After twelve long hours I had to get out and have a drink. Or I might go crazy."

"What's crazy is that Bubba and Tess are still there burning the midnight oil. I swear, we could work twenty-four hours a day and still not get everything finished," Big Jon adds. All this talk of long hours and hard work, I'm curious to what it is they do for a living.

"What type of work are you all in?" I ask, sipping on my Cosmo.

"Trading...stocks, bonds, annuities, futures. You name it, we buy and sell it." Matt may complain about his work demands, but he sure sounds proud of what he does.

"Um, sounds interesting," Chloe says to them all but zones in on the polished perfection that is Brice. Not surprising, he favors my brother in that he has light brown hair and steely grayish blue eyes. However, Flynn is much better looking than Brice. That's just my opinion. Although Brice seems nice enough, I feel he has this air about him. I'm getting the 'I'm better than you' vibe from him.

"So back to that accent I'm so fond of," Big Jon rumbles in his baritone voice. "Guessing you're not from around here."

"No, we're just visiting. Just some good 'ole southern girls in the big city," Chloe informs him.

"I knew it. Only wished you came from Texas. Something to look forward to when I get out of here," Big Jon flirts. "Although Bubba is gonna love meeting the two of you. If he and Tess ever get here."

"Can't wait to meet yet another Bubba," I say with sarcasm, but plaster on a smile. I hate how that name has turned into the quintessential stereotype of every male from a southern state. If I'd wanted to be introduced to a Bubba, I could have stayed at home. The hostess drops by to tell us our table is ready. While I'm paying our bar tab, Chloe invites the threesome to join us.

"I'm not sure how much room there will be, our reservations were for just the two of us, but feel free to squeeze in," Chloe suggests.

"I know the owner and can get your table upgraded to accommodate us all," Brice offers. I know he's only being considerate, but his arrogance and name dropping leaves a bad taste in my mouth. He saunters off toward the hostess stand to use his persuasive powers to get us a bigger table.

"Chloe? I specifically asked for that particular table because they assured me it was the best for watching the soccer match. I hope he doesn't screw that up for us."

"If he can get our table changed, I'm sure he can get a channel changed for our viewing pleasure. Don't sweat it, Suz. Just relax and enjoy," Chloe says with nonchalance. "And I'm probably more excited than you are about seeing Flynn's muscular thighs in action. Don't think for a minute I'd let these bozos get in the way of seeing the image that will later star in my dreams tonight." Chloe gives me a wink. Whew, so glad we are on the same page.

I have to give it to Brice...his connections actually paid off. Not only did we get a larger table, it's located directly in front of the mega screen that's broadcasting the professional soccer match. Chloe and I squeal like school girls when we see Flynn for the first time during pre-game warm ups. He looks great in his uniform. However, he seems nervous. Of course he'd be nervous...it's his professional debut. I'm sure millions are watching to see how he will handle replacing one of Spain's favorite players. His skills will be under a great deal of scrutiny tonight. I pray he does well.

While we wait for the official start of the game, we order more drinks and appetizers. The guys, who are frequent customers, make menu suggestions. All of them include the ahi tuna burger as one of their favorites. "I used to play a little soccer back in the day," Matt remarks tuning into the television.

"Where? On the beach?" Big Jon goads him. "You Cali boys wouldn't know a real ball if it hit you in the face. Bunch of pansies," he teases good naturedly. Looks like I had Matt pegged correctly. Hey, I can spot a beach boy from a mile away. Of course he's got that whole West Coast look going on. Shaggy blonde hair, blue eyes and all around California good looks.

"And what would you know about organized sports, cowboy? And the rodeo doesn't count," Matt inquires, trying to push Big Jon's buttons.

"I'll have you know I was a lean, mean fighting machine on the gridiron. Still hold the record at my high school for most sacks in one season," Big Jon says with pride. "We ever get out of the office to do something other than drink, I might teach you a thing or two."

"How big of you."

"Like they say, everything's bigger in Texas," Big Jon says with a smirk, raising his eyebrows up and down repetitively at me. He's shamelessly flirting and it's adorably cute. He makes me giggle. Both guys do...they are a riot. They remind me of the guys I grew up with, Landon, James and Patrick. They were forever kidding around with each other, ribbing back and forth. I miss those days of innocence. When things weren't so heavy and the most we had to worry about was getting our homework done. Since Patrick's wedding announcement, I haven't seen or talked with him. Landon was in and out, checking on Chloe before we left. He said he hasn't heard from him either. I knew he was trying to distance himself from us all. I hate that he has to deal with all of his issues...his engagement, impending marriage, his dad...all by himself. I wish I could help, but until he asks, I'm granting him the space he wants right now.

"Suz, look, look," Chloe interrupts my thoughts pointing to the television. The sound has been muted but the captions are on, alerting us that the commentators are discussing my brother.

> Commentator 1: So how do you think this Caulder kid will handle the pressure of replacing Salvador tonight?
>
> Commentator 2: Well, Salvador is a seasoned veteran. A real student of the game. He will definitely be missed by Real Madrid. Flynn Caulder has some pretty big shoes to fill. But from the coach's report, they think he is more than capable. He's showed some real talent playing on the semi-pro squad. He's a fast dribbler and has good foot speed. He's a threat to score with enough leg strength to strike from forty yards out. And he's a smart passer, always aware of where his teammates are. Overall, his skills on paper tell me he can get the job done.
>
> Commentator 1: I guess it was enough to convince Coach Gonzales to pull him up to the big leagues.
>
> Commentator 2: Not so fast, compadre.

"Holy shit, did he just quote Lee Corso? Wonder what that sounds like in Spanish," Matt ponders.

"Ssshhhh!" Chloe quiets the guys her eyes glued to the television screen.

Commentator 2: Unofficial reports have linked the promising soccer star, Flynn Caulder, to Isabella Gonzales, a rising star of her own. She was just featured in the Spanish version of *Sports Illustrated* infamous swimsuit edition. It has also been rumored that she has received a contract to model with Victoria's Secret as one of their angels.

Photos of a Spanish beauty wearing nothing but a skimpy bikini fill the screen. The men at our table, as well as others in the bar and restaurant, ohhh and ahhhh at the half naked creature.

Commentator 1: Wait a minute...is this Isabella Gonzales, Coach Gonzales' daughter?

Commentator 2: His one and only daughter, yes. Mr. Caulder and Miss Gonzales have been photographed together only recently, within the last week. Spotted at a coffee shop, sitting closely to each other and whispering, tells a spectator. Then pictures were leaked of the two of them burning up the dance floor at a local night club just two nights ago.

Photographs of Flynn and his model companion flash across the screen. I can excuse the incident in the coffee shop. Looks like two friends having coffee. Well two very close friends. But the photos on the dance floor...ever heard of dirty dancing? I hope it's dancing they were doing when the photo was taken. I glance at Chloe to see her reaction. She's still staring at the screen, head tilted with an inquisitive expression. Guess she's asking 'What the hell, Flynn?'.

"Damn, your brother doesn't mess around. He's basically banging that hottie on the dance floor," Brice so crudely states. As if I need another reason not to like him. He's nothing but an offensive son of a bitch.

Commentator 1: Are you suggesting his off the field antics may have helped him get a spot on the team?

Commentator 2: I'll leave that for the viewers to decide. I'm just laying out all the facts. His performance tonight will probably be the deciding factor. If he has a good game, then we can assume his skill level secured his place on the team. However, if he doesn't play well....fans could make the assumption that nepotism was involved, landing him the job. We'll have to wait and see.

Commentator 1: We won't have to wait long. The game is about to begin. Lots to think about folks. Stay with us for all the stats and highlights following the conclusion of the game. Enjoy!

The commentators are replaced with live action as the game begins. I try to concentrate on the game, especially Flynn's position, but I'm too concerned with Chloe. From the outside she doesn't seem to be affected by Flynn's latest European playboy status. But I know she's dying on the inside. I think she and Flynn started something before he left, something meaningful. I know Chloe felt it too. I could see it in her eyes, the way they would light up whenever he would call or Skype. Regardless whether or not a monogamous commitment was made, for Flynn to be dating so soon after leaving, it's like a slap to Chloe's face. And it's a colossal mistake on his part. Chloe will never, ever be able to trust him again.

So far Flynn's had a solid game. He's been credited with the assist which lead to the one goal of the game. At half time, Real Madrid is winning one nil. I've come to realize I'm probably the only person at our table that knows the score. Matt and Big Jon tried in the beginning to watch the action, but soon got disinterested, finding a professional baseball game more to their liking. Brice didn't even bother, choosing instead to flirt with Chloe. And she's been eating it up, never once paying any attention to the game after the newsflash about Flynn and his possible budding romance. Not that I can blame her. However, if she gets any closer to Brice, she'll be sitting in his lap. I'm not against her trying to find male companionship, or even just a casual hook up. But with Brice...ugh! Sure, he's handsome enough. But the whole alpha-male ego thing is a turn off for me. Maybe Chloe is into the dominance thing. It's doubtful...Chloe's way, way too independent to let anyone, especially a man boss her around.

With a break in the action, I decide it's time to visit the ladies room. I drag Chloe along for company. Okay, I really just wanted to get her away from Brice and his grabby hands. Plus, it's an unwritten rule that girls never go to the bathroom alone. Never. I try to keep the conversation light, definitely not mentioning Flynn. I'll talk with her about that later. For now, I just want us to enjoy our night out in NYC. I do, however, demand that I will buy us new drinks from the bar. "I just ordered another one before we left to go the bathroom," Chloe whines.

"I know, but I'll feel better getting your drink from the bar. I'll be certain I'm the only one that has access to it before you drink it."

"You're kidding, right? You really think Brice or Matt or Big Jon will spike my drink?" Chloe asks incredulously. No, not entirely I think to myself. I don't think Matt or Big Jon would ever do something like that. But the jury is still out on Brice. I wouldn't put anything past that guy.

"Chloe, we're in a strange city. And we just met these guys. I'm sure they would never do such a thing, but this day and time you can never be too sure. I'm just being extra careful. Indulge me, please?" I beg.

"Fine. But you're over the top. You know that?"

"Over the top about you. Just looking out for my bestie." I know I'm laying it on thick, but someone has to be smart in our situation. Guess that's gonna be me.

Walking back from the restrooms, I'm digging around in my clutch for cash to pay for our drinks. Not watching where I'm going I slam into Chloe's back, who just before was a few feet in front of me. "Hey, there they are. Girls, come meet the hardest working pair of our bunch. They finally decided to pack it in and join us for a drink," Matt calls out from a few tables away. Chloe stays cemented to her spot not moving, so I have to glance over her shoulder to see the newcomers.

Big Jon pats a guy on his shoulder pointing our way. "Bubba, you should take a real liking to these beauties. They come from your neck of the woods." The man begins to turn in our direction. Before I can get the complete frontal view, I already know exactly who they have donned with the nickname 'Bubba'. After the months apart, the sight of Wyatt still manages to take my breath away. He's similarly dressed like the other three, wearing a business suit. His tie had been loosened and he's undone the top buttons on his shirt. His thick dark brown locks look disheveled, like he's run his fingers through them a million times today. The unkempt hair style only adds to his sexiness. The big brown eyes, the ones that I used to get lost in, are wide with surprise at seeing me and Chloe in New York.

"Suzanna?" Oh my, that voice. It still gives me goose bumps and does a number on my nether regions.

"Eeeeekkkk! Wyatt McCain! I can't believe it," Chloe finally comes out of her stupor and races toward Wyatt. She jumps in his arms and he returns her hug. Our gazes remain locked on each other while he looks over her shoulder concentrating on me. "Who'd have thunk it ...a city of a billion and we run into you tonight."

"Yeah, wild, huh," Wyatt says clearly still stunned. "Good to see you Chloe. You look great!" He gives her a swift kiss to the forehead. With a beaming smile, Chloe looks up to Wyatt only to find his attention is focused behind her. He's still looking straight at me. "Well, go on. Go say hello. She's missed you," Chloe whispers before sidestepping around to the other side of the table, clearing the path between me and Wyatt.

Wyatt's hesitancy to close the distance between us stirs my feelings of being rejected yet again. Does he not want to see me? Talk to me? Well, too bad mister. Although our meeting is unplanned and earlier than I anticipated, here we are. Bravely, I take the first step forward. As if my movement was the permission Wyatt needed, he strides the remaining ten feet coming to stand only inches in front of me. "Hi," I greet him shyly.

"Hey," he responds back. He shifts, placing his hands in his pants pockets, seeming uncomfortable in my presence. The lack of conversation may seem awkward to outside observers, but the things we are communicating with our eyes need no words. His blank facial expressions give nothing away, but his eyes tell a different story. I see the hurt, the loss, and most importantly the love. Relief unlike I've never felt washes over me when I realize that Wyatt may still love me. It's a great starting point.

"Is this real? Are you real?" he asks still unable to believe that we are in the same place, breathing the same air, reconnecting after months apart.

"There's one sure way to find out," I suggest holding my arms out open and wide.

Now there's not a moment of hesitation on his part. He immediately engulfs me in an embrace, bringing me to my favorite place of all time. My head rests against his strong, hard chest and I melt with contentment, snuggling closer. I feel and hear his accelerated heartbeat and know the emotions coursing through him are in line with mine. If I could stop time, I'd stay right here in his arms forever. But forever apparently is not meant to be. I feel Wyatt tense against me before he begins to pull away. Our bubble has been busted as a pretty woman comes to stand beside Wyatt penetrating our inner sanctum. "Don't be rude, Wyatt. Aren't you going to introduce me?" she asks. This must the last of the five co-workers that I now know are interns with Galloway and Meads Brokerage Firm.

"Yeah, sure. Suzanna, this is Tess. We work together." Wyatt confirms what I already deduced. "Tess, this is Suzanna. My, um... my..." Wyatt finds himself at a loss for words.

"Friend from home," I supply. "It's nice to meet you Tess." I hope my smile is convincing.

"Wyatt, you didn't tell me you had friends visiting," she says ignoring me and focusing her undivided attention on Wyatt. She goes as far as touching his arm and I'm seconds away from slapping her hand away. I already don't like her for interrupting my time with Wyatt. Now, I'm on the border of hatred and soon to cross over if she doesn't stop touching my man.

"I didn't know," Wyatt says, discreetly adjusting his posture so her hand falls away. Good boy.

"So this is coincidence, you two running into each other? Of course, you're here vacationing over the long holiday weekend," she states, assuming she's figured out the purpose of my visit. Doesn't she know what happens to people who assume?

"Actually, I came to New York to see and talk to Wyatt."

"You did?" Wyatt asks in shock.

"I did. I was going to call you tomorrow. I think there are some things we need to discuss. But since we're together now, why wait until tomorrow?" I'm hopeful he'll take my subtle invitation and offer up suggestions for us to continue our conversation alone. I don't care where, just someplace away from his co-workers, specifically Tess. Also a place a little more private.

"We've got more work to do tonight on that acquisition. The reports are due tomorrow. Preferably early tomorrow, or else we'll get a late start to the Hamptons and get caught in all the holiday traffic. Brice said if we wanted to make it to his parents' place by dinner we needed to leave right after lunch," Tess reminds Wyatt. I don't remember asking for her permission to leave tonight with Wyatt. Not that she needs it. She doesn't seem to mind butting into our conversation. And when did Wyatt ever need someone to speak for him?

"Oh," I say glancing at my feet, feeling very small. My shoulders sag with disappointment as I realize that Wyatt and I might not get the chance to have our discussion. It was presumptuous of me to think he'd drop everything, his work and his social life, to spend time with me on my surprise visit. Why did I put off calling him? I should have been dialing his number as soon as I exited the airport. Now, it looks like he has plans of his own to be out of the city during the remainder of my visit. Guess it's what I deserve for being such a chicken shit.

Wyatt places his finger under my chin and presses up so I have no other choice but to raise my head and look him in the eyes. "If you really want to talk, my studio apartment is just a few blocks away. Or if you'd rather, there's a quiet little bar not far from here that we could go to. Have a few drinks. Both are within walking distance."

The corners of my mouth begin to lift and soon I can't control the smile that stretches across my face. "I'd like to see your place."

"Then let's go," Wyatt says through his own smile.

"But Wyatt_" Tess starts.

"Tess, the reports are basically complete. Just a few minor changes. We can easily finish them before lunch tomorrow," Wyatt says dismissing her. Their brief exchange is the only time his eyes leave mine. That's the only chance I have to get a good visual of the woman. Still in her work attire, a classy navy suit over a silk blouse, her outward appearance screams powerful businesswoman. But after Wyatt's words her pouty expression is anything but business-like. Of course, I had her pegged all along. She no more wants to work tonight than does Wyatt. But she does crave his company. I'm beginning to realize that Tess has a crush. Not that I can blame her. Wyatt is hard to resist. I know from experience. After tonight, I hope there will be no chance of Tess's crush for Wyatt developing into something more. If things go as planned, Wyatt and I will be well on our way to repairing our relationship.

"You ready?" Wyatt asks placing his hand at the small of my back to guide me toward the exit. Just that small amount of contact, with the thoughts of what might come later, has me suppressing a moan.

"Y-yes," I say sounding breathless. "I need to tell Chloe I'm leaving, first. You think she'll be okay to stay and hang out with your friends? They'll get her back to the hotel safely, right?"

"She'll be fine. They are all great guys...even Brice. Once you get underneath all his bravado you'll find he's a decent person. Not that Chloe needs help taking care of herself, but if it'll make you feel better, I can talk with Brice...call him off," Wyatt offers.

"Will you, please?" Chloe may be able to take care of herself. But with the recent news of Flynn, I'm don't trust her to make the right decisions tonight.

"For you Suz, anything. Let's go say goodbye." Wyatt leads me to the table to begin our farewells. I expected a round of questions about how Wyatt knows me and Chloe. But I'm thankful there are none. Luckily Chloe has already filled in everyone at the table about the history of our affiliation. After a quick word with Chloe while Wyatt chats with Brice, we say our final goodbyes and exit the classy sports bar.

Chapter Twenty Eight

We walk casually side by side as the natives race by us in their normal hurried pace. Occasionally, the crowded sidewalk causes me to brush up against Wyatt. Each time our hands touch I have to hold myself back from latching on and intertwining our fingers. Even though it's a balmy eighty degrees out on this summer night, I'm left cold from his lack of touch. The hug inside the restaurant and his guiding hand on my lower back were just enough to tease me. Now, I'm craving physical contact with Wyatt. I'm an addict and Wyatt is my drug.

As we travel the few blocks to Wyatt's place, he shows me some of his favorite spots. He points out the deli that he visits frequently for lunch. The pizza place he favors, going on and on about how they serve the best slice of pie he's ever put in his mouth. While we are waiting at a crosswalk, he points up into the sky indicating the high rise where his office is located. I'm a captive audience, soaking up every detail. I want to know as much as I can about Wyatt's life in New York.

Not fifteen minutes later, we stop in front of a twelve story tall apartment building. I follow Wyatt up the stairs and into the foyer. You can tell the building is an older one that has been refurbished recently. Fresh neutral paint is on the walls and the tile floor is shiny and new looking. As I'm looking around, Wyatt grabs my hand (finally) and pulls me over to a row of elevators. He presses the up button and we wait for a car, our hands still attached. Yay! When one approaches, we wait until some of his neighbors file out so that we can enter. When the doors close we are the only occupants on the elevator. Our first time being alone all night. He presses the button to take us to the fifth floor, but says nothing. I'm a little nervous, my palms beginning to sweat. Thoughts of the conversation we will soon be having swim in my head. Am I ready for the answers I seek? If Wyatt is truthful about the reason he broke up with me, will I be able to handle it? The ding of the elevator alerts me that we have ascended to the floor where Wyatt resides. Still holding hands, Wyatt pulls me down the hall to his door. Using his unoccupied hand, he searches in his pockets until he produces a key. Unlocking the door, he drops my hand to place his on my lower back again, ushering me inside.

"It's not much, but at least I get to live alone. Don't have to deal with a roommate," Wyatt says closing us in his apartment. He's right. It's not much at all. The open floor plan consists of a tiny galley kitchen with a bar that separates it from the living area. A couch and one other chair take up most of the living space. I can see the entirety of the short hallway with a door on both sides. I'm guessing one leads to his bedroom while the other one leads to the bathroom. Apart from being small, the place is clean. It doesn't even look very lived in. From what I heard tonight, sounds like Wyatt spends very little of his time here, the majority of it he is at work.

"It's nice," I say being polite. He's lucky to have this space, small or not. The real estate in the city is astronomically expensive.

"Um, thanks. Make yourself at home." He gestures with his hand toward the couch offering me a seat. "Can I get you something to drink? Beer? Water?"

"A water sounds good, thanks." I need to keep my head clear and stay away from all alcohol. We've got some serious topics to cover. Wyatt returns with two bottles of water offering one to me. Our fingers touch as the exchange is made and for a brief moment we both freeze. "Wyatt..." He pulls away with lightning speed and I have to flex not to drop the bottle.

"I've been in this monkey suit all day. Mind if I change real quick?"

"No, go on. Take your time." I need a few moments alone anyway to collect my thoughts. Wyatt takes the minimal ten steps it

requires to get to his room and shuts himself inside. Wish I had more
comfortable clothes to change into. At least I can get out of these
unforgiving heels. Once my feet are free and back horizontal, besides
Wyatt's touches, it's the best feeling I've had all night. I walk around
the small room working out the stiffness in my arches. I come to
stand by the only window in this part of the apartment. There's a
fire escape that obstructs most of the view. But if you angle yourself
just right, you can see the Manhattan skyline lit up in all its glory. I
feel Wyatt's presence first, before seeing his reflection in the glass
window. "You've got a view. It's breathtaking."

"Yes it is," Wyatt agrees.

"Can you even see it from there?" Wyatt is still clear across the room.

"I see it everywhere. Every morning when I'm in the shower, my
eyes closed letting the water wash over me, I see it. At work, on the
occasions I zone out for a minute or two, it's always there imprinted
in my mind. But I see it best at night, lying in bed with my eyes closed,
the vision so vivid I think I can reach out and touch it." Wyatt has
closed the distance between us and we are now standing toe to toe.
"But every time I try, it disappears. You disappear. Now, that you're
here, standing in front of me in the flesh, I'm scared it's not real. That
if I reach out for the touch I'm desperate for, you'll be gone." I don't
mistake the hurt and pain I hear in his voice.

"Oh," I manage realizing his breathtaking view isn't outside the
window. It's standing mere inches from him. It's me.

"Why are you here, Suzanna?"

"I thought we came back to your apartment so we could talk." We
discussed this at the bar, both agreeing we needed somewhere more
private to converse. So I'm confused why he'd ask me that question.

"We can talk on the phone. That is, unless you've deleted or lost
my number. It's a real possibility since the only time I've heard from
you since moving to New York was that random, simplistic text you
sent."

"I've still got your number."

"Then why didn't you use it? Would have been a lot less expensive than flying all the way to New York to '*talk*'." His use of air

quotes and the tone of his voice suggest he is slightly annoyed. "Why are you really here, in New York?" Okay, so I planned this trip to seek answers, needing to have a face to face conversation with Wyatt. And yeah, I wanted the vacation with Chloe. I wanted us to make some memories before we set out into adulthood. Plus, the trip let me escape the drama that seems to live in Garden City. All of those are valid reasons I decided to leave town and come to NYC. However, none of those are the real reason I traveled up the coast basically on a whim.

"I missed you," I answer truthfully. Wyatt raises his hand slowly and hesitantly caresses my face, obviously still scared I'll vanish. I lean into his touch assuring him I'm not going anywhere.

"You missed me," he states having to hear the words again.

"Every day."

Wyatt closes his eyes and breathes out heavily. "Suz, I....I needed.....I thought..."

"Shhhh, it's okay. I'm here now," I whisper placing my finger against his lips. His tongue slips out licking the pad before pulling the entire thing in his mouth. He sucks on it once, twice, three times before letting it fall from his lips with a pop. As if my entire body was wired through that finger, I heat up like a volcano. He pulls me into his body, which I find is also warmed with desire, and I'm close to the point of eruption. He buries his face in the crook of my neck nibbling the skin then soothing it with kisses.

"God Suz, I've missed you so much," he confesses, his words causing my knees to knock. He continues his assault on my neck kissing a line up to my jaw. Every kiss gets him closer and closer to my mouth. Finally, after paying attention to every square inch of my face, he stops just shy of touching my lips, hovering only millimeters away. "You're here, in my city. In my apartment. In my arms. That means you're mine, Suzanna. You. Are. Mine."

I nod eager for his mouth to stop talking and connect with mine.

"I can't go any farther with you until I hear you say it Suz," he demands making me wait. I'd say anything just to get him to kiss me. Truth is, I am his, always was, always will be.

"I'm yours, mind, body and soul," I tell him. That's all it takes for his mouth to come crashing down on mine. It's a battle, our lips, tongues and teeth fighting each other to convey through this one kiss the feelings we have kept suppressed during our separation. My hands, which sat at his waist, inch up over the dips and valleys of his abdominal muscles, sliding upwards across his bulging chest, to end clasped around his neck, trying to bring him even closer. His hands prefer to travel in the opposite direction, leaving my face, brushing down my sides and hips, coming to rest on my ass. He palms each cheek firmly, pressing my body up against his. The only thing that could make this better is if the barrier of our clothes were gone. I can't wait for us to be skin to skin. Just like the connection we have with our bodies, our minds seem to also exist on a parallel universe. I feel his fingers wiggle against my backside, sliding the hemline of my skimpy dress up into his grip.

"This dress looks amazing on you. But it's got to go. Now." I feel cool air touch my skin as he pulls the dress up my body and over my head, leaving me standing there with just my bra and panties. "I'll say it again," he starts looking me over from head to toe, "absolutely fucking breathtaking." When he begins to pull me up into his chest again, I push away.

"Oh no, I'm the tourist here. And there are some sights I'm dying to see," I tease reaching for the bottom of his t-shirt. I push his shirt up as far as I can until it bunches at his armpits and under his chin. He lends a hand, grabbing the material behind his neck and ripping it over his head. Taking my time, I not only enjoy the view but the feel as well. Lightly smoothing his bronze skin, I trace a line with each hand from the top of his shoulders to the prominent 'V' just below his waistline. My fingers tease the band of elastic that holds his sweat pants in place. Placing a thumb in the band on each side of his hips, I begin pulling down until the pants fall at his feet. He steps out of each leg kicking the pants to the side. He stands before me wearing nothing but a pair of black boxer briefs. The arousal he sports stretches the weaves of the cotton. They've got to go too. Repeating my actions, I manage to divest him of his underwear. I didn't allow his help with this final undressing, falling to my knees to finish the job. When he is completely naked, I'm eye level with his beautiful cock. And yes, his is beautiful. The smooth, velvety skin is stretched to the limit, encasing his hardened length. Veins strain against the thickness. I can't resist touching it, just one finger tip starting at the base and tracing a line to the mushroomed head. Just my feather light touch has his penis jerking with excitement. I brush over the slit at the end wetting my finger with his pre-cum. His hooded eyes lock with mine as I stare up at him through my lashes. Commanding his complete attention, I pop my finger tip into my mouth licking it clean.

"Suzanna," Wyatt moans. I'm not sure if he's giving me a warning to stop or begging me to continue. Needing more of his salty taste, I decide to go with the latter. Eyes still locked with his, I flick my tongue swirling it around the head of his cock. The jerking motions of his hips tell me I've got the green light to continue. Opening my mouth, I suck him all the way inside to the back of my throat. Relaxing my muscles, I'm able to cover his entire length from tip to base. Slowly, I retreat, sliding my lips almost to the end and then repeat the motion, over and over. "Damn, Suz, feels...so....good," he stutters. His compliment only spurs me on and I increase my pace. My hands rub up and down his inner thighs while his tangle in my hair. I caress his heavy balls in my palm and massage each one gently. I feel his entire body tense up and he begins to move away. I remove my massaging hands to grab his ass keeping him in place. I plan to take everything he has to give me, wanting his release in my mouth. With one last thrust, I feel his hot liquid hit the back of my throat. Swallowing quickly, I get another spurt of his release. After the third and last one, I lick him clean from base to tip letting him fall from my mouth.

It takes Wyatt a moment to catch his breath. But when he does, he uses his remaining strength to hoist me up off my knees. Standing toe to toe, he turns me around and walks us backwards until my legs hit the cushions of the couch. "Did you enjoy the flavor New York has to offer?" Wyatt says with a smirk.

"Mmmmm hummm. It was delicious," I say seductively licking my lips.

"Well, now, it's time for the locals to feast. And I'm starving," Wyatt pants in my ear. He begins kissing and nibbling down my neck as his hands work on the clasp of my bra. Releasing the undergarment, he immediately pulls a nipple into his mouth. He laps it with his tongue until it's hard and pebbled. Only then does he cover it entirely with his mouth and begins to suck. My head falls back and I moan my appreciation. Before he pops it from his mouth, he nibbles it with his teeth, the bite a mixture of pain and pleasure. As he repeats his assault on my other breast, I have to grab his shoulders to stay uprooted. My legs have gone weak with desire. He eases me back until my butt hits the couch. Pressing my legs apart he parks himself on his knees in between them. As he kisses a trail down my quivering stomach, he manages to rid me of my soaked panties. I'm laid spread and bare before him feeling self conscious. His ministrations stop while he takes a moment to stare at my privates, now fully on display. "You're glistening, Suz." I flush beet red as he appraises my state of arousal. Getting him off was such a turn on, a flood of desire soaked my underwear. Then, his kisses, starting at my neck, to my chest, stalling at each breast, and continuing downward, has me dripping like a damn faucet. He meets my eyes and I look away in embarrassment. "Hey, look at me," he commands. And I do. All I see is the look of satisfaction. He's proud, maybe even honored, that he still does this to me. "It's sexy as hell, Suz. You are sexy as hell!" I watch intensely as his fingers trace and separate my folds. He laps up my juices with one hand then brings his fingers to his mouth. Before they disappear between his lips, he places them under his nose and takes a sniff. Then he begins licking each finger, one by one, until he has tasted them all. "Still so sweet. Did I mention I was starving?"

I only manage to nod, the English language escaping me. He dives in, his tongue making a path from my entrance, up through my folds, and ending at my clit. He does this repeatedly as my body trembles under his attention. He thrust his tongue inside me like the starving man he claims to be. His tongue is soon replaced with two of his fingers while his mouth latches onto my sensitive nub. When he begins sucking my clit with vigor, I lose it, thrashing my head from side to side and screaming his name. I explode against his tongue, the orgasm hitting me with force. He continues to lap up my juices while I shudder with aftershocks from the most amazing orgasm I've ever had. Kissing a trail up my stomach, across my chest and up my neck, he finally stops to hover over my face. His lips, which are less than an inch away from mine, still shine from the wetness of my arousal. I lift my eyes from his mouth to see him looking at me with lust. But I also read in his expression the love he still has for me. And it's not just his facial features that enlighten me. I feel it too, his member hardening once again against my hip. Anxious with anticipation to feel Wyatt inside me, I adjust our positions on the couch. I lie back getting horizontal while Wyatt crawls up my body. Staring into each other's eyes, he covers my body and we become symmetrical with one another, like puzzle pieces fitting together just right. I open my legs to him and he rests his hips between them, his penis sliding through my wetness. I feel the tip of his erection at my entrance and I can't wait to accept him inside me. I wiggle my hips with impatience hoping to hurry things along. But what I've been anxiously awaiting doesn't come. Instead, he bolts up to a kneeling position his face stricken with a look of horror.

"Wyatt? What's wrong?" I ask with concern.

"Shit, shit, SHIT!!!" he yells, causing me to cower back against the sit cushions. "I don't have a fucking condom!" The realization of what he just said hits me and makes me want to scream a string of my own explicatives.

"You don't?" I question like that can't be possible.

"It's not like I have a frequent use for them. Plus, your visit was a surprise. Had I known you were coming, that we would be together like this, I would have stocked up." My heart swells with this information. Not that I really thought Wyatt was beating the streets of New York looking to hook up every night. I knew he was more than dedicated to his job, wanting to impress the hell out of his possible future bosses should they decide to hire him after this internship. Working long hours, morning to night, left him little time to socialize, especially with members of the opposite sex. I can't help but smile with giddiness. "This isn't something to smile about, Suz. I can't find any humor in this at all," Wyatt admonishes with a scowl on his face.

"Come here," I call to him wiggling my finger. He pauses momentarily before covering my body again and facing me. "I'm on the pill, Wyatt. You know that. I haven't been with anyone since you. I'm dying for you to make love to me. And I don't care if we use a condom or not. Actually, I would prefer we didn't."

"Suz, there is nothing more I'd like to do than make love to you with no barrier. The connection...I can't even begin to imagine. But..." He breaks our gaze and looks away with a guilty expression. He thinks the mask of guilt he is showing will remind me of his so-called indiscretion with Bridgett. But I know the truth behind the guilt he bears is due to the lie he is still trying to make me believe.

"Wyatt," I say, cupping his cheek and turning his head. I want his undivided attention when I tell him what I know. "You didn't sleep with Bridgett. You didn't cheat on me."

"I... um... How...." Wyatt struggles with words. But at least he didn't deny it.

"I ran into Bridgett a few weeks back. She told me...Ahhhhh!!!" My explanation is cut off when Wyatt thrust into me balls deep. His grasp on control snaps and he is no longer able to hold back from reclaiming me. He stills above me, looking deep into my soul. It's been a while so it takes some time for me to adjust to his thickness. Once I'm comfortable I try shifting my hips slightly, a silent urge for Wyatt to start moving. But he remains motionless. "Wyatt, please," I beg.

"Didn't cheat, Suz. Never do that to you. Hurts too much... to be ...cheated on," Wyatt declares in broken sentences. He's straining to maintain the little control he still possesses. I just want him to lose it all and let go. Just *please* let go and start freaking moving.

"I know, baby. I know."

"Do you?" he asks. I'm taken aback that he'd question me, especially at a time like this. Of course, I believe he didn't cheat. I was shocked at the time of our break up, too heartbroken to dispute what I saw in his apartment that day. Had I taken the time to really think things through back then, I would have immediately questioned the validity of the situation. He never said he slept with Bridgett. Now that I think about it, neither did she. I made my own conclusions when I found her naked in his bed. I assumed the worst, rightfully so given the scene, but what I should have done was pester them both that morning until they had no other option than to tell me the truth. That would have saved us months we have since spent apart, never to get back. Yet, Wyatt still wants to ask if I believe him? Or is he alluding to something else? I can't bare the pain I find etched on Wyatt's face. The frown he wears due to our discussion about the break up, tears at my heart. Yeah, I'm the one that insisted we talk. But talking is the last thing I want to do right now. Grabbing him behind his neck I pull his face forward until our lips meet, crashing together in a fervent kiss. I use my lips, tongue and even teeth to convey through this kiss how much faith I have in Wyatt. How much I trust him. How sorry I am I lost that trust from incorrect conclusions on my part. This is definitely not the time to dwell on the past...it's time to focus on the here and now. And the future. I pray Wyatt's sudden sullen mood will change.

"Ah, fuck it," Wyatt groans as he begins to move, almost slipping out of my body. But as his tip comes to tease my entrance, he thrusts back in, filling me completely. Over and over, he thrusts in and out setting a rhythm. Oh yeah, this is exactly what I needed. The only sounds I hear are those of our heavy breathing and the slapping of our skin. Wyatt rises up, bracing himself with his arms, and adjusts his hips. Increasing his tempo, he begins to hit that sensual spot deep inside of me. I'm literally lying back flat on his couch, but I feel as if I'm flying. The angle at which he drives into me heats my body to dangerous temperatures. I'm like a bottle rocket and he has just ignited me. I ascend into the air climbing higher and higher. When I can't take it anymore, I detonate, bursting into a million pieces. Colorful streaks of light explode behind my closed eyes. My body bucks and twists as the orgasm racks me from the core to my every limb. My inner walls tense around Wyatt's cock as he continues pumping into to me. His erratic breathing and drenched skin tell me he is close.

Using all my effort, I manage to open my eyes, not wanting to miss seeing the beauty of Wyatt's release. The look of pure desire is all I see when my eyes meet his. The added connection we feel as we gaze at one another is enough to send Wyatt over the edge. His face scrunches up in a painful expression and he closes his eyes. After one final thrust, he emits a guttural groan emptying himself inside of me. Completely drained and sated, he collapses on top of me. His hands play with the nape of my neck while I stroke his back. The calming effect of the soft caresses calms us both until we are able to breathe again at a normal rate.

"Suz," he mutters from the crook in my neck. "That was...."

"Amazing. Incredible. Earth shattering," I finish his sentence.

"Yeah, all that and more." I feel his lips turn up into a smile against my skin. I'm beaming too. I just had two orgasms, mind-blowing sex, and I'm currently enjoying some cuddle time. All with the man I love. I couldn't keep the smile off my face if I tried. We remain in an entangled heap on the couch enjoying the comfortable silence. After a few minutes I feel Wyatt's body weight ease from mine as he goes to get up.

"No! Don't leave me," I plead in a panic. The loss of warmth from his body pressing against mine has me grabbing onto his is wrist, keeping him in place.

"Hey, I'm just going to get something to clean us up. I'll be right back," he says and kisses the tip of my nose. I rush out a breath of relief. I'm not ready for our night to come to an end. Before I realize it, he has returned. With a damp, warm washcloth, he gently wipes between my legs, erasing the mixture of wetness still lingering from our love making. All cleaned up, he tosses the used washcloth on the floor. As if I weigh no more than a feather, he scoops me up in his arms and begins to carry me to his bedroom. I wrap my hands around his neck and snuggle into his chest. At the door of his bedroom he pauses.

"Don't leave me," he whispers looking down at my face, throwing my words back at me. "Stay with me tonight? Please?" As if he had to even ask. I strain my neck to bring my lips to meet his. Giving him a swift, yet passionate kiss, I break long enough to assure him I'm not planning to go anywhere.

"There's no where else in this entire world I'd rather be tonight," I say with complete sincerity. Hearing my words puts Wyatt in motion again. He enters his bedroom and deposits me onto the queen sized mattress. I scoot up toward the headboard while he fumbles with the covers pulling them down. I slide underneath the cool sheets and wait for Wyatt to join me. He shuts out the light before crawling in beside me. Face to face we lay, our bodies touching each other's from head to toe. From the city lights that cast a glow around the otherwise darkened room, I memorize the contours of Wyatt's handsome face. His strong jaw line has the beginning of a five o'clock shadow, a small dusting of dark stubble. I rub my hand across his cheek the dimple I love so much appearing as he smiles in contentment. Brushing a lock of his dark brown hair from his forehead, I'm awarded with a clear view of his gorgeous eyes. The intensity with which he stares at me with lust and love makes his normal brown irises appear obsidian in color. The beauty of this man still manages to steal my breath. The sight of him as the last thing I see each night and the first thing I wake to every morning....oh, what I wouldn't give for that to become reality. But to get there, we really need to talk.

"Wyatt, um..." I hesitate not knowing exactly where to begin.

"Shhhh, Suzanna. You promised tonight. Please, please let's enjoy this time we have together."

"But we need to talk," I remind him.

"Tomorrow. I promise we'll discuss some things. But for now, can we just be? I really need a good night's sleep. I haven't slept for shit since moving here. Well, even before that. I've missed having you in my arms each night," he confesses as his pulls me closer into his body, wrapping me in his arms. I lay my head on his chest, the strong rhythmic beating of his heart like a lullaby.

"Okay," I agree through a yawn. While exhilarating, the emotions of seeing Wyatt again have also exhausted me.

"'Night Suz. I...I...I'm really glad you're here." I feel like Wyatt wants to say more, but instead plants a kiss to the top of my head.

"Me too. Goodnight Wyatt." *I love you.* I want to add, but stop myself. I can't reveal my true feelings until I know why Wyatt broke things off a few months ago. So instead, I close my eyes and place a kiss on his chest, right over his heart. I hear his sharp inhale when my lips make contact and know the significance of my affectionate gesture is not lost on him.

Chapter Twenty Nine

"Morning, beautiful," Wyatt says leaning on the door frame of his bedroom. I slowly push up to a seated position. Rubbing my hands across my face I feel the remnants of caked makeup left on from the previous night. I'm sure my eyes are black with smeared mascara and eyeliner. Knowing only a good scrubbing will remedy my facial appearance I move my hands to try to detangle my bed head. My fingers get caught in multiple knots as I try to tame the mess that is my hair. And Wyatt's calling me beautiful? Yeah, right. He's the only one in this apartment that's earned that title this morning. My eyes rake over him. He is shirtless, his muscled chest on display. His bare feet stick out from the bottom of a pair of cotton drawstring pajama pants. My roaming eyes retrace their path as I turn them upward coming to meet his face. His hair is damp and I can smell his clean scent from my perch on the bed. He's obviously been up a while, at least long enough to get a shower. When I meet his eyes, he's wearing that smirk, that adorable dimple present, and I know I've been caught ogling him. But when he sees my frown of disappointment his smile disappears and he asks in concern, "What's wrong, Suz?"

"I didn't get to wake up in your arms," I confess in a whisper, turning away with shyness.

Not more than a half a second goes by before I feel the mattress dip beside me. Wyatt securely wraps both arms around me and pulls me back down to a reclining position on the bed beside him. "Close your eyes, Suz."

"Wyatt," I giggle.

"Just do it. I want this to be perfect." At his insistence, I close my eyes to fake sleep. When he sees me following his directions, he begins to feather light kisses across my face. I struggle to keep my eyes closed, but I can't keep the smile off my face. Finally his lips meet mine for a brief kiss. As he pulls away, my lids flutter open and I see him smiling down at me. "'Morning beautiful," he begins again, a redo of the first time I woke up.

"It is now. A very *good* morning," I say engulfed in his embrace. I snuggle closer letting his body heat warm me.

"How'd you sleep?"

"In intervals," I respond giving Wyatt a knowing look.

"Yeah, sorry about that. I just couldn't keep my hands off you," he admits. At one point during the middle of the night, I awoke with one of Wyatt's hands fondling my breasts while his other disappeared between my legs. The heavy petting and foreplay lead us to make love again. This time, it was slow and unhurried. We both took the time to explore every inch of each other's bodies. The connection was like none I have ever felt before. Our orgasms built and were reached simultaneously. It was perfection.

"Don't apologize. I'm not complaining. You have permission to wake me up for *that* any time." Wyatt nuzzles into my neck, his warm breath against my skin causing goose flesh.

"I just woke you up, Suz. Twice, as a matter of fact," Wyatt mumbles between kisses while his hands begin to roam across my torso. I know where this is going. While I'm more than happy to oblige, I'd like to at less freshen up. He's cleanly showered and well, I'm just gross.

"Wyatt wait," I force myself to say stopping his magical hands. He freezes looking up at me with apprehension. I can see the fear of my rejection all over his face.

"Baby, I want this. I want *you*," I reassure him. But he's still looking at me with confusion. "I desperately need to freshen up. I mean, I haven't even brushed my teeth." I slap my hand over my mouth hoping to trap my disgusting morning breath. "You're already cleanly showered. I just want to level the playing field, make things fair." My voice is barely audible through my fingers.

Wyatt grabs my wrist and pulls my hand from my mouth, replacing it with his lips. Firmly kissing me, he pulls back and declares, "I want you, no matter what condition you're in. Whenever. However. I just want you! But if you'll feel more comfortable, then go on and take a shower. I'll make some coffee and have it waiting for you."

"And then we can talk?"

As if my request were a bucket of cold water, Wyatt tenses before putting distance between us and jumping out of bed. He walks toward the hallway, glancing back over his shoulder. "Yeah, Suz. If you still need to talk, then we'll talk." Not waiting for my reply, he closes the door giving me some privacy. I sense a cloud of doom hovering nearby ready to rain on my perfect morning.

Twenty minutes later, I walk down the short hallway leading to the tiny kitchen. Wyatt is seated on the couch slouched over his laptop. He is so focused on his work he doesn't hear me enter. Not wanting to disturb him, I quietly pad barefooted to the kitchen in search of my daily dose of morning caffeine. I notice the mug and sugar he has left out on the counter for me. What I'm surprised to also find is a container of my favorite coffee creamer. Fixing my coffee just like I enjoy it, I walk over to sit beside Wyatt. He notices my presence when I'm just a few feet away, his fingers abruptly stopping from the furious typing he was just doing. Making no attempt to hide his appraisal of my entire body, I watch the expression on his face change from deep concentration to pure lust. His eyes darken as his gaze zeros in on what I'm wearing.

"I hope you don't mind. My dress was still in here," I point to the garment crumpled and lying on the floor. "Plus, I didn't really want to put that thing back on. And I didn't have any other clothes." Rather than stay wrapped in a towel, I rummaged through Wyatt's drawers until I found an old ratty t-shirt. The large shirt swallows my petite body, its length hitting me right above my knees. Hardly attractive. But you'd never know it by the steamy looks Wyatt keeps sending my way. From his appreciative gaze, you'd think I'd emerged from the bedroom wearing some skimpy sexy lingerie. "Um, Wyatt?" I ask when he continues to remain mute and stare. Shaking his head to clear his lust-fogged brain, he finally gestures for me to take the seat beside him. Situating myself, I slide close enough to feel his body heat but keep a small amount of space between us so that we don't touch. I know with just the least bit of physical contact, all bets will be off and we'll never have that talk. "You okay?"

"Yeah, I just...I really like seeing you wearing my clothes." I lift my coffee to my lips and take a sip, hiding the smile his words produce. I love how he never hides his feelings from me and always voices the effects I have on him. "There's only one other way that you'd look better."

"And what's that?"

"If you were wearing nothing at all," he says beginning to scoot closer. When he reaches for me, I back away to the far corner of the couch, my hand flying up to stop his progression.

"Wyatt, please. It's so hard for me not to jump your bones right now. But before we get distracted, we really, *really* need to have that talk."

Wyatt sighs in frustration. "Well, at least we are on the same page, about the jumping bones thing. But if you need to talk, then we'll talk. Honestly, I don't know what it is you need to hear that will convince you of my feelings for you. Haven't I showed you what you mean to me since I saw you at that bar last night?"

"Yes, and that's exactly why we need to talk. Look at us...haven't seen each other in months. Haven't even called or texted. Yet, the minute we're back together, we're back in each other's arms, sleeping together like we were never apart. It's obvious our feelings for each other haven't changed. So why, *why* did you break off things before leaving to come to New York?"

"I told you, Suz, I couldn't handle the distance," he answers, but avoids making eye contact.

"That's a lie!" I yell. "We talked in length about how hard a long distance relationship would be. Yet, we were committed to making it work. Or at least I was committed. The physical contact would be missing, but hearing each other's voice every day would be enough to take us to the end of the summer when we could reunite." I try really hard to hold it together, but my eyes fill with water and a lone tear slips down my cheek. Wyatt attempts to wipe away my tear, but I swat his hand away and demand an answer. "Please, be honest Wyatt. Why did you break my heart?"

Ring...Ring....Ring. My cell phone starts from my purse across the room. Ignoring the call, I wait for the annoying thing to stop ringing so that Wyatt can give me a truthful answer. He rakes his hand through his hair when he sees I'm not interested in taking the call. "And don't try to tell me it was because of Bridgett. I told you last night that I know the truth. How you saved her drunk ass from the bar, taking her to your place to sleep it off. You knew that lame excuse about not wanting the long distance thing wasn't going to fly with me, so you used her to make me believe you cheated. Convenient for you, yes. Heart breaking for me." I don't even try to contain my emotions anymore. I let the tears flow freely. Wyatt needs to see what all this has done to me.

"Arrrrgh. Suz, I don't know how to explain this."

"How about truthfully? Did you just not want me anymore?" I ask through a sob.

"No, never. I'll always want you, Suz. I love you."

Oh how I've waited to hear those words again from him. His actions have been silently telling me since I first laid eyes on him last night. But hearing those words coming from his lips solidify what I already knew. And begs me to ask again, "Then why, Wyatt? Why break things off?"

He opens his mouth to answer, but my damn cell phone starts again. "You gonna get that?"

"No. I'll call whoever it is back once you explain yourself." I'm so close to getting to the bottom of this mystery, I'm not letting anyone interrupt us now.

"Suz, when you play golf, what's your ultimate goal?" I narrow my eyes at Wyatt not appreciating the subject change. "I'm trying to make you understand why I did what I did. Just play along, please."

"O-kay. I play to win. My goal is always to finish first."

"Ah, first place. That's a nice place to be, right?"

"Well yeah, duh." This line of questioning is more confusing than ever. My patience is growing thin as he tries to explain himself. "I'm not following you, Wyatt."

"Hypothetically, let's say you don't finish first. Is it better to finish in second place or further down in the pack?" Wyatt's bound and determined to make his point through this silly dissection of my golf game.

"Well, technically second place is not a bad finish. But emotionally it sucks. To know you're that close to winning yet fail, falling a few strokes behind. I guess it's easier to deal with a larger loss, placing somewhere in the middle or even the bottom of the competition."

"I feel exactly the same way, Suz. And that's why I had to let you go."

"What?" *Ring...Ring...Ring.* My damn phone, again. Wyatt walks over and grabs my purse, bringing it back to me.

"You really need to answer that. It could be important." Wyatt takes our empty coffee mugs back into the kitchen, giving me privacy to take the call. In frustration I snatch my purse open to retrieve the offending phone.

"Hello," I answer rather rudely.

"Well thank God. Finally you answer your f-ing phone." Chloe ignores my harsh reception and dives right in. "Landon called and there's been an accident."

"Oh no. Chloe what happened? Is he okay?" I immediately regret not answering sooner.

"It didn't involve Landon. He's fine. Patrick however..." As soon as I hear his name I begin to hyperventilate. Breathing heavily I barely hear Chloe screaming at me on the other end of the line. "Suzanna. Suz! Calm down."

"I'm here. I'm calm," I say through shallow breaths. "Tell me what happened? Is Patrick..." I can't even finish the sentence, my voice shaking with thoughts of the worst scenario.

"He's in the hospital. Has a broken arm and some superficial cuts and bruises. But he's gonna make a full recovery."

"What happened?"

"Landon said Patrick and his dad were out late last night fishing. They crashed the boat. Not sure which one of them was behind the wheel. But Mr. Miles was blitzed. Had a blood alcohol level off the charts when they brought him in. And he's the one who escaped injury. Not a scratch on the MF'er." I hear the anger in Chloe's voice. It's really unfair how that evil bastard continues to cause trouble, yet comes out on the other side as clean as a whistle. Every. Single. Time.

"Did they charge him? He needs to be punished for what he's done to his son."

"They can't. Patrick won't press charges. Plus, he said he can't remember who was driving when the boat crashed. Since no other parties were involved, it's just Patrick's word, since his dad was basically sloshed."

"We need to go home, now. I have to see him. Talk some sense into him before his dad eventually kills him. Just like he did his mom." I'm rushing around the apartment picking up my clothes from last night. I've got to change and get going. I'll be damned if I let Jim Miles take the life of another person I love.

"Whoa, what type of crack have you been smoking, Suz?" Chloe asks totally serious. Then I remember what I just said. I told Chloe about my fight with Patrick when I mentioned that maybe his dad was the cause of the accident that killed his mother. But that was when Chloe was doped up with pain medication for her head injury. No wonder she doesn't have any recollection of our conversation.

"Just call the airline and get us on the next flight out of here. I'll cab it back to the hotel once I change. See you soon."

As I'm about to end the call I hear Chloe ask, "What about Wyatt?" Before I enter his bedroom, I glance over my shoulder to find he's been watching me the entire time, running around his apartment like a panicked fool. Although he doesn't have all the details, the gloomy expression on his face tells me he knows I'm leaving. Just when we were so close to repairing our relationship, me getting the answers I needed so we could start again. But now I have to leave. The entire situation is a disaster. But my conscience won't be at peace if I don't at least try to convince Patrick to get immediate help for his dad. God forbid he hurts or kills someone. I wouldn't be able to live with myself.

"Chloe, I'll explain things to Wyatt. Please, just rebook our flights. I'll be there shortly." On that final note I end the call and close myself in Wyatt's bedroom. While I dress I search for a plausible way to explain to Wyatt that the reason I'm leaving is because of Patrick. I can only pray he'll understand.

"I called you a cab. It's waiting downstairs," Wyatt says as I walk into the kitchen dressed in last night's clothes.

"Thanks," I sadly voice my appreciation. He acknowledges me with a head nod. "Wyatt?"

"Hum?"

"I still don't understand why we're not together. Actually, I'm more confused now than when I got here. You say you want me, always have, always will. Yet, I'm leaving with no answers, only some damn riddle you're requiring me to figure out." Wyatt doesn't respond just continues to stare at me with a blank expression. "Am I a distraction to your work? Dating me will get in your way of finishing first at your internship?"

"No, you're not a distraction. At my work or at anything."

"Okay, well...do you think I put my golf ahead of you? Will the travel of the pro tour cause us problems? If so I'll cut back and limit my schedule. That is, if I make it that far." I'd never let golf get in the way of my relationship with this man. Dream or not, he's the only thing more important, the only thing I definitely want in my future. If I had to choose, I'd for sure choose him.

"Absolutely not. I know how important golf is to you. It's a part of you. You wouldn't be the woman you are without it. So, no, I don't think you put golf ahead of me. And don't you dare rearrange your schedule for me, ever. Not only will you make the pro tour, you'll be a force to be reckoned with." His belief in my golf skills is unwavering. Although I'm happy he realizes how important golf is in my life, he has knocked down my last crack at solving his riddle.

"Thanks for your faith in me. But I'm still at a loss. Please, Wyatt, just tell me the real reason why you left me," I plead in my final attempt to make Wyatt explain.

"Can't Suz. Too much pride."

"Fine. Let your stinking pride get in the way of this, of us. I'm leaving Wyatt. Not just this apartment, but I'm leaving New York. Today. I thought when I returned home I'd have my answers. More importantly, I thought I'd return having you in my life again. But that's obviously not happening. It breaks my heart all over again having to leave you. Especially, this way, not having any answers and still no resolution to our relationship." I started my rant with anger that quickly transformed into desperation. By the end my speech I'm emotionally wrecked, my eyes too full of tears to keep them at bay.

"You don't want to leave and yet you're still going to," Wyatt finally responds sounding defeated.

"Yes, I don't *want* to leave you, but I *have* to go. It's complicated, Wyatt."

"It's complications that keep us from achieving that coveted first place finish."

"Good grief, would you stop speaking nonsense and just get to the bottom of it," I say in a raised voice, aggravation lacing my every word.

"You're a smart girl. Figure it out. Of course, after you deal with those *complications*," Wyatt says matching my aggravation.

Before things escalate to a full blown fight, I need to go. But not before leaving Wyatt with something to think about. Marching up to him, I wrap my hands around his neck and press my lips to his. At first my surprise attack is met with reluctance, but the more force I apply, the more relaxed Wyatt becomes. Finally he opens his mouth and our tongues begin an intricate dance, twisting around each other, fighting for dominance. I don't break the kiss until I'm forced to get air. Keeping Wyatt's face millimeters from mine and our eyes locked in an intense gaze, I make a declaration before saying goodbye. "I love you, Wyatt. I love you so much." With one final swift kiss, I turn and walk out the door to my waiting cab. I make a pledge that whatever it is Wyatt needs me to figure out, I'll go down fighting to do it. Last night gave me the hope I needed that this is not the end with Wyatt. It's just the beginning.

Chapter Thirty

"Is that Landon? How's Patrick?" Chloe and I are waiting for our flight to be called. She's been texting nonstop since we sat down. I'm trying not to be nosey, but I need an update.

"Suz, I told you a hundred times that Patrick's injuries are not life threatening." When she doesn't offer more I give her the 'And?' look before she can refocus on her phone. "If you must know, I'm texting with Brian."

"Oh, and how is Brian, the hot-shot writer, producer, director?" Brian, Chloe's ex fling and good friend moved out to California at the beginning of the summer when one of his scripts was chosen to be turned into a weekly drama. The production is about to begin and the drama is slated to air this fall. It couldn't have happened to a nicer guy. Plus, he's really talented.

"He's good. Busy, but good. Excited to start shooting soon." She looks away deep in thought before returning her attention back to her phone. I hope she's not jealous of Brian's achievements. She's always wanted to try her hand at acting, but her parents demand she finish school first. They're not as supportive as my parents have been with me and Flynn when it comes to Chloe following her dreams.

"Chloe, you okay?"

We will now begin boarding Flight 454 to Myrtle Beach, the announcement blares from the intercom. We grab our bags and walk to the boarding area where we wait our turn to enter the airplane. "Chloe?"

"Yeah?"

"I asked you if you're okay. You never answered."

"Sure, I'm fine. Just thinking about some things." Chloe stares off into the distance again, obviously inside her own head.

"Well, if you need to talk_"

"I'm moving to Hollywood," Chloe blurts out.

"Come again." Did she just say she was moving to Hollywood? Like in California, across the entire country?

"Brian thinks I'd be perfect for one of the characters in his drama. He showed the casting people some snippets of my performances from drama school and they have agreed to let me audition."

"Wow, that's great Chloe!" I give her a big hug almost knocking us over with the weight of our luggage. "Your parents must be so proud."

"Not exactly. I haven't told them. And I don't plan to."

"Chloe_"

"Suz, I'll tell them. Just not until I'm there. And don't lecture me. They won't understand the gravity of this opportunity. They'll try to persuade me to wait and finish school, earning that college degree they are forever reminding me that they are paying for. It'd only lead to a big fight. One I'd rather just avoid. So, please, don't say anything to your parents or anyone else. I'm not ready for it to get back to my folks yet."

"Okay, it that's what you want," I reluctantly agree. I can't imagine moving thousands of miles away without a send off from my parents.

"It is, and thanks. You wouldn't understand because your parents have always been so supportive. Mine, not so much. They look down on my preferred profession. Never thought I'd amount to more than a high school drama teacher or at the most the director of the local theater. And if for some reason I bomb the audition, I'd rather not have to hear the 'I told you so' lecture for the rest of my life."

"No chance you'll bomb the audition," I say with authority. I truly believe in Chloe's talent as an actress. Plus, she needs some encouragement from someone. Obviously she's not getting any from her family.

"You really think I have a shot? I'm getting really nervous."

"You'll be great. Before long I'll be reading about you in *People* magazine," I tease. "I'll know all the juicy details of your scandalous life in Hollywood." There's the smile I haven't seen in a while. Before long Chloe's beaming at the realization that she could be a star. "So when do you leave?" And there it goes, her beautiful smile fading into a frown. I'm suddenly not looking forward to her answer. We've made it to our seats, placing our luggage in the overhead bin and buckling up.

"I leave in two days," Chloe whispers her answer as I strain to hear her.

"Two days! But we weren't even scheduled to come back from New York until tomorrow. You were just going to have one day to get your things packed, tell me and then suddenly leave?"

"The production schedule has been set. Shooting starts in two weeks. They need enough time to finish at least eight full episodes for the fall season. If I get the part, I'll have little time to study the script, learn my lines, and all the other stuff I need to do," Chloe explains. "Plus, it's actually the perfect time for me to get away. You will soon be traveling the globe playing in golf tournaments. Flynn is overseas making a name for himself as a soccer stud, or maybe just a stud." I don't miss the hurt in her voice as she tries to make light of the new developments in Flynn's love life. But I don't get a chance to comment as Chloe continues to voice her list of reasons to move. "Landon is so busy with his job, in and out of town constantly. James has his head buried in a medical book at all times. And Patrick, well he'll soon be married and busy with law school. See, everyone else has life perfectly planned out. It's time for me to spread *my* wings, follow *my* dreams and see what life has in store for *me*."

"Where will you live?" I know this is a huge step for her future, but I'm not sending her to a strange new place without a place to stay.

"Brian is letting me stay with him until I can get my own apartment. Of course, I'll have to have a paying job in order to do that. I basically used almost all my savings from working at the restaurant this summer to purchase my plane ticket." Bless her heart. Not only does she not have her parents' support, she doesn't have their financial backing either. However, it doesn't seem to bother Miss Independent.

"Looks like you have everything worked out," I say sounding deflated.

"You're happy for me, right?"

"Of course I'm happy for you. You deserve to follow your dreams. I'm just sad that you'll be leaving, and so soon. We haven't been apart for more than a few days since we were in grade school. I'm just realizing how much I'm gonna miss you." I get choked up just thinking about not seeing Chloe on a daily basis.

"I'm gonna miss you too, Suz. So much." Both of Chloe's hands flap at a rapid pace in front of her eyes trying to dry her sudden tears. "And now you're making me cry!"

"Come here, superstar." I pull her into a hug and we both release our emotions. My tears are both happy and sad. I'm thrilled for the opportunity Chloe has, but I'm saddened that the same opportunity will take her away from me. I always knew our career choices would eventually send us in different directions. I just didn't anticipate it happening so soon.

The rest of the flight we spend talking about Chloe's move and I watch her excitement grow. That eases my despair about her move just a little. After a smooth landing we grab our luggage and head to the long-term parking lot. I drive straight to the hospital to see Patrick. Landon texted Chloe letting us know that Patrick was still there, but would hopefully be released later today. I've got to get there and talk with him without his dad being present. Bypassing the nurse's station, already knowing his assigned room number, we pause right outside his door.

"Suz, you go on in. I'm going to see if I can find Landon or Katelyn in the waiting area. See if they have an update about Patrick's release." When I make no move to enter the room, my feet cemented to the floor, Chloe gives me the nudge I need. "Hey, he's fine. Going to make a full recovery this time. Now, go on in there and tell him what it is you need to say. I believe you Suz, although your accusations about Mr. Miles are unfounded, I believe you. I've never seen you feel so strongly about something. I mean, you left the love of your life to come home early so you could sway the stubborn man lying in that hospital bed."

"Chloe, I'm scared. I'm terrified at seeing him lying there battered and broken. I'm scared he'll reject me, I mean, we haven't spoken much since our fight. But most of all, I'm petrified that I won't be able to get through to him, leaving him at the hands of his father's irresponsible drunken behavior. This time he's gonna pull through, but what about the next time, huh? I can't even think about it." Had the angels not been looking out for Patrick last night, I shudder thinking about the condition I'd find him in today. I can't let him take a chance with his life again. I fear the future outcome may not be so lucky next time. And if he refuses to get the help his dad so desperately needs, there will definitely be a next time.

"So what are you waiting for? Take your fierce protectiveness and determination and go in there and get the job done. It's a hard pill to swallow when the child has to become the parent in the relationship. No one wants to face the reality that their dad or mom is a sorry excuse for a parent. He may fight you tooth and nail on this matter. But at some point he's got to realize you're only looking out for him because you care. Plus, you're the only one of us that has that special power of persuasion where Patrick is concerned. You are taking one for the team girl....and I've got your back. Now, go!" Chloe nudges me forward until I'm standing right in front of the door. With a shaking hand, I grab the handle and twist the knob. Exhaling a heavy breath, I push the door open and enter the room.

The clicking sound of the door shutting behind me has Patrick whipping his head in my direction. "Suz?" He rubs his eyes with his un-casted hand, blinking rapidly. "Is that really you? I thought you were out of town."

"Had to see with my own eyes that you were okay." My gaze roams over his body from head to toe taking note of every injury he sustained. His wears a cast on his left hand that stretches from his palm to his elbow. Dark blue bruises dot his gorgeous face. Scattered around the bruises are scratches, irritated and red, but not deep enough for stitches. Although the injuries are small and will all heal, it still pains me to see evidence that caused him to hurt, landing him in this place. "I swear Patrick, I leave for a few days and look what you got yourself into!" I try for a joke hoping to ease the tension present since my arrival.

I think I've succeeded in cheering him up when the corners of his lips begin to lift. But his full smile I never see as his face begins to twist in agony and he grimaces in pain. Just the effort of forcing his bruised facial muscles to form a smile is too much. I rush to his bedside grabbing his uninjured hand and squeeze it tightly. "Oh Patrick," I say through a throat clogged with emotion. Tears build in my eyes and begin to run down my face.

"Hey, don't cry Suz."

"I hate seeing you like this," I admit.

"It's just some minor bumps and bruises. In a couple of days I'll be back to normal. I'm fine," Patrick assures me.

"Yeah, but you don't look fine. You actually look like shit!"

"Gee, thanks," Patrick grits through a half smile. The light teasing at least has him in a good mood. And he hasn't thrown me out of his room, rejecting me immediately. Now is my chance to try to get through to him.

"Seriously Patrick, you were extremely lucky this time. But what about the next? And we both know there will be a next time." He narrows his eyes at me in warning, but I choose to ignore him and continue. "You do know your dad's alcohol level was tested when they brought the two of you in. Big surprise, he surpassed the legal limit....by a long shot. Yet, they couldn't find a trace of alcohol in your bloodstream. But still, no one has been charged with boating under the influence because neither one of you will confess as to who was driving the boat."

"Suz..." Patrick's plea for me to stop falls on deaf ears.

"No! You'll not interrupt, but listen to what I have to say. We both know whose fault the accident was. You can lie to the doctors, nurses, and the police. But you can't lie to me. Your dad wrecked that boat last night. I'm so sure of it, I'd bet my golf career on it." Patrick's silence and his sudden interest in the blanket covering his legs, gives me all the confirmation I need.

"Dammit Patrick! Why haven't you pressed charges?" I ask angrily.

"Because he's my dad," Patrick shouts back.

"I don't care if he's the leader of the free world. He could have killed you. Just like he killed your—"

"Watch it now," Patrick demands in a threatening voice.

I'm so frustrated I could scream. All we are doing is going around in circles, this conversation leading nowhere. When will Patrick finally realize his dad has a disease? Alcoholism does nothing but transform Mr. Miles into an evil monster. A monster I've seen first hand. Is that what it will take to convince Patrick of the serious nature of his dad's condition? Will I have to confess my secrets, the real reason I bolted years ago, in order to keep Patrick safe? I never, ever wanted to tell Patrick about the sexual assault his dad attempted with me. But all my other cards are on the table. I have no other choice but to show my last hidden Ace.

"Patrick, I need—"

"What you need is to shut up and let me handle this." The harshness of his words have me dropping his hand and taking a step back. "Shit, sorry Suz. I know I'm being direct, but I've got to make you understand. Come here," he asks offering his outstretched hand to me. Slowly I take his hand intertwining our fingers and wait for him to continue. "I'm working on the situation. Please, promise me you'll stay out of it. You don't know all the players in this sick game that is my life. There're some powerful people who wouldn't think twice about keeping you silent if you cause too much of a stir. So please, for me, stop talking about my dad and what he may or may not have done. Promise me, Suz. I won't be able to sleep at night if I know you could be in danger."

"Danger? What are you talking about Patrick?"

"I can't tell you anything. You'll just have to trust me. Okay?" When I don't respond he immediately demands an answer. "Okay, Suz?"

"Okkkaay." What the hell did I just agree to?

Releasing a relieved sigh, Patrick squeezes my hand in his. "Thank you. Oh, and I'm gonna have to ask you not to make contact with me or Katelyn until I know things have been resolved."

"You're pushing me away again?"

"It's the only way to convince my dad that you're not a threat."

"Patrick, I'm so confused," I confess. He wants to keep me safe from God only knows what, but yet he doesn't want anything to do with me?

"I'm sorry I can't tell you more. Just trust me to figure this out. I've got a plan."

"If this is your plan," I gesture at him, circling my finger around his face to highlight his injuries, "then it sucks. It's got you lying in a hospital bed, for goodness sakes. You might want to consider a revision of this so-called plan of yours."

"Trust me, Suz," he begs.

The door handle to his room jiggles alerting us to company. "Doc says you're good to go, son....What the hell is *she* doing here?" Mr. Miles bursts into the room, his vicious gaze landing on me. I shake with fear, just like every other time I'm in his presence. And to make matters worse, Patrick drops my hand, breaking our connection, like it offends him to touch me.

"She's leaving," Patrick answers his father averting his eyes from me. "Now!" And just like that, I am being dismissed. Wow, that stung. I know he told me to trust him and that to be convincing we'd have to keep our distance from each other. But he never mentioned anything about being plain mean to me.

Pushing down the initial hurt, I keep my chin raised high. "Hope you make a fast, full recovery. Goodbye Patrick." The only sign that my statement even registered is the slight nod Patrick grants me. Turning to leave, I'm filled with dread at having to pass by Mr. Miles in my path to exit. Keeping my gaze toward the floor, I walk quickly to make my escape. A few feet from the door my steps falter as I hear Patrick's dad shift in my direction.

"Keep going, Suzanna. Crawl on back to that hole you came out of. Slumming with the likes of that bartender boy-toy of yours," he says followed by a menacing laugh. "It's no wonder you're trying so hard to get your hooks back into my boy. Need some help climbing back up the social ladder, huh?"

I should just keep walking. Make my exit and get out of the same breathing air as Mr. Miles. I know what it is he is trying to do. Goad me into a reaction so he'll have yet another chance to spew his hatred for me and convince Patrick what a no good person I am. But he's insulted the one person I'll defend until my dying day. A relationship with Wyatt is certainly not slumming it. Wyatt's got more work ethic and determination than Mr. Miles possesses in his pinky toe, if Mr. Miles has any at all. And if that's not reason enough to confront his attack, the fact that he suggests I'm using my friendship with Patrick for personal gain, for acceptance into his convoluted idea of societal standards? Well, that's bullshit! Like I care about my ranking in his so-called high society. Why would I want to surround myself with people like him?

"Excuse me?" I whip around and ask.

"Oh, you heard me. I have no idea why you're here visiting Patrick. Weren't you just on a trip getting hot and heavy with that no good McCain boy? Same boy you cheated with years ago? And don't try to deny it, Suzanna. I told Patrick all about seeing you leave the club cradled in the bartender's arms a few nights before you left town. No one believed that lie you told about your sudden serious concentration on golf. We all knew what a cheating bitch you were back then. Poor Patrick, heart broken because you left, thinking your golf was so much more important than him. Luckily he wised up when he found out the truth. Then, he was just embarrassed to have ever been associated with you."

"That's not true and you know it!" Yes, Wyatt carried me from the club to Chloe's car in his arms that night. But only because I couldn't walk, still in shock at having been nearly raped by Patrick's dad.

"Still trying to deny it, I see. Tsk, tsk, Suzanna...looks like you're becoming quite the habitual liar." His condescending tone makes my blood boil. So far, he's called me a user and a liar, neither of which I am. Looks like he's enjoying this game of insult throwing. Oh, and I'm so ready to play.

"You'd know a thing or two about habitual behaviors. Why you're an expert in bad habits. Better be careful, Mr. Miles. Never know when those habits might turn criminal." I stand my ground waiting for him to take the bait. I know I've pushed his buttons, watching as his jaw tenses and his lips press together in a straight line. His anger is obvious as his skin turns red and I can almost see the steam blowing out of his ears. The only movement he makes is the clenching and unclenching of his fists, which luckily stay stationary by his side. Don't think I wouldn't put it past him to take a swing. I'm a girl and all, but I know first hand the respect he has for women.

Through gritted teeth, Mr. Miles growls his words, slowly and with emphasis. "You. Should. Go. Suzanna." He breathes heavily around his anger. "Now!"

"And you SHOULD be in prison!" I yell right back.

Snap! The limited control Mr. Miles possessed is gone. He lunges at me wrapping his rough hands around my upper arms. The force of his abrupt movement pushes me backwards until I am slammed against the wall. I know he continues to rant and rave, probably calling me every name in the book. I can feel the spray of spit his mouth projects while he spouts angry words in my face. But I can't hear him as the blood rushes in my ears. My mind automatically leaves the present, going back in time over four years ago. As if I've been transported, I'm back in that dimly lit room at the country club. The feel of his hands on me again has me involuntarily trembling in fear, the only movement my body makes as I'm frozen in my memory.

His hands continue to grip my upper arms with strength that I know will no doubt leave marks. But my mind plays tricks on me and I feel his rough touch all over my body, roaming to my feminine parts, causing my skin to crawl. Not again, please no, not again, I silently repeat in my head. I still feel his hot, liquor laced breath, breeze across my neck and face, his lips making contact trying to suck and bite. The sound of my dress ripping is like an explosion in my head but the hospital room stays quiet, sans my heavy, erratic breathing. I'm close to hyperventilating, the struggle to fill my lungs with oxygen excruciating. I need to scream, alert someone of the danger

I'm in once again. But the memory and the fear that accompanies it, paralyzes my vocal cords along with the rest of the muscles in my body.

My wide eyes dart around the room, avoiding the monster right up in my face. I try really hard to take in the details of the room. Medical equipment, a bed, stark white walls, the smell of disinfectant....all signs that I'm actually in a hospital room, not back in the lounge of the club. But the memory battles fiercely, dragging me back to that horrid place in time. I try really hard to fight the onslaught of the details of that horrific night, details I've tried to bury. But I'm losing the war, as I remember the helpless feeling of being trapped up against another wall at the hands of the same man.

Succumbing to the pressure to stay in the here and now, I relinquish the tiny bit of control I held onto, and give up the fight. My body is drained as my mind continues to race. I'm zapped of energy, my body no longer able to hold my weight. Feeling the cold hard wall at my back, I slide down it until I collapse in a heap on the floor. *Here I am. Come and get me. Finish what you started and take from me what you want. Destroy me completely.* I've given up, nothing left in me to continue this fight.

"Ma'am. Miss....I need you to calm down and breathe." I hear the command, blinking at the unfamiliar female voice. I feel something being placed at my mouth, the sounds of crinkling paper faintly registering. Small hands cup a paper sack around my lips. "Okay, sweetie, in and out. I need you to take slow, yet big breaths. In and out." The same voice gives me instructions on something as natural as breathing.

"Come on, Suzanna. Listen to the nurse and breathe, please." Patrick. I'd know that voice anywhere. Even in the dark recesses of my brain, I recognize the sound. His voice is panicked as he pleads for me to comply. Closing my eyes, I call upon a force within to calm me, and begin taking small swallow breaths.

"That's it. Keep going. In and out." The female voice starts again. After a few inhales and exhales, it gets easier and I'm soon taking deep gulps of air. When my respiration calms completely, I push the bag away. Looking at my surroundings, I find the nurse and

Chloe kneeled in front of me at my feet, Patrick and Landon standing behind them. No sign of Mr. Miles anywhere in the room, thank goodness. They all watch me with concerned eyes. The attention of their intense gazes makes me feel uncomfortable. I lower my head and watch as I nervously twist my hands in my lap.

"Suz, you okay? What in the hell happened?" Chloe asks, taking my hands in hers.

"She had a panic attack which caused her to hyperventilate," the nurse informs the crowd.

"I've got to go," I softly say, pushing with rubbery arms to stand up. Chloe aids in my ascent as I lean on her and the wall. I'm dizzy and exhausted, the attack, and I'm not referring to the panic one, doing a number on me.

"Whoa there ma'am. I really think you should be seen by a doctor before leaving." The nurse, who continues to stand in front of me, is only trying to help. But I'll be damned if I'll let a doctor look at me and ask questions about what brought this on.

"I think that's a good idea, Suz. Let a doctor look you over," Patrick suggests. Bless his heart, he's the one that needs a doctor. Not me. He shifts on his feet, struggling to mask the pain of his sore body. Seeing him in a hospital gown, cast on his arm and bruises on his face, reminds me why I ended up here in the first place. His dad is to blame for his injuries, wrecking that boat last night. His dad brought on my panic attack, causing me to fight for every breath. Mr. Miles, the piece of shit that he is, continues to be a hazard to both our health. And who knows where the weasel escaped to, but I'm sure he'll be back.

Leaning into Chloe's shoulder, I whisper in her ear. "Get me out of here, now!" She must hear the urgency in my words.

"Landon, can you help me with Suz?" Landon walks to the other side of my body, wrapping his arm around my waist in support. "I'm taking her home. If she needs a doctor, I'll call James' dad. Come on, Suz. Let's get you home."

"No, wait! Chloe, she really needs medical attention. She totally freaked out. Scared the shit out of me," Patrick confesses. "I want her to see a doctor. What if something else happens and it triggers more anxiety, causes another panic attack?"

"That's why we need to leave now!"

"Suz?" Patrick questions. He is the only one other than his dad that witnessed the start of my episode. I'm sure he has plenty of questions which I can't answer. And I'm not waiting around for Mr. Miles to reappear sending me back to that dark place.

"I'm fine, Patrick. Goodbye," I say closing the subject. Chloe and Landon help me walk toward the door.

"No, Suzanna, please don't—" The door closes stopping his words midsentence. I don't need to hear what he has to say. What he has to ask. I'll never be able to be truthful with him as long as he continues to have his dad in his life. His plan to make it look like we are keeping our distance is going to work. Because I know I need to separate myself from him and Mr. Miles once and for all.

"I can't believe you're making me get on that plane, Suz!" I can't believe it either. I'm sending my best friend across the country, thousands of miles away. I need her now more than ever, especially after the episode that happened a few days ago. Chloe insisted she'd change her plans. She still planned to move to California, but was willing to push her departure date back. Of course, she'd miss that audition Brian had set up for her. The whole reason she was moving in the first place. As much as I needed her, I wouldn't hear of her passing on an opportunity that big. She has been my rock for so many years, helping me through the nightmares of my past. It's past time I repay the favor, pushing her to fulfill her dreams. If anyone deserves a break, a chance at stardom, it's Chloe.

"Yes, you can." I try to disguise the sadness in my voice with conviction. "And don't think about turning around and making a run for it. I'm standing guard until you've been through the security check and entered the terminal." This is as far as I can go with Chloe. She's stalling taking her place in line at the security check point which will take her into the terminal.

"Suz—"

"Don't *Suz* me! Now give me a hug and get in line!" I command through a smile, my words in contrast to what I really want her to do. I dread that she's leaving, wishing I could keep her by my side for a lifetime. But Chloe has given enough of herself to me, never asking for anything in return. It's my duty as her BFF to make her get on that plane, starting the life she's dreamt about.

Chloe throws her arms around me in a crushing hug. On instinct, I wrap my arms around her in a final embrace. The uncertainty of not knowing when I'll lay eyes on her again has me rethinking this whole thing and wanting to drag her ass back to my car, keeping her with me forever. The wetness I feel on my shoulder has me pulling back to look Chloe in the eyes.

"You're crying," I state. Chloe never cries. She's the strongest woman I know. Always keeping her emotions buried deep. She wears her bright smile, her façade as the happy, go lucky girl she comes off as being. But now, there's a crack in her armor, the tears of her good-bye streaming unabashedly down her face.

"Well, duh. Of course I'm crying, you ding wit! I'm gonna miss you so much," she forces through a gut wrenching sob. I'm the cry baby in this relationship. Often you find me in tears. Something as simple as a sentimental commercial on television has me tearing up. So this uncommon outpouring of emotion from Chloe sends my waterworks into overdrive.

"I'm gonna miss you, too," I manage to choke out. We resume our hug, ignoring the other passengers that breeze by. This is our moment. Our farewell until we meet again. After the emotional over-load has ended, only then do we break our embrace.

Watery eyes meet my own, as Chloe stares at me with concern. "Suz—"

"Hey, no worries. Not about me. Not about Landon. Not about Patrick, James, your parents, your sister. Nobody. Well nobody, except yourself. You hear me?" Chloe nods. "You've earned the right to worry about only you. Now, get on that plane. Go to Hollywood.

And show those casting agents, directors, producers, and everyone else the star I already know you are."

"I love you, Suzanna Caulder."

"I love you, Chloe Ryder."

I walk hand in hand with Chloe to take her place in line. When we arrive at the barrier that prevents me from going any further, I slowly unclasp my hand from hers, sliding our fingers apart until just the tips are connected. "Break a leg!" I recite the official good luck saying to actors.

"Keep stroking those balls," Chloe returns with the not so official offer of luck for golfers. We both burst out in giggles easing the ache we are both feeling. I'm grateful for the laughter, wanting my last sight of Chloe to be one where she's wearing her famous smile.

I create distance between us getting ready to walk away, leaving my best friend to embark on the promising future that awaits her. "See you soon?" I ask forcing myself to walk backwards, not trusting that I won't cling and beg her to stay.

"Hopefully, every week on the television," she responds with excitement.

"Can't wait! 'Bye, Chloe. Go get 'em."

"Goodbye, Suz." I walk away before my forced smile fades into a frown. I plant myself behind a pillar, watching Chloe snake her way up through the line. Before long she's being lead through the metal detectors, her luggage floating through the x-ray machines. Getting the all clear, she moves to the other side, the side only ticketed passengers can enter. Grabbing her things from the carousel, she begins to walk toward her gate. But before she disappears in the crowd, she pauses to glance over her shoulder in my direction. When our gazes lock, the love of a never ending friendship passes between us. No matter where our lives take us, the obstacles we'll face with our varying career choices and the distance that puts us apart, we know we'll always have each other. She waves her final goodbye for the day, her smile faltering for just a second. I wave back, planting an encouraging smile on my face, hoping it'll give her strength to carry on down the corridor. Watching her chest and shoulders rise with an intake of air, she exhales keeping her shoulders squared with confidence. Then she turns and walks with the other passengers until she gets lost amongst the masses. Only then do I let the tears flow again.

Chapter Thirty One

One Month Later....

The clubhouse at Harbour Town Golf Links is buzzing with people. My competitors for the weekend, along with their coaches and caddies swarm the place, passing and stopping at each table during the check in process for the qualifying tournament. Arriving late yesterday evening on Hilton Head Island, we secured our living accommodations for the week. This morning we are here for the official check in process. At first glance, it looks like we'll be here a while considering the mass of people crowding the interior of the clubhouse. But as if by the powers of a divine deity, the people part, clearing a path for us to go immediately to the first check in point. I'd like to think it has something to do with me. My competitors recognize that the Suzanna Caulder, golfer extraordinaire has arrived. They are so intimidated by my talent and skill level they give me the pass to cut in line. However, no one has really looked at me personally. Their eyes are glued to the obnoxious set of blinged out wheels in front of me, daring someone to get in its way. The driver, none other than the infamous Callie Young, is bound and determined to get to the front and start this tedious process. And people better get out of her way, otherwise they might find themselves with one less limb than when they entered the room.

If the bedazzled wheelchair isn't enough to stare at, Callie is. Her hair color was changed earlier this week, streaked now with kelly green highlights. Out of the blue, after one of my last practice sessions before qualifying, she asked what my favorite color was. I thought the question was odd but answered her anyway, stating that I preferred the color green. Lo and behold, she shows up at qualifying with green streaked hair. Normally, green hair isn't something I would consider pretty. But Callie rocks it and it looks fabulous on her. Plus, I love her even more for dying her hair in honor of me. It's her show of support and good luck during the biggest tournament of my life.

But it's not just her arrival and appearance that's got the crowd whispering. Everyone associated with ladies golf knows exactly who Callie is. They followed her brief yet brilliant golf career in college. She was so close to becoming a household name, getting ready to make a splash professionally. That was until the car accident that took the life of one of her friends and Callie's ability to walk. The details of the accident are sketchy to say the least, which caused rumors to run rampant. Callie received plenty of negative attention during the aftermath of the accident that shook the collegiate golf world. It's no wonder she dropped off the radar, only now resurfacing because of me. Makes me love her even more.

Having plowed through the crowd of onlookers, Callie stops short of ramming her wheelchair into the table, causing me and Drew, who have been trailing her the entire time, to come to an abrupt halt. "Well, look who we have here," the professionally dressed woman behind the table offers in greeting. I recognize the classy broad as Anika Besset, the reigning President of the Ladies Professional Golf Association. "What an honor, Miss Young. I didn't realize you were back out playing again."

"I'm not, obviously," Callie says, rolling her eyes dramatically. She makes a big production of smoothing her hands over every part of her wheelchair, just in case it needs pointing out. "I'm not playing golf at all. Especially not playing in this tournament. Not even if you had a paraplegic division."

"We both know you wouldn't meet the qualifications to compete in that division considering you're not paralyzed. You know, I still look at your medical records. I really wish you'd take my advice and meet with those doctors I conferred with. You'd be out of that god

awful looking wheelchair and back on the course where you belong."
Ms. Besset gives Callie a knowing look.

"Not gonna happen, Ms. Besset. Like I told you the other million or
so times you tried to get me to have those surgeries, I'm not going to do
it. All you want is some headlines, me being your attention grabber, to
get the ratings for LPGA out of the toilet. Well, no thank you."

"Callie, the only reason I continue to be persistent is because you
and I both know you could still have a promising career. Your natural
ability will still be there after__"

"Enough!" Callie yells, causing the room to grow quiet and all
heads to turn our way. Lowering her voice Callie whispers angrily,
"I'm not here to get yet another lecture from your highness. I'm here
to support and help coach my friend. She's your next big thing. The
girl's got game. So stop being rude and pay some attention to your
next big star...Suzanna Caulder."

I watch Ms. Besset finally raise her eye level from her focus on
Callie, seated in her chair, to me. At last, she begins to acknowledge
my presence. "Forgive me, um...I...." Ms. Besset begins. But the
words seem to get stuck in her throat. Leave it to Callie to make the
most powerful woman in golf stutter.

"Hi, I'm Suzanna Caulder," I say extending my hand. "Don't
worry, I'm used to fighting for attention when Callie is around." I
try to lighten the mood and put Ms. Besset at ease, sparing her the
embarrassment of totally overlooking me as a possible contender this
weekend.

"Miss Caulder, so nice to meet you." She begins rummaging
through the files on the table, locating the one with my name. As she
flips through the loose papers within the file, I wait hoping to sign a
few things and be on our way. "Um, looks like there might be a slight
problem." She continues to shuffle through the papers yet again still
not finding whatever it is that she's looking for.

"A problem? I don't understand." From my purse I begin to
pull out the envelope which contains every piece of correspondence
between the golf association, this tournament and myself. I'm a

stickler for record keeping and hope that my obsessive behavior will help alleviate whatever problem has occurred.

"It seems we never received the notarized copy detailing the caddy you chose for the tournament and his or her information. We have a copy of the online submission, but need the information verified and notarized before allowing you to compete," Ms. Besset explains.

"You should have received the official copy months ago. Look," I begin shuffling through my own paperwork, retrieving a photocopy of the document in question, "I have a copy of the one I sent to you."

Ms. Besset takes the paper from my hand and looks it over. "Yes, I see where you completed the forms, but we still need the originals, with the notarized seal. Did you mail them to us?"

"Yes,...I mean, no." Thinking back, I didn't actually do the mailing. I prepared everything, placing the important information in the priority mail envelope. Since I had an early morning practice, I passed on the envelope to Chloe to take to the post office during her trip home earlier this summer. I included it with her own stack of mail, putting it inside her purse so she wouldn't forget it.

"Well, which is it? Did you mail it or not?" Explaining all of this to Ms. Besset would be a waste of time. I needed to talk to Chloe. Even though she assured me that she had mailed the documents, I only asked her numerous times, I still needed some final clarification. The line behind us was getting restless, but they were gonna have to wait a few minutes longer. I whipped out my phone and punched in Chloe's number. I didn't care that it was only six in the morning west coast time. I'd keep calling until she answered her phone, not caring that I'd probably be waking her ass up.

"Hello," came a sleepy voice after about five rings.

"Chloe, it's Suz. Listen—"

"What time is it?" I hear her covers rustle as she moves around in her bed, no doubt looking for the time. "You have got to be kidding me, Suz. It's only six!"

"I know, but this is important. Remember that letter I asked you to mail, that time you and Flynn went home?"

"Yeah. I told you I mailed it. Told you like a hundred times. Are you really calling me to ask me about that stupid letter, again?" Chloe asks sounding irritated.

"That *stupid* letter as you refer to it may keep me out of qualifying!"

"*What*?" At least now I've got her attention and she sounds more awake.

"Looks like they never got it. So again, are you sure you mailed that letter, Chloe?" I ask slowly reciting each word. I need her to fully get the seriousness of the situation.

"Yesssss, Suz," she answers using the same verbal technique on me. "The entire stack of mail was dumped in the outgoing mailbox. I promise Suz, I mailed the letter. How it's not there is a mystery to me."

"Okay, thanks. And sorry for waking you."

"Can they really keep you from competing?" Chloe asks with sincere concern.

"Not if I can help it. I'll talk to you later. Go back to sleep." When I end the call, all eyes are on me waiting for an explanation. "She claims she mailed the letter. So...must be a postal error. Question is, what can I do now to fix the problem?" I nervously bite my lower lip waiting for a solution. Please, please let there be a solution.

"Well, I'll need an official notarized form, not a copy, from you by lunchtime today. That gives you a little less than three hours to find a notary. Better get a move on. Miss Caulder, I hope this all works out. I'm really excited about seeing you compete." Ms. Besset hands me back my copies and waves for the next person in line to step forward. Callie clears out a path for our exit. When we step outside, we all pull out our cell phones and start calling friends and family, hoping someone can get us in touch with a local notary.

Now, notaries are a dime a dozen. Had I been in my hometown I'd have this figured out with time to spare. But not knowing anyone that lived in Hilton Head I was starting to get worried. Dad came through, putting us in touch with an accounting associate of his that had a practice in the area. Drew drove like a bat out of hell across the island back to the mainland. The drive took a little over thirty minutes, having to navigate through the tourist traffic this time of year. Luckily, Dad's associate was waiting for us when we arrived, having been notified by my father about the urgency of the situation. He quickly looked over the documents and gave us the official notarization required by Ms. Besset and the tournament.

We were cutting it close with the time as traffic seemed to multiply on the trip back to the clubhouse. "Hey, don't worry. We're gonna make it. Even if we're a few minutes late, she's not going to keep you out of this qualifying tournament." I wanted to believe Callie but my nerves were frayed and I could only manage to nod while I bit my fingernails. The entire morning had gone so far from how I had planned, I hadn't had much time to think of anything but fixing the problem. But the more I focused on said problem, the more things weren't adding up. Unease crept in as the pieces I began to put together all pointed to one terrifying thought. If Chloe took her pile of mail to the post office, which she adamantly admitted to doing. And if her mail had been delivered, yet mine, the only one securely sealed in a priority mail envelope, was not. Then the only other option was that my letter was missing from her purse. But I had put it there myself, securing it in the bundle with a rubber band, my OCD organizational skills at work. Which leads me to the only explanation I can come up with...someone removed my letter on purpose, knowing it wouldn't get delivered thus jeopardizing my chance to qualify for the pro tour.

Wanna take a wild guess at who's on the top of my suspect list? Jim Miles, of course.

Patrick's dad hates me. His abhorrence of me was evident four years ago when he attempted to sexually assault me, stripping away my innocence. I could have made his life a living nightmare had I had the good sense to press charges back then. But I didn't, instead moving far away, never to bring that horrible night up again. You'd think he'd be thankful that my actions suggested I'd rather forget what he tried to do to me, rather than drag his name through the mud. But noooooo. Even after all this time has passed, he continues to despise me, going as far as to vilify me to his son.

Since our paths crossed this summer for the first time since the attack, he has taken each and every opportunity to scare, bully and threaten me. Our first encounter at Patrick's engagement party, he gave me a warning. Stay away from his son. Obviously he thought I re-emerged with the sole purpose to weasel my way back into Patrick's life. Which was so far off base. The only reason I attended that stupid party was to find some closure and finally put an end to the romantic relationship of my past. But Mr. Miles didn't see it that way in his intoxicated state. He was adamant that my presence was bound to cause a problem and threatened me with the consequence that should I be a distraction this summer or interfere in Patrick's engagement, he'd tell quite a different story of the events of that horrible night back in high school. Yeah, he still hated me. To think that keeping my mouth shut about his criminal act would somehow lessen his dislike for me was a total waste of time. The years apart had done nothing but cause his hatred toward me to fester to an even higher level. I can't figure out what warranted his disdain for me. All I ever did was date his son. Was that so bad?

In my mind, I'd already added to Mr. Miles' growing list of offenses directed at me. I pegged him as the one who busted up mine and Chloe's cars this summer. Even though the police officers thought it was a clean cut case of random violence, I knew the destruction of my golf clubs and bag was more personal. So, of course, I immediately blamed Patrick's dad. Now, I'm blaming him for the missing letter. The fact that he has it out for me is enough to find him guilty of this latest crime. However, if memory serves me correctly, Mr. Miles wasn't there at my house that night, the night the letter was mentioned and placed in Chloe's bundle of mail. So either he has someone else working for him, or I might have another enemy to contend with. Gee, what's wrong with me that people are turning against me, plotting and scheming to bring me down?

Mentally I make a list of all the people who were present the night the letter went missing. I immediately clear my friends, Patrick, Chloe and Landon. Also, I know Flynn didn't have anything to do with it, either. These people have been with me since I first picked up a golf club. I know in my heart they all want to see me succeed and fulfill my dream of playing professionally. So that leaves the only other two people that were at the house that night. Katelyn and Leslie.

Katelyn accompanied Patrick to my house that evening for our impromptu gathering. It was the first night we really got a chance to talk and get to know each other. That was the beginning of our developing friendship. Since then, we've talked and hung out multiple times. I'd hate to think Katelyn was using our friendship to do dirty work for Mr. Miles. I can't even fathom that scenario. Katelyn seems too sweet to get caught up in the evil dealings of Mr. Miles. I know she has her own secrets, secrets about the life she desperately longs for. I'm almost a hundred percent sure that her engagement to Patrick is a farce. Their interaction has been nothing but friendly. Well, except for the awkward display of affection Patrick put on after our fight. That was when he announced that the wedding was being pushed up to this coming weekend. Yeah, just another thing crowding my brain while I try to win this qualifying tournament securing my professional tour card. Anyway, my overactive brain is telling me that Katelyn isn't the suspect that fits this crime. So I'm scratching her off my list.

That leaves Leslie. Now, other than that one night way back in high school, when I publically showed my possession of Patrick to everyone during a party, putting a halt to Leslie's pursuit of my man, I have done nothing but be kind to her. Even as strange and one-sided as her relationship with Landon was, I was always supportive. I tried to include her in our close knit group of friends. And I never treated her differently, even knowing her not so stellar reputation in the past involving the opposite sex. So unless she's one of those grudge holding women, never letting things go, I can't think of any reason why Leslie would want to derail my future career.

This leads me straight back to the first person that came to mind. But how could Mr. Miles pull this off if he wasn't even there? I wouldn't put it past him to sneak into the house unseen and swipe the letter, making a quick escape. But unless he's solely focused on the destruction of my life that he's gone so far as to plant bugs in the beach house, listening to my private conversations, there's no way he'd have known the letter even existed. I think my brain is running into crazy town....suggesting things like bugs and shit. It's not like he's in the CIA or anything. He's a washed up small town lawyer, for goodness sakes.

While I've been in detective mode, I've paid little attention to our drive from the mainland back to the island. Only as we come to a stop, parking in front of the clubhouse again do I give my overactive imagination a rest. Drew exits the car and comes around the back, unstrapping Callie's wheelchair from its resting place on the lift. After he helps her from the passenger side into the chair, we all make a beeline to the front door. The parking lot is relatively full, so I know that many of the golfers are still in line waiting to finish their check in procedures. I beg Callie to let's not make a scene this go around, opting to stand in line like everyone else. Lawd knows I don't need any extra attention directed at me. I've got so much buzzing in my brain right now, if one person said something or even looked at me wrong, I might burst out crying.

"Fine, we'll wait in line like the normal folks," Callie begrudgingly agrees. "But let's just hope the line moves quickly. Your deadline for submitting the paperwork by lunch is fast approaching."

"We'll get it in on time," I say, but the definitiveness in my voice is missing. Please, please let this line move so I can just play some golf.

As if a higher power decided I needed a break, the line did move at a faster pace than this morning. I guess when you've submitted the proper paperwork prior, the check in process goes quite quickly. I and my entourage of two, Callie and Drew, come to stand before the first check in table once again. Ms. Besset gives us all a narrowing look, finally setting her gaze on me. With one eyebrow raised she asks, "Well, do you have the proper documentation this time, Miss Caulder?" I nod enthusiastically while Drew hands over the information. I had given the recently notarized pieces of paper, the papers that could decide the fate of my future, to Drew for safe keeping. I was such a nervous wreck my hands had begun to sweat profusely.

Last thing I needed was to turn in wet paperwork, the ink smeared from sweat thus becoming illegible.

Ms. Besset puts on a fashionable pair of reading glasses and begins to peruse the information in my packet. "I see you're getting out of the classroom to get back on the golf course, Drew. Having a change of heart about your MBA route?"

"Not a chance. I love the business world. Actually golf and business go hand in hand. Some of the biggest deals have been made on the golf course." Drew talks so casually to Ms. Besset, it's like they've known each other for some time. Plus, she knew of his enrollment in the master's program at CCU. I wonder what the connection is. "I'm just helping out a friend. She needed a caddy and since I've practically been her playing partner all summer while Dad coached her, who better than me to fill the job."

"Ah, yes, your dad," Ms. Besset remarks with a certain gleam in her eye. "Coach Moore always is more than accommodating to his students."

"Careful Anika, you're starting to turn green. And you can't pull off that color like I can," Callie injects flipping her colorful streaked hair. "Don't worry, Dad knows Suzanna is the real deal. A true student of the game. Not one of those bored housewife bimbos that use their husband's money for a little extracurricular activity." When Anika, as Callie so informally called her, does nothing but stare with an open mouth, Callie continues. "What I'm saying is Dad has no interest in getting into Suzanna's pants. No offense Suzanna."

"None taken, Callie." WTF! Does Coach Moore make a habit of carrying his lessons off the course and into the bedroom? And why does Ms. Besset seem to even care?

"Callie, no reason to be so blunt and crude. I never considered that to be the case in the first place."

"Yes you did," Callie taunts.

"I'll have you know, I've spoken to your dad frequently in the past several weeks. We even have plans to see each other during the tournament to catch up and talk."

"I bet you'll be *talking*," Callie continues, making Ms. Besset seem very uncomfortable.

A moment of silence descends upon us as Callie and Ms. Besset engage in a stare down. While they're occupied, I mentally connect the dots. My conclusion is that Coach Moore, Drew and Callie's dad, and Anika have other interests besides just golf. Seems to me golf balls aren't the only things they've been bumping. But to hear Callie, the relationship has been an on again, off again sort of thing. Coach Moore sounds like he has done some straying in the past and Ms. Besset is well aware. While I'd love to stand here and get all the juicy details, I've got more important things to do. Clearing my throat to get everyone's attention I ask, "Is this newly notarized document official enough now? Can I proceed and get my practice and tee times?"

Ms. Besset looks thoughtful as she presses her lips together. My nerves meet an all time high when she doesn't respond immediately. Finally, she speaks and I hope she'll put me out of my misery. "Well, I don't like making concessions for anyone. I could really get into trouble for not following the rules and allowing this last minute entry." My heart sinks to my toes. This is it...everything I've worked so hard for, disappearing just like that damn letter.

"But_" I begin, ready to choke out my final plea.

"Come on Anika, don't punish Suzanna because she hasn't done anything wrong. It's me you have the problem with." Callie speaks on my behalf.

"And...," Ms. Besset coerces for more. I don't know what power Callie yields that can turn this around. But I hold my breath and wait.

"Fine, I'll see those damn doctors. But they better be freaking miracle workers!" This all comes back to the prior conversation when Ms. Besset let me in on the little secret that Callie's condition might be able to be reversed. I'm not sure of all the details, but I know Callie holds a strong insistence to remain in that wheelchair. Why? That I'm not sure of. Wouldn't she have fixed this the minute she realized that her mangled legs could work again? However, I don't want her making life altering decisions about her health and surgeries just to get me into this tournament. No matter how important it is to my career.

"Callie, no. You don't have to do this." I touch her shoulder hoping she'll see the sincerity in my statement.

"Yes, I do. Otherwise, you won't get to fulfill your dream, Suz. Our dream." Tears fill my eyes as I realize the sacrifice Callie is making just being here. I can't imagine how hard it is to see someone else do all the things you planned to do before life took away that opportunity. "Plus, if these doctors are as great as Anika thinks they are, this it the last time you'll have the chance to win. 'Cause if I'm out on the course again, I'll beat your and everyone else's ass." I see the small glimmer of hope in her eyes before she masks it with her tough as nails persona.

"Well, congratulations Miss Caulder. You're officially listed as one of the competitors in this qualifying round. Good luck. You may proceed to the next station to receive your practice and tee times, as well as the instructions for having your equipment inspected before play begins." Ms. Besset stamps my paperwork and places it in her files. I feel like I might float away, the weight of not being able to participate gone. Raw emotions keep me from speaking so I nod instead, showing my gratitude. Continuing to the next table to complete the check in process, Ms. Besset has some final last words. "And Callie?"

Callie turns her head to the side and glances over her shoulder.

"I'll be in touch with the information about your appointments. I think you'll be happy to hear what the doctors have to say." Callie doesn't comment, only giving Ms. Besset a chin tip of acknowledgement. She turns her head back forward so that Ms. Besset can no longer see her face. But I can. And I rejoice when I notice the slight curvature of her lips. Callie is finally letting some hope bleed into her despair filled heart. This feeling of great expectations for both me and Callie is one I will hold onto to carry me to the top of the leader board. This win's not just mine any longer, but it's Callie, too.

Chapter Thirty Two

C allie doesn't bring up the deal she made, sealing my entry into the tournament. And the few times I ask about the little information I gathered about the possibility of her walking again, she gives vague short answers and then changes the subject. Usually to how I got in the predicament of almost being disqualified before play began in the tournament. Then it's my turn to give nondescript explanations. I never voice my suspicions that someone is trying to sabotage me. Although, Callie with her colorful personality would probably run with my assumptions, I'm not yet ready to tell her all the secrets of my past. And neither is she. I guess there are just some things that are too personal to bring into our fairly new friendship just yet.

As promised, Anika makes contact with Callie, even arranging several lunch meetings to discuss Callie's future medical treatment. While she's away, Drew and I attend our slotted practice times. As expected, the course is in pristine condition. We play each hole, studying pin placement for the various days of the tournament. When we are not on the course, we are constantly strategizing about which clubs to use, how to attack each fairway, and the slopes of the greens for every hole on the course. Quickly, the days fly by and soon it's the morning for the tournament to officially begin.

I arrived two hours prior to my tee time for the equipment inspection and some last swings on the practice tee. Tagging my bag and clubs, I wait my turn with the official to get the all clear that my equipment meets the association requirements. When my assigned time reaches, an elderly gentleman approaches with a clipboard. He gives me a warm smile which does little to settle my nerves. But I manage a smile in return and extend a shaky hand in greeting. "Hi, I'm Suzanna Caulder."

"Miss Caulder, nice to meet you." The elderly man gives my small trembling hand a firm shake. "I'm here to inspect your equipment. Are you ready?"

"Y-yes, si-rr." There's no hiding my nervousness with the wobble in my voice.

"Hey, no need to be nervous. This is just standard procedure for tournaments of this caliber." My nerves have nothing to do with the equipment check. I'm certain my clubs and bag meet the professional grade standards and restrictions. But I appreciate his kindness in trying to put me at ease. I watch as he does his job, making the appropriate checks on his clipboard. Ten minutes later he's almost finished when a gangly teenage boy rushes up to our spot. He's carrying a box about as big as him and I'm concerned he may be crushed under it's weight. Breathing heavily, he drops the box at my feet and addresses the inspector.

"Mr. Bill," he says between gulping breaths. "I was told to deliver this to Miss Caulder before the equipment check. I hope I've made it in time." Oh poor guy. His worried expression tells me he's frightened of getting into trouble. I'm sure he's a local student who volunteered for the tournament just to get out of his classes. He probably didn't realize what exactly he'd signed up for...delivering boxes the size of him, just squeaking in before the delivery deadline. If I wasn't so curious about the package at my feet, I'd feel sorry for him.

"Calm down son. I was just about to finish up. Don't sweat it." The relief in the boy's eyes is evident. "Well, Miss Caulder...could you do the honors and open this box. If it is equipment related I'll need to check it in before I can complete your inspection and move on to the next competitor."

Without hesitation, I begin ripping off the tape on the mammoth sized box, until I'm able to open the flaps and peek inside. I go to town littering the floor with the packing paper protecting the contents inside. Once everything is cleared, my hands still as I stare down at my gift in disbelief. Covered in a wrapping of clear plastic is my golf bag. The golf bag that I've been playing with since high school. The one that belonged to Marie, Patrick's mother. The one Patrick gave to me. But it can't be. That bag was destroyed this summer when someone decided to vandalize my car, along with other personal property that was locked inside. Taking a closer look, I see that the bag is not the original one. Of course this one has a new frame and casing. The leather, although the same color as my previous bag, is brand new, the scent intoxicating. My hands itch to feel the softness of the material against my palms. Stretching the plastic until it gives I tear it away and begin to physically inspect the golf bag. It's then that I notice that the leather is not as smooth to the touch as it looks. I run my hands over the seams that cover the bag and find that someone has hand sewn salvageable pieces from my old bag into this one. On one side of the bag, in the center near the top, is an original piece of leather from my old bag. It's not the wornness of the material or the small cracks and creases from age that clues me in to this fact. The marking of Marie's monogram, the same one she had sewn into her bag before her death, is the key piece of evidence. I trace my fingers over the letters like I've done so many times before. Lifting the bag to a standing position to look at it in its entirety, I can see the craftsmanship that it took to construct it. I notice on the opposite side of where I was just looking to find my own set of initials, monogrammed in beautiful script.

I rub my hands over the stitching, where both old and new are connected. I can't help but think of how fitting this is to my life now. I've just begun embracing the old, reconnecting with friends from the past, namely Landon and James. I'm also putting to rest relationships that ended, but needed the ultimate closure. I've come to realize my romance with Patrick wasn't meant to stand the test of time. However, it was a learning experience for us both. I'll always cherish the love we shared then and still share today. But I know the difference now between loving someone and being in love with someone. I love Patrick with all my heart. His gesture of taking the time to have such a beautiful piece of equipment made especially for me, shows he's just that great of a guy. But no amount of heartfelt gifts will change the fact that we no longer are romantically connected. No, I've given my heart to someone else. I've fallen far past the point of return to try to take it back. I may love Patrick, but I'm in love with Wyatt. My mini-realization comes to a halt when I feel the note attached to the handle of the bag. Untying it from the strap, I open it and read the words silently.

Dear Suzanna,

I promised you, when you were sobbing in the middle of the road clutching the remains of your destroyed golf bag, that I would fix it. I've made some questionable decisions of late, that may speak badly of my character. But I remain a man of my word. And if I say I'll fix something, I follow through. I hope you are pleased with how your gift turned out. I searched high and low for a seamstress who could take my vision and finish the project to my liking.

You may think you need a tangible piece of my mother to feel her presence. But I know she'll be with you regardless, her spirit always near. Just like me. I can't be with you physically...won't be there to watch you raise the winning trophy. But you'll be a constant in my thoughts. And you'll be forever in my heart. Even as I make a monumental commitment this weekend, there's a corner of my heart I've reserved as your home.

Good luck this weekend in the tournament. Not that you'll need it. I know the depths of your talents. They're as deep as my feelings for you.
All my love, forever,
Patrick

By the time I finish reading his note, my eyes are leaking. Tears fall steadily for various reasons. I'm overwhelmed at his gift. Only he would know how much the new golf bag, mended with pieces that connect me to his mother, means to me. To share that bond with someone who can relate is truly special. But I have conflicting emotions due to his touching note. As if our minds are running parallel, I see that he too has reached the realization that although we love each, a true all encompassing kind of love, we both are saying goodbye to the prospect of a romantic life together. I know it's a good thing to finally leave the indecision behind. We accept that we aren't meant to be together. But that doesn't mean his marriage this weekend is the answer. I still believe he is sacrificing his own happiness for reasons unknown.

We haven't spoken since the scene at the hospital. I kept my word and decided to trust Patrick. He asked me not to make contact so I haven't. He tried to reach out several times, I'm sure to check on me since he witnessed my panic attack. But I chose each time to ignore his calls. The farther away I distanced myself from that situation the better. But my heart is smiling at his latest attempt to reach out.

I'm startled from my thoughts when I feel a hand press gently on my shoulder. "Miss Caulder, do you want me to check in this new golf bag for the competition?"

"Yes, please," I answer wiping away the wetness from my cheeks.

"It's a really nice bag. Looks like it was made with love," the elderly gentleman comments as he inspects the detailed handiwork.

I think how very blessed I am to have the love of such a wonderful man. Whether it be Katelyn or some other woman, he's gonna make someone very happy one day. Even accepting our future label of just friends, he continues to put a smile on my face. "That bag, not only is it made of love...it's a true representation of the word."

At the start of the tournament I was still a bit jittery. But I still managed to par the first four holes. After that, I ran away with it, birdying the final twelve of the eighteen on the first day of play. The second day was just as good. I increased my lead and was ahead of the rest of the field, the closest person still behind me by seven stokes. Those first few days I played out of my mind. It was like I felt this presence which I couldn't explain. A few times, as my pairing partners were teeing off, I'd look around the crowd trying to locate the pair of eyes I constantly felt watching me. Of course, I knew they were all watching me and the other competitors. But this felt different. My parents were there always cheering me on. By their side was also Callie, her presence is where I drew my strength. But other that those people, I didn't see anyone else I recognized. Yet, that strange feeling of some- one else watching me, someone personally close enough to elicit the feeling, but still remain hidden in the thickness of the crowd, wouldn't go away.

Funny how when I began this journey, first finding out that I received an invitation to play in the qualifying tournament, I never thought I'd be basically doing this on my own. Not that I'm entirely alone. I've got Drew walking by my side, serving as my caddy. Also, Coach Moore is here, usually settled somewhere in the press room at the club watching and critiquing my every stroke on the live feed coming from the on sight cameras that follow us around. Plus, there are also my parents. They are ever present as they walk with the rest of the crowd that has decided to follow my group. Alas, there's Callie...as if I could forget her presence. Each time my gaze drifts to the gallery, her bright green hair is the first thing I see. She's usually giving me an imaginary fist bump, her hand punching air, as a sign of encouragement. So yeah, I've got a great support system.

But I can't help but think of the people who aren't here to witness this momentous occasion. As I shared my news with friends and family, everyone was so excited and promised me that they'd be here to watch me play. However, things always seem to change. Not that I haven't been showered with well wishes and good luck gifts. James and Lisa sent me a huge bouquet of flowers wishing me well. They weren't able to make the tournament because of Lisa's insane work schedule and James' medical school demands. Landon of course was somewhere in the state, guarding our possible future governor. He felt terrible that he wouldn't be able to make it to at least the first few rounds. His never ending text messages of encouragement keep coming though. Of course Flynn and I Skyped before the tournament started and he told me as only a pain in the ass brother can that I better kick some butt, or else. Don't know what he expected to do should I fail to make the pro tour with *his butt* all the way across the Atlantic. Through his teasing threat, I could still see how proud he was of me, win or lose. I know for a fact he'd be here if he weren't following his own dreams of playing professional soccer.

Then there's my BFF of all time...Chloe. Who knew she'd be across the country securing her first television acting gig? I'm so happy for her, but I really, *really* miss her. Especially now, during the biggest tournament of my life. Whenever I'm tied up in knots or stressed out beyond a reasonable limit, like now for instance, she's always been able to calm me down. Of course, we've been in constant contact for the past few days. She's called numerous times for updates on my play. And she's responsible for the edgy, yet chic, golfing attire I've been sporting during the tournament. The package containing my clothing was already at the hotel when I checked in. Her words, scribbled on a note, basically demanded that win or lose at least I should look good. Even thousands of miles away, she's still playing the role of fashion police. As soon as I win this thing, I'm going to see her. I need a dose of Chloe's sweet smile!

The list of people not in attendance just continues. There's Patrick...and his fiancée slash my new friend Katelyn. Like they'd even entertain the thought of making the drive to watch some golf. Can't say I blame them. I'm sure with their wedding this weekend they've got more than enough things to do to keep them busy. I'm really trying hard not to let the thoughts of their marital commitment enter my mind. But on this Saturday morning, as the field's been lessened by a third, some poor girls not making the weekend cut, the wedding seems to be the only thing I can think about. It's like a big mistake that shouldn't happen. Not because I don't want Patrick or Katelyn to get married. I do want them to find their forevers with someone...just not each other. And it has nothing to do with me wanting to take Katelyn's place. Sure, at first I thought maybe I'd be the one in Patrick's future. But that was before Wyatt. There's no comparison when it comes to my feelings for the two men. While I love Patrick, it's truly a platonic love. Wyatt...it's off the charts, smoldering, passionate, I'd die for you kind of love. Basically I'm in love with Wyatt and I don't see that ever changing. All I want is for Patrick and Katelyn to find that kind of love. And I know it's not with each other.

As I think of Wyatt, my heart hurts more. His absence is the one that really dampens my spirit. Sure, I'd love for everyone to be with me now. But the one person whose presence I crave the most is Wyatt's. He's really the only one I want to share this with. He's the only one I want to share everything with.

With the absence of those most important in my life, the wedding that will take place later today, and the loss I feel without Wyatt's presence, I can't really find my golfing mojo. Therefore, my third round play plummeted from the high standard I set the previous two days. And my score is a clear reflection of my lack of concentration. Finishing over par for the first time since the tournament started, I've lost my lead and I'm now in fourth place. My fairway shots were off, landing me in the rough several times. I couldn't get close to my target on the greens, my putting like that of a blind person. Overall, I played a terrible round and now I'm having to suffer the consequences of allowing my brain to get cluttered with thoughts other than those pertaining to golf. Drew and Coach Moore analyze every shot I made today, letting me know what adjustments I'll have to make in tomorrow's final round to have a chance at winning. But I know all about the technical aspects of my game and although they suffered today, it was my mental game that got the best of me. The pep talks from Drew, Coach, Callie and my parents help. But they are not enough. There's only one thing, one person, who can get me out of my slump. Locking myself behind the door of my hotel room, I prepare to turn in early after a light dinner. Before I try to settle in for some sleep, I pull out my phone and send a text.

I need you

Then I wait.

Chapter Thirty Three

Wyatt

It's almost like she knows I'm here. I'll catch her looking at the nameless faces of the crowd waiting for her to spot me. But I keep myself well hidden enough that she never confirms my actual presence. My girl is on fire. The last two days she's been killing the ball, placing herself ahead of the pack with a commanding lead. I wish I didn't have to leave this morning. All I want to do is watch Suzanna continue to demonstrate why she deserves to play professionally. But I have one last stop before I head back to New York. One last stop to make sure Suzanna gets everything she deserves. Even if it breaks my heart in the process.

The drive to Garden City Beach from Hilton Head takes most of the morning. Approaching the coastal community, I run into some traffic. The tourists are making a last ditch effort to vacation in the Myrtle Beach area before the summer comes to an end and schools start back. Crawling down Highway 17, I'm still on schedule to make it in time. Actually, I have about an hour to grab some lunch. Pulling into a sports bar, I'm not even thinking about the food on the menu. All I want is a place that might possibly have the golf channel so I can see how Suzanna's playing today. The waitress seats me at the one table that has the best view of the television that has the qualifying tournament broadcasted. The bar is not crowded at all since it's a beautiful day. I'm sure most people are taking advantage of the weather and enjoying the beach. Seems like I'm the only one interested in watching ladies golf.

After placing an order for a sandwich and fries, I concentrate on the screen in front of me. To my horror, Suzanna has already dropped a few strokes and is in jeopardy of losing her lead. And it's not just her golf game that gives me the indication she might continue to struggle. Although she looks just as beautiful as she did in person, her whole demeanor has changed. Her strokes have no power to them. Her posture is slumped and her head is down. Overall, she looks defeated. "Come on Suz, you can do this," I chant to no one. It kills me to see her struggle, but worse is seeing her basically give up. Maybe I should have stayed. Maybe I should have made my presence known. But I can't help but think that the change in Suzanna has little to do with me and more to do with what's happening in a few hours. Of course she'd be bothered that Patrick's wedding is so close to taking place. It's obvious she still loves him. Every chance she gets she's always running back to him. But she can't today...trapped in a tournament that she's dreamt of winning since being invited to play. However, her dreams aren't gonna come true if she continues to play like this. So I'm here to help her out. Pushing my pride aside, I'm going to give Suzanna her happily ever after. Too bad that doesn't include me.

By the time I finish my lunch, I've watched Suzanna's continued collapse. She's finished the first nine holes, getting ready to make the turn to start the back nine. The scoreboard now shows she's tied with another golfer, with a couple more closing in. My lunch settles uncomfortably in my stomach. I don't know if it's watching Suzanna's golfing failure or what I'm about to do. Either way, I'm struggling to keep my sandwich down.

The drive to the church takes about twenty minutes. It's still a good two hours before the ceremony is supposed to begin, but I spot several cars in the parking lot. I'm sure the bride and groom as well as their attendants are somewhere inside the church preparing for pictures to be taken. I bypass the front doors of the church knowing that more than likely, the groom has been sequestered in a room down the hall from the sanctuary. I walk slowly listening to voices, hopefully those of males, trying to locate Patrick. I don't need to wander into a room full of half dressed females getting ready for a wedding. Plus, it's obvious I don't belong here. I've come dressed in what I would have worn to watch a golf tournament. Didn't bother to even bring a suit seeing as I have no plans to stay for the wedding, should it even take place.

I stop in front of a door not quite pulled closed but shut enough that I can't see inside. It's not what I see that has me coming to a halt. It's the familiar commentator voices from a television or computer that lets me know someone else is interested in the happenings taking place on a golf course in Hilton Head. And I'd bet my life savings it's Patrick that's tuned in. Sure enough, when I press my hand against the door forcing it to swing open, I see Patrick sitting in front of his laptop watching the live stream broadcast of the tournament. He's so engrossed he doesn't hear me enter the room. He continues to sit there, decked out in his wedding tux, minus the jacket, watching the action unfold. My attention snaps to the screen when I hear him swear under his breath. "Shit Suz. A four year old could make that putt." Sure enough Suzanna has bogeyed another hole and no longer is tied for the lead. It's painful watching her slide down the leader board. All I want to do is turn around, leave this church, and drive back to Hilton Head and Suzanna. I'd take her in my arms, hugging and kissing the mistakes of her day away. I'd talk her up, preparing her for her great comeback on Sunday. Then I'd watch her raise that winning trophy, sharing in her accomplishment.

But when I glance over at Patrick and see the pain and shock on his face as Suzanna struggles, I realize I'm not the only one in this game. He's just as affected by Suzanna's success or failure as I am. And I've come here to give him the chance to show her. Hopefully, my "wedding gift" will finally give Patrick his freedom, thus giving Suzanna a choice. A true choice to make between a future with Patrick or a future with me. But I already know what she'll decide. I've known it since she decided to attend his engagement party without inviting me as her date. Actually without so much of a mention of it. I've know it since I saw that kiss, the one Patrick initiated, but also the one Suzanna participated in. And if the kiss wasn't enough, the fact she bolted out of my New York apartment after a night of love making, to catch the next plane back to South Carolina to check on Patrick after the boating accident…Yeah, that was enough to let me know she'd made her decision. Patrick was her one.

So, with the last piece of my heart, the one piece that belongs to Suzanna, lodged somewhere in my throat, I clear it making a noise and getting Patrick's attention. I can tell the minute he recognizes my presence, his eyes almost bugging out of his head. "Wyatt?" he questions like he doesn't recognize me. That or he can't believe I'm here.

"Hello Patrick. Long time no see," I greet, shutting the door until I hear it click. I need total privacy for this conversation. "I hear congratulations are in order."

"Um, yeah. Thanks." Patrick seems uncomfortable and I'm not sure if it's the congratulations I'm offering even though I didn't get invited to his wedding. Or if it's the wedding itself that's making him so uneasy. At least he has the decency to stand and approach me offering his hand. I give it a firm shake and release it as we proceed to stand in front of each other in an awkward silence. The commentator's voice fills the air and we both direct our attention back to his laptop. Looks like another competitor is making a run for the lead, and Suzanna gets bypassed again falling even further from the top of the scoreboard. Both Patrick and I make audible grimaces at the recent tournament events.

"Shit, she's gonna lose," Patrick mutters more at the screen of his computer than to me. His frustration at watching Suzanna's epic collapse is evident as he rakes his fingers through his perfectly styled hair. Hope those wedding pictures have already been taken.

"Maybe, the golf tournament that is. But she really won't be losing."

"What are you talking about?" Patrick asks.

"I brought you a gift." I take the small square package wrapped in standard brown shipping paper out from my back pocket. I begin to hand it over to Patrick, but have a moment of hesitation. When Patrick's fingers locked onto the thin square ready to take it from my hands, my fingers stay attached not moving. Moments later I reluctantly release my grip so Patrick can take sole possession.

"Is this a wedding gift?"

"No, I definitely wouldn't call it that." Patrick narrows his eyes at me for a brief moment before unwrapping the disc.

With a laugh Patrick says, "A compilation of your favorite love songs? How thoughtful."

"I wish it was something that lame." I pluck the disc from Patrick's fingers and remove it from the protective case. Minimizing the live golf action, I put the disc in the computer and wait for it to boot up. "You need to see this," I say, my finger hovering over the play button on the now dark screen. Patrick reclaims his seat in front of the computer and begins to watch what I can only describe as a horror film. Only this stuff is real, not that make-believe crap they produce out in Hollywood. When Patrick's attention is focused on the screen I press the button to begin unleashing Suzanna's secret.

The screen turns from dark to a picture of the lounge inside the country club. "Hey, isn't that the bar at the club? Where you worked?" I nod in affirmation, but Patrick doesn't see me. His eyes stay focused on the screen as Suzanna enters the door of the lounge bringing her into the camera angle. "Suzanna." Patrick whispers her name and it hurts to hear the longing in his voice. She walks over to the corner of the room to retrieve her coat that's hanging on the back of a chair. "This was taken that night of the Christmas party...our senior year." Patrick pauses to look up at me his features tight with confusion.

"Yeah, just keep watching." He returns his attention to the video even though I'm sure he's questioning why I'm making him watch something from over four years ago.

We both watch Suzanna, dressed in her cocktail dress, her face glowing under the dim lighting. She looks so young. She also looks beautiful. Man, I think the years have only made her more beautiful. I glance down at Patrick, his features now relaxed, as he takes in Suzanna on the screen. Yep, he's thinking the same thing. There's no way not to recognize how stunning she is. But our moment of admiration is brief when a male figure blocks our unobstructed view of our beautiful girl, turning this into something quite ugly. The man cages in Suzanna, basically pinning her to the wall. Even though his back is to the camera, when his body shifts, we get a clean shot of the side of his face.

"That's—"

"Your dad," I say with undisguised disdain. There's also a hint of aggravation in my voice. I'm sick of Patrick's verbal interruptions. I bet he's that annoying type who can't keep his mouth shut during an entire movie. Ugh! "Shut up and watch. You'll understand soon enough." Other than a quick glare in my direction, Patrick finishes watching the horrible events that happened that night. By the end of the video, Patrick's face is red with anger and his fists are clenched tightly by his sides.

"What... Why...," Patrick can't formulate a question or a sentence in his state of shock and rage.

"Now you know the real reason Suzanna left during her senior year in high school."

"That motherfucker!" Patrick roars, his voice echoing off the wooden walls of the room. No longer able to contain his emotions in his seated position, Patrick stands and starts pacing the room. Back and forth, back and forth, he strides huffing and puffing. Finally, his fury boils over and he stops in front of the wall and begins pounding his fists on the hard wood. I watch him unleash his pent up anger at his father, glad it's the wall taking it and not me. But when I see the cracks in his knuckles, the blood seeping over his fingers and spraying on his shirt with the force of each hit, I take action. Without thinking, I wrap my arms around Patrick's waist and pull him away before he punches a hole through the wall, or breaks his bones, whichever would have come first.

"Hey, man, you're gonna hurt yourself," I say as I cautiously back away.

Patrick takes a deep breath, not bothering to inspect the damage to his hands. "How could he do that to her? To me? To us?" He asks as if I'll have the answer. Which I don't. "He...he...oh god! If you weren't there he...he would have..." The thought of what could have happened had I not been there that night still sends shivers up and down my spine. "My dad was trying to rape, *rape* my girlfriend." Patrick's voice gets all panicky and he's started pacing again. I'm scared he might resume torturing that poor wall.

"But he didn't." I need to remind him of that so he'll calm the fuck down. Not that I can blame him for being so pissed off. What he just learned is a lot to swallow on any day. Just so happened he learned what type of monster his dad is on his wedding day.

"I hate him. You hear me? I. HATE. HIM! And I'm going to kill the bastard!" Patrick makes a move for the door presumably in pursuit of inflicting much pain to his father. Frankly, I couldn't care less what happens to Mr. Miles. I believe he deserves a slow, torturous death. But that's not the reason for my visit.

"Whoa! There'll be plenty of time for you to deal with your dear 'ole dad." I have to physically restrain Patrick from busting out the door in search of his father. "Look, you've gotta think about Suzanna." Her name is all I need to say to stop him in his tracks.

"Suzanna," he speaks her name like it's holy. At least his voice has dropped a few decibels letting me know he's starting to calm down. That is until we hear the muffled pleas from Suzanna coming from the video that I failed to stop during Patrick's rant. The video quality is outstanding, but audio was subpar at best. Still, the desperate sounds coming from Suzanna as she tries to fight off Mr. Miles is heartbreaking. "Turn that damn thing off!" Patrick roars. I quickly press the stop button and watch the computer screen turn dark again. However, I leave the disc in the computer. It's no longer mine. I'm putting it in Patrick's hands to do with as he pleases.

"Why didn't she tell me?" Patrick asks after moments of silence which he needed to control his rage.

"To protect you."

"What?"

"She didn't want to take away your only living parent, seeing as you had just recently lost your mother," I explain.

"I'd be better off without him. And for the record, I no longer consider him my parent. He may as well be dead to me." I have a feeling Mr. Miles' attempts to destroy other people in order to control his son's life have been going on since that awful night. I don't even want to hear what else the monster has done. I'm starting to feel sorry for Patrick, even though I'm the one giving up everything. "She should have told me."

"You have to understand. She was trying to protect you from a scandal. When I mentioned pressing charges, she wouldn't hear of it. You can imagine the types of things that would be said about your dad and her from the society snobs that inhabit our small town. They would have had a field day with a story like this. And I'm sure your dad nor Suzanna would come out of it unscathed. That's why she bolted. Took off to escape and protect you at the same time." This is hard for me to admit, but I have to be honest with Patrick. The only reason I'm spilling Suzanna's secret is so she'll get what she wants. And I know she wants Patrick. So I need him to understand the tremendous sacrifice she made all those years ago. "Suzanna didn't leave you because she wanted to concentrate on her golfing skills. Nor did she leave you because she was having a relationship on the side with me. I know all about those rumors some jerk started just to stir the pot. And I assure you that they are not true. Not one bit!"

"But you and Suzanna did have a relationship. She finally told me when I pestered her enough about that random, sudden trip to New York."

"Yes, but our relationship didn't start until a few months or so before she graduated from college. *College*, Patrick. Almost four years after high school." I make sure to emphasize the time frame so he can't question Suzanna's morals. I should throw in there that other than Patrick, I'm the only other guy Suzanna dated. All those years she never bothered to pursue a romantic relationship, obviously because she was still so hung up on Patrick. But I don't elaborate. Let him come to that conclusion all on his own. I think I'm providing enough.

"So why now? After all this time and the fact that you two were recently involved, why show me this video and tell me her real reason for leaving me? Forgive me for seeming dense, but I just don't get it."

"Because I love her."

"Huh?"

"And because she loves you. Always has, and probably always will." I have to look away to hide the pain of saying those words out loud. I think I'd rather someone pull off my fingernails one by one than to have to hear how Suzanna loves another man more than she loves me. "Listen, I don't have the first clue about what your relationship is with your fiancée. Katelyn, right?"

Patrick nods, but doesn't give me any insight into his and Katelyn's relationship.

"Well, if you love Katelyn, and I hope you do if you asked her to be your wife, then by all means go ahead and get married today. You have my blessing for a future full of wedded bliss. But if there's any doubt that Katelyn may not be the one for you...if you feel anything other than friendship for Suzanna, any lingering romantic interest where she's concerned, I beg you to think twice about getting hitched today. Think one last time about Suzanna and if you're really, *really* ready to leave her behind." There, I said it. I'm basically handing Suzanna to him on a silver platter. Damn, I must be the stupidest man alive. But I love that girl so much I'm willing to sacrifice my own happiness for hers. And if Patrick is truly the man to make her happy, then my job is done.

Having said all I came to say, I start to make my way to the door. I stop before exiting the room when Patrick asks, "So you really love her?"

"With all my heart."

"But you're going to give her up?" Patrick questions.

"I'm giving her you. Don't make me regret it," I say in warning, my words commanding. If he so much as hurts one strand of hair on her beautiful head, I will hunt him down and make his life a living hell. His look of understanding tells me he seriously heeds my warning.

"Thank you," Patrick adds before I depart. I can't acknowledge his gratitude because my surrender hurts too badly. Maybe one day I'll be able to tell him 'You're welcome'. It just won't come anytime soon.

After leaving Patrick alone in his room, I get in my car and drive straight to the airport. I don't have any desire to stick around for the fireworks that I'm sure will explode when Patrick confronts his father. Nor do I want to find out if the wedding gets cancelled. All I want to do is park myself on a barstool inside the airport and drink until I'm numb. So as I arrive hours before my flight is scheduled to board, I find the only bar in my terminal and proceed to get drunk as I wait for my flight to be called. Thirty minutes into my second drink, straight whiskey, my phone vibrates in my pocket. I've been avoiding the incoming texts I've received since leaving New York. I'm sure the majority of them are work related. But I don't think the mighty conglomerate of Galloway and Meads will fall while my measly intern self takes a couple days of vacation.

I'm also avoiding the texts from Tess, my co-worker. The only female co-worker on my team. I've got the impression that Tess wants more between us than just being colleagues. She's been a little touchy feely the last couple of times we've worked late into the night. I've brushed off her advances as politely as I can, basically ignoring them and pretending they didn't happen. It's not that Tess isn't appealing. Although she hides behind her tougher than nails business persona, she's actually a sweet girl. Not only that, she is easy on the eyes too. Long auburn hair, usually fixed in one of those classy up dos, big jade green eyes, and smooth fair skin, all combine to make Tess a real beauty. Yeah, so I've noticed her attributes. Can't blame me with the amount of time we spend together. And under normal circumstances, that green light she's been sending my way would have me making the next move. But since arriving in New York, not Tess or any other beautiful woman could stop the thoughts of the one person that's constantly consuming my brain. Suzanna. Even those few months when I thought I'd never see her again, after I broke up with her under false assumptions, I still couldn't fathom being with someone else. Then, after our brief encounter over July fourth weekend, when she unexpectedly came to New York to seek me out and get some answers, there wasn't another woman who could touch my radar after the time we spent together. Well, the short amount of time we spent together. I'd wanted to show her my new world, wanted to keep her with me as long as possible. But she chose instead to run back to her long time ex, concerned about minor injuries he sustained in a boating accident. Didn't matter if he just had a hangnail...she'd still run back to him. Always would, and probably always will. I drain what's left of my drink and motion to the bartender for a refill at the disturbing thought. It shouldn't still hurt when I realize I'll never be the top priority in her life. I mean, I realized that as soon as she left New York. That's exactly why I'm sitting in the airport now. Having come to terms with the fact that Suzanna's one true love is Patrick, not me. So being the great guy that I am (although I don't feel so great, I feel like a dumbass), I did the only thing I could think of in my last attempt to make Suzanna happy. I laid out the truth to Patrick in hopes that he'd put the brakes on his marriage and run. Run straight into the open arms of Suzanna. Ugh, that visual makes the liquor in my stomach rise up my throat.

Quickly I need something else to visualize. Maybe it's time to look at Tess in a different light. I conjure up some erotic scenario of the two of us working together late at night. She loosens that hair of hers, letting in fall down her neck and back. She loses the stuffy suit jacket and unbuttons her blouse, just enough for her ample cleavage to be on display. Then she makes her move. In what's supposed to be an innocent exchange of papers, she drops them on the table in front of where I'm sitting. Her breasts make contact with my back as she leans over, slightly pressing her body into mine. Normally, this is when I ignore her blatant body language signaling her desire to do more than investment banker work. But this time, I'm letting myself give in. Since I've given up Suzanna, letting her go to find her true happiness with Patrick, it's time I take something for myself. Turning in my chair, I'm eye level to Tess's chest, her breasts straining against the fabric of her shirt demanding to be released. Sliding my hands around her waist, I pull her closer until my face is almost buried in her cleavage. I inhale, her feminine scent the agent that spurs me on. My lips make contact with her skin and I can't stop the flick of my tongue, wanting to see what she tastes like. I feel her body tremble as my licks against her increase. The sounds she makes are foreign to me. Sure they are sexy moans and meows, but they don't contain the familiar tone and pitch I'm used to hearing in my dreams. Because they don't belong to Suzanna.

No! Stop it! I command my brain pushing thoughts of Suzanna away. I'm letting her go. Therefore, she has no right to appear in my imaginary sex scene. Amping it up to keep her away, I decide I'm gonna get down to business with Tess. Like really fast. Having enough of this teasing, I grab the edges of Tess's open shirt and rip it apart, the buttons on her ruined blouse bouncing off the wall and the floor. Still keeping my eyes on her torso, I watch as her chest rises and falls as she takes rapid breaths. Impatient to get her naked, my hands skate across her flat stomach inching around her waist to her back to find my target. I quickly unsnap the clasp of her bra and remove the last of the clothing from her upper body. Then I quickly start to work on undressing the rest of her. Her skirt falls to her feet when I unzip it. I don't take any time in removing her underwear, pushing them down her legs in haste. Finally, I have a beautiful willing woman standing before me wearing nothing but a pair of heels. I'm starting to feel the first signs of my arousal, my cock twitching in my pants. Then she speaks. "Wyatt," she whispers and I can't miss the desire in her voice. This should have my dick straining against my zipper. But it only has the opposite effect. Because her voice isn't the one I want to hear full of longing. *Dammit Suzanna, quit plaguing my dreams!* The girl is becoming a real pain in my ass, acting as a cock blocker even in my head! Oh no, I'm not letting that happen.

Needing to fulfill this fantasy, I let my hands wander over Tess's hips and down her thighs. Retracing my downward movements, my hands travel up and slide inward their destination being the apex between her legs. Landing on my target, I find Tess hot and wet. She begins to speak my name again, but before the 'W' sound is out of her mouth I bark, "Don't speak. Don't make a fucking sound!" Harsh, I know. But I've got to finish this without you know who making another unwelcome appearance. I watch my fingers disappear in the patch of dark curls, cropped short and tight. I run my finger through the wetness of her folds spreading her juices from her entrance to her clit. I hear the sounds Tess struggles to keep at bay. At least she's being submissive and adhering to my demands. Good girl. Circling her hole, I push in one finger, then add another. In and out, in and out, I finger fuck her hoping to regain my own arousal. The thought of another piece of my anatomy other than my fingers, doing the exact same thing, gets the job done. Soon I have no choice but to release the beast from the confines of my pants. Hey, this is my fantasy so if I want to call my dick a beast, so be it!

With one of my hands still going to town between Tess's legs, my other one stokes my dick. Fully ready to complete this, I stand letting my pants and boxers fall down to my ankles. I'm still looking downward as I turn switching our positions so Tess is now backed up against the conference table. My body presses into hers, giving her no other option than to sit on the edge of the table. She does so, immediately spreading her legs. So willing. I take my position between her knees, my dick twitching to make contact. Still looking downward I rub my head against her glistening pussy. Watching as I position myself at her entrance I'm prepared to push in, finally engaging in the act of sex with someone other than Suzanna. Well, not really. I mean, this is just my imagination at work. But at least it's a start. Baby steps, I remind myself. Just as I'm about to get inside Tess, she cradles my face in her hands lifting my head to meet her face. *Shit!*

This is all wrong! Where's the honey wheat colored mane, streaked with natural golden highlights? Where are the steely blue eyes, looking at me with so much love and devotion? Where is the sun kissed skin, from long days of being outside? I see none of those things. All I see is auburn hair, fiery green eyes, and too fair skin. The total opposite of what I crave. And with this sighting, there goes my erection. There goes my whole fantasy. Up in smoke. I'm still so wrapped up in Suzanna Caulder I can't even finish my imaginary sexcapade. Pathetic!

Shaking my head to rid it of that mental disaster, I formulate a new plan. If my head won't cooperate, then I'll just have to make my body get the job done. What I need is the real thing. Actual flesh and bones standing before me. There's no way I'll ever be able to stop if that's the case. Yeah, it's time to move on. Leave Suzanna as an afterthought and focus on what I can have waiting for me when I return to New York. So while still under the effects of alcohol I'm determined to follow through with a life that no longer includes Suzanna. I know just how to do that. I pull out my phone anticipating seeing a text from Tess. I plan to text her back with more than an invitation to get caught up on work. But it's not a text from Tess that I see. Lo and behold, Suzanna has made contact. And it's not just to say hello. Although it's only three little words, those words stab at my heart like a freshly sharpened dagger. *I need you.* Ah hell, what have I done?

Chapter Thirty Four

"Please help me in congratulating the winner of the 2014 Southern Qualifying Tournament and the newest card holding member of the United States Ladies Professional Golf Association...Miss Suzanna Caulder." The crowd breaks out in thunderous applause as Ms. Besset announces me as the winner. We do the traditional hand shake before she hands me a trophy half the size of my body. "Well done, Suzanna. Congratulations."

"Thank you," I say as I raise the trophy over my head. I don't think she heard me because the crowd noise increases as I show off my new hardware. I slowly turn so that every patron of the game who came to watch can catch a glimpse of my accomplishment. I spot Callie in her wheelchair hooting and hollering like a cheerleader on steroids. My parents are standing behind her watching the trophy presentation. Dad is beaming, a smile full of pride stretched across his face. Mom smiles too, as tears of joy run down her cheeks. I find it hard not to shed my own tears. But I manage to keep them at bay, although my eyes fill with water. However, there's no keeping the happiness off my face. I'm positive I'm showing all my teeth as I pose for pictures with my winning trophy. The big wig sponsors are all here on the last day of the tournament to take part in the post tournament presentation. Also, the reigning president of the LPGA, Ms. Besset, is here as well, smiling for the camera. Bet she's glad Callie went along with her bribe to let me in the tournament. The golf I played today was nothing short of amazing.

It was hard waking up this morning to find my text to Wyatt had not been answered. Maybe I should have elaborated. But who pours out their feelings in a text? It's no secret to him how I feel. Since leaving New York, I've reminded him everyday how much I love him. And the times he did respond, his answers were short and to the point. One day he responded with 'I know'. Another day his response was texted back as a one word question...'Enough?' I kinda got the gist of what he was getting at, but it still hurt that he didn't return my sentiments of love. Not once. So, when I was down in the depths of failure and despair, at a critical moment in my life...miserable play on the third day of the most important golf tournament of my life...the only person I wanted to help make it better was Wyatt. So I sent him the text with those three significant words...I need you. I wanted him to know that I not only loved him, but I needed him, in every moment of my life, during the good and the bad. But he either didn't get the text or chose to ignore it.

So when Callie found me this morning, mourning not only the loss of my lead in the tournament but also the loss of the most important man in my life, well she was none too happy. She threatened to bitch slap me if I didn't manage to get it together. I tried to rein in my tears, and yeah, my sobs finally turned into to sniffles, but she still wasn't impressed. After sitting me down and giving me the vague details of the events leading up to her accident, I finally began to emerge from my funk. Callie told me that she is no longer able to compete on the course all because of a guy. A guy she once loved. Up until now, I never really saw Callie as the committed type. But apparently she was head over heels for someone during her college years. She left out a bunch of the story, breezing over some important parts. But her raw deep pain was evident as she recounted how she let a personal relationship mess with her head, so much so it eventually took away her dream of playing golf professionally. I was shocked speechless when she finished not really knowing what to say. Seeing Callie stripped bare of the walls she erected to hide behind was something I wasn't accustomed to. When she begged me to let everything go, thoughts of Wyatt, wondering where Patrick and Katelyn were headed on their honeymoon, worrying about Chloe in Hollywood, hoping Flynn was behaving and keeping it in his pants in Europe, just about everything that was cluttering my brain, I couldn't not try when I heard the pleading tone in her voice. I don't think I'd ever seen Callie be more sincere and honest.

So I mustered up every fiber in my being and demanded they give me the strength I'd need to get to the finish line today as a winner. I pushed all thoughts of everything and everyone else in my mind away and concentrated on the one constant in my life...golf. Well, Wyatt did try to sneak in a couple of times. And since I was using all my will to fight to win on the course, a few times I let him enter my thoughts. But the sadness I felt earlier when I thought of him was replaced with reaffirmed determination. Just as I was refocusing on my golf game, hitting every shot like it'd be my last, I decided I'd take the same approach with Wyatt. He wanted my all? Well as soon as I won this blasted tournament, I'd show him all I had to give. He better watch out.

I played like a woman possessed today. Having to dig out of the hole I created yesterday with my crappy play, I approached each hole with a vengeance. At some holes I played conservatively, just hoping to make par. This was only effective enough to get back within second place. Which by my standards wasn't good enough. Who wants a second place finish? Then it dawned on me. That strange conversation I had with Wyatt before I left him in New York. He was being very cryptic using my golf game to make a point. I told him then that it always felt worse to finish in second place rather than further down in the field. Because second place was too close to first and the failure of not getting to the next step hurt more. Well shit! Is that how Wyatt felt about my feelings for him? Was he always comparing himself to Patrick and the rest of my friends, never thinking he finished first with me? What's worse is what if I made him think that? It couldn't be more far from the truth in my eyes, but my actions as of late told a different story. I'd have to prove that I could finish first in this tournament. Then I'd make it my top priority to prove to Wyatt that he will always be my first place prize.

From that revelation on, I attacked each golf hole with a renewed fervor. When the other golfers were laying back, I'd swing for the stars praying I'd position myself closer to the green, thus eliminating a shot. And it worked. The calculated risks I took paid off. So when I found myself putting on the eighteenth green with a two stroke lead, I could barely believe it. Although I had to wait for the pairings behind me to come in and finish the course, I still was hopeful seeing as only one other competitor had a chance to beat me. When she faltered on her tee shot on the eighteenth fairway, I knew I had won.

Now, as I hug my trophy close to my body for one last photograph, I'm almost full of elation. Almost being the key word. See I've come to realize that yes, I've fulfilled my dream of becoming a professional golfer. And I know there's a promising career in my future. But a future without the man that I love, a future without Wyatt, keeps me from feeling completely happy. I guess when someone is a part of you, a part of your mind, soul, and body...it's hard to be anything other than a percentage to the whole. I won't be whole until I have both golf and Wyatt in my life.

The post tournament chaos has me enjoying the quietness of the locker room. Most of the competitors have filed out, offering me their congratulations as they departed. Dad's been busy since my win was announced, hounded with phone calls from potential agents and sponsors. Mom is on her phone as well, telling anyone she knows about my win. After the obligatory photographs, Callie gave me a humongous hug in which no words were needed. Her silent thank you for doing what she failed to do years ago was received as she wrapped me up in her arms, a very un-Callie like show of emotion. Drew was gracious when I told him I'd never have been able to win without his abundant knowledge of the game and his caddying skills. And Coach Moore, well, he was so excited he invited everyone out for dinner and drinks on his dime. God bless him! I'm sure they are waiting for me to join them so the party can officially start. But I need just a few more minutes for this to all sink in and figure out my next move.

In the silence of being alone, I close my eyes to clear my mind. In my meditative state I don't notice when someone enters the locker room until I hear a voice. "That was quite a show you put on out there today."

The deep baritone is all too familiar. I look up in a state of confusion when my eyes meet his. "Shouldn't you be on your honeymoon?" I ask Patrick.

"If I'd gotten married, yes, I suppose so."

"You cancelled the wedding?" I question again.

"*We*, both Katelyn and I, cancelled the wedding. It was a mutual decision, one we both feel good about." Patrick approaches me slowly and I can see the weight that had been lifted off of him. I knew there was something fishy about their engagement and I can't wait to find out the details.

"Tell me what happened," I say and pat the seat beside me.

"I will, but not now. It's a long story that will take too much time."

"You have somewhere you gotta be?" Here I go with yet another question. But he's got me so confused by being here I just need to get some answers for any of this to make sense.

"That depends." *Really?* My frustration builds at his vagueness. I think back to the moment he alerted me to his presence. He must have arrived early enough to watch the final round of the tournament considering his statement about how I played. Maybe once the wedding was called off he bolted from the church and drove straight here. I would have knowing how his dad would react. Oh gosh, his dad? I bet he is furious. For some unknown reason he was set for this marriage to take place. And he was holding out on treatment until Patrick tied the knot. That's the only way Patrick would consider entering into a loveless marriage...his father's promise to get help once the wedding took place. But now...

"Wait! If you didn't get married, then what...what's gonna happen to your dad? Is he still gonna get help?"

"The fact that you care whether or not my dad gets helps or drinks himself to death makes me love you that much more. But to answer your question, I checked Dad into a treatment center this morning in Charleston. It was either that or jail."

"Jail? What in the world did he do?"

"Suzanna," Patrick says softly. He turns so that we are face to face, our eyes locking onto each other's. "I know."

The sympathetic and apologetic look in his eyes tells me he is aware of my secret. But I have to ask anyway. "I, um....I don't.... understand. W-what...do...you know?" I avert my gaze to stare at my hands that are now twisting nervously in my lap.

"I know what my dad did to you. What he tried to do to you." Patrick shudders as if he's visualizing the entire thing. His hands are fisted so tightly his knuckles turn white. Taking a deep breath, he slowly releases his death grip and calms down. "Suzanna, look at me."

Moments tick by before I garner enough courage to look at him. When I lift my head, tears spill from my eyes. He gently takes his hand and wipes away the wetness from my face. His tenderness is too much and I have this overwhelming need to explain. "I'm so sorry. I didn't know what to do. I didn't want you to find out, like ever. That's why I left when I did. I couldn't tell you. It was wrong, but I was so scared. I'm so sorry. I should have told you." The words run out of my mouth at such a rapid pace I have to stop to catch my breath. That and to release the sob clogging my throat.

"Hey, Suz. Don't cry. And don't you dare apologize. You did nothing wrong. Nothing! Yes, I wish you had told me. But I understand why you didn't. I can't imagine what you were going through..." Patrick pulls me into his chest as I continue to let out tears from four years ago. I'm soaking his shirt, but he doesn't seem to care. "I'm the one that's sorry. I can apologize for my dad, not that it'll do much good. I don't expect you to forgive him. God knows I'll never be able to. But I am sorry I just let you go. I was so heartbroken when you left I let my emotions cloud my judgment. I thought the worst of you because that was the easiest way to deal with what I was going through. I wanted to hate you. I really did. But I couldn't. Granted, when you told me you were leaving for golf of all things, I was so angry. That you would pick golf over us, it was mind boggling. I never quite believed that excuse completely. That's why when I saw you again after all these years it was one of the first things I asked you. When you held strong to your story I made it my mission to find out the truth. Now, I wish it had only been golf that sent you packing."

"Yeah, me too," I say through a sniffle. I pry my face from Patrick's chest and look up to see he has tears in his eyes too.

"I'm so fucking sorry, Suz. I should have tracked you down, begged you until you had no other choice than to tell me the truth, whether I wanted to hear it or not. I should have fought harder for you. And I'll have to live with the regret of not doing that until the day that I die."

"Patrick, please...no regrets. No about us." He nods and pulls me back into his arms. We sit like that releasing all the pent up emotions of years gone by. This is the closure I was searching for at the beginning of this journey. And though it's heartbreaking, in its own way, it's also freeing.

Once our emotions are stabilized I mutter the thought that runs through my head. "I can't believe your dad confessed. I can't believe he told you."

"He didn't."

"What? Then how...?" My brain spins out of control about who else knew about the events of that night. It's only a small amount of people, and other than Patrick's dad, they are all currently out of the state. Well, with the exception of Mrs. Stokes. But I doubt she'd make Patrick privy to my secret. All this time I thought she was Team Wyatt.

"Wyatt paid me a visit yesterday at the church. Right before the wedding." That can't be right. Wyatt is in New York. Isn't he?

"Suzanna, let me ask you a question. What gave you back your mojo today?"

"Don't throw a bomb like that and then just change the subject."

"I'm not changing the subject. Just answer the question, please." If I have to play along to Patrick's silly games to find out the whereabouts of Wyatt then so be it.

"I don't know. A few things, I guess."

"Elaborate." I narrow my eyes at Patrick, but he continues to wait patiently until I decide to confide in him. Whatever.

"Well, Callie for one. We had a heart to heart and she shared some personal things that put me in the right mind set."

"And two…"

This is uncomfortable talking to Patrick about Wyatt, but he was the one to help force my comeback. I decided if I could risk it all on the course, then I could risk it all on my heart. I pledged on the course just today that I wouldn't give up on Wyatt being in my future. Plus, we've already bypassed any levels of comfort when we discussed how Patrick's dad attempted to rape me one night. So sharing my feelings for another man, to the man I once loved shouldn't be a problem, right?

"If you must know, I was thinking about Wyatt. You happy now?" I ask in embarrassment. Wow, this is awkward. But I'm surprised to see Patrick smiling at me like he just figured out the answer to global warning.

"Just as I thought," he says smugly. "You love him?"

"More than I thought possible."

"Then we've got to go."

"Patrick, what the hell are you talking about?" I'm not going anywhere until he gives me some answers.

"Look, Wyatt's convinced that you love me."

"I do love you, just not like that. Not anymore."

"I know, Suz." Patrick's smile slips just for a fraction of a second, but he recovers it quickly. "Believe me, I know. And I'm okay with that. I'll take whatever kinda love you're willing to give me. But you've got to go tell Wyatt. Immediately."

"O-okk-aaay."

"Listen, he loves you. And I know this not because he told me he did. But I know how much he loves you because of *what* he did. Not only did he save you from the hands of my father that night. He also had the foresight to make a copy on a disc of the events that happened which were captured via the security camera. Then he erased the footage from the security video so no one else could see it."

"Oh." Wyatt never told me he did all that. To think he's had that disc all this time.

"He showed me the video so that I'd finally realize the real reason you left me. He wanted me to see that you didn't all of a sudden fall out of love with me, but you left because you were trying to protect me." Patrick looks around the room, averting his gaze from me. I can tell by his tense features he's back to thinking about that horrible night. I could try to tell him to forget about it, to let it go. But I've been affected by what happened that night for years now and still haven't been able to put it to rest completely. I can't expect Patrick to do that either, especially since he just gained knowledge of what actually happened.

"I guess his hope was that I'd call off the wedding and come back to you. Which of course, I did both. He thinks for some reason that I'm the one you want, that you're still hopelessly in love with me. And he was trying to make sure that you got your happiness in the end, despite the devastation he'd feel in giving you this final gift. So, he's giving us a second chance. And, well..." Patrick leaves it hanging out there like I might change my mind. I'm not sure if he's being serious or not, but regardless I have to be careful with his feelings.

"Patrick, like I said earlier, I do love you. I always will and hope that you'll continue to be a part of my life. As a friend. You see as much as I love you, I'm not *in love* with you. I'm *in love* with Wyatt." I see the light dim in his eyes and that's when I know he came with the slightest bit of hope that that second chance we'd been gifted might be given a go. But he deserves my honesty. I kept so much from him in the past, I'm not gonna make the same mistake and start lying to him again now. "But I do need to thank you. Because of you I know what true love is. You were the first person that I got to experience that with. And I'll always cherish our time together. We were two young people brought together through friends. And when things developed into more, we handled ourselves with maturity. Even after years apart, the bumps in the road that were no fault of our own, we still manage to stand in front of each other with a friendship that will stand the test of time. I mean, how many people can say that, huh? We're the lucky ones."

"Damn Suz, you're killing me." Patrick pulls me back into a hug and holds on tightly. "That heart of gold you've got is making this next part even harder."

"Next part?" I ask peeking up at him.

"I'm taking you to the Savannah airport. I've booked your flight to New York and reserved you a room for tonight."

"You did?" I'm getting all teary eyed again that Patrick would do all that for me. Especially when he knows I'll be going determined to win back Wyatt. "Why?"

"Because, Wyatt is a saint. Everything he did all those years ago... man, I'll never be able to repay him. But what he did yesterday? He was willing to let you go because he loves you so much. So now it's my turn to let you go. Because, yeah, I love you that much too." The intensity with which he says that last part shakes me to my core. So maybe he hasn't resolved his feelings yet to just a friendship basis. But he'll get there. I know in my heart his one and only is out there waiting. Waiting to meet the one man I've been blessed to have in my life, both at a romantic and platonic level. And I'll be the first one to tell her how lucky she is. Patrick pastes his smile back on and tries to lighten the mood. "Plus, every saint deserves an angel. And you Suzanna Caulder are definitely an angel." He releases me from his embrace and walks around me like he's searching for something.

"What?" I ask after he's circled me twice looking me up and down.

"Just trying to figure out where you're hiding your wings. And your halo."

"Shut. Up!" I say and burst out laughing. Patrick is such a corn-ball. He starts laughing too and I'm so glad we've ended, what began as something serious and dark, on a happy note.

"Come on, oh angelic one. Your chariot awaits!"

Chapter Thirty Five

I wake up with the sun. It takes me a moment to remember I'm in a hotel room in New York City. But as soon as I do my nerves kick up a notch. Of course I've been a nervous wreck since my plane landed late last night. I have to give props to Patrick. He booked me in a really nice hotel. Nice enough that they have a few stores located in the lobby thank goodness. Since I arrived with nothing but the clothes on my back and my winning trophy that was the first stop I made after checking into my room. I bought some essentials...a toothbrush, some clean undies, and a few snacks. Not that I had an appetite. I was much too nervous to eat. The clothing store was just about to close before I ran in to purchase a pair of pjs and some clean clothes to wear today. It's not the most glamorous attire, just a pair of black slacks, a printed flowy blouse, and a pair of black ballet flats. But it sure beats having to put back on my stinky golf clothes from yesterday. Yeah, didn't think I'd have a chance to win back Wyatt's heart if he could barely stand the smell of me. Yuck!

I order a light breakfast and shower while I wait for it to be delivered. When it arrives, I set it on the table by the window and try to eat. Mainly I just push the food around on my plate while I watch the sidewalks down below come to life. As the sun rises the flow of people scurrying to work increases. The traffic becomes heavy clogging the streets. The sounds of horns blaring become more frequent as cars and trucks navigate through the morning rush hour. The city is bustling this morning and it gets me excited. Well, excited and nervous. I can't wait to get out there in the mix of things. But the short walk to Wyatt's office building isn't nearly long enough to calm my nerves.

Give Patrick another star...not only is the hotel nice, but it is centrally located in the business district. I just have a short few blocks to walk before I'll arrive at my destination. A few blocks before I'll come face to face with Wyatt once again. A few blocks before he'll make me the happiest person alive. Or, a few blocks before he'll crush my heart for the second time this summer. Nothing to be nervous about, right? Yeah, right.

After a few bites of breakfast, I can't stomach any more. I head into the bathroom to dry my hair and use the minimal amount of make up I keep stashed in my purse. Thirty minutes later I take one final look in the full length mirror attached to the bathroom door. It's not the best I've ever looked, but it is not the worst either. I just hope it's enough to convince Wyatt to give us one more shot. *Please, please be enough,* I pray.

By 9:00 a.m. I can't wait any longer. I'm jittery enough with the two cups of coffee I've downed. Surely, Wyatt has arrived at work by now. I grab my purse, not forgetting my hotel key card, and begin to exit the room. The shiny metal of my trophy stops me in my tracks. On a whim, I grab it. I might look like an idiot walking the busy sidewalks of New York carrying this hunk of metal around, but its presence is gonna play a big role in convincing Wyatt that we belong together. I hoist the trophy close to my body and begin the trek down the sidewalk, being extra careful not to bump into someone. To my surprise, no one pays me any attention even though I'm hugging a big shiny metal object to my body like it's an extension of a limb. I guess New Yorkers see crazier shit than this on a daily basis. I'm really beginning to love this city. I'm a little winded by the time I arrive at the big glass doors of the high rise that houses Galloway and Meads Investment Bank and Brokerage Services. I almost get run over by the amount of people trying to enter the building. I choose to wait for a lull in traffic seeing as I don't know exactly where I'm supposed to go once I enter. The lobby is massive with banks of elevators on both sides. At the center, there's a receptionist sitting behind a massive desk. I also see several security guards. A couple of them are stationed at the elevators and another is sitting with a receptionist, watching footage from the live security cameras. I approach and offer a smile before asking, "Which floor is Galloway and Meads located?"

"They are on the 12th floor. Just take the elevators to your right," the receptionist answers with her own smile. Who said New Yorkers were rude?

"Thank you very much." I walk away and wait in line for an elevator car to open. Several people enter the small elevator that I'm on so I crunch into the corner to make room. The doors are about to close when someone yells, "Wait!" A kind lady presses the open door key and lets the gentleman enter. He spots me immediately...I mean who wouldn't look twice at the girl hunched in the corner carrying a trophy half the size of her body. The initial puzzlement on his face turns into recognition and he maneuvers between the packed bodies to come to stand by me.

"Suzanna, right?" I'm startled at first that he knows my name. But after taking a good look at the guy he too seems familiar.

"Yes, I'm Suzanna. Please forgive me. It seems we've met, and you do look familiar. But I can't recall your name."

"Of course you wouldn't remember my name. We had barely been introduced before Wyatt whisked you out of the restaurant. After he called me off your friend. I'm still pissed at him for that, by the way." Then it hits me. Brice. We met briefly when Chloe and I were in New York. The same night Wyatt and I reconnected.

"Brice, it's good to see you again."

"So, you do remember?" He gives me that smile that I'm certain has an effect on many women. However, I still think of it more as a smirk, not at all genuine. "Wyatt didn't say anything about you being back in town."

"He doesn't know. It's a surprise."

"You're fond of surprises it seems," he comes back quickly. "I think last time he was surprised by you then as well."

"Yeah, well, I've got some groveling to do." I look down at my feet embarrassed to have to admit that to Wyatt's co-worker/friend. "Anyway, I'd like to keep it from Wyatt that I'm here until I see him. Can you help keep it a secret?"

"I'll do you one better. I'll sneak you into his office."

"Really? Oh, that would be great. But is he not in yet?" I thought these interns worked extremely long hours, early mornings until late at night. Especially those that want to get noticed and get offered a permanent position. That would definitely be Wyatt.

"Yeah, he and Tess arrived earlier today, but they are both in a meeting on another floor."

It's not the elevator stopping at the next floor that has my heart dropping to my feet. No, it's the information Brice just shared so easily. Almost like Wyatt's and Tess's arrival today is an everyday occurrence. What if I'm too late? What if Wyatt has moved on with Tess? I try to hide my disappointment, but apparently it's written all over my face.

"Hey, what did I say?" Brice asks, but then doesn't have to wait for my answer. As if a light bulb went off inside his head, Brice immediately starts explaining. "Oh, you think Tess and Wyatt are together, like together together? No, that's not the case. Unless I've missed something. I just meant they arrived at the same time. From different locations. You got it?"

"Um yeah, sure. No need to explain that to me." But he did need to explain it. Not that I entirely believe him. I can't say I find Brice to be the most trustworthy guy. Plus, after seeing the possessiveness Tess displayed during our one and only meeting at the bar, I could totally detect that her feelings for Wyatt might have crossed that work relationship line. At least, in her case. Wyatt was quick to dismiss her that night. But with everything that has happened since then, I can't be sure he's still holding off her advances. My stomach is tied up in knots and I'm regretting the few bites of breakfast I forced down. These new developments are enough to have me thinking about bailing. But because I can't be certain about what has or hasn't gone on between Wyatt and Tess, I deserve to at least hear it from the horse's mouth. My nervousness has spiked and I'm also full of trepidation, but I choose to forge ahead.

Luckily I don't have to stand and feel Brice staring at me for too long. The elevator quickly rises to the 12th floor. When the doors open, Brice leads the way and I follow. He says hello to the pretty girl on duty as the receptionist for this floor. I peg her correctly as one of the women I thought of earlier that are indeed affected by Brice's charm. What, with the way she bats her eyes and juts out her chest, you'd think Brice was on the verge of asking for her hand in marriage. All he said was good morning, for goodness sakes. There's a lot I'd like to tell that woman, but she's too busy ignoring me for me to waste my breath on a lecture. So I continue to remain invisible as I slink behind Brice down the hallway.

We walk through a maze of cubicles and more reception desks, until I think I'll never be able to find my way out. Finally we stop in front of a slightly opened door. Brice pushes it open to reveal an office the size of a walk-in closet. There's only room for a desk and a small filing cabinet. "Well, this is it. Wyatt's home away from home. It's not much, but you gotta start somewhere, right?" I squeeze through the door. With just us two inside the small room feels crowded.

"You need anything while you wait?" Brice asks.

"No thank you, I'm good." Brice nods and makes to leave. "Hey, do you know how long Wyatt will be in his meeting?"

Brice looks down at his shiny watch. I'm sure it is a luxury brand. "They've been in there for over an hour now, so it shouldn't be that much longer."

"Okay, thanks."

"Good luck Suzanna...with that groveling thing and all. Wyatt's a good guy. I hope things work out the way you hope." Brice leaves then and I start to reconsider my opinion of him. Other than insinuating that Wyatt and Tess might have a thing, he's been nothing other than accommodating and nice. And he didn't even say anything about the fact that I'm lugging around a trophy. Well, he is a native to the area. I'm sure he has seen his share of crazies. Still I'm glad he didn't see the need to call me out on my crazy.

I watch the minutes tick by slowly on the clock hanging above the closed door. Ten minutes in, I hear footsteps outside the door. I listen as mumbled voices talk rapidly about figures and numbers that I both don't understand nor have any interest in. But my interest is peaked when I hear the softer sound of a female that enters the conversation. As the footsteps and voices get closer, the conversation changes from business to personal. "So, you want to celebrate tonight with drinks?" the unidentified female asks.

"Sounds good. Let's just see how the day goes and we'll check with each other later?" Now that voice is unmistakable. Wyatt must be standing right outside his door for his words are clear as day.

"Come on Wyatt, you know what they say...all work and no play..." the female teases in an annoying whine. I guarantee I know her identity now. It's got to be Tess.

"Yeah, yeah. Okay one drink, then I'm turning in early," Wyatt relents.

"We'll see about that," the female responds, her voice fading away. "Catch you later, Wyatt."

"Later Tess."

Bingo! I knew it, knew it was Tess that was flirting with my man. While I compile a mental list of all the nasty things I want to tell her, like how she'll be lucky to ever have a drink with Wyatt again, the sound of the door knob turning puts a stop to my bitchiness. I take a huge breath and press my body back into the corner I'm hiding in. The door opens and I get the first glimpse of Wyatt. Boy, does he look hot! All dressed up in his business attire...the man wears a suit very well. Can't really blame Tess for trying now, can I? What with him looking like the very sexy, powerful hot shot he is... *Not the time to drool, Suz*, I mentally chastise myself and redirect my thoughts. He is looking down at the papers in his hands when he enters his small office. He walks the few steps to his desk before he notices anything different. It's not until he has almost rounded the largest piece of furniture in his small work space that his stride falters. He takes a few steps back and quizzically studies the two and a half foot tall trophy that sits atop his work space bearing my name.

"I won," I say.

He whips his head around and spots me leaning against the wall. "Suzanna?"

I take two small steps forward bringing me closer to Wyatt. "I won the golf tournament."

"Yeah, I can see that," he says his eyes darting between me and my trophy. "Congratulations."

We stand looking at each other neither of us knowing how to continue. I was at least hoping for a smile, but Wyatt seems perplexed, angry even. His brows bunch together and there's tension in his face. "Suz, what are you doing here?" he asks finally breaking the silence.

"I've come to collect my first place prize."

"Isn't that what the trophy is for?" he asks gesturing with his hands to the metal object. "Looks like you've already received recognition for your winning finish."

"A prize for my golf accomplishment, yes. But I'm looking for more. I'm looking for the prize that represents more than just four days of playing great golf. I'm looking for the prize that doesn't come with a trophy to place on a shelf. I'm looking for the prize of a lifetime. The prize I'm determined to fight for until it's mine. Forever. That prize is you Wyatt. You are and will always finish in first place with me. And together, whether we win or lose in this life, you'll always be with me in the final pairing."

"Don't do this Suzanna," he warns his voice deadly serious.

"Why?"

"Because I'm not your number one prize. We both know you're only here by default."

"Default? What are you talking about?" I have a pretty good idea where this is heading, but I want him to clarify, just so I can prove how wrong he is.

"Don't play dumb with me. Even while you were trying to win a golf tournament, I seriously doubt you forgot what else was happening in South Carolina this weekend."

"And what would that be?" I ask already knowing the answer.

"Patrick's wedding," he says raising his voice. He rakes his fingers through his hair in frustration. He mutters, "Damn him, that stupid fuck," under his breath but I manage to hear each insulting word.

"Ah yes, the wedding that everyone keeps talking about. Seems I did hear something about that," I say nonchalantly playing along.

"Thought you'd be a little more torn up about it. But I guess you can't really break out in tears in front of me. Especially when you're trying your best to win me back. That's why you're really here, isn't it Suz? You can't have Patrick since he's officially a married man so you're settling for the next best option, which is me, right?" Whoa, this is worse than I thought. I knew he had some insecurity about any lingering feelings I might have where Patrick was concerned. But he is honestly convinced that I'd choose Patrick over him. Well, it's time to set him straight, once and for all.

"Patrick isn't married. Actually, he is very single." I wait and let Wyatt comprehend those words. I know the moment they sink in. His jaw slacks open and his eyes round in surprise.

"W-wh-aaa-t?" he stutters, too shocked to speak normally.

"Patrick and Katelyn cancelled the wedding. I'm surprised you didn't know already, what, with your visit to Patrick on Saturday. Isn't that what you wanted?" I ask walking closer so that I'm standing right in front of Wyatt, totally invading his personal space.

"Suz," he begins but I cut him off.

"That was your plan, right? Spill my dirty secret so Patrick would stop the wedding and run straight back to my open arms? You thought you had it all figured out. But you were wrong, Wyatt. So very wrong. You see, Patrick and Katelyn never wanted to get married in the first place. It's too long of a story to get into right now, but let's just say they were both being coerced into a loveless marriage that would benefit their parents. Sure, you provided Patrick with the leverage he needed to go up against his dad and stop the wedding. But it had nothing to do with him wanting to be with me or vice versa."

"I'm sorry, Suz," Wyatt apologizes sounding guilty.

"You're sorry? For what exactly? Telling Patrick my secret? Or not coming to me first to talk to me about how I felt?" I should be angry that he took such drastic measures without consulting me. But I can't really be angry at him. In all honesty, what he did only makes me love him more.

"For everything."

"Don't be sorry, Wyatt. You did nothing wrong. I'm the one that should be apologizing. If I ever made you feel like you ranked anywhere other than at the top with me, well then I'm the one so very, very sorry. I let you wrongly interpret me helping Patrick with all the drama he was going through with this engagement. And I don't blame you for coming to incorrect conclusions every time I ran back to Patrick. I didn't make you privy to some of the information I learned this summer. So you had every right to think my feelings for Patrick trumped my feelings for you. I was only trying to protect Patrick, just as I've been doing for years now. However, Patrick no longer needs my protection thanks to you. I'm grateful that Patrick finally knows the real reason I left him during high school. We've talked about it and now he is trying to deal with knowing the ugly truth. I'll be supportive and help him if he needs me, because that is what friends do. And Patrick and I are friends, only friends. He'll continue to be a part of my life, but only in that capacity." For me, my explanation will never be enough for the way I made Wyatt feel inferior. I vow to work every day to make it up to him, show him how much he means to me, if he gives me the chance.

"So now that I no longer have to be his protector, I'm here today to set the record straight." I cup his face in my hands so that I can look directly into his eyes when I say what I have to say next. "Never, and I mean never, have I loved a man the way that I love you. What Patrick and I shared all those years ago was special. But it pales in comparison to what I shared with you. You are my every thing, the one I want to wake up to every morning and the last person I want to see when I close my eyes at night. I can collect all the first place finisher trophies to fill an entire house. But they wouldn't mean a damn thing if the one person who finishes first in my life wasn't there with me in victory. There's no one else that's even in the same league as you that could compete for my heart. Actually, there's not even a competition because you've already won it. You've won my mind, my body and my soul, Wyatt. Now, I'm asking you to let me be a real winner. Let me win your heart. Because there's no other prize in the entire world I'd like to have."

With a sigh, Wyatt closes his eyes. I maintain our physical connection keeping my palms against his cheeks. I want him to not only hear my words, but to feel their meaning. Plus, selfishly I just like touching him. I don't want to think it, but if he doesn't give us a second chance, this may be the last time I feel his skin beneath mine. A few moments later, Wyatt opens his eyes and our gazes lock. He remains stoic so I can't get a good read on his expression. But since he hasn't pulled away from me, I take it as a good sign. Just when I'm about to close the gap between us, desperately needing to feel his lips against mine, he takes several steps back. The distance he creates causes my hands to fall from his face breaking our contact. I feel the loss immediately. I take a step closer, but he takes a step back, shaking his head. "Suz, I um....I," he mumbles. Then he steps around me and covers the short distance to the door.

"Wyatt? No, don't leave me" I beg, but he's gone, disappearing out of his office door and down the hallway. "I love you," I whisper although I know he can't hear me. I knew there was a chance he'd reject me, but I didn't give it much credence. I thought once he heard everything I had to say, he'd gladly let me back in his life, picking up right where we left off. But obviously I was too late for him to consider giving me that second chance. Even though I know he loves me and God knows I love him, I guess the hurt I caused him is too much to get over. Tears leak heavily from my eyes. I turn my back on the door and brace my arms on his desk, needing it to keep me upright. My tears turn into sobs, racking my entire body. I'm so, so sad. But I'm also angry, not at Wyatt for walking away, but at myself for waiting all summer to tell him how much he means to me. My anger builds until I feel like I'm going to explode. Needing to release my pent up frustration I scream loudly while my arm swipes across the desk, taking the contents on its surface to the floor. The noise in the small office intensifies as papers, files, a phone, a laptop, printer, and finally my trophy all come crashing down on top of each other. I don't care about the mess I've made nor about the damage I have caused. The only thing remaining atop the desk is the tiny puddles of water where my tears have landed.

I'm still standing in the same spot, bracing myself against the desk, when I hear the door reopen and close again. Frightened that my earlier outburst may have been misinterpreted as a disgruntled client, I wouldn't be surprised if security had been called. I calm myself enough to stand without the aid of the desk. Now, with free hands, I wipe away the wetness on my face. Taking a deep inhale, I prepare myself to leave...that or be escorted out. "Give me a minute to clean up this mess," I say kneeling at the pile of destruction I created on the floor, "and I'll be on my way."

I sense the presence of someone closing in behind me. A warm breath blows across the skin of my neck, causing goose bumps on my flesh. The feather light touch of lips makes a trail to my ear. "Where do you think you're going? Forever Suz, remember?" Wyatt whispers. I'm too caught up in what his nearness is doing to my body that at first I don't register his words. Slowly, I turn my head to see his gorgeous face just inches from mine. "Forever," he says again replaying my words from earlier. He extends his hand and I eagerly grab it. He helps me up so that we are now standing toe to toe. His finger gently glides across my face, wiping away a stray tear I left behind in my hasty effort. "What's this?" he asks lifting his finger to show the evidence of my crying.

"I...you...," I struggle to say it out loud. "You left. I thought... you didn't love me anymore. I thought I was too late." I break down again, reliving the moment he walked out of his office.

"Suz, no, no, no. How could I leave you when I've been waiting all summer to hear you say those words? I love you, Suzanna. And from here on out, it's you and me, babe. You're stuck with me. So you sure about all you said? Because if you are, I'm not letting you leave me again. Ever!"

"I've never been more sure of anything in my life."

The conviction of my statement is the green light Wyatt's been waiting for. *Finally*, he crashes his lips to mine in a searing kiss. He barely gives me time to open my mouth before his tongue plunges inside. There's nothing soft or sweet in his actions. Our lips collide in an epic battle, both of us displaying our passion for one another, passion that has only grown exponentially during our time apart. I surrender to his control, melting into his body and relenting to his dominance. Because, really, there's no reason to fight it. He owns me...my entire being belongs to Wyatt.

I wish I could survive on the taste of Wyatt alone. But that little thing called oxygen; yeah I need that to breathe. Reluctantly, I pull out of the kiss before I faint from the lack of air. We both struggle to catch our breaths, the rapid and heavy sounds of our panting filling the otherwise silent room. I'm still wrapped up in Wyatt's arms as his hands roam up and down my back. I have a vice grip around his neck that not even a crow bar could pull a part. He looks down at me resting his forehead against mine. "I love you so much, Suz," he says brushing his lips against mine.

"I love you, too." When Wyatt begins to deepen the kiss, attacking my lips again, I have to pull away and ask, "Hey, where did you go when you left earlier?"

"Oh, that," he grins showing those dimples I adore. "I went to clear my schedule with the boss and tell the receptionist I'd be out the rest of the day. I didn't trust myself to touch you until I could get you back to my apartment and ravish your body into the night."

"Oh," I say as my body heats with thoughts of all the things we'll do at his apartment.

"But since you've cleared my desk..." he throws out as he adjusts our positions so that I'm now pinned against the piece of furniture. He gently leans me back until I'm horizontal with the desk top and he covers my body with his. I'm more than ready to consummate this new beginning of our relationship. I can feel the wetness pooling at the apex between my legs. Not to mention the throbbing ache that accompanies it. But since this is the "new" us, the beginning of our future together, I don't want our love making to take place at his workplace.

"Wyatt," I half giggle, half moan.

"Hummmmm," he says between kisses he plants up and down my neck.

"Take me home."

My body screams at me when he stops lavishing my neck with attention to look down into my eyes. "You want to go home? Like South Carolina home?" he questions.

"No, home...with you. Your home, my home, *our* home. My future is with you, so I'm thinking wherever you are is now home." With my official professional tour card, I can basically live anywhere in the world. As long as I have a place to practice and can travel to the various tournaments. I didn't plan to make this trip permanent, but I can't think of leaving Wyatt ever again. So if he'll have me, I'm moving in. I was serious about this whole future thing and him being a constant in it.

He looks deep in my eyes, reaching the deeps of my soul. "Really?" he asks softly.

"Yes," I whisper confirming my decision with a quick kiss.

"You've made me the happiest man in the world today, Suz."

"And I plan to do that everyday, from now until forever."

He helps me up from the desk. With our hands clasped together, fingers intertwined, he drags me out of his office down the hallway and into the elevator. The ride down to the first floor doesn't take nearly as long at it did when I arrived. Probably because Wyatt kept me occupied the whole time, his mouth and hands doing things that shouldn't normally be done in a public place. Outside the building, he hails a cab, even though his apartment, or should I say *our home*, is only a few blocks away. He continues to rev me up during the short cab ride, so by the time we make it inside his building I'm so hot for him I can't think straight. Good thing he has enough sense to close the apartment door before clothes are being shed until we're both stark naked. He leads me to *our* bed then makes good on that promise to ravish my body. We make love well into the night. When we can no longer fight our exhaustion, he cradles me against his body whispering into my ear, "Goodnight, Suz. I love you."

"I love you, too," I say as my eyes close. But there is no darkness. All I see is the future ahead of me and it glows brightly. I've managed to find the closure I needed in order to move forward. And I couldn't be more excited to make that move with the one man nestled beside me, cradling me in the protectiveness of his arms. My love, my life, my everything....

My ultimate and most cherished prize.

My Wyatt.

THE END

Epilogue

Patrick (Six Months Later)

"Thanks for listening, Lisa," I say as I throw out our empty coffee containers in the hospital bin designated for trash.

"Anytime, Patrick. And thank you for the coffee. I needed that break to get me through the next hours of my shift," Lisa says through a yawn. I can see the effect the long hours working as a nurse are doing to her. I swear, if I didn't know any better, I'd think she lived here at the hospital. She's forever working, taking extra shifts in addition to her regular forty hour week.

"You work too hard," I comment as we walk from the cafeteria to the lobby.

"Hey, medical school is expensive," she says in her defense. James, one of my best friends from childhood and Lisa's live in boyfriend, is close to finishing his first year at the University of South Carolina Medical School in Charleston. And from what I've seen and heard, it's been a difficult year, what with all the studying and exams. James has always been a smart dude and top notch student, but I think he's finding medical school is no joke. Lisa's comment about expenses doesn't sit well with me. It's not like James' parents aren't able to afford his tuition. His dad was my pediatrician all during my childhood and still has a thriving practice in Florence. So his parents certainly aren't hurting for money. Maybe Lisa feels obligated to be the sole provider and cover their costs of living while James is in school. I guess she wants to prove to James' parents that she can pull her own weight. But James' parents love Lisa...as we all do. I'm sure if things were tight they'd be more than glad to help out. The elevator arrives and the doors open, so I don't get to question Lisa about the money issue. She skips inside the car ready to return to work. "Hey, dinner later this week?"

"Absolutely! Maybe we can get James to join us if we can pry his head out of one of his many books."

"Doubtful. Exams are coming up so he's amped up his studying efforts. I may as well be living alone with how much James and I see each other." I don't miss the loneliness in her voice. But she's quick to cover it up. "Why do you think I'm inviting you, huh?"

"And all this time I thought it was because I was irresistible," I tease placing my hand over my heart. "You wound me Lisa. Now that I find out you're just using me for my company."

"You know it, Patrick," she says with a grin. "I'll call you later in the week."

"Sounds good, 'bye Lisa."

"'Bye Patrick. Oh, and think about what I said. I promise it'll get easier." The doors of the elevator close shut before I can disagree. Lisa and I have been meeting regularly during the past six months. My dad is still in the alcohol rehabilitation center located adjacent to the hospital. Although he is finally sober, he still struggles with the demons of his past. And he's got a lot of them. It finally came to light that he caused the car accident that ended my mother's life. Of course, he never intentionally set out to harm my mother, but because of his addiction to alcohol, he made the unwise decision to get behind the wheel of the vehicle while intoxicated, thus crashing the car into a tree. He could have been put away for involuntary manslaughter, but charges were never filed. Thanks to his good 'ole buddy Judge Bostick, who now serves as our governor, evidence was buried to keep my dad out of trouble. My dad would later find out that no good deed goes unpunished. Years later, when Judge Bostick got the opportunity to run for governor in a special election, he knew he needed to convince the citizens of SC that he and his family were good clean cut individuals, with no skeletons hidden somewhere in a closet. Problem was his only daughter, Katelyn; the rebellious debutant who cared nothing about images and wanted only to pursue a career in the music industry. Knowing he wouldn't win an election with the constituents of our conservative southern state, while his daughter was off performing rock and roll shows, baring tattoos and throwing devil horns, he constructed a plan. Enter me. He bribed my dad with the threat of revealing the circumstances surrounding my mother's death. In exchange for my agreement to marry his so-called wayward daughter, he'd keep his mouth shut. He'd also continue to let my dad work at the law firm *my dad* built from the ground up, which Judge Bostick had recently taken over at a steal. My dad's drinking only got worse after my mother's death, which had a dismal effect on his business. Close to going bankrupt, my dad sold the business to Judge Bostick and offered me as a sacrifice in order to continue working as an attorney at the law firm. Thinking I'd be saving my dad from losing his life's work, I agreed to not only the arranged marriage, but also to attend law school so that I could be exploited during the campaign as not only the soon to be perfect son in law, but also as the next generation of great attorneys to take over the "family" business.

It sounds preposterous, I know. But what was even crazier was that I was going along with it. Of course I didn't know the real reason my dad was so persistent that I become engaged to a practical stranger. I just thought I was helping my dad out. He'd been so depressed since the loss of my mom. Plus, he was the only immediate family I had left. So yeah, I agreed to marry Katelyn. Stranger yet, Katelyn agreed to participate in the farce set up by our parents. I'd like to think it was my winning charm and handsome looks that convinced her to give up her future, but she had other reasons for being pushed into the arrangement. We played the loving couple so well, that for months no one questioned our out-of-the-blue, sudden engagement. That was until the night of our engagement party. That's when Suzanna Caulder, my high school sweetheart and the only girl I ever loved, reappeared in my life after years of being apart. Seeing her again only stirred up those unresolved feelings I had suppressed since she left me during our senior year. At the time she claimed it was her decision to attend some swanky golf academy out of town to focus on her goal of playing professionally someday. But I never bought that excuse, seeing how that was the first time she ever mentioned moving away for golf and completing her high school days elsewhere other than with me and our friends. Initially, I had been devastated when she ended our relationship and left me. Then that devastation turned into anger. I believed the rumors flying around our social circle, those that hinted that Suzanna escaped from town to avoid being caught cheating on me. People were quick to believe that Suz and Wyatt, the bartender at the country club, had some type of ongoing affair. When Wyatt quit his job shortly after Suzanna's departure, it was easy to think that there may have been some truth to those rumors. My anger intensified until I wanted nothing else to do with Suzanna Caulder ever again. Putting her out of my mind, I went to college and did the typical guy thing...joined a fraternity, partied hard, hooked up with different girls. But no matter how hard I tried, I never truly eradicated Suzanna from my thoughts.

So seeing her again...yeah, that put a major kink in my dad's plan to marry me off quickly. He, as well as several other people, noticed the magnetic pull that still existed between us. While I continued to play the doting fiancé, I secretly planned to spend as much time as possible with Suzanna before the wedding. After I crossed the line one too many times, sneaking a kiss here and there, she only agreed to see me during our summer at the beach under her guidelines of just being friends. Taking whatever she was willing to offer, I agreed to the whole friendship thing. There were times when I thought she may want more, and believe me, had she caved I'd have gladly called off my engagement, my dad and Judge Bostick be damned. However, I came to find out that I totally misconstrued her feelings. She did love me, but only as a friend. I learned later her heart belonged to someone else. A few months before she graduated from college, she and Wyatt (same guy), took their years of friendship and turned it into something romantic. Although they had broken up at the beginning of the summer, Suzanna never stopped loving him. I used to think that Wyatt was the stupidest man alive. I mean, who takes the love of a woman like Suzanna and just throws it away? But my opinion of

Wyatt changed when he paid me a surprise visit on my wedding day. Not only did I find out how very much Wyatt loved Suzanna, but I also learned how I'd come to owe him a debt I'd never be able to repay.

Wyatt dropped a bombshell that day. He showed me a video tape which I still have nightmares about. The footage was taken from the security cameras at the country club. It revealed the real reason Suzanna left me all those years ago. And after what I saw, I couldn't blame her for leaving like she did. I'd get the hell out of dodge too if something so horrific happened to me and I knew the only way to protect the ones I loved was to live with what happened alone, keeping the secret to the very end. Seems dear 'ole Dad, in just another one of his drunken states, tried to sexually assault my girlfriend. Although Suzanna fought hard against him, his size and power would have eventually won out, and we all know where this story could have ended. But thank heavens Wyatt was there to save the day. He busted into the lounge of the club, pushing my dad off of a terrified Suzanna. Then he carried Suzanna out of the club and to safety, watching over her the entire night. He begged Suz to press charges, but she wouldn't hear of it. Her only concern was how this would affect me. The next morning Wyatt arrived to work early enough to make a copy of the video surveillance before erasing the footage for good from the security files. Lucky for me, Wyatt held onto the evidence all these years. And how fitting that on my wedding day of all days, a wedding day I never wanted, he gifted me with the only copy. I hated seeing what was on that disc, but it did give me the leverage I needed to stand up to my dad and break our agreement. After talking to Katelyn, we mutually decided to cancel the wedding. Then I went to have a little chat with Dad. He's lucky he's still alive and breathing. Had Landon not been with me to calm me down, I might be the one averting criminal charges. After revealing the newly acquired information, I gave my dad one of two choices...rehab or jail. Wisely, he chose rehab and here we are today.

My relationship with Dad is strained, to say the least. After I admitted him into the rehab center in Charleston, I vowed I'd never have anything else to do with him. But the doctors and counselors insisted that patients with supportive family members had a better recovery rate than those without. On the verge of hating my father, deep down I still wanted him to kick his addiction. Eventually, I moved to Charleston, selling our family home in Florence. Even as a family of three, we didn't need all that room the palatial house offered while I was growing up. Although the house held memories of happier times, when my mother was alive and we were a normal family, there weren't any other reasons to keep it. The housing market in Florence remains above the national average so I managed to make a nice profit from the sale. Using that money, I bought a three bedroom beach cottage on Folly Beach. Chloe's Aunt Tina knew the previous owners were anxious to sell. So when I called about possible locations in Charleston, she put me in touch with the owners. Now we are neighbors, Aunt Tina and Uncle Aiden just a couple of blocks down the road. Aunt Tina has become like a surrogate mother, bringing enough casseroles and baked goods to satisfy my healthy appetite. And, like Lisa, she always lends her ear, especially if I need to vent about my father. Which I often do now that we have begun group counseling sessions. Usually I stop by the rehabilitation center a couple of days a week after class. Yes, I decided to continue my education and attend law school, but since the wedding didn't go as planned, my tuition and acceptance from the University of South Carolina Law School in Columbia was pulled, thanks to my ex-father-in-law-to-be, Governor Bostick. I never thought I even wanted to be an attorney. My passion has always been in journalism, more specifically sports journalism. I have always enjoyed writing about sports figures, stories about not only what they accomplish on the field or court, but also investigating the personal driving force behind their competitive nature. My strong desire to get personally attached to the subjects I write about lead me to the decision to earn my law degree. Hopefully, armed with the tools to negotiate and write contracts, I can continue to pursue a career in the sports world, not as a writer, but as an agent. I still dabble in journalism. Actually, I've had a few pieces published locally and state wide. I'm still waiting for ESPN to decide to use the many articles I've submitted. Until I see my name in print or online under the sports conglomerate's banner, I'll just keep trying. Hey, you never know. Maybe with my sports journalism undergrad and law degree, I might be invited on as an analyst. One can only dream.

Exiting the hospital, I pull out my sunshades to ward off the glare of the afternoon sun. It's a gorgeous southern winter day, crisp, clear and cool. Grabbing my keys from the pocket of my jeans, I set off across the parking lot for the drive to my house. I'm anxious to get home to my girl. And since I've been gone all day I know she'll be waiting to welcome me. Shouting from the entrance to the orthopedic wing of the hospital has me looking that way. The first thing I spot is a female with...*purple hair*? She's giving an orderly a mouth full, waving off his attempts to help her walk. Then I notice the walking apparatuses she's using to hoist one leg in front of the other. She's moving at a snails pace, but remains stubborn in her resolve not to accept any assistance. There's a familiarity I'm sensing as I watch the patient stride closer to the doorway. Colorful hair, nasty attitude, a potty mouth...could it be? No, Callie Young is bound to a wheelchair. What in the world would Callie be doing at a hospital in Charleston anyway? I haven't seen Callie since this past summer when she agreed to help Suzanna's golf game in her efforts to win a spot on the pro tour. I assumed she was still working with her dad, Coach Moore, in Myrtle Beach. Callie and I formed what I guess I would call a friendship when I would drop off or pick up Suzanna from practice each day. We spent some time together talking while Suzanna was out on the course. In the beginning, the journalist in me only wanted to get the details of the car accident that resulted in Callie losing her ability to walk. It was a big story years ago when it happened, but sources close to the individuals involved remain tight lipped still to this day. Why such a big deal? Well, Callie Young was the equivalent of what Tiger Woods was when he played at Stanford. People already hailed her as the next superstar of the LPGA. But one night after a fraternity party everything changed. My ulterior motives to dig deep into the story transformed into something else the more I really got to know Callie. I can't describe the feelings I had during the time we spent together but it was strange, especially since my goal for the summer was to win back the heart of Suzanna. Yeah, that didn't happen. I often think about Callie and what she's up to. No doubt getting into trouble. Could that really be her in my new hometown? I begin the trek to the orthopedic wing to get my questions answered, but by then the familiar, yet unidentified girl has already disappeared into the building. Turning back toward the direction of my car I pull out my phone when it begins ringing. Landon's name appears on the display screen.

"Yo, what up, bro?" I answer.

"No wonder you haven't sold any of your articles. If you write like you talk," Landon quips.

"Well at least I'm writing and doing something I enjoy rather than wasting my time guarding the devil," I add. Landon is still working for the security team that keeps our great governor safe. I don't know why he still works for the slimeball after everything he learned when Katelyn and I cancelled the wedding.

"The pay is great?" Landon responds more as a question.

"Like you care about money."

"Patrick, just know I have my reasons." And that's about as much as I'll get on the subject from my normally brooding friend. Let's just say Landon is a man of few words.

"Fine, so really, what's up with you?"

"I've got the weekend off and I thought I'd come visit, that is if you'll give me a place to stay."

"Yeah, yeah sure. Love to have you." I haven't spent much time with Landon with his job keeping him so busy in the capital city of Columbia. It will be great to see him and catch up.

"Cool, I'll see you sometime Friday afternoon."

"See you then," I say ready to end the call. But Landon isn't yet finished.

"Um, Patrick....have you heard from her?" he asks like he does almost every other time we talk. And I give him the exact same answer I have each time the subject comes up.

"Landon, Katelyn is fine. And that's all I'm allowed to tell you until you quit working for her father. Remember, her words, not mine."

"Yeah, okay. See you later in the week. 'Bye Patrick."

The call ends and I actually feel bad for my friend. Don't think I didn't miss the connection that seemed to form between Katelyn (my fiancée at the time) and my best buddy Landon over the summer. When we called off the wedding, I thought maybe Landon and Katelyn would have a chance to explore their feelings for each other. But once Landon decided to stay on as an employee of Katelyn's father, Katelyn saw Landon as just another team member of the enemy. The night we were *supposed* to get married, she bolted, leaving with her friend Beau and his band members. Trading in her cardigans and pearls for leather and chains, Katelyn reclaimed her true self and she never looked happier. She and her band, The Gardians, have been touring the country doing gigs here and there hoping to get picked up by a record label. We have kept in contact and she assures me she's happy and the band is doing great. The times we have talked, occasionally I bring up Landon and his never ending persistence to ask about her. She vowed me to secrecy about her whereabouts, wanting to keep her location hidden from her family. I think she misses Landon and would love to have the chance to see if anything would develop between the two, but she doesn't trust him as long as he works for her father. I can't say I blame her. I know what a sneaky MF her dad can be when he wants something. But I do trust Landon. I don't think he'd play the go-between between father and daughter. However, I will follow her wishes and keep Landon in the dark for the time being.

Pulling in my driveway, I hop out of the car and run to open the door. "Stella, I'm home," I call as soon as I enter the house. Big brown eyes almost completely shielded by a thick mane of golden hair peek around the doorway from my bedroom. "There's my girl!" I say throwing my backpack on the floor preparing for my welcome. Within seconds, Stella takes off down the hallway sliding on the hardwood floors a few feet away from me. She crashes into me licking my face. Now that's a welcome I'll never tire of. "Whoa, girl. Let me up so we can go for a walk." She managed to knock me on my back, all four of her paws pressed against my chest. She continues to lavish my face with her slobber. I don't mind because I love the smell of her puppy breath. "Wanna go for a walk?" I repeat finally getting her attention. She runs to stand by the door waiting while I grab her leash. Yep, I'm in puppy love. After moving to my new home on Folly Beach, I quickly got tired of coming home to an empty house. Having too much going on to seek the company of a female *human* companion, I opted to get a pet. One look at Stella and I was sold. She's the cutest golden retriever puppy I have ever seen. And her personality is equally adorable. For the time being, she's the perfect cure for my loneliness.

Attaching her leash, we begin our journey over to the beach. I stop and collect the mail from the mailbox. I'll read through the contents of the letters and magazines while Stella tires herself out chasing the seagulls. Once at the beach I let Stella loose and she takes off. I sit and begin sifting through my mail. I notice a few bills have arrived, which I'll pay online, some information about spring registration from the College of Charleston Law School, plenty of advertisements and special pizza offers which I'll put in the junk pile, some letters and a couple of magazines. I choose to leaf through the magazines first since it'll take a while to tire Stella out. Boy, does she have a bunch of energy! I grab the entertainment gossip rag that the previous owners subscribed to, but I'm now receiving. Taking a closer look at the cover, my eyes almost bug out of my head. Standing dead center under the tag line "The Hottest New Stars of Television" is none other than my childhood friend, Chloe Ryder. Or should I say "Runt", the nickname she was given by the fab five all those years ago. I think we got that wrong because she definitely doesn't look like a runt. Not that she ever did. She earned the name only because she was a year younger and a grade behind the rest of us. Of course she's always been beautiful, but now, whoa...she's down right smoking. Her normally dirty blonde shoulder length hair now falls down her back and chest and is the lightest shade of blonde I've ever seen. Her big brown eyes are heavily made up giving them a sultry look. The bright red of her lips compliments her sun kissed skin. She's surrounded by other actors so only the top half of her body was photographed. But her toned, thin arms and shapely shoulders are sexy as hell in the skimpy tank top she's wearing. The only thing missing is her brilliant smile. Guess the photographer was going for the pouty, sexy look. Well, he got it.

I recognize the man standing close behind her on the cover. He's her male costar, the guy all women from the ages of twelve to fifty are going goo-goo crazy over. What's his name? Ben...no, Bennett something? Like I'd know. I have to admit I'm not an avid viewer of the number one rated cable show on this fall. Not that I don't support Chloe, because I do. It's just that between everything I'm juggling – attending classes, therapy sessions with Dad, studying for said classes, and the little bit of writing I do in my spare time – leisurely television watching is not in the cards for me. The few nights I did remember it was airing I made a point to turn on the television with the volume muted. This one time, I happened to glance up from my law notes to see Chloe on screen involved in an intense love scene. She was rolling around in the sheets with that costar of hers that I can't remember the name of. I saw a little too much than I wanted of my dear friend. Let's just say the premium cable channel her show airs on has much more liberties than the networks when it comes to the showing of skin. Quickly, I turned my TV off. However, it was too late to turn off the memory of seeing Chloe in a state of undress. So for that reason alone, I'll support Chloe in all she does, I just won't watch her show.

I'm still so mesmerized by Chloe's magazine cover, I haphazardly open the remaining mail without glancing at the envelopes. Once the mail is open, only then do I inspect it to see if it's worthy of keeping or if it's going in the trash pile. I'm still looking at the magazine as I grab the last of the envelopes and tear into it. Inside I find another envelope and glance down to read *Mr. Patrick Miles and Guest* beautifully written in the center. Before diving into the presumed invitation, I look out across the sand to check on Stella. She's happily digging a hole near the shore, running away each time the tide rolls in to fill it up. I chuckle at her antics, knowing a bath will definitely be in order when we return to the house. My thumb and forefinger pry the heavy cardstock from the envelope. Looking down, all thoughts of my dog and Chloe's magazine cover are forgotten. There in the grip of my hand is a picture of Suzanna and Wyatt. His arms encircle her waist as his chin rest on her shoulder. Her head is tilted ever so slightly that her gaze meets his. Although neither is looking directly at the camera, the photographer captured the moment perfectly. Both are wearing ridiculous smiles of happiness. For a moment, I focus on Suzanna and marvel at her beauty. She's not at all made up like Chloe on the magazine cover, yet she's just as beautiful if not more so. For a fraction of a second, I'm jealous it's Wyatt and not me in the picture. But then I don't think I'd ever be able to put a smile that bright and full of pure happiness on Suzanna's face. So I let go of my irrational feelings and decide to be content that Suzanna has found her one true love. Flipping the picture over, I already know what I'll find. Sure enough, it's the announcement of their engagement with details about their wedding slated for late April. But what really gets my attention is the hand written note Suzanna scribbled at the bottom of the paper.

Dear Patrick,

Just months ago I received a similar invitation from you, announcing your engagement. You personally asked me to accept and join you in your happiness. Although your engagement wasn't based on true love and didn't end in marriage, I'm still thankful it occurred. Had it not been for that invitation, I'm not sure you would be in my life today. This past summer we were able to reconnect and find our friendship again. And I plan to never let that go in my lifetime.

I hope that you'll join Wyatt and me on our special day. It wouldn't be the same without you there to share it with us. Just know that Wyatt makes me deliriously happy. My complete happiness is knowing that you Patrick, my friend, are

just as happy for me. Plus, I hope you'll bring that guest...I'm dying to meet the lucky lady. I want you to find your happily ever after, too. You deserve it.
Love always,
Suzanna

Rereading her handwritten note several times, it occurs to me that I am truly happy for Suzanna and Wyatt. If I had to handpick someone for Suzanna, I'd definitely choose Wyatt. They were meant to be together. Smiling down at their picture one last time, I'm at peace with the fact I'm not the man to complete Suzanna in a romantic way. I'm just happy knowing that I'm the man who she considers a friend 'til the end. Grabbing the strewn pieces of paper from my mail pile, I stand up and call to my dog. Stella comes running over so I can attach her leash for our walk across the road. I'm thinking of all the things I have to do tonight once Stella has had her bath. Mentally, I add one more thing to my list. There's still a couple more months until Suzanna's wedding. I better get a move on and start working on *my* plus one.

Acknowledgements

I began writing the second book of the Fabulous Five Series before the first book, Beneath the Lie, was ever published. I fell in love with every character I created and wanted to tell all of their stories. Although The Final Pairing is the completion of Suzanna's story, it is also jam packed with tidbits of information about the rest of the fab five. This is all thanks to my readers. I was overwhelmed by the outpouring of support and compliments I received from my first published work. Many of you bonded with the characters just as I did and couldn't wait for more. Well, now you have it. Sorry it took a while, but I wanted to give you Suzanna's ending as well as plenty of information about future reads in the series. So a big thank you to my readers and fans! I love bringing my stories to you.

Thanks once again to my husband. He is always supportive of my writing career and now, with this book, has read a total of two romance novels in his lifetime. I'm soon to make him a diehard fan of the romance genre. Thanks again to my children who waited patiently while I typed away behind the computer. Even though they aren't yet old enough to read my books, they remain my biggest fans! I love all of you very much.

I huge shout out to Sarah at Okay Creations. She is responsible for my awesome cover. It was a pleasure to work with someone so creative and talented. With just a few emails back and forth, she took my ideas and turned them into exactly what I envisioned the cover to look like. I look forward to working with her again in the near future.

It takes a lot to make me look good. But somehow through the lens of his camera, Milton, with Milton Morris Photography, worked his magic. Thank you Milton for lending your talents and capturing a great author photo I'm proud of.

I'm so blessed to have great friends. Friends with fulltime jobs and families of their own, yet they still volunteer to read and reread my manuscript over and over again helping me get it polished and just right. Once again, Lisa and Bethany, you have gone above and beyond and I don't know where I'd be without you both. You are both so very special to me. Thanks for everything, especially your friendship.

A final note to my readers. Thank you, thank you, thank you! It is an honor to bring my stories to each and every one of you. I love hearing from you so please consider leaving a review. As a self published author with limited marketing resources, your reviews are a great way to let other readers know about this book and others in the series. Want more of the fabulous five? Connect with me through Facebook and LIKE my page www.facebook.com/VirginiaCHartbooks. Or find me on Twitter @VCHartFab5. Thanks to my brilliant friend Sunny who continues to be my social media expert. My viral presence would not exist had it not been for Sunny's mad computer skills. Even though I have a constant technology cloud hovering above my head, you are a ray of light...literally. Finally, if social media is not your thing... believe me, I feel your pain. I'm still scared to post fearing I might accidentally blow up the world. So if you're as old fashioned as I am, you can always reach me through email at thefabfiveseries@gmail.com.

And as always...Happy Reading

About the Author

Author Photo credit –
Milton Morris Photography

Virginia C. Hart resides in her beloved state of South Carolina, where she was born and raised. Married for fourteen years, she and her husband have two beautiful children. After graduating from Francis Marion University with a bachelor's degree in accounting, followed by a master's degree in education, Hart has been teaching part-time at the local technical college for nearly a decade.

When she's not teaching or chauffeuring her kids around, Hart is likely to be found typing away at a new book, furiously reading yet another book, or visiting her favorite South Carolina coastal spots.

Inspired to write her own romantic fiction when she was reintroduced to her love of reading a few years ago, Beneath the Lie, was published in February, 2014. The Final Pairing is the second book in Hart's Fabulous Five Series.